THE GARDENER'S APPRENTICE

A novel

Robert Ketchell

Published by Worthybridge Press

2017
© 2017 Robert Ketchell
All rights reserved.

ISBN: 1545059799
ISBN 13: 9781545059791

ACKNOWLEDGEMENTS:

This novel has been many years in the making as most novels are. To write a full length work is a labour of love, not too dissimilar to climbing a mountain perhaps. Several people have helped to advise, correct and read through various drafts at various stages. I would like to thank Jemma Kennedy, Jacquie Blakeley, Jacqueline Brouard, Ali Easton and Tilly Young, who all contributed invaluable insights and support as the work progressed. I bear responsibility for the final product, but remain grateful to those who helped guide this work into life.

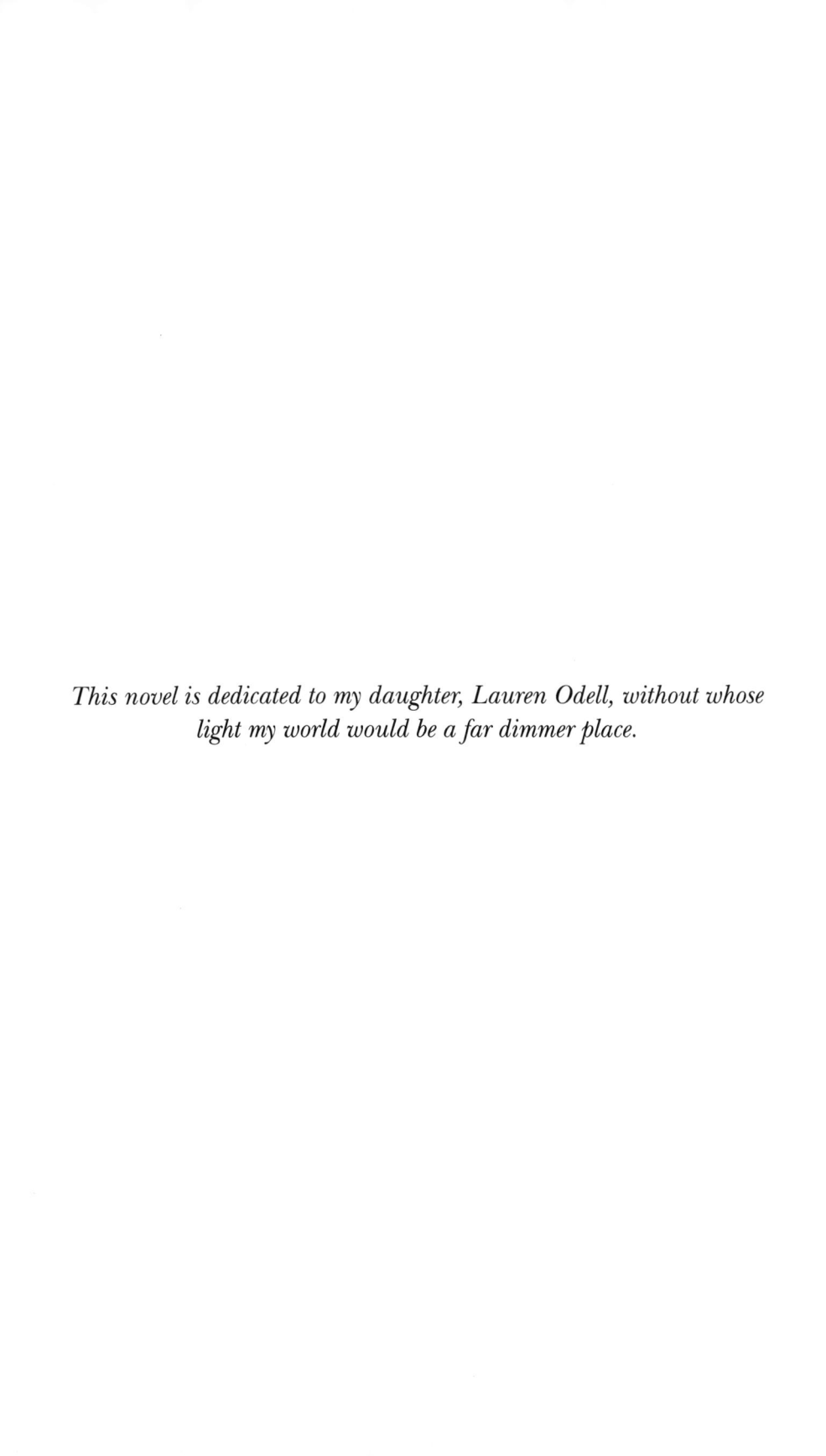

This novel is dedicated to my daughter, Lauren Odell, without whose light my world would be a far dimmer place.

PART I

CHAPTER ONE

September 1583

The young boy was running, running as fast as he could across the open space, a glittering tapestry of high summer grasses. "Look Mama, look at how fast I can run," his voice high pitched, sharpened by excitement, and the very thrill of it all. "Look, Mama, look…." and as he ran, he left a hand trailing behind him among the stems parted in the wake of his passing. Light sparked and played among the slender stems and pale slivers of leaves. Then as he paused for breath he looked back towards where his mother stood watching him, shafts of the late afternoon sun angling between them. Motes of dust raised by his scampering feet spiralled into the light sending sparkling flashes into the air as if dancing fireflies. The illusion delighted him. "I can do it again, look, Mama, I can do it again. The earth is on fire." Running, always running, under an immaculate blue sky, with the wind never seeming to touch him, perhaps even running faster than the wind itself.

Shigoto Okugi's mother watched him as he ran in ever widening circles about her. A smile creased her face, instinctively softening it. It was a smile for this being who was her only child, not the kind of smile intended to be shared with the rest of the world. Only she knew the difference, and she kept the reason to herself. They were standing in the silken midst of a sea of silvery-green swaying grasses that stretched out from where they stood until it was halted by a woodland, the trees crowding together as if unsure whether to proceed further. In the other direction toward where the sun slanted in, the grasses appeared to come to a sudden end, the earth that bore them seeming to fall into the sky. In fact the ground simply fell gently away beyond view.

She loved to stand there, near the point where the earth met the sky. It pleased her to accompany her young child there, and watch him run in circles around her. At this place she would allow herself to smile, her eyes dissolved into the tenderness that she ordinarily kept hidden behind the mask of who she was expected to be. It was a time when she felt a sliver of relief from the weight of the ordinary, familiar way of being. For those precious moments, that had about as much substance as the fragile beauty of cherry blossom, were time stolen from the ironclad grasp of reality. He was running now, in ragged steps so relatively recently learned it seemed, with his stiff arms outstretched, a flightless, fearless bird, running in circles through the parched grasses of late summer. She barely appeared to move; yet her eyes followed the boy's every step. Here at this place, this moment, she could feel something that she felt nowhere else. Not simply for herself, but through her child, her son. Through him she could catch a glimpse of some other place, which lay out there beyond the point where the grasses dissolved into the sky.

If she had walked on a little further towards that dividing line between the heavens and the soil layered by time and geology, she would have seen the ground gently sloping away to the lapping sea. The land creased into a series of undulations, broken only here and there by clumps of trees, their crowns leaning inland shaped by the wind. Down by the pebble strewn shore a tangle of crude fishermen's dwellings were ensnared in extended lengths of drying nets strung between poles. But she never walked that far any more. They had once, and as mother and child stood side by side without a word between them looking out over the immensity of the sea, the smile slipped from her face and she felt only sadness and longing. She never went that far again. For the sky she could smile, but not for the sea, the sea that reached out without end.

"Come, Oku-*chan*," she called out to him, using the suffix of familiarity to his name. "Come now, we should be making our way back, it'll be dark soon. Hurry now." She turned away from the source of the light, and with her shoulders pulled back, she set off back the way that they had come without looking behind her. Momentarily the young boy hesitated as if the ground was holding him fixed in place, then casually abandoned whatever fantasy he was enacting in the moment and ran after her. Just as he caught up with her with his hand reaching blindly for hers, he turned and saw to his disappointment that there were no 'fireflies' left now. They had all fallen back to earth, fallen stars, burnt out and exhausted of purpose. All there was, was the grass sward stretching toward where sky and land flowed one into the other, a luminosity of light that seemed to promise everything to those who could reach out for it.

"When I am big and grown up, I will run as far as the sky, and I will be this huge dragon and run as fast as the wind, and I will be bigger than everything that there is," he said with a quiet satisfied determination, carefully observing his mother's reaction.

Shigoto's mother turned to him. "You are a funny child, did you know that? Where do you get such ideas from?"

"I will, you know," he stated, now with an even greater determination, buoyed by the teasing. It was all the proof he needed. But her hand had tightened its grip on his.

"Come on, we need to get back home. Oba-chan, your grandmother, will be waiting for us. Who knows, maybe your father will be coming by too." Her voice was flat, all expression and emotion neatly stowed away, even from her son. Together they walked along the trace of a path through beaten down grasses until the trees opened up and embraced them before finally swallowing them whole. They left the wide-open spaces falling away into the unseen lap of the ocean, and the last fragile embers of the sunlight falling across waving grasses. The deepening sky rode above them and beyond it all.

Through the last days of summer mother and son came to this place and through the first creases of change that came with the autumn weather, until the wind veered around and brought sufficient chill to bring the landscape to a pause. Not everyday, as not every day did time allow them to make the walk from the small house they called home: past the last of the dwellings, stores, workshops, stables and sundry other buildings, past the convoluted shoreline of a large pond before they finally plunged into the dense woodland that enclosed and protected the gardens. It was a walk that took them perhaps twenty-five minutes to reach the point where the woodland began to thin, so creating a ragged edge, a boundary, and a point of transition. Beyond that were the grassy fields that stretched on toward sky and sea. In late summer or early autumn men in numbers would gather there, and cut the grasses with swinging blades, or horses would be turned out to roam and graze their way across the open space. During the winter months when the storms rolled impatiently in from the sea, the grass swathe now close-cropped and silver-withered reaching out before them, their strolls would end at the boundary between the shelter of the trees and the raw, open space. If they even got that far they rarely lingered for long. Spring brought freshly minted greens and a temporary carpet of tiny dazzling white flower heads, and then as if released from some invisible shackle they would venture once more beyond the safety of things.

To Okugi Shigoto, mere young boy that he was, the subtlety and lyrical beauty in all this was by and large lost. To him it was all so much simpler: they either did or they did not reach the field. If they did he could be like a hound released from the leash, a harrier unbound from its stays; if not, then there would always some other consolation to be found. He lived after all in a rich world of his imagining. Unlike his mother he had not lived long enough, nor experienced enough to have formulated a distinct sense of past, present and future. For him each and every day stretched on endlessly in an unsegmented continuous present, and in the main his living was unfettered. Life was as unmeasured by notions or realities of what had been, and what was yet to come. Life was all together much simpler than that. His home was where the hearth lay, with its wisp of palest grey smoke spiralling into the air, transitioning from the square of the timber framed heart to the circle of the sky. His mother, always his mother was the rock he swam out from, out into the world in carefully calibrated and crafted strokes, always for now destined to return.

CHAPTER TWO

February 1574

"So, all these rumours we have been hearing are true. I know now who's coming to stay."

The whispered words sent a shiver through the listeners. It was something they had been hearing as idle chatter for several days, and now that its final confirmation was apparently about to be unfolded, there came a certain sense of release. Oyadori exhaled as silently as she could, a polite smile ghosting across her thin lips. When she returned her attention again to the dried flower stalks being crushed between her fingers, her face was passive once more.

For a moment none of the three maids-in-waiting spoke.

Oyadori sat with the two older women on a broad polished veranda that lay between the women's apartments and the walled garden which shielded them from general view, one of three maidservants engaged with the domestic chores that filled their days. At sixteen years old, Oyadori was the youngest of the three by some way, and such things mattered in the rigidly ordered world within which they lived. She had come to know her position, as they all knew their place in the greater scheme of things. Gradually, drop followed by drop the rest of the story emerged, in such hushed tones that their heads at times almost came together, as they strained forward to try to catch every morsel. Kobuto san had, to her inner delight, gathered up all the fragments, real or imagined, and had bound the morsels she had gleaned into a rich tapestry now known to her as truth or fact.

"It's true," Kobuto repeated. "A visitor is coming, and very soon too... perhaps within the next few days even." She leaned back to observe with a barely concealed delight the effect of her words on the others.

"Are you sure? Who is it? Come on tell us who it is," Awayuki san, the oldest and thus most senior of the three, asked breathlessly in her surging excitement. Kobuto san merely nodded her head slowly by way of an answer, her full lips set in her well-rounded face pursed, though her eyes were directed at the tangle of plant stems lying idle across her lap. From a distance she would have appeared as someone momentarily pausing to contemplate her next action, and for what seemed to the others as a long drawn out moment. Kobuto san said nothing, holding her silence. It was as if she was refining her words and thoughts into their correct order, and until that order was established beyond doubt she could not possibly continue.

"Certain as I can be," she finally said in her most conspiratorial voice, and then she lapsed into another teasing silence as her hands blindly resumed what they were supposed to be doing.

Oyadori could follow the import of this scrabbled, coded conversation. It had been the talk of the palace staff for days; rumour and cross rumour, wild speculations and wild guesses had been flowing unimpeded through the place like shooting stars arcing across the night sky. Where it started no one knew, but soon enough, to the observant or the blatantly curious, it had become obvious that something was afoot. An important guest was expected at the palace, and the rumour mill had moved into working overtime. Orders had gone out for the renovation and cleaning of some seldom used rooms, and very particular attention was being paid to the highest of standards of all aspects of the work being done. In quiet moments, away from the chill hand of duty, everyone was engaged in the game of guessing the identity of the visitor.

A few days earlier Kobuto san had implied that her suspicions lay in the direction of an Imperial connection to the expected visitor. Awayuki san had at the time dismissed such a notion as being fanciful and unlikely. Neither of the two older maids-in-waiting had turned to Oyadori to ask for her thoughts or opinion on the matter. Being the youngest of the trio, they did not invest her opinions with any gravity. They did share some of the information their position allowed them to winnow, but by no means all. Given her age and status, Oyadori having had been in service but a couple of years, something which placed her firmly at the bottom of the pecking order, the two older maids rarely passed up any opportunity to remind her. Particularly Awayuki, who seemed to take a certain delight in any such opportunity to put her younger companion in what she regarded as being 'her place'.

'What do I really care?' Oyadori thought to herself in a quiet moment. Her fingers were stripping desiccated flower heads and dropping them into a bowl. 'So, some important person is coming to stay at the palace, someone grand; well, it'll only mean more work for the rest of us. If what Kobuto san says is true, then there will only be the two of us to look after Madam. Awayuki will be assigned to the visitor, not me. It'll be the usual thing, "You are too young to serve," or "You are too clumsy". Whoever it is, I probably will not even get to see them in person'. Oyadori found real enthusiasm for the whole episode hard to retain for long, particularly since the conversation she had had earlier that morning with Lady Saeko. Thus when Kobuto was finally ready to reveal the actual identity of the imminent mysterious visitor, Oyadori's mind was only half engaged with this latest bout of palace gossip.

"The Emperor's brother is being sent into exile. He is coming here. There has been trouble in the capital, and he is being put, how should one say? Out of harm's reach. That's who's coming, the Emperor's brother no less. Prince Hotaru." Kobuto finally unveiled her pièce de résistance, a trump card to sweep the table clean with. "You must absolutely keep this to yourselves, nobody is supposed to know." The words were spoken so low that Awayuki and Oyadori barely caught them before her whisper evaporated completely into the air about them. In such a closed and inwardly focused society, gossip was a commodity that could be, and invariably was, traded for favours. Knowledge was power in the hands of those who knew its real value. Awayuki let out a stream of air through her nose, her eyes glistening with delight.

"That's not all either." Kobuto san looked about the otherwise empty veranda, before continuing. "One of us will definitely be assigned to his retinue. He is travelling with a small party, and it has been ordered that we provide additional staff to look after him."

Now Awayuki's mouth was but a thin horizontal slash across her delicately boned face, some inner flame lighting up her eyes. She reached out her hand and gently laid it on Oyadori's forearm.

"Don't worry, they won't chose you. You have nothing to worry about," she said as she slightly tightened her grip. She smiled, almost laughed as her dancing eyes met Kobuto's. Oyadori said nothing in return; her gaze was firmly fixed on the bowl in front of her. Slowly, and with great deliberation, she resumed to rub the dried flower heads between her fingers gradually reducing them to a coarse dark dust.

"She's just disappointed because she will not get to serve the guest. Well, that's just the way of it, that's all. It will take someone who knows their job well, not a mere…" There was already the voice of triumph in Awayuki's voice. "You are too young yet."

"Not from what one hears. Evidently he greatly enjoys the company of women," added Kobuto.

"Really?" As Awayuki drew closer to Kobuto her eyes were shining bright as stars. "But he is of divine status isn't he?"

"Maybe that is the case, but he is a man too, so one hears, and that may have been part of the reason why he has been exiled to Mikura in the first place," Kobuto replied very quietly, and she and Awayuki dissolved into soft peals of laughter.

"Divinity in the form of a man, a real man of flesh and bone! Now there is something to behold. This I may care to experience for myself. And I thought that there was only one thing that men were capable of being interested in," said Awayuki, her mind racing along with her voice.

"Keep your voice down, that is probably sacrilegious to say, let alone to think it," scolded Kobuto san without particular menace. "We do not know anything remember, absolutely nothing at all. Bear in mind who it is we are talking about here. This is not some ordinary visitor to the palace. Even the Master of the Palace Guard knows nothing of the identity of the visitor. Right now probably less than a handful of people know he is coming. Imagine that!" she added with a final flourish.

The three women resumed their tasks in silence, each now lost in their own thoughts. Then Kobuto san leaned over to Oyadori, "We know nothing of this, that includes you too," she reiterated, this time with a pronounced vigour.

"Yes, Kobuto san," Oyadori uttered in a low voice.

Very soon after her father had passed away during the influenza outbreak that had swept through the island two years previously, she had been appointed to her present position as a junior maid to Lady Saeko. There had been no element of choice in the matter, she had simply received word to report for duty immediately, and that was the beginning of her life in service. In doing so she made the leap from the world of a child to the paradox of being an adult in a trice, and from that time she had been expected to make her own life wholly available to the needs of her mistress. At night she slept on the floor just outside the closed door to her mistress's sleeping quarters. Her life such as it was before soon began to pale into the clouded realms of memory. One life ended and another began.

Just as the fissures of loss had opened in her life, she had been pitched into another world. Now it seemed every moment of her long waking hours were filled with tasks and errands to be done. Her mistress was demanding, as was expected of her status. Also her fellow (more senior) maids, Kobuto and Awayuki, would rarely fail to point out the gaps and inconsistencies in her knowledge of etiquette and various relevant procedures relating to her duties. Despite this Oyadori had soon became aware of the relative importance of her position in respect of being able to divine something of the mood and temperature of the palace and the household as a whole. She had developed an image of the palace being like a musical instrument: when a note was struck, the sound reverberated out and everyone would hear it. She gained a sense of being part of a delicate web constantly vibrating with anticipation and fuelled by the expectancy of service. When Oyadori came to this understanding, the image of being close to the epicentre of that world intrigued her and made her feel in some way touched by the importance of it all. She felt that she was capable of seeing some things that the others could not glimpse, and it would became part of her secret knowledge, something that maybe one day she could trade to her advantage.

Several times a day, as part of her duties Oyadori would visit the kitchens to collect or return something. The kitchen area functioned as the practical hub of the palace complex, and as befitted its status and practical importance, it was a sprawling ever-lively area. Here, rice was cooked in huge vats, vegetables and fruits according to the season were delivered by cart or basket load, to be washed, cut up or used whole, raw, steamed, fried in oil, simmered, stewed, or pickled in rice bran and salt. Delicate silver fish which had been trapped in wicker baskets in mountain torrents had their bellies split open and were grilled whole over an open flame, slabs of pink and white flesh drawn from the depths of the sea were divided or delicately filleted, cooked or salted down in solid wooden lidded tubs. Rice and plum wines were fermented in aged dark-stained barrels and teas of delicate shades of green and brown stored, each carrying its distinctive blend of the scents of grass, sun and the earth, were dispensed with brightly coloured sweetmeats on demand.

A kitchen though is not simply about processing foodstuffs; messages, requests, orders, even soft whispered yearnings, tales of darkly imagined intrigues, suspicions, vanities, desires and hopes were all carried there by invisible currents. It was here that by a confluence of forces, all rumour and conjecture concerning many different aspects of the intimate life of the palace was drawn to, simmered down, dissected and embellished, eventually to be returned into the hot house world of the palace.

For the past three days the kitchens had been sizzling with a renewed intensity of speculation, the flames of which were hotter than any stove. Each time Oyadori entered the bustling area she would immediately be assailed by questions as to the identity of the rumoured imminent visitor. Being so close to the centre of power it was generally assumed she must have insider's knowledge, been privy to light which could be shed and shared to ever widening circles. Her appearance in the kitchens would cause a brief scrum to occur, as a welter of questions would be proposed, suppositions, proposals and counter arguments of every hue made, each seemingly even more absurd than the last. On one such occasion recently, a basket containing live crabs was kicked over in the melee her visitation caused, and the confused crustaceans ran temporarily amok, scampering fruitlessly about searching a way back to the sea. She would just smile serenely, and say nothing. Then the grumbling, unsatisfied, stonewalled crowd would dissipate as rapidly as it formed. Oyadori knew how to keep a secret, she knew when not to say anything at all, and as to all the questions, she brushed them off as lightly as if it were the wind racing through the needles of a well-anchored pine.

"Pah! She doesn't know anything. She's too young to know anything, anyway." One of the disgruntled kitchen workers turned away in disgust at Oyadori's apparent lack of interest in engaging in conversation. In truth she was now quite tired and fed up with the whole matter. 'What did it really matter who the visitor was?' she thought to herself.

'So, a member of the Imperial family is coming to stay on Mikura,' thought Oyadori as she continued to pluck at the dried flower heads and drop them into a bowl beside her. She tried to lose herself in the privacy of her own thoughts. 'No wonder those two are all excited. There is not much else to fill their lives with, but gossip and chatter. Does it really matter that much, anyway, who ever the visitor is? Soon enough everyone will know and then what happens? Nothing. Life just goes on, one chore replaced by another, one season rolling into the next, life goes on, that's all there is to it.' It was true though that to a certain extent she had been caught up in the excitement of the moment and she had listened to the various pieces of ill-informed speculation that were circulating. It was, after all, something that helped to break up the grind of daily life, but she was also capable of holding herself aloof from other people, as if she had cast a thick carapace about her for protection. After all, when Kobuto san had finally revealed the identity of the visitor, she had felt a sense of mild anticlimax. Her own, more personal concerns were weighing far more heavily on her mind.

She had just returned from the long walk to the kitchen and back to fetch an arm-stretching pail of hot water, when she was summoned to attend to Lady Saeko, in person. The room was dark, as the night shutters had not yet been withdrawn, and there was only a solitary candle that struggled to emit a dim light. Oyadori moved over the threshold into the room on her knees, set down a broad bowl with some of the warm water, then slid the door closed behind herself and waited, downward pointing fingers resting lightly on the tatami mats, and her eyes cast down in front of her. Apart from herself and Lady Saeko there was no one other in the room.

"Come here child, come closer to me. Leave the bowl. I wish to speak to you." Lady Saeko beckoned with a long thin arm out of the gloom. Oyadori inched forward still kneeling on the floor, head bowed.

"I have to inform you that some thought has been given of late to your position in the household," the voice of the older woman bore down on the back of Oyadori's head as she knelt motionless before her mistress. "My husband has a man who needs a wife. It was thought that you would make a suitable wife." Lady Saeko paused, the light from the single taper shadowed most of her face. "I have consented on one condition, and that is that you will remain in my service, at least until you are heavy with child. I cannot afford to be losing my maids just like that. So you will continue as before, is that understood?"

"Yes, Ma'm," but Oyadori was not sure if she had actually fully calibrated and understood the words. The news came rolling down on her in a rush, throwing her equilibrium to one side. It felt to her that the words were being addressed to someone else, a mistake had been made surely, and she was simply the wrong person in the wrong place. She had not asked for this, had never yet even for a moment considered the possibility nor the desirability of marriage.

"Anyway, we will see what happens in the future, but for now you continue in your present role." There was now an irritated, soured tone to Lady Saeko's words, as she looked through the gloom at the young girl nearly prostrating herself in front of her. "Now you can fetch me a towel, and tell Kobuto to prepare my clothes for the day. Nothing with green in it mind. Now go."

"Yes, Ma'am." Oyadori edged herself backwards to the doorway. It was the sheer strength of willpower that helped her to move and to respond without revealing what she felt inside herself. "I will leave the warm water here for Madam."

"No, put it on the stand there. That's where it goes, are you not taught anything?" Lady Saeko snapped out her irritation at Oyadori and the world in general.

"Excuse me Ma'am."

"Oh, and this man, your husband-to be, I mean. His name is something like Shigoto. Shigoto Kanyu, I think. My husband thinks a lot of him evidently." She paused, as if she had run the course of what she had to say. "Now you may go and fetch Kobuto," and Lady Saeko waved her hand in Oyadori's general direction with as much concentration as if she were ridding herself of a distracting flying insect. After Oyadori had slid the door shut again from the outside, she remained on her knees for a long time, head bowed low to the bare wooden boards of the corridor floor. She pressed her face as tight into her sleeves as she could, as if she wanted nothing more than to shut out the light of the new day. Even as she did so she knew in her heart that nothing, nothing at all, could halt the forces of fate, and that what she might want or not want for herself, was like mere dust thrown up into the wind, just as the light of day would arrive whether one was ready or not for its rebirth.

CHAPTER THREE

May 1584

"It's time it happened. It's the right thing to do. Otherwise the boy will just continue to be a burden. It's time he became useful to someone. Anyway, he is growing up, and he will need to be found a trade. He will be a garden apprentice, it has been decided." The man's voice was gruff, impatient and sounded as if its owner did not wish to make this a discussion. He was not particularly tall figure, and sat cross-legged on the floor with his shoulders hunched forwards and head tilted toward his chest, he looked even shorter than he actually was. His face was pinched, the cheeks slightly sunken with deep-set shaded eyes, and his skin had the pallor and delicacy of someone who on the whole avoided the strong light of the sun. Shigoto's mother was kneeling close by him as he spoke, her face impassive and composed, with her eyes downcast before her.

"Would you like more tea to drink?" she said quietly, as she reached out and picked up the teapot that sat on a small lacquered tray. She turned with the pot, the spout now facing towards the man, the fingers of her other hand hovered expectantly over the lid without actually touching it.

"No, enough. I must go," he replied looking down at the cup before him, as if he expected to find something there that would relieve him of his discomfort. But all there remained were the traces of the unfinished tea.

Shigoto looked from one parent then to the other. He could sense the strain within his mother. She seemed to be pulling at something that would not move, perhaps could not move. The tension between the two adults was as palpable to him as the thin coil of smoke spiralling from the incense stick in the corner of the room. He hated these brittle angular scenes between them, and had so often in the past run either to his grandmother, or fled the house altogether and locked himself within the safer confines of his own imagination. These visits never lasted long, and he had noted that they usually ended with his father making an abrupt exit. He wondered now how long it would be before his father would rise to his feet and leave. For now that moment could not come soon enough for himself, and it could only be better for his mother too, he reasoned to himself.

His father had arrived unexpectedly at the house that evening, as he always seemed to do, when suddenly there would be his looming presence in the small entry porch, and his hard voice calling out for attention. On this occasion having settled himself awkwardly in the main living space, he had called for Shigoto to be present. "I suppose that it is only right that the boy be here. He should be grateful that there are people who are considering his situation. Anyway decisions have been taken, so he may as well hear this for himself, no harm in that." He spoke quietly, with his face averted from Oyadori, so that he might have been speaking aloud merely for his own benefit, not hers.

'No harm in that?' thought Oyadori as she prepared the tea to offer Kanyu. 'Is that the way to consider this? What he means is there is no harm in letting my son know that his life is merely some inconvenient detail to be decided by others. That he cannot be free to find his own way in this world. That he too is just another insect caught in a web.' She thought back to the conversation, which had apparently sealed her own fate, when she was informed that the man who now sat before her would be her husband. She could recall with icy clarity the sense of helplessness she had felt then, and also the gnawing anger she had buried in a place deep enough that the sun would never reach it. 'They are doing to him, to my son, what they have done to me. My son is being punished for my sins. They cannot see him for who he is. There is 'no harm', because he is also no threat to you, is that what you really mean, husband?'

Sheepishly and uncertain as to why his presence was required, Shigoto had entered the room, shuffling his bare feet across the floor as he did so. He came and knelt a little way behind his mother, instinctively putting as much space between himself and his father as he could, whilst still remaining covered by the protective shadow of his mother. He had grown to fear his father's sudden arrivals, as he was well aware it left a trace of tension behind when he had finally gone, a scent of gloom that needed to be exorcised, as if it were a recurrent, persistent stain on their lives. His grandmother, who lived with them in the small home on the fringes of the palace grounds, usually found some reason to be on her way out of the house when Kanyu arrived, and would often light some incense before the small family altar, as she fussily made her way out. Thus he associated the scent of incense hanging in the air with the brooding presence of his father.

The Gardener's Apprentice

"There will be notice given at the Ceremony of Appointments and Promotions. The list has been drawn up and it will be passed to the scribes soon. The matter is taken care of. Lord Saeko will make the announcement at the ceremony." Kanyu, his face now lit with an inner satisfaction, turned towards Shigoto whose own eyes were looking towards the open doorway and beyond. "That's right, isn't it boy, you can't be hanging around all day at your mother's breast, can you? You understand well enough what I am talking about, don't you?" He was not expecting a reply.

Even if he did, Shigoto usually said nothing at all. He had already learned it was best to keep his thoughts to himself. 'He will get up soon and go. I can see that he wants to be gone. He's not like a proper father anyway, and he does not live here with us. He's just like a visitor. I don't know why he calls himself my father. When he goes then I can go back to what I was doing. Why did they want me here anyway? What is any of this about some ceremony to do with me? I don't want to go, I shall refuse to go. They will have to drag me there. Drag me there by the hair, which will make them feel bad. Then they will feel sorry.'

"He's still only a child yet..." his mother started to speak, then fell back into a resigned silence. She replaced the teapot on the tray with a dull, dry sound. Her movements seemed to be taking place in a world where everything ran at half speed or less. Where every action had to be fully thought out and weighed in the minutest detail, before the ensuing re-action could begin to unfold itself. Shigoto glanced first one parent then to the other. He was waiting for his father to be gone, and then life in the house could resume its more equitable course once more. Time for him seemed to be standing still, and it made him feel uncomfortable, as if a stream had been dammed, temporarily halted in its tracks.

The conversation had been hard to follow and he hadn't really been listening anyway. His parents had been speaking to one another in clipped tones scattered with mainly unfinished sentences and the significance of what was being spoken about largely passed him by. Through an innate sensitivity to the silences between words and the concealed yet readable gestures, he knew that in some way others were deciding upon his future and there was nothing he could do about it at all. Nor even could his mother.

"Another couple of months and it will be official. Until then you are not to say anything to anyone, not even the old woman." Kanyu momentarily jerked his head up, as if he half expected the 'old woman' to be standing before him, arms raised high and about to about to viciously strike down. Then he slowly slipped back once more into the opaque depths of his own thoughts.

"You mean my mother?" said Oyadori softly, though as she spoke the words were hardening as an accusation in her mouth.

"It is a matter of protocol, that these things are done right, and that they are seen to be done correctly. It's important to maintain proper face. That's all there is to it." Kanyu lifted a hand to mop his brow with a handkerchief that he had extracted from inside the folds of his kimono. "It's not a matter that can be questioned, that's all. My father… my father would not hear of him being trained as a *samurai*. He felt it not to be appropriate, in the circumstances, that is." Once again Kanyu nervously dabbed away at his forehead with the cloth that he had crushed in his fist.

"He is my son, he is barely nine years old, he is still a child," Oyadori said with such a hiss of emotion, that Shigoto looked up towards her back as she sat facing his father. He did not need to see her face to read her mood. He saw it reflected back to him clearly enough in the cold, dark pools of his father's eyes.

"It's a matter of protocol. Protocol and duty. You would be wise to remember that yourself. We all have our duty to perform, and you must understand what that means, don't you. I don't

The Gardener's Apprentice

have to spell that out for you. The family, the Saeko clan comes before everything, that's right isn't it? That's how everything works. It's the glue that keeps this world together, and puts food before us. Anyway, the time for discussion is finished. I have to go. There are important things I need to attend to." He stood up and straightened the folds of his bland coloured kimono marked with the crest of the Saeko clan, and without a further word left the room. He said nothing to Shigoto as he left, and did not even look his way.

"Yes, I know what you mean," she said to herself after he had gone, "I know just what you mean."

Later that evening, Oyadori came to sit beside Shigoto, when he lay covered by a thin quilt, his eyes heavy with sleep. "There are matters that you do not yet understand, my son. Things from the past that's all, but they do not need to be a burden to you now. Maybe, just maybe, you can escape the past when you are older, throw it off like a layer you no longer need, just as the snake sheds its skin. There will be a time enough for all that, a time of reckoning will come to us all for sure, either in this life or the next. For now there is nothing to be done, just live each day as it comes. Just live each day as it comes, that's all you have to do."

Oyadori reached out her hand and brushed it lightly across his head, smoothing down his hair. She wanted so much to take him up in her arms. If she could have taken him back into her womb at that moment she would have done. She would do anything to protect him from the world outside the walls of the house they called home. But she knew she could not do any of those things, and she felt a surge of frustration. Some day he would have to know everything, and then he would be better able to judge for himself. Until then she was determined to give him all the succour she could. She had vowed it, it was there fixed in her, something sacred to the memory that she kept locked so deep in her heart, that it was never allowed even the slightest trace or suggestion of light to fall on it. He was her son after all, the tissue of her tissue, blood of her blood, he had been born into her love, and nothing could change that. What other reason did she need to nurture him, anyway? That she knew, and she fully accepted was her fate that she willingly acquiesced to. It was part of what she could not and had no wish to escape from, nor any desire to leave behind. He was all she had, the one and only only person she could really permit herself love in this world.

"Mama?"

"Yes, Oku-chan," she used the soft, diminutive term of endearment she reserved for when they were alone together.

"What were you and father discussing? It was about me, wasn't it? Does he want something from me, is that it?"

"Your father has arranged for you to be a garden apprentice. Now sleep, go to sleep, there is nothing to think about," she said with a soft smile.

"What is a garden… a garden apprentice? Is it something bad? Is that why you are sad?"

"No, no, nothing like that. Not at all," she paused finding a soft smile for him. "It's never easy somehow when your father is here. But that is not for you to worry over. All you need to do is to sleep now. Everything will be fine in the morning." She said it as sincerely as she could, and with a fervent desire that it could be so, that it would be so.

"Why does father not live here? With us that is." The words barely escaped his lips.

Oyadori laid her hand on his warm shoulder.

"He comes to see us when he can. He is such a busy man your father. He has many responsibilities for his work. That's why he is not here much. He helps to look after the affairs of Lord Saeko. You could say that your father is an important man, that's why he is not here so much. He always has so many things to do, so many duties to attend to."

Shigoto pondered her words for a little while. He knew that there was something that did not fit together well; there was some niggling inconsistency that kept him from grasping what was really being said. But in the end it lay beyond him, out of his reach. As he lay there his eyes never left his mother's face. He kept them fixed there, trying to understand her beyond her words, always trying to reach out toward her.

"What does a garden apprentice do?" he asked.

"Now, sleep, I said, didn't I? There will be time for all the questions in the world in the morning. Now it is late, look even the candle is feeling tired." Oyadori looked across at the candle that had begun to splutter, throwing uneven fits of mellow light across her son's small face.

"No, I need to know," he said beginning to struggle to sit up, until her hand pressed down on his shoulder.

"All right, I will tell you, if you promise to go to sleep straight-away, and no more questions. As I say there will be time enough tomorrow." Shigoto settled back down once more, blinking his eyes as if a tacit agreement had been reached, but said nothing. His gaze though remained fixed on her.

"A gardener tends the gardens for Lord Saeko. He works to keep everything in its proper place, neat and tidy. He helps to make the garden beautiful and clean. So that when Lord Saeko, or his wife, looks at the garden, everything is as it should be. It is said that when the garden is healthy, then so is the family strong. It is an important job." Her hand remained resting on Shigoto's shoulder until she could feel the peace of sleep had carried him away. Oyadori remained kneeling by the child in the flickering candlelight as the shadows chased themselves about the room. "Yes," she continued in a voice the room could also hear. "A gardener loves the garden he looks after, every tree, every plant, every rock can be as his child, something to look after, something to love. There are those who would not agree, but there are far worse things to be in this world. Nobody will ever know your name, you will not be remembered, but maybe the trees and stones will know and remember. The priests and poets say this world is but a fleeting glance, nothing but a wisp of smoke, after all. Perhaps it's better not to have any real expectations of this life; better not to have to shoulder all that for a burden after all. No, my son, you go and be a gardener, it is what has been decided for you anyway, and who are we to say otherwise? What choices are we really given? You do what you are supposed to do, may be you will find some joy in that. Let your dreams carry you on, my son. Let them carry you on to a better place than this. If you let them they will."

Shigoto heard none of these sentiments. He had slipped away from her, left her waiting and watching on the shores of wakefulness. His breath came in long, languid pulls, and his face was clear of worry and doubt. There would be another time for questions.

That night in his dreams he was walking across a field, so wide and far, that his sight did not reach to its edges. He was walking with giant strides, his pace eating up distance as if it were mere dust. His head reached up into the clouds and beyond: he was a colossus striding across the domains of empire and nothing could prevent his progress. In his hand he grasped a thick wooden stick. Burnt silver smooth by the sun and wind, it twisted in his hand as he strode along. His stick was alive as he was; it was its own living force that connected with his vital being, as if they were inseparably entwined. The stick was his covenant of power, his instrument of authority, and also the endorsement of his will. In his hands it could be a fork of lightning zigzagging down into the earth, a bolt of energy, so pure and fierce, that everything it touched was atomised, vaporised into the dust of dust itself, all forms utterly destroyed once and forever. He was the source of that spume of destruction, for as he strode he became a fierce fire-breathing dragon racing across the sky. With bulging, glistening, blood-red eyes and the lids stretched tight back, the five claws of each foot raking with furious blind violence at the air, its mouth agape and spitting a stream of lightning down onto the mountains and waters below. The sky, an infinite bowl containing both light and darkness above and around him. The dragon was the master of its universe, the beginning as well as the end of all that it chose.

Then in the centre of the space that he was aware of stood his mother. She was dressed in a kimono of the palest pink overlain with an abstract shower of falling white flowers, her hair combed back tight enough for it to glimmer like a polished helmet, and her face wearing a passive mask of motherhood. Her body flickering and glowing in an inconsistent light, she seemed at that moment to be as delicate as a soft breeze rustling dry leaves.

CHAPTER FOUR

Late February 1574

The wind was rustling among leaves that had fallen crisp and bleached into the garden below the veranda, Oyadori was making her way back from the kitchen area to the women's apartments carrying a large closed lacquered box. She walked with as quick steps that the narrow girth of the kimono allowed, her head looking down and feet skating across the smooth polished boards. Lady Saeko had retired to her rooms, the sudden onset of chill unseasonable weather had laid her low with a mild fever. The illness had not, though, diminished her demands, but sharpened them and her maids were being hard pressed to live up to her expectations. The box was divided into sections and contained a variety of delicacies to tempt the patient back to full vigour. Oyadori had not herself eaten since first light and her stomach grumbled as she made her way.

Turning a corner as she approached the women's apartments Oyadori almost collided with a kimono clad figure rushing in the opposite direction, and she nearly lost her grip on the box as she lurched to one side to avoid the impending collision.

"Watch where you are going. Don't you look where you are putting your feet?"

"Oh, it's you, Awayuki san," said Oyadori.

"Yes, it's me. That's no reason not to look where you are going. You almost knocked me over. I could have been injured by an accident like that."

"I am just taking the Lady's lunch to her apartments," explained Oyadori, recovering her comportment. "She is not well, she has not left her rooms all day. She is keeping us terribly busy, especially now there are only the two of us to look after her."

"No reason not to take care where you are going," repeated Awayuki needlessly, and she glared at Oyadori, making a show of readjusting her robes.

"I'm sorry, but I must deliver the Lady's food," said Oyadori, hoping that she could proceed, she was becoming anxious and uncomfortable at the unforeseen delay. Kobuto san would be waiting, and she knew that any further delay would potentially evoke a sharp-tongued comment from the other senior maid.

Awayuki smiled. "Well, all the more reason to be looking where you are going then. You could have dropped the box, and then what a mess you would be in then, eh?"

For the briefest moment Oyadori thought that Awayuki was going to bring her fist down onto the box in order to cause just such an accident. But Awayuki merely patted down an imaginary stray hair in her coiffure.

"So the Lady's not well then?"

"Yes," replied Oyadori anxious to proceed.

"I know, Kobuto san was just telling me. She needed my advice on the preparation of some herbs. I have just been talking to her. She said that you were struggling to cope, without me, that is. I thought you would. I don't know why Lady Saeko ever thought to take you on as a maid. It's a job you do not seem to be quite ready for somehow. Isn't that so?"

"That's not fair, Awayuki san," protested Oyadori.

"Fair? Who ever said anything about fair? Still I have plenty to do myself, looking after His Majesty. That's demanding enough. Not that you would appreciate that." Awayuki looked disdainfully towards the young woman, then she lowered her voice. "Especially as he clearly finds me attractive, as a woman. But oh, I'm sorry, of course, you would not know anything about that either. Well I haven't the time to spend it chatting with you. You had better hurry along hadn't you, the food will be going cold, no doubt." With that dismissive comment Awayuki gathered up several folds of the kimono cloth in one hand and made to move off. "Kobuto san told me to tell you to hurry if I saw you, her Ladyship is calling for food, and she was wondering where you had got to."

But Oyadori had already started on her way, she was glad to have reason to be out of Awayuki's path.

When she arrived back at the private apartments, she was nervously expecting a dressing down from Kobuto san for having taken too much time. She found Kobuto san sitting alone in one of the rooms that served as an antechamber to Lady Saeko's private room.

"Excuse me for taking so long, Kobuto san. The food was not quite ready when I arrived," Oyadori paused, "then I met with Awayuki san briefly on the way back." She gently placed the box on the floor. Kobuto san would be the one who would take the food through to the inner sanctum, yet she did not make any move to do so.

"It's alright, Lady Saeko has fallen asleep again, she has been asleep for a while, probably the best thing for her really," Kobuto san spoke with a flat voice that betrayed neither anxiety nor anger, and Oyadori could feel her whole body relax as she realised that she was not about to be scolded. "Leave the box over there, we'll see if she wants to eat when she wakes up again." The older woman continued with folding a pile of cloths that lay scattered about in front of her.

Oyadori gently placed the box with its decorated lacquer top onto a low table in one corner of the room. The screen doors were slid fully back and the light flooded into the room. Beyond the wide opening the small garden seemed to shine and shimmer in the light. There were several tall shrubs toward the rear of the garden that had been clipped into domed shapes, and luminescence caught in some of the dark, green-black leaves, causing them to sparkle as they moved stiffly in the breeze that came and went at random. For a moment Oyadori stood watching the garden taking in the subtle shifts of light playing across the various surfaces and textures.

"You can finish folding these cloths if you have nothing else to do. There is some sewing to be done as well. We may as well get on with those jobs whilst we have a few minutes peace and quiet," said Kobuto san after a little while.

"Yes, of course," replied Oyadori. The garden with its composed and balanced beauty made her feel good, as if the qualities she could see in it were filling her. "I love this little garden," she spoke softly almost to herself. "It's so pretty, it does look so lovely whenever you look at it. You know I have noticed that even though the seasons may change, the garden always keeps certain strength, a dignity to it. It changes all the time but it is so subtle really."

"My, you are in a philosophical mood today," said Kobuto san. "Here. If you can tear yourself away from the garden, help me fold and put these cloths away. Then we can sit on the verandah to do the sewing for a little time."

Before they had settled on the broad expanse of the verandahh, Kobuto san went and checked on Lady Saeko. She was back a few moments later.

"Still asleep," she reported. "A few more moments of peace and quiet."

They sat in silence working busily with needles and fine thread stitching back together lengths of fine kimono silk that had been taken apart for washing. Every now and then Kobuto san would raise her head from the work, as if to listen for any sounds that may indicate Lady Saeko had woken, before her plump fingers resumed their task.

"I have always enjoyed the gardens of the palace grounds, when there are a few moments to myself I love to walk in the gardens. My mother and father used to take me around there when I was a child," said Oyadori, her eyes lingering on the small garden, as if it held an answer to some deep question for her.

"Yes, they are nice," replied Kobuto san absently, as she pulled at an end of silk thread. "Not that I have the time myself to spend wandering around the gardens with an empty head."

If the remark was intended with any cynicism then it missed its mark. "My father loved the gardens, he knew the names of many of the trees, and would speak to the gardeners too sometimes. You know I remember that he once said to me that if he had not been a samurai in the service of Lord Saeko, he would have enjoyed being a gardener."

"I am sure he was just jesting with you," said Kobuto, her lips curled ever so slightly, and she shot a glance across at her companion.

"No, it's true, he spoke about the garden being just like nature. He wrote poems you know. He presented a poem about spring maple leaves to Lord Saeko once, and the lord praised him for it. I recall my mother telling me."

"Well just be grateful he was a samurai, not a gardener, then. Imagine what your life would have been like if he was a gardener. You would not be sitting here now in the service of Lady Saeko if he had been a gardener, that's a fact." Kobuto

The Gardener's Apprentice

smiled as she delivered these last words as if she were laying a trump card down.

"I suppose so," said Oyadori with a slight sigh as she absently drifted deeper into the well of her own thoughts and memories.

"Be grateful for who your father was, be grateful to the Buddha for that," said Kobuto with a certain emphasis. "Incidentally I hear that there is to be a new head gardener, a priest from Kyoto, no less. Poor fellow, I wonder what he is doing coming here from the capital?"

But Oyadori was not quite finished with her own musings. "You know if I had a son, maybe I would not mind for him to be a gardener. I think that it could also be a noble way of life."

Kobuto set her hands down in her lap and looked sharply up at the young maid. "Now dear, I know you are young and your head is no doubt full of foolish thoughts, but really, what a thing to say! At least allow your son the honour of being a priest. Really, you do have some foolish notions in that head of yours. What is the world coming to?"

They both then lapsed into silence and privacy of their own thoughts, which was only broken by the occasional gust of wind catching the leaves of cherry trees just beyond the garden boundary.

"Oh, that reminds me, I meant to say…" she said after a little while had passed, each of them fully engaged with what was in front of them. Oyadori looked up in bright anticipation.

"Yes," but Kobuto san's hands continued working for a few moments before she continued. "There was a visitor whilst you were away to the kitchens."

"A visitor? Oh you mean Awayuki san, I know I met her on my way back, she…" Oyadori paused to weigh up the possibility of launching into a complaint about the petty bullying attitude of Awayuki, but then given the relaxed nature of the moment she decided not to pursue that line. After all, she knew that Kobuto san usually tended to side with Awayuki, as if they were the best of friends.

"No, I was not thinking of Awayuki. Oh, she just came by to brag about her new situation. Serving the visitor seems to have gone to her head somewhat. No, there was someone else, a man, no less."

Oyadori looked up surprised; normally men were not permitted to approach the women's apartments, unless they were on official business. Even Lord Saeko himself would tend to send a messenger to deliver messages for his wife. He rarely appeared in person in her quarters.

"Yes, a visitor came by, for you, as it happens." Kobuto san's voice never wavered, and remained quietly pitched at a volume that retained discretion, as if she were sharing, or about to share something that was intended only for Oyadori's hearing.

Oyadori was shocked, and she could feel the skin on her forearms bristling with nervous tension. She looked across at Kobuto san, but the older woman's eyes were focussed on the sewing she held in her lap and her hands continued their work without a break. Her face revealed nothing at all of she might be thinking.

"Me? Someone came to see me? How could that be?' Oyadori could not hide her concern, though it was somehow tempered by the casual way in which Kobuto san had broken this startling news to her. What had she done? For a few moments she looked down at her now idle hands without really seeing, her mind a turmoil of possibilities. None of them particularly appealed to her. A wind stirred through the garden before settling itself down again.

"Yes, I was surprised myself, but apparently the visit had been sanctioned," said Kobuto, this time the slightest of smiles playing across her face. She was clearly enjoying drawing out the revelation.

"Oh, Kobuto san, tell me, tell me who was it who came. I was not expecting anyone," said Oyadori.

"Are you sure? You have an admirer apparently, wonders will never cease I suppose," and she looked across at the face of Oyadori before her. Oyadori was not a woman anyone would have regarded as a particular beauty, though she had the benefit of youthfulness. Now her delicate, rounded face was etched with the tension, her eyes, deepest brown shading towards black, were staring intently at the older maid. Her thin lips that had yet to fill out into sensuality were slightly parted as if they were waiting for the next words to form.

"Who, who do you mean came to see me? Is there anything wrong? Perhaps with my mother?" Oyadori's voice was now full of concern as she turned her head to look toward the garden, but it was no longer with an admiring gaze. "Please, Kobuto san, who was it, what do they want of me?"

Kobuto san's hands finally stopped what they were doing, and she set the cloth down in her lap. She was about to say something, to reveal the identity of the visitor, and to either assuage or confirm the anxiety felt by Oyadori, when a reedy voice came drifting out from the depths of the apartments.

"Kobuto. Kubuto. Where are you, I need you now. Kobuto."

"Coming Madam, I am on my way right now," she called out, and with a speed that belied her rounded frame, Kobuto rose to her feet and without a backward glance moved quickly towards the closed doors behind which her mistress lay in the cloying envelope of her malady.

Oyadori looked up from the sewing in her hands to the garden again, as another gust of wind raked the leaves of the trees that were just beginning to reveal the first signs of the coming change of season. Somehow this time the garden did not seem to quite have the same soothing balm. She felt a prickling of anxiety moving within her. A deep foreboding that change was coming swept through her, that once again life was being presented to her in such a way that she felt that she had little, if any, control over the events. Then another sharp gust of wind came swirling, racing through the garden before her, the trees twisting and leaning over in response to its force, and the wind chased along the veranda threatening to scatter the lengths of cloth that were lying in front of her. Oyadori had to move quickly or they would have ended up in the garden. She had just recovered some order when the doors of the private apartment slid open and Kobuto san stepped backwards out of the room, bowing deeply as she did so, then kneeling on the wooden boards she eased the doors together again until they shut with a soft sound.

Kobuto san came over to where Oyadori was gathering up the lengths of cloth.

"It's alright, she is resting again. She just wanted some water to drink, that's all," she said with a soft sigh and bent down to help Oyadori.

"The wind was beginning to rise, I thought it better to take these things inside," said Oyadori, by way of explanation of what she was doing.

When everything had been gathered up and put away again, Oyadori once more returned to the conversation that had been interrupted. "You said that someone came by to see me earlier, who was it? A man I think you said."

"Oh yes, that's right," Kobuto feigned indifference, as she resumed her teasing out of the growing tension in the younger maid. "Maybe you could go to the kitchen and get some food for us. I'm getting hungry, I am almost tempted to eat what's in there," she said indicating the lacquered box that lay unopened on the table.

"Kobuto san, please, who was it who came?" This time Oyadori's voice revealed the strain of the anxiety she was feeling.

The Gardener's Apprentice

Kobuto looked across at her and observed the face looking anxiously at her. "It's nothing much to worry about, I don't suppose, he was just here a moment or two, he asked after you, if you were here, then disappeared as quickly as he had appeared. He is a clerk in the offices of Lord Saeko, as far as I know."

Oyadori did not quite know what to make of this, as the job title was not one she was familiar with.

"Yes, but what was his name, why did he want to see me? It's not normal that a man should just appear at the women's apartments like that, even Lord Saeko would not do that. Why was he asking after me? Kobuto san who was he? You know more of what happens around here than most people, please don't tease me like this, it's not right. Who was he?" She spoke the words in a rush.

"His name is Shigoto. Shigoto Kanyu, if I remember correctly. Yes, that's right, Shigoto Kanyu".

Shigoto Kanyu: those two words came to Oyadori like stab wounds thrust deep into her soul. Of course, it was the name of the person that Lady Saeko had told her had been chosen to be her husband. The sound of the words carried a chill that made her shiver and quake. Kobuto san stood serenely before her with a faint smile playing across her face, as if the whole matter was but a game, something to be amused at.

"Shigoto Kanyu," Oyadori turned the words over and over in her mind, though she realised that there would be no possibility that she could ever forget them, they had silently haunted her ever since she first heard them, and she did not know why.

"You should be pleased, Oyadori. What I have heard is that he is to be your husband," said Kobuto san with a note of triumph in her voice. "Of course I only saw him for a moment, but he seems like a pleasant enough person to me. For a husband that is."

Oyadori did not hear this last comment, she rushed out of the room and ran as quickly as she could along the veranda. Her ears were full of the sounds of a wind screaming through a thicket of trees, tearing at the leaves and scattering them far and wide in its wake. She did not know where she was going, she only knew that she had to run, run before the wind tore her into pieces too.

CHAPTER FIVE

June 1584

"Oke Kaiba, son of Oke Ikan, to be made Stable hand, 2nd Class, appointment immediate.

Jiimi Kokageko, daughter of Jiimi Tsuyoi, to be made Wick trimmer, from 9th month onward.

Shigoto Okugi, son of official Shigoto Kanyu, to be made Apprentice Under Gardener, appointment immediate.

Hone Sakana, son of Hone Himono, promotion to kitchen apprentice, appointment immediate …"

On droned the monotone voice of the aged patriarch, his voice scarred and undermined by the accumulation of the years and the cares of statehood, barely reaching into the first of the packed ranks of the crowd assembled before him. Hence each announcement sparked murmuring waves of sound running from the front to the rear of the assembly, as the news spread out into the world at large. Each name mentioned, each pronouncement was like a pebble thrown into water with the ripples reaching out seemingly touching lives at random. Every fresh announcement would inspire a soft, muted explosion of joy, resentment, resignation or indifference in those assembled on the expanse of the gravel courtyard below the broad veranda. Above them all the great patriarch Lord Saeko sat, flanked by his two sons, encrusted and resplendent in his finest kimono. About him gathered his extensive family, also his closest and most trusted retainers, who leaned inward ever so slightly, so as to publicly display their profound loyalty, also to be seen to be straining to catch every regal utterance. The steps leading from the courtyard to the veranda were lined with ranks of hard-faced soldiers, whose sole duty, and single expectation was to lay down their lives in the service of the family that fed and watered them, should that be required.

On hearing Shigoto's name and formal seal of appointment being read out, the faintest shadow of a smile fluttered over the firmly closed lips of the loyal, though junior ranked retainer, Kanyu. The younger Shigoto himself heard nothing. He was still contemplating the manifest unfairness of the severe injunction from his mother and father that had banned him from bringing his favourite toy as a companion to the ceremony.

Shigoto was rehearsing again the retribution he could impose on his vile parents, his father in particular, for refusing the perfectly reasonable expectation of his to bring his stick, when his father's elbow caught him sharply at the side of the head. Then he caught the trace of his name having been mentioned, and one of the strangers in the pressing crowd turned to look down towards him with a smile and a nod of the head. "You are to be a garden apprentice," the father whispered to him, the words barely escaping sideways from the clutches of his stiffly drawn lips.

All of a sudden Shigoto felt a seismic shift in his world, the safe certainties of a few moments ago were now suddenly being challenged by a new order. Dark clouds appeared to be massing on the horizon that was not as far off as he had thought. He moved away from the side of his father and nestled in closer to his mother, slipping his small hand into the comfort of hers. Shigoto felt as if a severe sentence had been imposed on him, a dull grey blanket of confinement and oppression had been thrown over him. It was the end of something, but he could not identify exactly what that thing was. No doubt it would soon become clear enough, but for now as he appeared to be on the verge of entering the wholly bewildering world of adults. Shigoto was not sure he wanted to go down that route. All his imagined games and playful scenarios were after all but inverted reflections and observations of the world as perceived through a child's prism. At the precise moment of the transformation, when fate finally reveals a part of its hand and thus lays down a marker for the future, in that initial millisecond of time when perception is most acute, his overwhelming emotion was one of dread.

His father had appeared at the house earlier that morning, Shigoto had been playing in the small space that passed for a yard, and he had seen his father march purposefully through the gateway. At first he had not recognised the visitor. His father was wearing the two swords, which were his by right to do so by the virtue of being a *samurai* however lowly ranked, though it were not on every occasion that a sheathed blade appeared tucked into the left side of his belt. He had also freshly shaved the crown of his head, in the manner of his class, leaving a telltale smudge of blood drying on his pale, exposed pate. There was a frown of concentration across his face as he strode towards the entry porch of the modest dwelling, with the preoccupied air of a man of no little self-importance, trying to recall something he had perhaps overlooked to do. Shigoto went to duck behind a bush that grew by the corner of the house, but his father had spotted him.

"You, boy, come on. It's time we were going. This is not the time for games and frivolity now. Come on," he shouted out louder than was really necessary in the circumstances. He stood in the centre of the yard, his hand moving nervously to and from one of the handles projecting at his waist. Shigoto peered through the thin foliage at him, his hand tightly clasping the stick he had been playing with. "Come on," Kanyu bellowed, even louder this time. "It's not time for playing damn stupid games. Where is your mother?"

At this Oyadori appeared in the entry porch, alerted by the shouting.

"Oh, it's you husband, I am here. What are you shouting at? The neighbours will hear you yelling like that. Is it really necessary? Please come in a moment, we are almost ready. Please come in."

"Well, I am ready now," said Kanyu, though this time he managed to modulate his volume slightly as he saw that his wife standing a few paces away. He looked slightly abashed. "Come on, why are two you not ready? You should be ready by now. This is causing delay and it will not look good to be late. We need to be near the front of the veranda for the announcements. I am not standing at the back of the crowd. It simply is not fitting for a person of my status. My father will be seated on the veranda with the family. I need to be seen." He was almost pleading in his exasperation.

"Of course, of course," said Oyadori, trying her best to placate Kanyu's temper. "We are ready, give me a moment and we will be with you. Just please don't shout in that voice; the whole neighbourhood will hear. With the greatest respect, of course."

"Bah! You should have been ready, waiting for me when I arrived. I call this disrespectful, this, this is not what being ready means. It's an important day, you should have known that."

Kanyu spluttered on until his rage finally subsided into simple frustration.

"Oku-chan, come in now. Come here at once please. Look your hair needs to be tidied again. Put that stick away. Your father is impatient to be going." Oyadori's voice had a firm tone, and Shigoto knew that she meant business. But he did not want to walk past his father who was now standing with his feet apart and fists resting on his hips, the perfect picture of a man confounded by events seemingly outside his reach or control. Instead he made his way round to the far side of the house and clambered up onto the thin veranda and made his way into the building via his grandmother's room.

"You should not act like that with your father," Oyadori scolded him mildly as she straightened his hair and his costume. "Come on now, and let's be on our way, before he really does explode into a shower of sparks and sets fire to the building." This latter part she said quietly, so that the words would not carry as far as Kanyu who was now pacing in the yard. "There," she said, "you look presentable enough now. Just like a *samurai*, eh? A grown up boy, who is going to be a fine man, I'm sure," she added with not a small measure of pride in her voice.

"I'm taking my stick," said Shigoto in the most defiant tone he could muster.

"No, no, you cannot do that, Oku-chan. Leave it here, it will be here when we get back, then you can play with it again. But it would not be right to take your stick to the ceremony."

"I'm taking my stick," repeated Shigoto, his knuckles whitening as his grip tightened.

"No'" said his mother firmer this time. "Leave it here. Now come on we really must be going, this very instant."

They exited the room with Shigoto clasping his stick as if his life depended on it.

"How can it take you so long to get ready? What is it that takes so much time?" Kanyu's frustration had not entirely left him, as mother and son appeared in the entry porch ready to join him and complete the family group.

"We are ready to accompany you, husband." Oyadori said in the sweetest of voices.

"Right, well, let's get a move on. I am sure we will be late now because of you. This family will lose face arriving late like this. It's an outrage, a slur on my name, it really is." Then Kanyu noticed his son bearing his stick. "And what the hell is that?" He pointed a long trembling finger at Shigoto standing at his mother's side.

"My stick, for fighting as a dragon," mumbled Shigoto, choosing to avoid the incandescent glare of his father.

"Well, throw it away before I break it over your head. I've been kept waiting long enough as it is. I am not tolerating this one moment longer. I am your father and I am issuing you with an order. Throw the damn thing down. Now!"

"Husband, you are shouting again. The neighbours…"

"Damn the neighbours, damn you both, and damn it all. Throw that stick down this instant or I will take out my sword and remove your head. I have every justification. More than every justification, I am being driven demented by this insolence." Kanyu reached for the handle of the long sword at his waist. Slowly and with great deliberation Shigoto turned and set the stick down to carefully lean against the side of the building, then he reached for his mother's hand, eyes cast down, refusing to look toward his father's florid face.

"Right, we are ready husband, lead the way," said Oyadori with great calmness.

❖ ❖ ❖

The reading of the roll call of appointments and promotions wound its laboured way to a conclusion. His Lordship lowered the scroll listing new appointments, and then raised his fan with its motif of mountains and clouds with orchids painted in the Chinese style. It was a gesture that heralded the end of the ceremony, and the moment at which the onlookers tightly packed toward the base of the steps began to break up and the crush of bodies began to resume being individual beings. Released now from a tension arising from the blend of personal anticipation and a strict adherence to the ultimate supremacy of clan loyalty, most headed cheerfully toward the colourful, billowing awnings, beneath which an array of dishes of food had been laid out like treasures. Shigoto's father hurried off to be at his Lord's service without another word to mother or son. Still clutching his mother's hand, Shigoto drifted along with the flow of the crowd towards where the delicacies were being displayed. Occasionally his mother would stop to exchange a few words with another kimono-clad lady, and Shigoto with a silent acceptance would reluctantly receive the few words of formal praise and encouragement directed towards him.

The kaleidoscopic colours of the women and men dressed in their finery brought a gaiety and glamour to the whole occasion. The sight of the throng of people milling in front of the red and white striped awning tents adorned with the Saeko crest, three fish chasing each other's tails in a circle, was sufficient to lift the gloom which had temporary settled about Shigoto. Now it was his mother who was holding fast to his hand, anchoring him to her side. In front of them people were jostling to get to the food and refreshments provided generously by their Lord and Master. Shigoto was eager to get to the front of the crowd before the tables were entirely laid waste and stripped bare of the last of the temptations. Straining at his mother's grasp he attempted to penetrate the wall of bodies opening and closing before him. As he pressed forward he pushed roughly against the side of someone wearing a midnight blue kimono, with a broad brimmed straw hat shading the owner's face from view.

The tall figure looked down to see who or what was attempting to push past him. "Ah, how fortunate a meeting is this? If I am not mistaken it is young master Shigoto. I do not think that we have been properly introduced."

The words fell down on Shigoto, their articulation and steady intonation with a certain steely edge came down like a sharp shower of hailstones stopping him in his tracks. He looked up as the man removed his hat to reveal a dark tanned head devoid of any trace of hair, and two piercing eyes looking down at him from what seemed an great height.

"Maguro Sensei, greetings to you on the occasion of Announcements and Appointments. I trust you are in good health, Sensei. You certainly look as healthy as ever." Shigoto's mother recognising the person her son had almost knocked to one side in his haste, instinctively came to the rescue of the young boy. "Please excuse my son, he is enthusiastic for everything. We are most grateful to Sensei, for accepting our son as an apprentice. We, that is, my husband and our family are most honoured at your agreement to instruct our son, Sensei. We are most grateful for the kindness and consideration you show to us." The mother dutifully spoke up for all the family, even the absent father. "Oku-chan, this is Maguro Sensei. Show your respects to your teacher."

With this she bowed purposefully and elegantly before the erect figure of Maguro Sensei, pulling on her son's arm in such a manner as to make it clear he was to bow too. The lower the better in his case.

"I shall be discussing the matter of the appointment of your son as an apprentice with his Lordship," he said with a voice that precisely carved out the words, and then he paused for a moment before finishing his thought. "I have no particular need of additional help in the gardens at present." That angular voice came down once again.

The figure of the priest, erect and lean, loomed over mother and child. Maguro Sensei's look once more came to rest on the head of Shigoto standing below him. He seemed to be studying something intently, the way a bank-side heron would stare hypnotically into the water flowing before it. His eyes narrowed to two barely perceptible slits. Shigoto held himself stock still, with his attention turned toward the gravel and dust at his feet, not daring to move, least of all look up. Maguro Sensei reached out a thin, finely sculpted hand with his long fingers and gently tilted Shigoto's face upward. Now his look could fall directly onto the boy's face. Shigoto felt the full force of Maguro Sensei's gaze. It brought with it a peculiar warming sensation, which gradually spread throughout his chest cavity. For what seemed like an eternity to Shigoto, but probably lasted no more than a few seconds, the Zen monk held Shigoto's complete and utter attention. Shigoto felt his very being laid wide open, and he was rendered defenceless before his putative teacher. Maguro Sensei had the complete freedom to enquire into whatever aspect of his being he might choose, to see everything he might possibly have need to know, to weigh the balance of possibilities and probabilities, and listen in to the lapping chatter of the river of Shigoto's fate. Was it that he recognised something of his own soul in there? If Maguro Sensei was a heron, he appeared to be poised at the point of striking into the waters rushing past his feet, just when a new unheralded factor entered the delicate equation of chance and destiny. Maguro Sensei turned to Shigoto's mother, who was tightly clutching her son's hand to the point where her knuckles were gleaming white under the taut skin stretched over them.

"He is young yet to be an apprentice. He can't be more than eight or nine years, I would say. While I am all in favour of children learning their way in this world, we all require a childhood too. I am sure that Lord Saeko will be most concerned to respect that notion too. I appreciate the desire of a family to send their son out into the world equipped to make a living, to be set on a righteous and noble path. But there are many considerations that need to be taken into account in this matter. It is a question of sensitivity, too. Preparedness and sensitivity to the kind of work proposed. You will know well madam, that as a gardener he will regrettably not be granted any particular status in our society. There again, you must appreciate there is a model of proper order and progression that exists all about us, if we but look carefully enough. To know and to follow the river is all we can expect of life." Sensei paused in his thoughts, as if he had decided that it was necessary for the import of his words to sink deep enough to take root.

"Yes, Sensei, I'm sure you are correct in what you say," said Oyadori after a moments pause, though in truth she was not entirely certain as to the veiled meaning of his words.

Maguro Sensei looked again at the top of Shigoto's head, his lips pursed in thought and judgement.

"I will send word for him when the time is right. In due course we will discover no doubt if the boy is ready to become the apprentice, if he is prepared to take the path to being a creator of gardens. For now, for the time being he may accompany me on occasion on my garden inspections and supervisory duties. I will send word when the time is suitable." His eyes never flinched, never strayed, never revealed what really lay behind the deep tanned surface of his face.

Maguro Sensei bowed toward the mute mother and child before him. It was, like everything else about the man, a precise and measured inclination of the head, accompanied by the merest suggestion of the upper part of his body leaning forward. As he straightened again, to return his posture to its full height, he brought the broad, round straw hat, which he had removed and was holding in front of his chest upward and settled it back on his head. Mother and son stood motionless, her arm now round his shoulder, pulling him in to her side. Shigoto was staring with eyes the size of rice bowls into the face of the priest. In his own good time, Maguro Sensei adjusted the thin black cloth straps of the hat under his chin, his gaze rested gently on Shigoto. Then he appeared simply to vanish, for in the next moment he was out of sight of the mother and son who were left gazing into the empty space he had left behind.

"Come on. There will not be any food left unless we get a move on," said Oyadori finally coming to, as if she was waking from sleep. Somehow her son's hunger had left him. It was the inscrutable face of Maguro Sensei that dominated his imagination now.

CHAPTER SIX

March 1574

For the first time in what felt to have been an age, Oyadori was briefly released of her responsibilities and duties. She had received permission to take some time to visit the Shinto shrine and offer her prayers for the departed soul of her father. Oyadori slipped a shawl over her shoulders, checking to make sure she had a few copper coins to throw into the offertory box and set off towards the shrine. The afternoon had a lingering crispness about it, with low puffball clouds suspended in the branches of trees shorn of their leaves. She was relieved about being able to spend a little time on her own. Lady Saeko had been particularly demanding of late, and that combined with Awayuki's absence had placed extra demands on the staff who looked after her daily needs. Were it not for the fact it was the anniversary of her father's death she might not have been granted to time away from the palace. Oyadori needed time to be able to think, to try and settle her thoughts. As she made ready to leave, the conversation she had had with her mother recently came back into her mind, about the proposal relating to marriage set to her by Lady Saeko.

"Yes, I know," said her mother.

"You know?" Oyadori's voice rose in surprise.

"They came and spoke to me, it is only polite to tell the family." Mother and daughter were sitting in the small house they had been granted to live in since the death of Oyadori's father two years previously. Her mother's delicate frame folded into a kneeling position by the ash-lined hearth, a metal kettle suspended over the glowing charcoal. Oyadori was on her feet pacing the room.

"What did you say? Did you agree? Did you give your consent? You know, no one had spoken to me about this. I do not even know the man. This man who has been chosen to be my husband. This man whose children I will have to bear. You know he came to see me without even a letter of introduction or anything. He just came on his own to the Women's apartments. Just turned up like that one day. And this is supposed to be someone with manners? I may not be a grand lady of the court, I may be young and just chambermaid, but I know something of what is good behaviour. It was fortunate for me that I was not there at the time. How dare he? Does he think that he already owns me, just on the say-so of Lord Saeko? At least my father was a samurai, and what is this man? Some administrator? He probably does not even own a sword." She spoke passionately and quickly, her tone stung by the sense of bitterness and iniquity that now erupted inside her.

"Sometimes it's just better to accept things as they are," her mother had said finally. Her face, lined by age and the endurance of cares, remained defiant.

"So you had no objections to your daughter being treated as if she were the property of someone else?"

"Oya-chan, calm yourself. It is not like that, not like that at all. Think of yourself, think of your future, you will need a man to look after you. You are coming to an age where children will be expected of you. I am sure that the Lord Saeko has chosen carefully for you."

"Pah! What does he care for me? Does he even know my name? My face? I am just to be a gift to some retainer of his that he wishes to favour, that's all. I am as much worth to him as a barrel of rice wine at best, some thing to be traded for a favour, or as a reward for some good conduct. "She put the cup that was in her hands down with such force that it clattered loudly on the floor.

"Calm yourself Oya-chan. It is not like that, not like that at all. You are young yet, and will get used to the idea in time. It will be for the best, you will see. Your husband will give you fine sons, something to be proud of, you will see."

Oyadori had looked across at her mother who was avoiding direct eye contact with her.

"So, to have a daughter has no merit then." It was not a question; it was a statement of all the hurt and anger that was welling inside her. "If my father were alive he would not agree to this."

"It is not like that, not like that at all," her mother repeated, her voice hushed. "Your father would agree it is for the best, I am sure. We are who we are. He understood that very well, very well indeed."

"How can you say that? What do you really know what he would think? Maybe he would have preferred to have had a son, and not a daughter, is that what you mean?" Oyadori resumed her attack.

"Oya-chan, please, have some respect, do not speak of your father in this way. May his soul be at peace now," said her mother, and the conversation then faltered, and mother and daughter lapsed into the silence of an uneasy, unspoken truce.

As Oyadori entered the narrow tree lined lane that lead in the direction of the shrine, those last words came back to her with particular resonance, 'may his soul be at peace'.

'Is that what it takes to be at peace I wonder, do we have to die first to find the grace that seems to be so lacking in our lives? Unless we are born into the right family that is.' She thought of her mistress Lady Saeko, surrounded by all the privileges and riches of her position, with servants and maids to answer to her every need, day or night. She was aware then of the huge gulf that lay between them, of what seemed to be an unbridgeable divide, which no matter what merit she might gain in this world she would never be able to cross. Then she saw a little way ahead of her the bright orange and black painted *tori* gate that marked the entrance to the shrine compound and she stopped by the side of the lane. She wanted a moment to recover her equilibrium, her calmness, as she did not want to enter the compound with the acidic rancour of her thoughts still fizzing and festering inside her.

Beside her was a huge tree, its girth far wider than the span of her outstretched arms, at its base a small upright stone with a crudely carved figure on its face nestled in among the exposed roots. The stone had been there perhaps as long as the tree. Its steep sides had been eroded away by the years into gentle slopes, though the figure was just about recognisable even as it faded back into the matrix from which it had once been released. Oyadori looked back down the lane whence she had come. It was empty and there was no one to be seen from the direction of the shrine, no sounds apart from the wind in the crowns of the trees, and the calling of unseen birds. She knelt down and brushed away a few dried twigs and leaves that had fallen onto the stone figure. Then she put her hands together and clapped three times, muttering softly to herself 'Namu Amida', evoking the Buddha's name. 'Please help me, please help me find my way.

Please help me gain some merit in this world. I am trying to be a good person, to do the right things, really I am.' She offered her prayer before the silent Jizo figure at her feet. As she stood upright again her head swam dizzily, and she put one arm out to brace herself against the rough bark of the monumental tree. As she did so, she thought she could feel the trunk tremble ever so slightly, and she looked up towards the towering height of its crown that seemed to be lost somewhere in the sky. She felt a strong affinity, a personal connection with the tree; it seemed to her that the aged colossus was trying to communicate something to her. "What?" she said. "What is it you want to tell me?" But all she could hear was the sound of the wind filtering through the branches, and the stone figure by her feet remained as passive and as silent as before.

Oyadori passed beneath the arch of the *tori* gate and made her way into the grounds of shrine. The whole shrine complex, a scattering of single storey timbered buildings, was surrounded by a dense growth of tall trees which served to cut it off from the landscape beyond, and gave it an atmosphere of profound tranquillity. There seemed to be no one else about. The palpable calm of the shrine eased her, and she felt herself being brought gently back down to earth. She headed for a small building that stood over a spring in one corner and entered it. The light was dim inside, and the temperature felt cooler to her cheeks. She knew her way well enough, having visited the shrine many times with her mother, and on several occasions with her father too. There were two uneven stone steps that led down to a small pool of water. In one corner the water murmured and bubbled contentedly to itself. Oyadori crouched on the lowest step and picked up a bamboo ladle that had been set on a flat-topped stone to one side and dipped the cup into the inky water. She rinsed her hands and her mouth, momentarily savouring the draught that set her teeth on edge with its metallic coldness. It felt to her as if the chill water was finally dousing the last embers of her anger, and that she could at least for the moment set aside her concerns. Having made her ablutions, she remained crouching there for a moment, absently twisting the handle of the ladle that allowed the remnants of water to return to the dark pool.

As she left the building and re-emerged into the light of the day, it took her eyes a moment to adjust. She halted, and sighed deeply. She felt ready now. She had put her cares to one side and felt prepared to offer her prayers with a clear and empty mind. She began to walk towards the main shrine building, in front of which stood the offertory box and was about to reach for a silk purse tucked into the broad cloth band around her waist when something caught her attention. People were making their way along the lane. Whether they were coming to the shrine or heading elsewhere was not immediately clear, but there were the unmistakable sounds of voices, of chatter and even laughter drifting towards her. She frowned: she had hoped to hold on to this moment of peace and quiet at least until her prayers were said, and she instantly resented the intrusion. From where she was, she could see the *tori* gate and just a little way down the lane, but whoever it was on the path must have been further down and they were out of her line of sight. She suddenly felt exposed and unsure whether or not to continue.

'Don't be foolish,' she said to herself. 'Many people use this shrine, and they have every right to be here. Just as much as you.' But there was something in the gaiety of the voices that contrasted with her own mood and struck a wrong note for her, and she felt the muscles in her chest tighten. 'Why is it that it is so hard to find a few moments on one's own?' She looked over towards the gate again, but could see nothing more than the foliage and trunks of the trees lining the beaten earth of the lane. Whoever was there, and it seemed to be obviously more than a few, must have stopped a little way down the lane. She resolved to continue, after all she had come here for a specific purpose, and she felt that there was no particular reason why she should be deflected from that. She walked on with her eyes firmly fixed on the shrine.

Standing at the front of the shrine, she reached out with both hands and grasped the thick rope that hung limply down, and gave it two or three vigorous shakes that set the cluster of bells it was attached to rattling dryly. Then she clapped three times, before bringing her hands together and with head bowed offered her prayers to the deities of the shrine. When she had finished she pulled the purse from her belt and tossed the copper coins into the wooden offertory box where they clattered to a rest. She had done what she needed to do: she had fulfilled her duty to her father, and felt lightened having relieved herself of that duty. She was just about to turn and make her way back, when she heard the voices accompanied by more merriment again, and this time there was the sound of a horse whinnying as if impatient to move on. A horse. That could only mean one thing: whoever was on the road was not some group of local farmers. It must be a person or persons of some status, a member of the Saeko family most likely. Oyadori could feel the blood draining from her cheeks, and her heart instinctively started to sharpen its rhythm. Not that she was doing anything wrong, or even out of place: she was perfectly entitled to be here at the shrine, but she did not want to have to explain herself to anyone. This was supposed to be her time, a few moments to herself, and the intrusion of someone in a position of authority would only serve to undermine her currently fragile confidence.

In an instant she knew what she would do. Gathering up the folds of her kimono with both hands she took one final look towards the gate - there was no one in sight though the voices were clearer, louder now and she fled into the cover of the vegetation that surrounded the shrine compound. Barely noticing the whiplash stings of the branches, she plunged into the undergrowth until it swallowed her up. The woodland she had entered was very dense and within a few strides she was out of sight. When she stopped she was breathing heavily and her heart pounding. 'What is the matter with me,' she thought. 'I do not normally react to things like this. I am just making a fool of myself. What if they saw me running away? Perhaps they would think I was a thief, and come after me. If anybody were to find me here, what would they think?' But nobody came after her, no one called out in alarm, she was quite alone.

As she gathered her scattered wits, the voices came filtering through the leafy cover, more clearly. Whoever it was had now entered the compound of the shrine. The words were indistinct, but she could confirm that there was more than one voice; a small group of people was visiting the shrine. Then after a few moments the bells clattered into life as someone shook the rope they were attached to. Despite her instinct telling her to stay still, to stay where she was, Oyadori started very slowly to edge back in the direction from which she she had just fled. Using her arms stretched in front of her face she cautiously parted the screen of branches and leaves until a chink opened up in front of her, just wide enough to allow her to see who it was visiting the shrine, but small enough for her to remain hidden from casual view.

    Standing in a group in front of the shrine were a group of men, maybe half a dozen in all. They were dressed in fine kimonos and seemed relaxed as they talked among themselves. If they had any idea of her presence, they betrayed no suspicions by the way they behaved. Oyadori breathed softly, sure now that neither her flight nor presence had been observed. It was simply a group of people visiting the shrine, as if they were touring the area and taking in the local sights. She did not recognise any of those people she could see. If they were relatives of the Saeko family or members of Lord Saeko's court she would have at least recognised some of them, if not all. Her curiosity increased and she remained in concealment wondering who the visitors might be.

Though their attitude seemed to be casual and relaxed, Oyadori became aware that in addressing one of their number, they seemed to adopt a particularly respectful and polite manner. Whereas they would look each other in the face when talking together, the person whom she had not been able to see closely, the one who had stood in front of the shrine and rung the bell, always stood slightly apart from the main group. He stood with his back to her, but she noticed that whenever he moved in the direction of one of the group they would step back. Clearly it was someone of importance, someone who commanded a high degree of respect.

Then suddenly it came clear to her just who it was she was spying on. When the truth dawned, her hand trembled slightly. She instinctively drew back, closing as she did so the gap in the screen of vegetation that kept her hidden from their view. 'How stupid I am! Of course, it's him. Who else could it be? No wonder I did not recognise those men, they must be part of the retinue of people who came with him.' She shuddered at the thought that she had been in effect spying on the brother of the Emperor, a member of the Imperial family, no less, and someone whose societal status was so far above hers that it did not bear thinking about. 'No wonder they are all so respectful,' she thought. 'Who else could it be but him? The Imperial houseguest in exile.' And she knew then that she had placed herself in a position of some delicacy, for if she were caught and exposed, she would most likely, if not inevitably lose her position as chambermaid to Lady Saeko at the very least.

Her initial instinct was to withdraw, find some way through the thicket of trunks and leafy cover, and make her way back onto the path that would lead her to the palace, and the relative safety of Lady Saeko's apartments. She moved her foot to step backwards and it collided with the base of a small tree that she had stepped in front of to gain a better view. Then her curiosity began to get the better of her, and instead of quietly withdrawing, she made up her mind to take one more look in the direction of the voices. Given the relaxed and casual tone of the conversation, she could judge that the men had no idea they were being watched. Once again she very cautiously lifted her arms and slowly parted the foliage to gain a better view. The group had moved off from where they were standing in front of the main shrine, and had begun to drift towards another nearby structure. This was an open platform set to one side of the main shrine, and was a place where ceremonies were enacted for special occasions during the year. In doing so the men came closer to where Oyadori remained hidden. Now she could see clearly the fine garb of the distinguished exile, she could make out the lustre of his kimono; moreover as he turned to address the others, she was able to see his face.

'I am not supposed to look into the face of someone who is of divine origin. I will be damned,' she thought to herself, but there was something about the face that held her attention. Far from being stern, or even malevolent, it struck her that she was looking into the face of a man who had the capacity to enjoy life. He appeared to Oyadori to be considerably older than her. She guessed his age to be about his mid forties perhaps, though she really had no way of being sure. His slightly florid cheeks and the unlined face carried the look of someone who had borne the tribulations of life lightly. But it was his eyes that held her attention the most, they appeared jet black, as if they were pools of pitch tar, and now she could even see the network of fine creases that radiated out from the corners of his eyelids. When he smiled, as he often did, the mesh of lines became more prominent, and his face radiated a charm and a surprising openness that she had rarely, if ever encountered before. 'Clearly he is someone who has enjoyed his life, lived his life to the full,' she mused, and she recalled the subtle admonition of her fellow maids, when they had insinuated that the visitor was a man with a reputation for enjoying the company of women. Something stirred in her, some feeling buried so deep that she barely recognised it, and she was genuinely surprised when finally the thought surfaced in her mind, as if a bubble of air had been released from captivity deep beneath the surface of a pond. 'He's an attractive man, that's for sure. No wonder they say he has had much success with women. He's a very attractive man indeed.'

One man had run back to the gate, where the horse had been tethered, and now reappeared with paper and writing utensils. 'They are going to write poetry,' she realised. 'Now is the time I can try to make my way out of here while they are busy with that. Oh, Buddha, forgive me for what I have been doing. I should not I be spying on others I know. Please don't hold it against me.' Slowly and quietly as possible, Oyadori released the sprig she was holding onto and closed off for the time being any further opportunity to spy on the group who had now settled themselves on the open platform. Then she turned and began to push her way with utmost care through the undergrowth, careful to check where each foot was landing in case she made any sound that might give gave her presence away.

It took her a while but eventually she made her way back to the lane that led up to the shrine. Before she stepped out on to the path she listened intently, and carefully confirmed that the lane was indeed empty before emerging onto it. When she did, she realised that her heart was beating at a rapid rhythm again and her breathing was slightly laboured. She felt warm enough to have raised a slight sweat, despite the chill and damp air of the woodland. Glancing up the lane towards the shrine one more time, she set off at a quick walking pace trying to put as much distance between herself and the men as possible. After a little while she slowed her pace, and looking down at her clothing brushed off a few specks of dirt. She ran a wooden comb through her coiffure to try and restore any stray hairs to their proper place. Then she walked on. Now Oyadori could feel a light heartedness sweeping into her, she smiled, and even began to take a certain delight at what she had done. She had got away with something that few people would have dared to do, of that she was sure, and it almost made her giddy to consider it.

As she came into view of the palace grounds, a thought rose up from the depths of her unconscious. When it emerged into the realms of her mind where she could recognise the idea for what it was, she had to stop walking. It was something so outrageous, so outlandish, that her primary instinct was to bury the thought so deep that it would never see the light of day again. 'Oh, no,' she thought, 'not that, no, no. What am I thinking of?' Her cheeks reddened in an instant, but her eyes had a certain glisten to them, and she could not stop the corners of her mouth curling fractionally upwards. 'That would put an end to all this nonsense of marriage proposals. He would never want to marry me then.' By the time she passed under the gateway into the palace she had regained her usual opaque composure, and no one could have assumed she was anyone other than a maid returning from her pious devotions, ready to resume her duties and be at the beck and call of her mistress once more.

CHAPTER SEVEN

July 1585

"Excuse me. Sorry to disturb you, but Maguro Sensei instructs Shigoto san to meet him on the path to the hill of the tall waterfall in the shortest possible time." The voice called out from just inside the frail gateway at the front of the house. There was a moment's pause in the house before it burst into a mild frenzy of activity.

"Oku-chan, Oku-chan," Oyadori called out to her son. "Where is that boy?"

"He was at the back of the house, playing in the dirt again. What ever else did you think?" replied Shigoto's grandmother, Oba-chan.

"Oku-chan, come here at once. Sensei has sent for you, you have to get ready, now. Come on there is someone waiting to take you to him. One of the gardeners is here, hurry now, you cannot keep Sensei waiting, Oku-chan," her impatience growing with every passing moment.

"Oh that boy, stubborn as his father, no doubt," said Oba-chan.

"Now mother, it is not the time to be saying things like that. I had no warning Sensei would send for him otherwise I would have got him ready. Oba-chan, please go and wrap up some rice balls. He can take them as a gift to Sensei, as he must not go empty-handed. Oku-chan, I want you here, now!"

Shigoto appeared in the house, looking crestfallen, he had been dragged away from his play by the urgent calling of his mother.

"Do I have to go? I was busy, doing things. It's not fair all this," he whined in protest. He could vividly remember, with a shudder, that first meeting with Maguro Sensei, when his teacher's eyes had seemed to burrow into him, to see into him in a way that he had never experienced before. He knew in his heart that he would have to go. This man, Maguro Sensei, his teacher had called for him and that was reason enough. "It's not like it's really important or anything. Please, let me stay. I was busy. Can't you say just say I am not well or something like that?"

"Look at the state of you. Get out of those clothes at once. Now." Oyadori's voice was firm and controlled, leaving no room for negotiation.

When he was dressed in clean clothes and presentable enough to be sent out into the world, a small parcel clasped under his arm, Shigoto left with the gardener who was patiently waiting to deliver him to Maguro Sensei.

"Some woman, your mother, eh?" The gardener turned to him once they were a little distance from the house, and out of sight of Oyadori who had come as far as the gateway to see him off. "After a woman like that, you will find Maguro Sensei a pussy cat to deal with. That's for sure," and he laughed aloud. Though

Shigoto did not see the amusing side of it, his ears still ringing from the scolding he had received as he left.

"It's not funny," said Shigoto after a brief silence.

"No? I thought it was one of the funniest things I have seen in a good long while. Oh yes, some woman that mother of yours. I would hate to cross swords with her, that's for sure. I bet your father does not get a word in at home, eh?" Good-natured laughter spilled out of him at the thought.

"What does Maguro Sensei want me for?" Shigoto had calmed down. His fate was inescapable, that was as clear as his mother's final word, and he began to resign himself to an afternoon of tedium.

"Sensei? Maguro Sensei, well, he wants to turn you into a gardener, I suppose. He's quite a man is Sensei you know. He's another one not to cross swords with, if you see what I mean."

"Does Maguro Sensei have a sword?" asked Shigoto as the pair made their way to the gardens.

"A sword?" The gardener stopped and put his hand on Shigoto's shoulder. "Listen, and listen good to me. Maguro Sensei is a priest, eh. You know what they are, I suppose?" Shigoto nodded his assent to this self-evident question. "Well, let me tell you, I have seen Maguro Sensei cut a man down just with his eyes, at ten paces and all. Fierce? You have never seen a man who can project fireballs out of his eyes, have you? Well, Sensei can. I tell you young man, never get him mad, he will send you into the next world before you remember what you had for breakfast. Best do what he asks of you, and do it the best you can. That's the sort of man your teacher is, the rest of them, mere pussycats. 'Cepting your mother of course, with due respect to her. Remember my words though, eh. Remember my words good, the words of Kamaboku the gardener here, I have seen it all, seen it all." Then Kamaboku the gardener, laughed again.

Shigoto pondered this new and potentially alarming news. But there was something in the way that it was delivered which gave him a certain comfort that he was not in imminent danger of being consigned to the afterlife, not just yet anyway.

"Is that your name then? Kamaboku san," he asked as they continued on their way.

"Yes, that's right, Kamaboku. I am the garden foreman. Not a man to play about with either, eh." Kamaboku's smile was wide, and the broad gap where his upper front teeth used to be was prominently on show.

"What does a garden foreman do?" asked Shigoto, having decided that perhaps caution was the best approach to the unknown this time.

"He runs errands for Sensei, that's what he gets to do," came the reply. "And looks after the other gardeners, and makes sure we get done what we are supposed get done."

"Do your eyes send out fireballs too?" Shigoto was perplexed and intrigued at this novel idea. He thought that he might adopt it for his playmate, the terrifying dragon, which merely spat out an all-consuming jet of flames.

"No, that's Maguro Sensei's speciality. It takes years to learn. Anyway, you are about to find out, he's just there." Kamaboku had stopped and was pointing up the path to where a tall slender figure was standing waiting.

Kamaboku stopped, and ushered Shigoto forward with a nod of the head, then he turned about and headed off down a side path and disappeared from view. Maguro Sensei stood with his back to Shigoto peering intently at a waterfall that was crashing down with a good flow and a heavy sound between large boulders. Shigoto approached him with a degree of caution. He had twice before been summoned to meet Maguro Sensei and on both occasions they had simply walked about the gardens, with barely a word being exchanged between them. Shigoto was not even absolutely sure afterwards that Sensei had even noticed he was there.

As he came within a few paces of his teacher he stopped, and waited. Maguro Sensei's back was still turned to him. He seemed to be wholly absorbed in observing the water's flow. The lip stone of the waterfall was tall enough to be above the head of Maguro Sensei. The water slid over a large flat stone before it cascaded down in a curtained rush and crashed into a pool below, before gathering itself again, before running off along a stream course, which Shigoto knew would eventually disgorge itself into the large pool known to all as the Great Dragon Pond. Shigoto waited, and waited, until impatience got the better of him and his attention began to wander.

"He is not interested in me,' he thought. 'I wonder if he even knows I am here. Oh, adults are such strange people. I do not wish to be like them. Now if I had my dragon stick with me I could sneak up on him an...'

At that moment Maguro Sensei wheeled around to face Shigoto. "Ah, the young garden apprentice himself, Shigoto Okugi, if I am not mistaken," he said looking directly at Shigoto.

Nervously his attention now very much focused on his teacher, Shigoto held out the small cloth wrapped parcel his mother had thrust into his hands as he left the safety of his home. "Maguro Sensei, please accept this humble gift. I...I... hope that you will excuse it only being an offering... a... umm, token offering. I wish to learn from you... and that you can teach me..." Shigoto tried to remember the words his mother had spent hours drilling into him by way of a polite formal greeting to his teacher. Maguro Sensei did nothing, nor did he say anything, his piercing gaze rested on Shigoto's face. Shigoto could feel his cheeks reddening and the deafening sound of water seemingly filled his head to the exclusion of any thoughts at all, threatening to wash away the greeting he had laboriously memorised. Then Maguro Sensei walked right past where Shigoto stood rooted to the spot, his arms still out stretched holding forth the gift of rice cakes, and started to make his way down the path at a good pace.

For a moment Shigoto half expected to be hit by a fireball crashing into him. Then as he turned and saw the now rapidly retreating back of his teacher striding away, a feeling of anger arose in him.

'What have I done? I said the words that mother taught me. I was polite to him, and he just walks off. That's not fair, he is my teacher, and he should be teaching me something about being a gardener, or something. How am I ever to learn anything if he just walks off like that? It's not right, not right at all. I am going to set my dragon on him. Let's see if he can really spit fire from his eyes. Well, my dragon can beat him anytime, I'll show him.' Then disregarding any consideration of his personal safety, he set off at a run after his rapidly disappearing teacher.

As he ran the anger inside of him blossomed, and he determined that when he came up to Maguro Sensei again he would have no compunction in showing him how he felt. Never mind that he did not have his 'Dragon stick' with him, he felt capable of enacting the role of the dragon himself, stick or no stick. He rounded a corner in the path, and nearly collided head first with his teacher who was standing there facing him, waiting for him. Shigoto skidded to a halt. Suddenly faced with his nemesis, his confidence and anger dissipated faster than he could have dared imagine.

"Maguro Sensei, please accept this humble gift. I..." he began to recite once more the polite phrases of greeting, which was the only thought that did form in his mind. Maguro Sensei put his hand up to stop him.

"Tell your mother I appreciate her kindness, and that I am grateful for her consideration," he said then stepped forward and extended both hands palm upwards before Shigoto. As he moved closer, Shigoto involuntarily took one step backwards. When he realised that his teacher was merely acquiescing to the gift, he stopped and set the parcel down in the hands and bowed low. Much to his surprise Maguro Sensei bowed in return, so Shigoto bowed once more. This time Maguro Sensei remained upright, though his eyes had regained their cloud-piercing quality. They remained in that position for a few moments, the tall willowy figure with the sun glinting from his shaved head, and the diminutive uncertain frame of the prospective apprentice.

"Tell me one thing Shigoto," Maguro Sensei spoke with a firm, strong voice. "Why should I accept you as an apprentice?"

This perplexed Shigoto. It was so unexpected that he had no ready answer rehearsed for the opportunity. In the couple of previous occasions that he had accompanied Maguro Sensei, his teacher had simply accepted the gift from his mother, with a polite nod of the head and a murmur of thanks and they had continued on their seemingly purposeless tour of the gardens. True, his teacher had not spoken a word to him at all, but equally he had never questioned why he was there. He had apparently accepted that Shigoto would follow him on his rounds, and then at some point would dismiss him and tell him to return to his family.

"I…I suppose because Lord Saeko told you to, Sensei," Shigoto said after a pause to consider the matter. He hoped fervently that this was the correct answer to the question posed to him.

"Indeed, is that so? But if I recall clearly, Lord Saeko appointed *you* to be a garden apprentice, am I right in that?"

"Well, yes, Sensei, I suppose so." Shigoto spoke carefully, as if he were picking his way through a thicket of thorns that threatened to tear into his flesh.

"But that does not answer my question, does it?" His teacher continued.

Shigoto was stumped by this development. He did not know where the exchange was heading, but he was sure he did not really want to go there.

"Well, Sensei, I suppose you have to be my teacher because Lord Saeko said so." Shigoto tried again, hoping very much that he had found the right form of words this time.

"That, Shigoto, was Lord Saeko's wish, let us accept that for the moment. Whether it really was the wish of his Lordship or the wish of others, let us set that matter to one side for now. For the time being it is of no practical consequence anyway. Am I right on this matter?"

"Yes, Sensei," Shigoto replied with a degree of hesitancy. He had no clue as to what he was agreeing to, only some vaguely realised instinct informed his answer.

"Then, perhaps you will agree that for you to become an apprentice to me, it is better that the matter has *my* agreement too. After all, if I am to be your teacher, and if I accept you as such, it puts us on a better footing, no? So my question remains the same: Why should I accept you as an apprentice."

This time the anger that had been subsiding in Shigoto came boiling up to the surface again. Never mind that it was some fire spitting adult that he was confronted by, that was of no concern to him at this moment. "It's because I want to be a gardener, that's why, Sensei." The words escaped him before he could even consider their potential impact or effect. "I want to learn about being a gardener, and you are the person who can teach me, that's why. And walking off and leaving me behind, and not speaking to me at all, will not put me off. I will follow you, and I will keep following you, until you teach me something about being a gardener." As soon as he said it, Shigoto knew that he had stepped over a mark, crossed an invisible boundary. Punishment in some heinous form was sure to come down on him for this outburst, if not from Maguro Sensei, then most surely from his mother, or even worst of all from his father, for Sensei was bound to report him for his insubordination and rudeness. He stood in front of Maguro Sensei, head bowed and waiting as a condemned man does for the swishing sound of the executioner's descending blade.

Nothing happened.

When he finally raised his eyes enough to look towards his teacher, Maguro Sensei was tucking into one of the rice balls Shigoto's mother had made. His eyes were not blazing flames, and his face was unnervingly relaxed and carefree. Once again Shigoto did not know what to make of the situation at all. Maguro Sensei was proving himself to be a person who was quite capable of confounding every expectation that he had of how adults behaved. If he had confronted his father in such a way, a swift kick or a slap across the head was the retribution he would have expected to swiftly follow. Howls would have been heard and tears would have been shed. Instead, here was his teacher contentedly eating a rice ball, while giving him what appeared to be a quizzical look. Shigoto shuffled his feet and waited whilst Maguro Sensei finished his mouthful and then extracted a handkerchief from within his kimono and slowly, deliberately, wiped his fingers clean.

"Delicious," he said. "Shigoto, please send my compliments to your mother."

"Yes, Sensei," Shigoto replied hesitantly. "And Sensei, I…I am sorry, please forgive me for speaking out of turn. I…"

Once again Maguro Sensei lifted up his hand to stop the flow of words. "No, no need for an apology this time. I asked you for an answer and finally it came out of you. I have no problem with that. But tell me Shigoto, and in this I also expect you to reply with honesty, do you really mean what you say?"

"You mean about wanting to be being a gardener? Yes, Sensei, I really want to be a gardener, I do." This time Shigoto spoke with an even tone that reflected a certainty and conviction he felt within himself, even if he understood nothing of why he gave the answer that he had.

"Good," said Maguro Sensei, "good. Right, in that case let us resume our walk shall we?"

As they walked around the gardens Maguro Sensei would stop every so often, and he would explain to Shigoto something about what they were looking at. They were standing by the Great Dragon Pond. The lake had a highly convoluted shoreline with many hidden bays, pebble beaches and stretches of rock-strewn shoreline, which tiny windborne waves would lap against with a pleasing sound.

"Would you say, Shigoto, that this was a natural pond?" Sensei asked him, as they stood together looking out over the sparkling surface that caught the sun as it appeared from behind the scudding clouds.

"Yes, Sensei, of course" replied Shigoto, it had never occurred to him that it could have been anything other than natural. Then Maguro Sensei explained to him that the body of water had been carved out of the earth many years previously, during the reign of the third Lord of the Saeko clan. He went on to explain that the pond had been dug out by prisoners of war brought to Mikura; during a time when fierce inter-clan warfare sporadically broke out as unpredictable bushfires across the land. It was even said by some that a dragon that lived in the pond and had lined its nest with the bones of the men who died in its excavation, guarding over its ossified hoard so that the souls of the departed would remind the living of the price of beauty.

To Shigoto, the Great Dragon Pond had always felt huge and mysterious. It was as if it was a continuation of the sea surrounding his island home. Now he looked at it with a renewed interest and respect. They followed a path that wound its way around the pond with the hidden dragon resting in the unplumbed depths.

The body of water would appear and disappear from view, as if it were flickering in and out of focus. One moment it was hidden from sight by trees or the underlying tucks and folds of the land, and in the next, a glimpse of water would appear suddenly framed by an opening in the vegetation. Sometimes they would take a path that would take them in a direction heading away from the pond, only for the path to make an unexpected turn and lead them back towards the water again. The pond was fed by a winding stream, which Shigoto knew began at the waterfall where he had met Sensei earlier. They crossed over the stream, broad and shallow now, by means of several flat-topped stones placed just above where it disgorged its burden of fresh water murmuring softly as it slid into the pond.

They made their way slowly around to the west side of the pond where the outfall was, across the mouth of which a low fence of thin bamboo canes had been interwoven, and in front of the barrier a raft of leaves had become trapped. When Shigoto saw this he puzzled over the upright stakes. He asked Sensei if they were intended to prevent the dragon from escaping from the body of the pond.

"No," Sensei smiled at the thought, "It's so that the leaves will catch there, as you can see. The gardeners will remove them from time to time. If too many leaves fall into the water they will rot, and the water will turn sour. If the water turns sour the dragon can become angry and people may suffer from its wrath and distress," he explained. Shigoto on hearing this now eyed the leaves with some degree of concern, and he felt inclined to bend down and remove them.

There were several places where they could get right down to the edge of the pond, places that were hidden from view from the main hall of the palace complex. Crouching here Shigoto felt as if he were quite in another world. From there he could watch the dorsal fins of the carp cleaving clean lines across tranquil patches of its surface. Out in the pond were several islands of different shapes and sizes, some were very low while others rose higher and were completely encircled by great dark boulders emerging directly out of the water. Growing on the backs of the islands gnarled, thick-barked pines leant in different directions; some tall and thin, others squat, with branches reaching finger-like over the silvery water. These islands, Sensei explained, represented turtles and cranes, and he pointed at certain stones and asked Shigoto to imagine them representing a head, a leg, or part of a shell back. As he did so, Shigoto had no trouble engaging his own vivid imagination to see amphibians and birds prowling across the water.

"So why are the birds in the water, Sensei?" Shigoto asked, amid the variety of questions now jostling for expression in his mind.

"It's an ancient Chinese story," Sensei explained. "The Chinese believed that paradise was a series of islands, each one of which was supported on the backs of giant turtles. If people were good in their lives, if they lived a life of kindness, piety and virtue, they would be carried on the backs of cranes to paradise when they died. When we build a garden, we are creating paradise on this earth, perhaps that people maybe do not have to die before they can taste paradise."

Shigoto felt a sense of awe at this idea of creating paradise. It was far beyond anything he had considered before. If that is what gardeners did, then he definitely wanted to be a gardener. He wanted to create paradise too.

Bridges connected some of the islands, and in places long flat slabs of rough stone connected one island to its neighbour. There was also a large wooden bridge, cheerfully painted with a bright orange-red colour, which arched like a cat from the shore across to one of the larger islands. This bridge was especially prominent from the direction of the palace buildings, so it was normally strictly out of bounds to anyone but the Saeko family. They paused at the centre of the bridge and Maguro Sensei showed him how to stamp his feet on the wooden boards. This brought the carp in the pond arrowing towards the bridge in the expectation of morsels of food to come raining down from the skies, which would then be swept up into the wide gape of their gasping mouths. Soon there was a lively scrum of brightly coloured carp milling about below where they stood, churning and frothing the water much to Shigoto's delight.

"Well, Shigoto," said Sensei as they made their way back to the shore once more. "I have to attend to various duties now. You have seen an aspect of the garden, and there is much more to see, but that will do for the time being. This is an ancient place, Shigoto, it holds many secrets, and they do not yield themselves to those who do not have the sight to see. Gardens are like that. Very few understand what they are capable of, and not even every gardener comes to know about these things. Assume nothing, and maybe you will learn something. Be like a carp; try everything, reject what is not right, and accept that which sustains you."

"Yes Sensei," said Shigoto, his mind reeling with all that was so new. He felt Sensei had opened a door, so giving him a glimpse into another world he had not known existed.

"Anyway, I trust you can find your way home from here. Do not forget to pass on my thanks for your mother's gift, and please tell her that it will no longer be necessary to send a gift when you come. Now run along, and go directly home." Maguro Sensei dismissed him with a wave.

All the way home, Shigoto's mind was churning over with the wonder of what he had seen. It really was as if scales had dropped away from his eyes. He could not wait to get home to tell it all to an audience of his mother and Oba-chan. Perhaps he was going to enjoy being a gardener, after all.

CHAPTER EIGHT

March 1576

At some point during the night, Oyadori emerged into wakefulness. She was sure she could detect what seemed to be soft rustling sounds, followed a muffled thump as if someone were moving clumsily but cautiously about in the next door room. Her senses were now alert and she was about to sit upright. She was poised to lift her arm and sweep back the thick futon that shielded her from the chill air, when she felt Kobuto san grasp her shoulder and hiss a barely audible warning. "No, stay where you are. Go back to sleep. It's nothing. Go to sleep." Oyadori settled herself back into the warm folds of the covering. For a little while longer she lay awake, primed for any other noises but silence had settled once again, so she let go and gratefully slid back into the depths of sleep.

As the first light of day began to seep into the small antechamber to the apartment of Lady Saeko, Oyadori awoke. Since Awayuki had gone to attend to the service of the distinguished visitor, she had shared an adjoining room at night with Kobuto. Kobuto had wasted no time in acidly pointing out that it was was to be regarded as a favour, given out of the kindness of her heart, but not something that should be taken for granted. Oyadori blinked a few times feeling reluctant to relinquish the envelope of musty warmth that cocooned her and begin the day. She looked over towards the dark mass, which was the still sleeping Kobuto lying nearby, and Oyadori thought she would wait until the other woman stirred before finally getting to her feet. It would give her a few more precious moments to hang onto the dream she had surfaced with.

In her dream, Oyadori had been walking someplace that was littered with huge smooth rock outcrops and many stands of trees huddled together as if for protection. The slabs of rock were baked by a brilliant sun and felt warm to the touch of her hands, whereas the ground under the trees was dank, dark damp and cool. She saw herself at certain times in the dream making her way in a grim masked silence between the trunks of the trees. Her back was bent over to avoid the low branches, and the ground beneath her unshod feet uneven and pockmarked with patches of spongy mosses. Then at other moments she could see herself stretched out under a brilliant azure dome of sky, spread-eagled on a huge mass of smooth rock which glittered and sparkled brilliantly, the air filled with the calling of thousands of unseen birds. The pleading voices of the birds would be caught by the wind, and bent and twisted into shapes, colours and even voices in song. As she awoke the realisation came to her that the one was conditional, dependant even on the other. Had she not known of the dark compressed space beneath the trees, she would have felt threatened by the sun and the vast sounds of the birds sculpted by the wind.

'I feel as if I have travelled with the spirits in my dreams,' she thought. 'Is that what we do? Because if that is the case, the world that I see with my eyes cannot be the only world that there is. Perhaps the priests are really right, and that there is a heaven somewhere. A world far away from the Kanyu's and the Lady Saeko's of this world. A world where we can be free to live as we wish.'

Kobuto was starting to stir, perhaps even rising up from the depths of her own dreams, and Oyadori knew it was time to bring herself back into the light of the day. The working day was here, and she pushed back the cover and got slightly unsteadily to her feet. There was only the faintest sound of Lady Saeko's deep breathing coming from beyond the thin paper screens that divided the two rooms. Oyadori went to prepare the hot water to make tea, her first task of many that would seamlessly fill her day.

Later that afternoon when Lady Saeko was visiting her husband and Kobuto and Oyadori were on their own, Oyadori brought up the subject of the sounds that had woken her in the night.

"I thought perhaps some animal was in the room. I was afraid, it was so dark too." She said.

Kobuto looked quizzically at her, as if she were trying to get a gauge of the height or the depth of something.

"Sounds? I heard nothing in the night. You must have been dreaming."

"No, I heard something, really I did. I thought you did too. You awoke too. Don't you remember?" Said Oyadori." You put your arm out to me and said I was to go back to sleep, and I did," continued Oyadori trying to dredge up the memory once again.

"I am sure you are mistaken, dear," said Kobuto with a patronising tone.

"No, you did. I know you did. I did not dream that, I know. It sounded as if something was moving."

Kobuto held her eyes on Oyadori, and for a long moment said nothing.

"You are never to mention the subject up again. Certainly never in company, do you understand?" She spoke with a firmness and conviction that took Oyadori aback.

"No, no. Of course, I will never," she uttered, confused and taken aback.

Kobuto san eye's never yielded their predatory intensity.

"You know what the sounds were made by, don't you?"

"No," protested Oyadori. "I thought it might have been an animal, that's all. It sounded as if it may have come from Lady Saeko's, on the other side of the screens. I was concerned for a moment. That's all."

"It was some kind of animal, if you like," said Kobuto, and Oyadori instinctively raised her hand up to her mouth in fright. "But this animal has no fur, and scuttles about in secret." Kobuto gave a slight nod of her head.

Then the realisation dawned on Oyadori as to what Kobuto san was referring to, and her hand clamped even tighter at her mouth, as if she were afraid now that even the slightest breath would leave her body.

"You mean…? You mean it was Lord Saeko visiting his wife in the night?" Oyadori whispered when she had recovered the function of speech. Once again Kobuto gave her a long piercing look before replying in an equally low voice.

"I never said it was Lord Saeko, now did I?" Oyadori's eyes were round as copper coins. "Now you understand why you heard nothing. You heard nothing and you thought even less. If even a breath of this were ever to get out, do you know what would happen?"

Oyadori mutely shook her head.

"The Captain of the Guards would arrive with two or three men and they would take you to the fields. There he would cut off your head with his sword before you even knew what was happening to you." Kobuto continued, her eyes were glacial and fixed on

Oyadori's. "That's what would happen," she added, though she had no need to. The meaning and the message had got through clear enough to Oyadori. She did not need to reply and for a long time nothing more was said about anything.

As she went about her tasks Oyadori tried to summon back the dream she had had during the night. But the memory was fractured and hopelessly broken, only shards remained in her recollection now. She could not recall all the rich detail, nor the full sequence of events and places.

'I wonder where I went in the dream,' she mused to herself. 'It all felt so familiar somehow, as if I had been there before. I remember a priest talking to mother about dreams once and he explained that we travel in our dreams. It was only in our dreams that we can taste paradise. Father refused to listen, sweeping it all away as being nonsensical 'women's talk'. I must have been quite young then, it was many years ago, perhaps they did not realise I could understand what they were talking about. I have carried that memory inside of myself since that time. I have always wanted to see paradise. Sometimes I even pray for dreams to come at night so that I may travel away from this world. Funny isn't it, the things we desire. Did I visit paradise last night, was that what it was? But there were some parts that were not nice, some parts I did not like, I remember that. Some of it was good and some bad. Surely paradise is not like that. It can't be....'

"Oyadori," Kobuto's sharp voice cut across her dreamy thoughts, snapping her abruptly back into the immediate world. "Oyadori, come this way girl. Madam wants to see you, hurry."

"Me? Now?" Instantly she felt her stomach tighten. But Kobuto had the traces of a smile across her face, which settled Oyadori back down again into mere suspicion and ill ease. "Is it something that I have done?" She said as she needlessly straightened the neat folds of her kimono, and touched the back of her cool hand to her warm cheek.

"More something you are about to do," said Kobuto, and this time the smile broke out across her face, like oil spreading languidly across the surface of water. "Hurry, now girl."

Oyadori was kneeling in front of the closed door of Lady Saeko's apartments, she took one last deep breath and called out aloud.

"Excuse me Madam, you wanted me?"

"Enter."

She slid back the door just enough to get her frame through, and moved over the threshold, her head bowed. Once in the room she slid the door closed behind her with the merest sound, then turned in the direction of her mistress and bowed low. There she remained.

"Come, Oyadori. Come and sit over here."

The request so surprised her, also the tone of voice, she had to pause to equate the voice with Lady Saeko's presence. There was gentleness in the voice's tone that she had so rarely heard in the context of being personally addressed. As she glanced up and edged her way forward still on her knees to the place Lady Saeko was indicating, she realised that Lady Saeko was not alone. Across from her, kneeling, were two men. Given the nature of the conversation she had had with Kobuto, Oyadori felt her face colouring at once, even as she did she repressed the thought that was rising in her mind. She bowed again, deep to the floor to hide her blushing cheeks.

"Sit up, sit up, for goodness sake, Oyadori." Lady Saeko snapped at her in a more recognisable tone. That was the second time she had spoken Oyadori's name, and she used it in the manner of one who has found a new tool and was relishing the novelty of its use.

Lady Saeko was sitting on a broad thick cushion made of pale blue silk; beyond her the doors had been slid open to allow a view of the private garden. Oyadori could see a stand of bamboo

The Gardener's Apprentice

lean in the breeze, and the murmur of water running along an unseen stream percolated through the room. The air was cool, almost chill, as there was no heating in the room at all. About five paces away on the opposite side of the room was the kneeling figure of a man in a sombre coloured kimono, a broad dark coloured belt was wrapped around his waist at which he tugged at nervously with his fingers. Behind him and to one side sat another man, older, with greying hair and his forehead shaven in the manner of *samurai*. The garden set out beyond him he ignored completely, even though the chance was he had never in his life been granted access to these chambers before. He was looking intently at Oyadori. So was the younger man, though his eyes flickered on and off her, as if he were not sure he should be looking at her. When Oyadori bowed toward the men, the younger one had seemed almost embarrassed for a moment.

"Oyadori, you are here so that I can introduce you to someone. I mentioned about him some while ago to you, as I'm sure you will recall well enough. This is Chamberlain Shigoto Sembei, who is in service to my husband." The older man never reacted to his name being mentioned, nor took his eyes off Oyadori. "He is here with his son, Kanyu, for whom Lord Saeko in his wisdom, has picked you out as being a suitable wife." The younger man's eyes darted wildly towards Oyadori's face, and then flew away again in an instant.

Oyadori felt her heart miss a beat or two, but she was well enough acquainted with what the situation required and she bowed deeply again. It was also a way of avoiding looking at either of the two men, and when she straightened her back, she kept her eyes looking down at the fine woven texture of the *tatami* mat, an arm's length in front of her. Her face bland, impassive and composed, her hands folded quietly in her lap.

"Yes, Ma'm," she said to break the silence that she felt threatened to suffocate her.

"Well, Chamberlain Shigoto is here to formalise the marriage. Unfortunately your father is not with us any longer, but discussions have been held with your mother, and she has agreed to the union proposed." Lady Saeko took up the task of officiating proceedings.

'Discussions?' thought Oyadori, still keeping here eyes on the floor. She was tense as a bow about to release an arrow into the sky.

"Your father was well acquainted with Chamberlain Shigoto. Your family has raised no objections. My husband has agreed to raise the stipend received by the Shigoto family, in recognition of the additional responsibilities being taken on."

'A responsibility, is that what I am to be. A wife and a responsibility to someone?' Oyadori remained mute. Chamberlain Shigoto coughed.

"Your husband, Lord Saeko, is a great man, Madam. The Shigoto family have been in the service of the Saeko clan for generations. Our blood has been spilled alongside yours, and will do so again in the future if that serves to protect the Saeko clan."

"Yes, yes, Chamberlain Shigoto, I am sure." Lady Saeko waved an impatient hand in his direction. The older man bowed, and the son followed suit moments later. "We are here to discuss the marriage, not speak of blood being spilled and other such matters of the past."

"With your indulgence Lady, but I feel the young woman should know that the family she is about to enter has been granted leave to carry two swords for many a long year. She should know that we are not some peasants." The older man spoke with a firm voice, tinged with pique and bruised pride.

"May the thought of that burn in the flames of hell, Chamberlain. No such insinuation was made," said Lady Saeko without elaborating on precisely which thought in particular was to be consigned to the fiery furnaces.

"Young lady," Chamberlain Shigoto now turned his attention towards Oyadori. "We are indeed an old and loyal family, and my son is a *samurai*, as will be his sons too." His words seemed to carry threat as much as a boasting tone now, as if he were sure he had his quarry trapped and ready to be dispatched to the afterlife. "That my son serves the Lord Saeko and his family as an administrator should not mislead you to the martial qualities of the Shigoto family. We are fighters by nature, young woman, we are…"

"Yes, yes, Chamberlain Shigoto, please. All this talk of fighting is well in front of my husband, but may I remind you where you are now. This is neither the time nor place, please. May I remind you we are here to discuss a marriage, not to recite battle honours and such like. No one questions the integrity of the Shigoto family, I am certain you have served with distinction, and will continue to do so in the future. That is why my husband has looked kindly on your family, and the matter of a wife for your son. It is indeed an expression of his gratitude that he has consented to involve himself with this matter at all." Lady Saeko's words were laced with exasperation.

"Our family is deeply honoured by his Lordship's consideration," said the Chamberlain and bowed his head. "And to yours Madam, of course."

"Good, then the matter is settled, I take it." Lady Saeko sought to bring the interview to a close as rapidly as possible.

All the while Oyadori had sat with her eyes cast down, though she found that by imperceptivity relaxing her head, she could bring her line of sight up enough to be able to glance across at the younger Shigoto in her peripheral vision. He had stayed quiet during the exchange, his demeanour seemingly aloof from what was happening before him, as if he were engaged with wrestling distant thoughts of his own. Every now and then his eyes would slide across towards Oyadori, but they never rested for long, and he looked downwards every time Lady Saeko spoke.

"Our family will take engagement gifts to the girl's... I mean to the bride's family. I will see to it in person, myself that is. Also, further gifts will be delivered in person to the Saeko family, for your indulgences, Madam. To show respect and recognition of our gratitude," he said pointing at the folded paper envelopes that lay on the floor in front of him.

"Yes Chamberlain, I am sure they are gratefully received too," sighed Lady Saeko. "Your kindness in the recognition is noted. And when is this event planned to take place? I trust an agreement has been reached on that matter too? I would though wish to reiterate my consideration that she remains in my service until she is heavy with child. I have made that clear all along. After any birth we will reconsider the situation. She is after all one of my maids. I have some say in the matter, do I not?"

"Yes, indeed Madam, of course that is the case. Indeed, of course, that is just so, and agreed by all parties. The marriage is planned to take place in three months time. Excuse me, next month that is. There seems to be no good reason to delay things. It is an auspicious time, so we are told, that is. The priests, I mean, the shrine priests have been contacted about that. We have been most thorough in looking into every matter. The girl is of good age to deliver fine sons. We are anxious that nothing should hold up the course of nature, so to speak, that is. In a month's time, the wedding ceremony is planned for. My son, Kanyu, he is... he is of a suitable age to marry, and accepts to take on the responsibility of being a husband. At his age, he is a mature man, and trusted by Lord Saeko with the response... I mean, the responsibility of office, that is." Chamberlain Shigoto stumbled over his words. The blunt, gruff warrior in him wanted to cut to the chase, he was less comfortable with the conventions and the required delicacy of addressing women such as Lady Saeko. He was far more comfortable rattling a sword, or banging his fist onto his broad armoured chest to conclude a discussion in his favour.

The Gardener's Apprentice

Subtlety or diplomacy made his teeth grind, he considered himself primarily a man of action, not feathery words.

"Good, then that is settled," said Lady Saeko with no little feeling of relief.

"This is impossible. Am I dreaming all this? Nobody seems to know I am here,' thought Oyadori. 'They are discussing my future, me as somebody's wife, and where am I in all this? Do they even see me? Do they really know I am here? What do I mean to anyone? What do I mean to him?" And she dared to glance at Kanyu, to look him full in the face. Her face was a rigid mask that she had fixed in place, and which was held there by an iron clad determination, but Kanyu was looking towards his father, his shoulders rounded. She felt hot stings of anger pulsing in her chest, and she fought to keep the flames down. Silence became the blanket she threw over the blaze raging inside her, to smother them and to prevent them bursting through and devouring the room, and all in it.

"Oyadori, fetch us something to toast this meeting with." Lady Saeko clapped her hands making Oyadori startle slightly in surprise.

"Yes Ma'am, right away. Excuse me," she bowed to the three now motionless bodies that had temporarily suspended their task of spinning a web, and made her way out of the room. As the door closed with Oyadori on the outside, the voices took up once more inside the room as polite conversation resumed.

"So, I am trapped, like a fly in the spider's web,' she thought to herself. 'This is a dream I suppose, and this is the part of the dream I did not want to arrive. I did not enjoy being there. So where is paradise supposed to be in all this, then?'

When Oyadori walked into the anteroom where Kobuto was bent over the hearth, warming a bottle of sake, she appeared calm again. She knew that there was nothing she could do; to refuse the offer of marriage would throw her life and that of her mother into complete chaos and disarray. It seemed inconceivable to her that she could do that. Not to her mother, her father's memory, the family name, and perhaps even to herself. The union had been ordained by Lord Saeko who was her ultimate Lord and Master, who was she to refuse? 'After all, I do want a child of my own,' she clung to that one glimmer of hope.

"So, the meeting has gone well then?" said a smiling Kobuto san hurriedly, as she gathered three small drinking cups and set them on a fine lacquer tray.

"I suppose so. I am to be married in a month's time. Though I am to remain in her service for the time being at least," replied Oyadori, her voice a flat, windless surface.

"You'll get used to it. Marriage, that is. It's no different to being a maid really. Now take these things through to them. Make sure you do not let the cups rattle when you put the tray down. Put it down near Lady Saeko, and keep your hands steady when you pour out the rice wine. Only a little mind though, and she will only have but the merest taste, that's all. The men will have half a cup, no more than that. No point in them getting merry, it's just a toast. Besides she will want them out of there as soon as possible, I'm sure." They went together to Lady Saeko's chamber, but only Oyadori went in with the tray.

As Oyadori re-entered the room, she felt a calm inside herself, a detachment from the fate that was there before her. For as the door of the chamber slid back, an image had sprung into her mind. She saw herself once more lying flat on a bare expanse of rock, the sun high in the sky enveloping her in its protective warmth. As she poured the *sake* to each person in turn, her hands were steady. She knew now what she had to do, and that this would be for herself, herself alone. If she were to be condemned to the tides of fate in this way, then at least she would try all she could to gain a taste of paradise, may be even of love, even if it were only for the briefest of moments.

CHAPTER NINE

August 1585

"I wonder if he has changed his mind for some reason,' thought Shigoto one wind-strewn afternoon as he trailed wordlessly a few paces behind Maguro Sensei. Word had come to him via Kamaboku as usual that Maguro Sensei wanted his presence that morning, and that he was to accompany Sensei as he made his garden inspection. Since that occasion when Shigoto had made what felt like a pledge to accept becoming a gardener in front of his teacher, they had continued to meet sporadically. There was no particular pattern to these occasions, days would stretch out between meetings, and sometimes, even weeks would pass by. Over the last winter he had hardly seen Sensei at all. Not that he minded escaping the chill winds of those coldest months. He would rather stay at home on those occasions engrossed in the world of his play, and occasionally spending time with other children in the neighbourhood.

Spring had come with an effervescent flurry of cherry blossoms. The flowers never stayed long on the trees, and soon the slightest breeze showered the ground with falling petals like an unseasonable snowfall. Now the trees were heavy with leaf, and the days stretched out in languid warmth, yet despite the beauty Shigoto felt an impatience weighing him down.

"Why does Sensei not send for me? It's not right, I should be doing things, learning to be a gardener," he complained to his mother one afternoon when they were together. Since his appointment she had returned to serving Lady Saeko, though it was more by way of a part-time occupation, in the times when she was necessarily absent from the home, his grandmother would look after him.

"Perhaps he is just busy, Oku-chan," she replied in an absent minded way. "I am sure that Sensei has not forgotten about you. He will call when he is ready for you."

"But I am ready. I want to be a gardener. I told him that. He said that he would teach me. He told me stuff about the pond and its dragon, and about paradise and things. But now..." the words trailed away in disappointment.

"I trust Sensei has your best interests at heart. He will send for you when the time is right. You are still growing. Maybe he thinks you need to be a little stronger, a little bigger. After all being a gardener involves heavy work I should think. Be patient Oku-chan, strong and patient."

"I'll tell father when he comes next. He speaks with Lord Saeko. Lord Saeko will order Sensei to teach me things," said Shigoto with a defiant voice, his mother's explanation having provided him with no satisfaction at all.

"Just be patient, all things will come in their good time," his mother said as she picked up her sewing and resumed what she was doing.

"It's all so unfair. I hate being a gardener. Maybe I will not be a gardener after all," said Shigoto with a bad tempered tone.

Oyadori let her hands drop into her lap and looked up at her son. "Life isn't always fair," she said. "We do not always get what we want, or expect. That is just the way of things, you have to accept things as they are, not expect everything to be just as you want them to be. Things will be easier that way, you will see." She looked up past where Shigoto was pacing about the room like an animal confined to a cage, her gaze settling among the branches of the only tree in their yard, which was suddenly full of a flock of squabbling sparrows. "See, even the birds cannot agree among themselves sometimes," she said wistfully.

Shigoto stopped his pacing about to follow where she was looking, then he rushed over to the open doorway and stamped his feet on the boards of the veranda and waved his arms.

"Yaaagh," he shouted in his high-pitched voice. The birds exploded from the tree as they took off in fright. They wheeled once as a synchronised unit over the house before heading off elsewhere to continue their noisy discussions.

"Oku-chan, you should not have done that," Oyadori scolded him sharply. "What ever have they done to you?"

"They were making too much noise. I hate birds, "he said sulkily, his arms now swinging loosely and dejectedly at his sides.

"When I have finished this sewing, we can go out for a walk together. We can go to the field, and look at the sea if you like," she said. "For now be patient, we will go in a little time, just let me finish what I am doing then we will go. It will be nice there now."

But Shigoto had jumped down from the veranda and had gone in search of something to do.

As he tried to absorb himself in the comforting domain of his own imagination Shigoto tried to figure out what lay behind his dissatisfaction. For now his imaginary games could not fully drag him away from his concerns, in particular, his relationship with Sensei.

'I don't do anything apart from just following him around,' he argued the matter over to himself. 'That's what's not fair. I should be doing things, like the other gardeners. I want to, but he does not let me do anything. Maybe Sensei is reluctant for some reason to accept my position as an apprentice. I told him I wanted to be an apprentice, to be a gardener, he should know that by now. So why does he not just do what he is supposed to do? Maybe I will mention it to my father next time he comes.' But that thought made him shudder as if he felt a sudden chill wind. 'Lord Saeko gave an order that I was to become an apprentice gardener, so why does he not treat me like one? If I get told to do something then I get into trouble with people if I don't do it, then Sensei should get into trouble too. These adults just do as they please, they make up the rules to suit themselves, that's all they do, and that's not fair at all.'

Shigoto picked up his favourite stick and thrust its point so hard into the ground that with a sudden crack the tip of the stick broke off. He looked morosely at the broken piece of wood. Then with a fit of pique he threw the piece he had in his hands across the yard. It clattered against the fence, and he turned anxiously to see if his mother had heard anything. There was no reaction from within the house. He returned to his musing in an even more sullen frame of mind than before.

'Is this what was meant by being an apprentice, just following aimlessly behind your teacher? Surely being an apprentice is also in some way connected to being a gardener, a gardener who does proper things. Someone who runs about doing work, taking orders from Maguro Sensei, delivering urgent messages, climbing into the tops of trees, and being part of a group of workers who sit in a group eating lunch together.' It suddenly came clear to Shigoto what was what was missing in all this. He was not actually part of the crew of gardeners. He remained fixed on the outside looking in from the wrong side. What seemingly stood in his way was the tall figure of Maguro Sensei, this person who was supposed to be his teacher, yet he was all too obviously teaching him nothing. Shigoto knew what learning was from the efforts his mother continued to persevere with regarding the matter of Chinese characters and writing. Learning was hard work that made your head spin and ache.

A couple of days later Kamaboku made an appearance at the house.

"Excuse me, but Maguro Sensei asks that Shigoto meets him in the garden as soon as possible." He called out from the gateway.

"Ah. Kamaboku san, please come in. Oku-can will be ready in just a moment. Will you have some tea," Oyadori answered from inside the house.

"Oh, that would be very kind, but please do not put yourself to any trouble for me, eh." The smile lit up Kamaboku's face.

"Please wait here by the veranda, the tea has been made, and Oku-chan will be with you directly." Oyadori continued from the doorway.

Kamaboku sat down feeling pleased as could be. He was in no hurry. When he had supped his tea and Shigoto had emerged somewhat sour faced from the house, the pair of them left together.

"Hey, what's the long face for, eh?" asked Kamaboku, as they walked up the lane that lead towards the gardens.

"Nothing," said Shigoto. Kamaboku for all his gap-toothed smile was after all just another adult. What would he understand about the way things were?

"How's it going with Maguro Sensei then? You getting on well with him?"

"I suppose so," replied Shigoto after a long pause.

"You'll get used to him. He has his own ways, you know, but he is a fair man, got to say that about him, eh."

When he joined Maguro Sensei, he exchanged his ritual greetings with his teacher. Maguro Sensei said little but gave his young apprentice a quizzical look that once again made Shigoto feel that he was being observed from the inside out. "Come on then Shigoto, we cannot be standing about all day," said Sensei, who then strode off, Shigoto almost had to run to keep up with him. The pair of them had reached to top of a small hill that gave a fine view across the Great Dragon Pond. Here Sensei paused, and a distant look came into his eyes. Shigoto was gradually becoming more sensitive and observant as to his teacher's moods. He knew not to intervene at these moments, so he buried his chin deeper into the collar of his kimono and waited patiently for the instruction to move on. Having taken in the scenery for a few moments, Maguro Sensei turned to Shigoto.

"Well, Shigoto, what do you make of this then?'

"This, Sensei? Umm, I'm sorry, what exactly is *this*, Sensei?"

There was no reply from the tall man, who seemed as far away as ever, as if he was travelling in some far off place in his own thoughts. Maybe even lost there trying to find a route back. Stillness hung between the two figures, as if a drape of thin gauze had been lowered between them.

"Do you have any questions, Shigoto?" Sensei eventually asked, his voice still seeming to come from a long way away.

Shigoto had been caught ill prepared, and he blurted out the first thought that came into his mind that appeared reasonable to share with his teacher. "What is a gardener, Sensei?"

"That, Shigoto, is what you will find out in good time." Then he turned about on his heels and left Shigoto hurrying to catch up with his quickly retreating steps. Once more Shigoto felt the anger born of frustration with his teacher coursing through him: he had asked, he felt, a perfectly reasonable question, and received by way of reply an answer that answered nothing. He felt his patience slipping. Having once again run to catch up with Sensei, he appeared right at his teacher's side, and for the first time spoke directly to him.

"But Sensei, excuse me Sensei, but what is a gardener supposed to do?"

Maguro Sensei stopped where he was, having been caught by surprise, for there was real urgency, even passion now to Shigoto's voice. The heron-like figure carefully observed the upturned face of his student for several minutes before carefully replying.

"A gardener creator, Shigoto, is an artist, an artist and a magician dealing with energies and spirits. A gardener is someone striving to become a garden creator, somebody searching out those tools to be able to create with Nature. Looking everywhere, all about him, in rocks, in water, in mountains and valleys, trees, and in flowers. Searching above in the sky, searching below in the earth, searching inside and out, turning everything over, to find what it is he is looking for. A true artist, Shigoto, will pay any price for that which he searches for, any price at all. A garden creator is someone who builds whole worlds through which people pass, yet the likelihood is that they will only see but a small part of what is actually there, knowing nothing but a fraction of what exists. There are three parts to our art, the past, the present and the future. Yet the garden creator sees them as one, as a continuous flowing, like a stream running past his feet. That is as it should be. To the outsider, they are separate parts that may or may not connect in time. As I say the garden creator sees them all as one process."

He paused to gather his thoughts, Shigoto stood before him entranced by the unexpected outpouring of words.

"When we walk under the tree, do we take it all in and know every twisting branch or every leaf? Of course not, we see only a tree and we recognise it for what we know it is. That type of tree there, Shigoto," Sensei pointed his finger in the direction of a tree growing nearby where they stood. "It has a name people have given to it. That plant growing close beyond it, the small one with yellow flowers, its roots when mashed together and mixed with water will produce a dye people have learned to fix the colour of silks with. These are the useful things and many people know about them. Beyond that..." he paused as if to re-gather his thoughts, also to give Shigoto a chance to catch up with him.

"...Beyond that, beyond that there is another world of the garden all together, Shigoto. For example an incorrectly placed or badly balanced arrangements of stones can bring disorder and illness to the master of a house, can condemn him and his family to suffering, ill fortune and death even! You think I exaggerate? The ancients knew all too well of these matters. If the gardener does not learn what is the difference between right and wrong, between the right way and the wrong way, he can bring misery and destruction, not beauty and life to the household. Make no mistake in this, the garden creator works with powerful energies, very powerful energies indeed."

Maguro Sensei paused once more as if to draw breath and let the import of his words sink in. When he resumed expressing his thoughts his words came raining down on Shigoto, and he did not pause this time to consider if his young charge was following the meaning of what he had to say. He made no concession to Shigoto's age and inexperience, the words bubbling up from a wellspring of experience and knowledge. He spoke from a place of experience beyond words. It was as if he spoke for himself too.

"A garden creator is searching for a truth, Shigoto, that is all. It is as simple as that. Trying to work with that which may not always be manifest to our eyes, but that which is always there. The true nature of our work is that we are working with energy, the ebb and flow of energy. I call this force energy; there are some who have called it love. It matters not one bit what label we attach to these things, for labels are changeable, perishable, and even liable to be lost and forgotten over time. But what the garden creator seeks to do is to see beyond the surface of things, to know their true heart, to understand this energy as well as he

The Gardener's Apprentice

recognises his own hands. The true gardener, Shigoto, is always searching for the tools he needs to be a garden creator. Anyone can work in a garden, be a gardener, Shigoto, and that does not take any particular skill or even great strength of body or mind. Not everyone can be a garden creator though, for that you are chosen by the garden, by the place itself, you do not choose that Way. It chooses you, seeks you out itself and buries itself deep in your heart. Never forget that, it is the first lesson, the first step on a very long path."

Maguro Sensei fell silent again, and Shigoto felt himself spun about by the force of what he had just been told. He went and sat down on a low flat-topped rock nearby where they were standing and rested his chin in his hands. No one had ever spoken to him in such a way before. The flood of words opened up a stream of images, thoughts and feelings that threatened to engulf him. Then, he could see in his own mind an image of a wave falling back to the ocean from a stony beach. He was walking, walking alone; to his right side a lively sea pounding with relentless energy against the shore; to his left, the trees were crowding thickly together, jostling one another for space and light. A wind was blowing hard from behind him pushing him onwards as its impatient blasts filled his hearing. Though he could see the canopies of the trees surging, first one way then another in a maelstrom of motion, all he could hear was the wind. Pushing him onward.

"When will I become a proper apprentice, Sensei?" His voice quavered with excitement. He felt a desire to be accepted, a wish to be taken into the fold, as he wanted to go deeper, much deeper, into this world that Maguro Sensei had sketched out before him.

"Is that what you have chosen for your own self, Shigoto? Is that really the path you wish to follow, or are you taking that route because you have been told to do so, by the Lord Saeko, or by your parents, perhaps out of filial respect to them?"

A dense silence fell between the two of them. There was only the rustling of leaves in the trees and the excited chatter of birds, but Shigoto heard none of this. He had arrived at another place all together.

Now Shigoto was walking along that same shore, but the wind had gone, stillness had replaced the wild motion of the wind, the sea softly lapped against the shore. There was no sound in his ears, no thoughts in his mind, no effort in his legs as he walked along a narrow path with the sea reaching to infinity on one side, and land stretching away on the other. Shigoto looked over toward Maguro Sensei who was standing a pace or two away and he looked up towards his face. With the light above and behind him, Sensei's face was in deep shadow and his features all but indistinguishable from Shigoto's position below. The gulf between them, as pupil and teacher, as man and boy, was enormous, yet the rising, filling pressure in his chest pushed him on, he was prepared now to take the risk of speaking directly. He knew then that he had the complete attention of Maguro Sensei, who was willing to set aside any distinction between them, to listen without prejudice to what Shigoto may have to say.

"When will I become a proper apprentice, Sensei?" Shigoto repeated. "I want to be a gardener."

"You know, and I am saying this because I happen to like you, if you are going to survive in this life, then you are going to need to be strong. I am warming to who you are, Shigoto, and I am not just saying this to annoy, or put you down in some way, but ... to be an apprentice is a hard choice, you will have to commit yourself completely to me as your teacher. Whatever you may think you know now, it is nothing, nothing but smoke in the wind. You will be called to loosen all attachments. Do you understand what I mean by that? There is something called fate, which all human beings have to accept. There are circumstances in life that we have to come to embrace, because that is what we have been given to do. This we have to accept without question."

"You mean that now *you* are my father, and the person who I thought was my father is no longer my father." Shigoto had no prior warning of the words, they just seemed to form in his mouth and emerge of their own accord.

"That is correct in a way, Shigoto. Your father and mother are no longer here just to be your father and mother. Your mother and father will still exist, but you who were their son no longer will be there before them as before. The reasons for this are complicated and will pass beyond your understanding for now. It is better that you simply accept the workings of fate and not to question this matter further for now. Our master Lord Saeko has asked me in his wisdom to be your teacher. That is a duty as fate given to me, and one that I have had to accept. In time you will be trained as a gardener, and it is your fate is to accept that your life and work is to be at the service of the Lord Saeko, just as it is mine. Shigoto. We are simply two leaves at the mercy of being tossed and tumbled about by the wind."

"You mean fate," a concept with which Shigoto was not altogether familiar, but was beginning to intuit implied something in which he had little or no choice, "it is something that I have to agree to?"

"Yes, Shigoto, in a way, you have a choice to make, yet there is really no choice to be made. You have to come to accept life as it is, for what it is. There is something called fate, which all human beings have to accept. What I mean is that there are circumstances in life that we have to come to submit to. Your fate I suspect is to be a gardener. My fate is to be your teacher. You can just take it all as a light-hearted matter, just see it as spending time in a pleasant place, but, there can be more to it than that. What I am saying is that you will need to be strong to cope with it all. Build strength from the inside out, then you will stand more firmly on the ground. Remember Shigoto, things are not always what they appear to be, that is always very important to bear in mind. Perhaps it is the most important thing of all. When you really understand that, then things will become easier for you. We all have had to face that fact. It's part of learning to be an apprentice, as well as learning how to be a human being. I have not known you for long, and maybe you have had an easy life so far, and you are young after all. In this world, Shigoto, one thing is for sure, you are going to need to be tough on the inside, as well as becoming strong in the arms, back and legs." Having spoken Sensei took a step back as if to give his young charge the time and space to consider his words.

It seemed like more than one thing to Shigoto, but he was beginning to get a grasp on of what he was being told, even if at that moment he could not really appreciate the full implications of it all. Shigoto knew Sensei was warning him of the difficulties of what lay ahead, and yet was seemingly also holding the door of change open in invitation for him to step through should he wish to do so. It dawned on Shigoto that the path along the shore he had seen in his mind, that he had been blindly following at first, and then had been driven along by the wind, must have been made by others passing that way before him. He had noticed no one else on the path, yet he had felt unthreatened and unafraid.

He was back on that path once more and now a side path, narrower than the one he had been walking on. It branched off towards his left and began winding a way through the trees. He took it and was soon swallowed by the forest crowding down towards the shore. The light changed as he entered the forest, from a sharp contrast out in the open to a soft focus, the air was cooler and lighter here with rich scents rising up from the damp ground. The path wound first one way then another; though slender it remained clear enough for Shigoto to follow without searching. He felt he was walking without effort, and so he could give all his attention to what he was seeing and experiencing. The path reached the top of a rise, where the canopy had thinned sufficiently above his head and was now open to the sky in places. Shigoto realised he was in the Hirame Palace gardens, but he could not quite place where. It felt comfortable to be back on what felt like familiar territory, and when he turned around he could no longer see nor hear the sea. He pressed on expecting to catch a glimpse of the Great Dragon Pond. As he wound around a group of evergreen shrubs clustering together, he looked up and saw the figure of Sensei in the distance. He waved towards Sensei, who returned the gesture, and Shigoto forged on toward the unmistakable shape ahead on the path. As he came up to the spot where he had seen his teacher, he found himself quite alone. There was no one there. He shook his head to clear his mind.

"That will be all for today then, Shigoto." Sensei's voice brought him back to the rock he was sitting on. "You can make your own way home from here I am sure. When the time comes, Shigoto, you will become an apprentice gardener, according to the wishes of Lord Saeko. Whether you become a garden builder of repute, who can say for sure. The mountains and water know but do not speak of that at this point. Live your life as it comes, one day at a time. Your fate is laid out before you Shigoto; those choices have already been made and cannot be undone. Hurry along now, your mother waits for you. Of that, I am certain it is true."

CHAPTER TEN

End of March 1576

"Oyadori, Oyadori, come on, hurry with those things now. What is the matter with you, you are so slow this morning, have you not woken up yet? Come on, what is the matter with you?" Kobuto's voice cut across Oyadori's thoughts as if a knife sinking into soft tissue.

"I'm sorry. I am coming, but this basket is so heavy, it feels as if it is pulling my arms off. There was nobody in the storerooms who could help me carry it, I had to bring it here by myself." Oyadori put the woven bamboo basket containing summer clothing down on the floor. It landed with a thud.

"Oh for goodness sake be careful with what you are doing, the room shook then as if there were an earthquake. What's the matter with you? You are young, you should be strong enough to lift that." Kobuto scolded her again with an irritated edge to her voice. "All these clothes need to be taken out of there and

The Gardener's Apprentice

hung out to air. Then the winter kimono can be packed away and placed in the basket, then taken back to the store. Don't forget to put the herbs here between the layers of clothes when they are packed. Now get on with it."

"Yes, Kobuto san, right away." Oyadori bent to her task, trying very hard to keep the way that she felt inside from spilling over on to her face. She did not want to reveal anything more than she had to, it would only cause more anguish and tension. There was enough of that about as it was. Her back hurt, and her arms ached from carrying the heavy basket, but she did not dare to show what might be construed as any sign of weakness, not this morning, not in front of Kobuto san. It would only cause her to twist the blade deeper. Kobuto was in a furious mood and she was lashing out in every direction. All it had taken was a few words and tension between the two women had erupted. Ever since then Kobuto had not let Oyadori have a moment of calm as she made the younger woman the object of her anger and frustrations.

Kobuto had been to see Lady Saeko earlier that morning, following a series of visitors to the apartments, and had come back to join Oyadori stony faced and serious.

"So, I do not know why you have been chosen, but there is a job for you to do," she had said, it was as if the words were paining her to utter. Oyadori was taken aback by the change of mood in the older maidservant.

"Oh, what is that then, Kobuto san?"

"It seems that Awayuki has hurt herself, she has fallen and twisted her ankle. She is no longer fit enough to be in service of the visitor. We have to find a replacement for her." Kobuto had spoken with some venom, and Oyadori had innocently assumed the reason for the sour face was Kobuto san's irritation at having to arrange a replacement.

"Well, I am sure there will be someone who can be sent, presumably it will only be for a short while. I can go and speak to the Chamberlain myself, if that would be easier for you." Oyadori was familiar now to the mercurial temperament of Kobuto, and she wanted to try to help ease the situation, before she felt the weight of Kobuto's jealousy being heaped further on her.

"Hah, that matter has already been decided it seems," said Kobuto. Then she looked across at Oyadori, her face twisted into a mask of repressed, internalised anger. "They want you to go. It's you who have been chosen, not me. It should be a question of seniority. I should have been the one to serve the visitor, but for some reason they have selected the youngest and the most inexperienced member of staff to serve a person of such distinction." Oyadori blanched at the prospect, and at the memory of her thoughts when she had spied on the distinguished visitor at the shrine. She said nothing, nothing at all, merely bowed her head and tried to busy her hands, hoping that the beating of her heart would not show and so reveal her inner feelings.

"So, so what are you waiting for, a formal letter of introduction to take with you? Go, I have passed on her Ladyship's instructions. You are to be in attendance during the day until the sun sets below the horizon, and then you are to continue with your duties here. They will find a replacement for you, not that that will cause any great headache to anyone. An insect could do the job as well as you."

"Yes Kobuto san, I will leave now," said Oyadori. She was trembling inside.

As she walked through the palace building to the apartments where the visitor had been installed, she vividly recalled the face of the man she had watched from her hiding place. Everyone referred to him as "the visitor", as if it were somehow sacrilegious to even utter his name. Though she had previously learned through Kobuto san that his name was Hotaru, Prince Hotaru. The 'Firefly Prince'.

'I must be calm,' she reminded herself, 'after all what am I to a person like that, a mere servant, someone so far below his status and position in life, that even if he did look at me, his sight would pass right through me. No, put your wild and stupid ideas away, lock them away deep inside you, there are some things that can never be allowed to see the light of day, no matter what the situation may be. You only thought about such matters because of the pressure of marrying this man, Kanyu. Remember who you are, mother is right after all, may be it will be for the best to just accept this situation. Marry this man Kanyu, bear his children, and that will be the best you can expect of life. It will be enough, be satisfied with that. May be you can find in time that there can be some love for Kanyu, I am sure he is a good and honest man. His father is strong willed, that's for sure, though I am not really certain of the character of Kanyu, he seems to be doing what his father wants. Perhaps he looked at me and wondered why he has to marry me. Maybe he is not sure? He is older than I am, and he has not married yet, perhaps there are reasons for that. He does not much look like a *samurai* that's for sure, his face looks softer somehow, and he does not wear his arrogance on his sleeves. Well, they say he is a bookkeeper, an accountant for Lord Saeko. Maybe he does not have the temperament for fighting, that's all. Perhaps he will be a gentle, kind man, a good father to his children.'

As Oyadori made her way along the corridors approaching the apartments where the visitor had been installed, there were several grimfaced guards stationed along the way. She instinctively bowed her head to them as she slid past. None of them moved a muscle. 'They look completely bored,' she thought to herself. 'Perhaps it will be no particular pleasure to be in service to the visitor after all.' Despite this thought, her stomach was tightly knotted as she gently knocked on one of the doors to an antechamber, and waited outside in the corridor for permission to enter.

After a couple of days had passed, Oyadori felt as if she had settled into the routine of her new responsibilities. 'After all that,' she thought to herself,' it is not really any different to be in service to a man than to a lady. It is still all about being at someone's beck and call, the endless rushing about, and running errands to the kitchens, fetching this, carrying that. They are all the same really.' Hotaru had a small retinue of servants who had come with him into exile, and they were the persons who were immediately tasked with looking after him. Oyadori had barely set eyes on the visitor, let alone been in his presence for more than a few moments. 'It would not surprise me if he does not even know I am here at all,' she thought. 'So all this excited chatter that Awayuki would come out with when she came by to see us, about the onerous job she had, it was just idle chatter. Just something to puff herself up with, and try and make us feel inferior to her. I should have guessed, should have known better than to be taken in by all her fine words and airs.'

The light was beginning to stretch out into the late afternoon, shadows stealthily creeping across the courtyard garden outside the apartments. Oyadori was thinking that soon she would need to return to Lady Saeko's quarters to resume her duties there when the sound of laughter caught her attention. The visitor and a number of his retinue had been away for the best part of the day. Oyadori had been told that Prince Hotaru was going hawking with Lord Saeko; now with their return the apartment was alive with the animated chatter of the returning party buoyed up by the day's exertions. Oyadori was struck by the contrast between the atmosphere here in the prince's quarters, and that of the quarters of Lady Saeko; it was unusual to hear laughter and merriment coming from there. 'Maybe exile does not weigh too heavily on his shoulders,' Oyadori thought, not that she could really imagine what it must be like to be forced away from your home. She had never travelled beyond the bounds of Mikura, and barely beyond sight of the Hirame palace itself.

One of Prince Hotaru's retinue came through into the room where Oyadori was busying herself. She recognised him as the pleasant mannered older gentleman, who had once explained to her that he had been in the service of the prince for many years.

"Ah, young lady," he said as he caught sight of Oyadori. "Perhaps you could hurry to fetch something to drink, his Highness has a thirst after the day's hunt. Be sharp about it if you would. His Highness would like to quench his thirst before he takes his bath." There was no pretence or malice at all to the way in which he spoke and Oyadori immediately got up to go to the kitchens.

"Yes sir," she said. "I will be as quick as I can." She returned shortly with a tray bearing a bottle of *sake* and small cups.

When she returned, the doors of the rooms occupied by the visitor were wide open, and she could hear the conversation proceeding in the usual jocular manner as they discussed the highlights of the day's activities. She set the tray down on the floor by the open door and kneeling knocked on the doorframe to call attention to her presence with the refreshments.

"Ahh, at last, something to calm the raging thirst of a weary hunter, excellent. Even if the quality of the rice wine is not as good as one may expect in the capital, at least it will wet the throat. Enter, enter, do not keep us from a drink any longer than we must." The room burst with the soft explosion of several people laughing, and Oyadori slid the tray into the room and still on her knees and keeping her eyes on the floor in front of her, entered herself. Beginning with Prince Hotaru she served the group in the room, then she set the bottle back on the tray and was about to make her way discreetly out of the room again.

"Oh, wait, one moment," it was the voice of the distinguished visitor. Oyadori remained frozen where she was, not daring to look up as the conversation died away. She felt exposed and uncertain as to what was expected of her. "No, don't go, after all it's not so often that we have the opportunity to spend some time with a young lady. After that last sour faced maid, I was beginning to wonder if there were any pretty faces around here anyway." The room filled with laughter once more, and Oyadori felt the blush rising into her cheeks, instinctively raising a hand to her face to cover her mounting embarrassment. "Nothing gives one such pleasure as a young girl's blush, even prettier than the cherry blossom of the Imperial palace, I would say, worthy of a poem perhaps." The room convulsed with merriment again. Oyadori felt wretched, and wished that the floor would open up and swallow her whole, all she wanted at that moment was to run and hide.

"Excuse me, Sirs," she stammered out her voice barely audible." I have duties to attend to. If you will excuse me." She started to turn whilst still kneeling, so at least she could attempt to cover her discomfort at the tone of the remarks.

"Nonsense, nonsense, look these cups need filling again, they are dry as our throats now. Come, fill our cups, then you can replenish the supply. We have been hunting and have our success this afternoon to toast. One bottle will hardly do justice to our pleasure, isn't that right Shunrai?"

"Yes, indeed Sire, after a day such as today, celebration and poems are in order indeed." One of the men seated to Oyadori's left spoke up in a teasing voice. "Come on girl, you heard my Lord, the cups, fill the cups, quick as can be now."

Oyadori needed all her inner strength to remain calm enough to pick up the glazed bottle and pour another round of drinks as the men held out their cups to be filled. The air was filled with their bonhomie and amusement, the only person who felt out of place and uncomfortable was Oyadori.

"Now if you will excuse me Sires, I will fetch another bottle from the kitchens."

No one paid her much heed as lively conversation had broken out again.

"Well, she is pretty as peach blossom, is she not? We should write a poem comparing the tender beauty of peach blossom with that of cherry. Taoru, fetch out the writing utensils and bring paper, the bath can wait. We must write poems whilst the fragrance of such beauty is still vivid in our minds." Hotaru declaimed to general amusement.

"And perhaps as the scent still lingers in the air, it is after all late in the year for such blossom to appear, not to mention particularly in such an unlikely place." Someone else added and the room exploded once more into gales of laughter. Oyadori made her way out as fast as she could, her cheeks felt as if they were burning red hot and her head was spinning wildly as if it had been her who had emptied the bottle. As she made her way with the empty bottle to the kitchens she a discreet smile played across on her face.

Over the days that followed, Oyadori found herself being called again and again to the service of Hotaru. Even after Awayuki had returned to work, Hotaru would specifically call for Oyadori to attend to him. She was aware of his apparent interest in her, but she tried to shut out such thoughts from her mind, and was mindful to do whatever was required and then leave as soon as possible. The truth was she was flattered by the attention she received, though she would never have dared to reciprocate in any fashion. Any thoughts or ideas she may have harboured, any lingering trace of affection or attraction she may have felt towards Hotaru she strove to bury deep beneath the placid mask of the servant simply doing her duty.

Oyadori had just finished with her duties at Prince Hotaru's apartments, and she was ready to make her way over to join

Kobuto once more. She slid back the door of the antechamber and slid on her knees out into the corridor. When she saw Hotaru walking alone towards his room, she hesitated for a split second before starting to duck back into the room.

"Ahh, our Maid of the Blossoms," Hotaru's cheery voice called out to her. Oyadori bowed deep and remained where she was. Hotaru stopped opposite to her instead of walking on past. She could feel her cheeks starting to colour again, and she clenched her fists tight, digging her fingernails into the soft tissue of her palms. She said nothing and dared not move until he passed on. Instead nothing happened, he remained where he was.

'Oh, please continue on your way. Return to your rooms or wherever you are going. Please,' she pleaded silently to the figure she felt looming over her.

"So, I am always honoured to see such a fresh pretty face," he said with a voice that was light and teasing. Oyadori remained where she was, bowing even lower not daring to move.

"Is there something I can do for you, Sire. I have to be in attendance at Lady Saeko's apartments... I... I am expected there," she said, he voice so low it hardly left the floor.

'Please let me go, just be on your way, what do you want from me?" Her internal voice pleaded with him too. Oyadori sensed the weight on his feet shifting, he was that close to her. 'Oh, please just move on, Kobuto san will be furious with me for being late, it just gives her another reason to be mad with me.'

Hotaru moved on, and Oyadori was just beginning to let the breath she had been holding back ease out, when he stopped again at the threshold to his rooms. She had remained as if she were frozen in terror where she was. "You can fetch me a drink, *sake*," he said, his voice was tighter this time, as if he had been affected by the strain she felt herself under.

"Yes, Sir, I'll go at once," she managed to let the words out.

The Gardener's Apprentice

Hotaru strode into his rooms closing the door gently behind him.

As soon as she heard the door slide shut Oyadori leapt to her feet, and walking as quickly and calmly as she could, she headed off down the corridor. She swept past the guards on duty there, whose blank stares seemed to suggest that they had seen nothing, though they must have been aware of at least the outward appearance of what had transpired, her heart pounding heavily in her chest. 'Nothing happened, nothing happened,' she kept repeating to herself as she moved along, not even caring where she was headed for the moment.

Her blind motion had in fact carried her close to the apartments of Lady Saeko, to the Women's quarters, not in a direct line to the kitchens. The day was rapidly beginning to fade now as evening threw its dark cloak over the palace, and the gloom of corridors and walkways under the overhanging roof eaves was thickening with the approach of night.

'I should go and tell Kobuto san that I will be late, that I have another task to do, before I can come to the apartments,' she thought. 'That way I can at least avoid being told off. She won't like it, but at least what can she say, she could not refuse for me to carry out an order, not from him.' But when she reached a junction in the walkway, where to take a left would lead her towards Lady Saeko apartments, she continued straight on, now she was practically running as she went.

By the time she was back outside Hotaru's apartment she had composed herself, as if the tensions she had experienced had somehow been resolved. She set the tray with a bottle of *sake* and three cups down on the floor, and looking quickly along the corridor she straightened her perfectly neat kimono. Then she knelt by the tray in front of the closed door, and lifting her hand rapped lightly on the dark stained timber framework.

"Excuse me, Sire, I have your refreshment here."

For a short time nothing was heard from inside.

"Come," Hotaru's voice called out. Oyadori reached up to the recessed handle of the door and slid it far enough ajar so she could enter. She slid the tray into the room and followed it still kneeling, and then bowed low to the floor. "Come in, come in for goodness sake, I cannot drink *sake* from there. Perhaps you can light some lanterns, the room is getting dark." Hotaru appeared to be alone in the room. He was sitting on a cushion at the far end of the room. The paper screens had been pushed back and he was looking out on to the small garden beyond.

"Ah, that's better," he said when she had lit several of the paper lanterns that sat on the floor. "Come, you can serve me the wine. There is no one else here to serve it to me." His voice was once again filled with the boyish charm that she had noticed at the shrine. He was alone. She edged over to where he sat looking over the now rapidly darkening garden, where the shapes of the plants only retained congealed outlines. She set the tray on a low table in front of him and waited with eyes looking downward, until he picked up a cup and held it silently out to her. She picked up the bottle with both hands, and tipped a little of the clear liquid into the cup. She noticed her hands were steady.

Hotaru drank it down with a gulp, and held the cup out to be refilled then he drank it down again, this time in two movements. He set the cup back down onto the tray with a soft click.

'Ahh," he sighed, "a beautiful evening, no? I wonder if the fireflies will be playing tonight. Maybe it's still a little early in the season for them yet." Oyadori remained where she was, her eyes cast down, waiting, waiting for his next instruction, waiting for his next move. There was a long moment of quiet, when the only sound was the languid calling of crows roosting in a tall pine beyond the garden's enclosing wall. The day was shutting down.

"I take it you know who I am," he said eventually. "In my experience servants often know more than their masters do. Strange that, don't you think? Sometimes I think we live like exotic birds in a cage," and he laughed softly to himself and held the cup out to be refilled. "We like to think that we have all the freedom in the world, but we are just birds that have had their feathers clipped. Oh, we look and sound pretty enough, but what do we do? Where do we fly to, I wonder? We end up in places like this, whilst life goes on in the capital," his voice trailed away, and he drank again, then held out the cup to be filled again.

Oyadori could sense now the arc of longing in Hotaru. She could feel the pain of the separation he must be feeling in his heart. She heard it in his voice as if those were the words he had spoken. "I know just what you mean,' she thought. 'I understand what you are saying, even though there is such a distance between us. I know what is in your heart, because I feel longing in mine too. Maybe we are not so different after all. If I could only speak my mind to you, then perhaps you would understand as well, and see life as we ordinary people know it.'

"What is you name, girl?"

Oyadori remained silent, looking downward at the bottle of *sake* sitting on the low table at Hotaru's side.

"I asked you a question," he said now more urgently.

"Oyadori, Sire," she said very quietly.

"I cannot hear when you mumble, speak up. I asked what is your name?" His voice, mellowed by the alcohol, floated down to her.

"Oyadori, Sire. I am a personal maid to Lady Saeko."

"Oyadori, such a pretty name. Do you write poetry, Oyadori?"

"No, Sire," she shook her head.

"Pity," he said, and then held out his cup for a further refill. As she poured the liquid into the cup he held out to her, she glanced fleetingly upwards. Hotaru was looking at her full in the face. She dared look back at him and saw that his face was smiling gently, his skin lit golden by the lanterns. His eyes were sparkling with life, vivid and vibrant. She felt something shift within her, as if a sack had burst open and its contents were now running wild and free.

"How old are you. Oyadori?" he repeated her name with great deliberation, as if he were teasing out every nuance of sound.

"Sixteen, or thereabouts, Sire. I am not entirely sure," she felt herself blushing slightly at her inability to recall exactly. She did not want to appear stupid before him.

"Are you married yet?" Hotaru asked.

"My mother is alive, though my father… my father died just over two winters ago." She stammered, and the image of Kanyu, looking hopelessly lost and forlorn, briefly flickered across her mind.

"I asked if you were married yet," Hotaru was smiling as he posed his question again.

Oyadori shook her head. "No, no, Sire. I am to be married in a month's time."

"I see. Do you know the husband-to-be?"

Oyadori shook her head from side to side slowly. "No, hardly at all."

Hotaru held out his cup to her. Oyadori picked up the bottle, which she found she had been holding all the while in her lap, and started to raise it to the cup. Then Hotaru placed the cup down on the tray, and his hand came out to meet her face. His long fingers touched her chin and he tilted her face upward, it required next to no pressure to do so. Now she was looking directly into his face, and the candlelight fell across her visage lighting her eyes as she looked into his.

"Very pretty," he murmured, "so very pretty indeed." A shadow fell across her face as his hand dropped away and his lips met hers. She closed her eyes tight, but the light remained burning so bright that she saw nothing else; she only knew the world through pure sensation. "I think you had better put the bottle back on to the table, otherwise it is going to end up on the floor," he said. He took it out of her hands and set it down.

Oyadori clasped her hands to her waist, she felt as if she could not speak, not with words anymore. She had been swept out past the point where words had any meaning left to them. They were but empty vessels now, shorn of purpose or need. The space that she existed in, the space that she could register was so flooded by sensation and feelings, that the concerns and connections to the everyday world had been utterly washed away by the flood that was bearing her out to sea. She was helpless in the force of the energy that tore through her, beyond caring, beyond knowing. The only thing she could do in response was to allow herself to go with whatever was happening. In some part of her mind she recognised a warm glow spreading through her body. It made her feel safe, secure, and it gave her the strength to finally open her hands and let go.

As Hotaru's weight came down on her body, Oyadori saw a herself in a wide field of grasses, the wind bending their heads over revealing a silvery underside to the vivid multitude of greens. There was no sound, nothing but the wind moving, playing its own games and creating gentle arabesques across the open expanse of the field. The whole world was shifting, nothing was still, and oscillation infused every particle. Yet everything had its own perfect logic, one movement fitted into the next without any friction at all, one motion created the space for the next to seamlessly appear. Then she felt a sharp tug of pain as he began to move inside her. When her mind had cleared again she was at the very edge of the field, where the grasses with their constant sweeping energy transformed themselves into waves lapping at the shore. One following onto the other, in a ceaseless series of subtle caresses that stretched out into an infinity of space, past the point where the sky touched the edge of the cold silvered grey sea. Oyadori stretched out her arms and legs as far as she could until she felt that she could encompass the dome of the sky in her span. 'So, at least, I know what it is to feel love' - the words were the first thing that she recognised as she fell back into the embrace of solid earth again.

"I think that you had better be getting back to your mistress," the liquid voice of Hotaru came to her, and she opened her eyes again to the room with its velvet shadows and golden patches of light. She got unsteadily to her feet, puzzled at how disarrayed her clothing was. She straightened out her kimono's layers. "Leave the bottle here, I can pour for myself." They were the last words she heard, as she left the room barely able to feel the glassy smooth wooden boards beneath her feet.

CHAPTER ELEVEN

September 1587

"Mama?"

"Yes Oku-chan, what is it?" said Oyadori.

"Why does Sensei keep disappearing?"

"How do you mean, 'disappearing'?"

"Well, it's as if one minute he's here, and then he has gone, I don't see him. I don't hear from him. One time he is telling me things, the..." Shigoto's voice trailed away.

"Oh. You know Sensei, he is a busy man, and has many things to do. He is a priest as well as a gardener, so I suppose sometimes he has to do the sorts of things a priest does, and sometimes he has to do the sorts of things that a gardener does. It must be hard for him, I suppose."

"How can that be hard for him?"

"Well, you know, being one thing one time, and another, another time. "Oyadori's voice had a slightly dreamy quality to it, as if her mind was not really concentrating on what she was saying, rather that she was plucking the words from someplace far away.

"Is Sensei married?"

"Oh, Oku-chan, so many questions." Oyadori looked towards her son and considered his question. They were sitting together in the same yard of the house where they lived, the earth radiating a warm dampness after a rain shower that had fallen earlier penning them in the house with its sudden intensity.

"Well, *is* he married?" Shigoto insisted.

"How should I know? You are the one who sees him, maybe you should ask him," she smiled to herself.

"I could not do that," said Shigoto seriously. "It would not be right."

"Maybe not," said Oyadori after a moment's pause. "Anyway I heard that Sensei had gone over to the mainland. Someone in the kitchens mentioned that when I was there yesterday fetching some things for Lady Saeko. Though he may be back by now. Why, do you miss your walks with him?"

"Has he gone to Kyoto? That's on the mainland too isn't it? He sometimes speaks of Kyoto. He was born there, it's the capital, I know that. Kamaboku told me so," said Shigoto a certain pride creeping into his voice

"No, I don't think so. Well, I would guess may be not anyway. It's a long way to Kyoto from here. It's a very long way, and takes many days to get there."

"I want to go there." Shigoto was looking at his mother with an intense curiosity, the mention of the capital had pricked his attention. But Oyadori was busily engaged with what she was doing, and for now he decided to hold back on the question uppermost in his mind. They lapsed into silence, held apart by their own thoughts. Oyadori was sorting through a basket of small green bean pods, picking out those that were turning brown and setting them to one side, though from time to time she would

The Gardener's Apprentice

absently drop a brown stained pod in among the green ones. Shigoto held onto his question until he felt he had to let it out, as if he had been holding on to his breath.

"Have you ever been to Kyoto?" he asked.

Oyadori stopped what she was doing. There was a wistful look in her eyes, which Shigoto did not know how to reach beyond. Her hands were picking through the basket of pods but she was simply letting them slip through her fingers, again and again.

"Well?" said Shigoto, his impatience was finally getting the better of him. He instinctively felt that he had touched on something, but he had no idea what it was, nor how to get any closer to what he really wanted to know.

"Umm, well, what?" answered Oyadori her voice was again sounding as if it were coming from a place far away, very far away.

"Have you ever been to Kyoto?" he repeated, this time his eyes never left her face, as if he might find some clue as to what it was he was looking for there. But Oyadori had brought an veil down and all he could see was the slight smile creasing her mouth.

"No," she said finally and firmly. "No never." Then she got to her feet and brushed her lap with the back of one hand, before bending down to pick up the basket. "Oku-chan, I am going to make some supper. If you want to hear about Kyoto, why do you not speak to Oba-chan. Her father went to the capital with Lord Saeko's father one time, how about that then?"

"Oba-chan invents things, she makes them up. I never know if what she says is right or not, she gets confused and talks too much sometimes," he said.

"What a thing to say! Now that's not nice at all. You should be ashamed to say something like that. Poor Oba-chan, I hope she did not hear you speaking out of turn like that. That's not nice at all." Oyadori's face tightened slightly.

"Sorry," said Shigoto looking down at his feet.

"I should think so too," and Oyadori turned and made her way to the entry porch, leaving Shigoto sitting alone on the wooden bench. Beside him a small heap of brown pods were the only reminder of her presence.

"It's true though," muttered Shigoto to himself, then he brusquely swept the pods onto the ground and got up. "I'm going to the gardens," he called out loudly to his mother now inside the house.

"Don't be long now, and don't get into mischief," she called back. But he had gone already.

Shigoto was sitting cross-legged by himself on a large flat-topped rock that overhung the 'Great Dragon Pond', lost in his own thoughts and idly throwing pieces of gravel to the koi carp, which had gathered in an eager crowd in front of him. Their great gaping mouths thronging at the surface of the water churning it into a living iridescent froth. Something made him turn around and as he did, there was Maguro Sensei standing higher up the bank, hands on his hips watching him. Shigoto was suddenly afraid of the scolding he would receive for feeding gravel to the fish, and he felt as if he were an animal caught exposed in the glare of the sun far away from the safety of its lair. Pinning him with a stare from those hawk-like eyes, and bowing deeply from the waist toward Shigoto, Sensei said, "The apprentice is not yet the Master, young Shigoto. The empty carp swims more easily than a stone falling through the water. Perhaps it is time that the young apprentice was holding something more useful in his hands." With this he turned about and simply seemed to disappear, leaving Shigoto somewhat unsure whether his teacher had been there or not, whether he had actually seen him or simply imagined him. Shigoto stared at the empty space for a long while, then returned to throwing gravel to the seemingly ever hungry, never satisfied fish exuberantly roiling about in front of him.

The Gardener's Apprentice

A few days later, Kamaboku arrived at Shigoto's home. "15th Grade Gardener Shigoto is to appear for work at the Southern Courtyard immediately." He called out from the modest front gateway. Oyadori appeared instantly at the front of the house. "Is it true, Kamaboku san, for work, you say?" she said, her voice tinged with surprise.

Kamaboku was smiling his broad gap-toothed smile. "Yes, for work this time. Walking days are over it seems. This time it's for work. Mind you, work does give a man a thirst, you know."

Kamaboku stood on a large broad flat stone set deep in the ground in front of the low unassuming narrow veranda that ran across the front of the house. Oyadori was kneeling, one hand holding onto the open sliding paper covered screen.

"Kamaboku san, can I offer you some tea? Okugi-chan will be but a moment, and I will need to prepare some food for him to take. Please accept some tea. I won't keep you long, I promise."

Kamaboku's face lit up with delight, and he sat on the edge of the veranda, his feet resting on the stone.

"No problem at all. Maguro Sensei will not be there. Kamaboku will show the young man his tasks himself. There is time for your kind offer of tea this morning." From inside the house muffled sounds drifted out. Kamaboku sat leaning forward with his arms resting on his knees looking out through the open gateway onto the bare earthen lane beyond, his deeply etched hands lay quiet one in the other. By his side a small bowl of bright green tea now sat, the faintest insinuation of steam rising from the still surface bearing a flavour as fine as any incense to him.

As Kamaboku and Shigoto arrived in the Courtyard, two gardeners were getting ready to leave and they shouted something indistinct to Kamaboku who waved back at them. They had left a bamboo rake, brush and a wicker basket by the foot of the steps leading up to the veranda in front of the main hall of the palace. Shigoto stood looking about him at the vast empty expanse of the Southern Courtyard stretching out in front of the *shinden*. The courtyard was bounded on three sides by buildings, and was open on the fourth side, where it ran down to a long curved pebbled shore of the Great Dragon Pond. Because of its intimate proximity to the principal reception rooms of the palace it was not a place he ever ventured outside of festival days, or those occasions when the inhabitants of Mikura were called to appear before their lord and master. Then the courtyard would be a bustle of colour, movement, familiar and unfamiliar faces, and a thousand different things to catch the eye. The bulk of the main hall loomed over the two figures, its immense and imposing structure appeared to Shigoto to resemble some huge ancient beast struggling with the twin burdens of age and grave responsibility trying to get to its feet. Shigoto looked up in awe at the expanse of the roof and imagined all the tiles cascading down in an uncontrollable tidal wave towards him. His mouth was dry, and he felt very small indeed.

"Ah, here are your tools," said Kamaboku as he strode towards the rake, brush and basket, and then brought them back to Shigoto who was still standing looking unsure about him. "Come on now, look lively, it's your first day at work, Shigoto san. Here take the brush, eh. Now what you have been assigned to do is to sweep and clean the Courtyard. You must leave it in perfect condition, not a leaf on the ground, and not a weed to be seen."

Kamaboku held out the long handled brush towards Shigoto. The end of the bamboo handle of the brush reached above his head. He looked at the tool in his hands, the head of which had been made by bundling and lashing together very thin long bamboo side shoots into a flared tongue-like shape, and the worn ends of which curved lightly upwards through repeated use.

"So, here you are, set to, somebody will be back to see how you are doing. Until then you are to be on your own. These are Sensei's instructions. He is very strict, as you know well, so do a good job of it, eh." Kamaboku edged in closer to Shigoto and in a quieter voice, said, "If I were you I would start in one corner, say over there, and make your way across to the other side, all the way along the front of the building. Then make your way back again to the side you started on. Tidy a section a few paces wide each time. Work your way backwards and forwards, backwards and forwards. That's the way to do it. Easy as anything, eh. Oh, and make sure to brush out any scuff marks."

"What are scuff marks?" asked Shigoto, holding his brush and feeling hopelessly lost with the enormity of the task before him.

"These ..." replied Kamaboku with his trademark smile, as he dragged one foot across the loose gravel surface, leaving a faint mark on the ground, and with that he left Shigoto to his own devices, and made his way across the courtyard in the direction of the gardens.

Leaving the rake and basket behind, Shigoto took the brush, with its oversized handle, and walked slowly and carefully across to where Kamaboku had indicated a good place to start. He set down the head of the brush on the surface, and looked up toward the building. The veranda was at a height where, if he pushed himself up on his toes, he could see a distance along its length. There was no one there. Then Shigoto turned to look down the length of the open corridor that led on towards a pavilion set over the Great Dragon Pond. The pavilion was empty, and the corridor vacant and still, but for the breeze humming softly as it passed through some ornamental fretwork under a low handrail. Shigoto looked down at the brush, then, cautiously started to walk sideways along the front of the veranda of the main hall towards the steps dragging the brush behind him. Arriving at the side of the steps he looked up, and could see from his new vantage point that he truly was alone. He set off back to where he has just come from, dragging the brush behind him. For an hour or so Shigoto marched quietly backwards and forwards across the courtyard.

When he came to the first of the two large trees in the courtyard, he stopped. One was an ancient cherry tree, its trunk split open like a rotting fruit, at its centre a gaping vacant space emptied by time and decay. Several posts had been driven into the ground around the tree, and a girdle of rope prevented the last morsels falling apart completely. Still, several live branches hung on defying antiquity to reach weakly up into the sky, and every spring it would blossom, just as it had been doing for over two hundred and eighty springs. On the opposite side of the steps, on the west side of the courtyard, was a citrus tree, with a dark, deeply fissured trunk of exaggerated girth twisting about itself. In its great age, it seemed to be caught between being pressed down from above, and forced up from below, as if it alone were responsible for keeping the sky and earth apart. Above the trunk there was a dense series of domes of dark evergreen leaves, and now in the late summer, small orange coloured bitter fruits peeked shyly between the dense masses of foliage.

The rope girdle wrapped tight around the waist of the cherry had been coiled very neatly with tight abutting turns. Shigoto walked around the tree following the turns of straw-coloured rope, looking for a beginning or an end. The binding had been done so neatly, with such great dexterity, that he could not see how the ends had been fastened in. From around the base of the tree, he collected a few dried leaves that had tumbled down from the branches above. Putting the crisp fragments of leaf together in a neat pile he went to collect the basket where it sat waiting for him. Arriving back by the tree, Shigoto was surprised to find the leaves where no longer where he had left them. He looked up, half expecting to feel a breeze or wind. The air hung still. Walking around the tree, looking to see where his hoard had scattered to, he came across the leaves on the opposite side of the trunk.

'I did not put the leaves here, on this side, I am sure I did not,' he thought to himself. Then as he bent down to pick up the leaves to deposit them in the basket, he noticed that the leaves were not in the small neat heap he had created, but lying in loose lines running out from the base of the trunk toward the centre of the Courtyard. He crouched on his haunches and carefully picked up the leaves one by one, dropping them into the basket as he went. From time to time he looked up, his eyes scanning along the veranda, running the length of the corridor, and also behind him across the expressionless space of the courtyard. Though he appeared to be alone, he could not avoid the feeling he was being watched. When a bead of sweat ran down from his forehead and dropped onto the back of his hand, he fell back startled for a moment. When he realised what it was, he laughed. "Hey, I am a gardener now. I am Shigoto Okugi, 15th Grade Under Gardener," he said aloud, to reassure himself.

With the leaves collected and in captivity, he continued his wandering backwards and forwards across the space dragging the brush behind him. When he came across a leaf or any other foreign body, he would stop, drop the tool he was using, walk over to the basket and deposit his collection there. Then walk back to his brush and resume his meandering course.

Later in the day Kamaboku called in on him. He stood next to Shigoto, and the pair of gardeners looked about them. Kamaboku pushed his lips out and nodded his tacit approval to Shigoto.

"You are doing alright. Not a bad job, not a bad job for your first day. You hungry? It's time for some lunch, I brought mine over, and we can sit and eat together. Better to be out of the way, someplace where nobody can see us." He jerked his thumb back in the direction of the main Hall.

Gratefully dropping his rake from his now weary arms, Shigoto ran over to the corner where he had started his day, and ducked under the veranda into the dank earth-tainted shade beneath the building. He emerged a few moments later clutching a cloth bundle, and holding a small ceramic lidded water jar by its cord handle. Then he ran to catch up with Kamaboku who was striding over toward a pavilion where musicians would sometimes sit and play. They passed around the back of the pavilion and finding a grassy patch sat down on the grass to sup and eat.

"Nobody from the Hall can see us here," he said conspiratorially, "and we get the view across the lake to enjoy with our lunch. Not bad, eh. Like a proper couple of *samurai*, sitting eating lunch, enjoying our leisure." Kamaboku roared with laughter at his own humour, and in the process Shigoto learned he had but a very meagre collection of crooked teeth left standing in his mouth. Sitting cross-legged they opened their cloth bundles, and began to eat the food contained inside in silence. Shigoto's mother had wrapped each of his rice balls with broad bamboo leaves, pinning them closed with a thin sprig of bamboo. Kamaboku started laughing when he saw this, and gesticulating at his companion's lunch with a finger, and slapping his thigh with his other hand, he all but choked on a mouth full of food. Tears rolled down his inflated cheeks.

"Ah, Shigoto, you are a good one. We will get on just fine the two of us." Kamaboku addressed him, once he had recovered his poise, and emptied his mouth. "Tell me something, does your mother always wrap your lunch like that?"

"Yes, I guess so. Why?" Shigoto looked at his lunch lying on the dark green square of cloth in front of him, puzzled as to what could be so amusing.

"She is a good woman, that mother of yours, eh. Looks after you well, no? Looks after Kamaboku too. With a fresh tea for

Kamaboku, when he comes to call for you in the mornings. I like that, one could get used to such a thing, eh."

Shigoto said nothing, but just let out a low sigh. Kamaboku was clearly as demented in his eyes as all the other adults he knew. 'Maybe that is what getting old does to you,' he wondered. 'I do not want to get old and be like that.' After they had eaten and drunk a little, Kamaboku settled himself back comfortably on the grass.

"Hey, Shigoto, give me a nudge if anyone comes, eh," and closed his eyes and seemed to promptly fall asleep. Shigoto looked out across the still surface of the pond and watched the clouds drifting by, lost in his own thoughts. 'Well, I suppose this is what it means to be a gardener.'

Soon enough Kamaboku roused himself, and with a cheery, "Right, let's get back to work then, eh," the pair parted, and Shigoto trudged back to where he had left his rake.

❖ ❖ ❖

"Hey, Shigoto. How are you getting on?" It was the friendly voice of Kamaboku striding towards him from behind. "It is time to stop work, Sensei asked me to come over and tell you it's alright to go home now." Kamaboku came up to where Shigoto was stood. "Hey, is that the rubbish you have collected in your basket. You have done well today, eh. Out to impress on your first day, eh?" Kamaboku ruffled Shigoto's head with his hand, a gesture that Shigoto detested coming from anyone, his mother in particular. "Come on, collect up your tools, I will show you where to leave them for the morning."

"Is Sensei, coming today? To see what I have done, that is?" he asked Kamaboku.

"No, no," Kamaboku chuckled. "Sensei is busy over the other side of the gardens today. He'll be over there a while yet. He is always a busy man is Maguro Sensei, that's why he sent Kamaboku over to tell you to finish for the day. You can resume again tomorrow. After Kamaboku has had his tea that is, eh," as he laughed his farewell.

CHAPTER TWELVE

May 1576

"They are going to have to be told, you know, something like this cannot be hidden for long. Then we will be ruined, that will be the end of this family," the woman's voice trailed despondency and gloom in its wake. There was nothing in what she had been told that she could find remotely optimistic. "I suppose there are some options open to you, but none of them are good." She looked across at her daughter sitting opposite to her, but her eyes were discarded empty shells.

"What can I say? I am sorry, Mother," said Oyadori, her head bent.

"What you can say is that he forced you. He will deny it of course, it will be your word set against his, and yours will count for nothing. You know that don't you," she spat the words out as if she had finally found a way of expressing the anger she felt. "Then there is the other family, all the arrangements will have to be undone. It's a disaster. Perhaps we would be better off dead. But even then our names will be held to shame and abuse. You know how it is, it would be a worse punishment to stay alive. Maybe, if we bear that now, then in the next life we will not have to carry so much of this burden upon ourselves."

"Why do you talk of death all the time? There is life in me, a new life. I am going to have this child. I will bear whatever punishment comes my way, but I will be there to take care of my child."

"You may not have the chance to honour your fine words. Be careful, be very careful what you say, how you say it, and to whom you say anything. Your life, our lives, are hanging by a very thin thread just now." Oba-chan paused to reflect and then reached up to her head and taking a single strand of hair between her fingers, she pulled sharply at it. Then she extended the strand out towards her daughter.

"See this, you see this," the single hair hung limp from her grasp between them. "That is about what is between us and death, either by our own hand, or that of one of the palace guards, or even by the hand of the man who was to be your husband. Damn it."

"You exaggerate," protested Oyadori.

"Exaggerate, me exaggerating? Oh, you think so do you? Then that only goes to show you know nothing about these people and how they are, or what they are capable of. They will lose face over this, that's enough for them to act." Her voice was now reduced to a hoarse whisper. Then she fell silent, spent.

"Then I will speak to him," said Oyadori at last, there was a quiet determination about her. "It's his child too, he was the one who gave me this seed. He will at least want the child, if I die after that, at least the child may live…" she was at the verge of breaking down completely, her ears filled with the sound of doors slamming shut, and her hands clasped knot-tight in her

The Gardener's Apprentice

lap were blurred, swimming in her vision. Nothing was clear anymore.

"Child, you are a dreamer, you always were. What does this man care for a child borne by a servant? Wake up from your dreams, will you. Come back to this world, live in this world a moment. Men are different to us. I suppose if your father were here now, he would tell you to put a knife to your throat. Perhaps he would even do it himself. He would not stand for this, he was a man of honour, and it was everything to him. He often said to me that we should think that our lives are nothing; we simply exist to serve the Saeko family. To him it was a noble thing to die for the clan, and an honour. He was a real *samurai* your father, he could not have stood to lose face like this. I suppose we women are weaker than men in that way. We see things through different eyes. For men everything is simple, you either breathe or you die. No, this man, this visitor to our shores, what would he care? He has had his pleasure, you are nothing to him now, but the bones he spits out. He has taken what he wanted after all."

"It's not true what you say," Oyadori protested. "He is a kind man, I saw it in his face. He was concerned for me, he took an interest in me. Who is this man Kanyu? I am nothing to him. He does not even like me, I felt that when we met, when I saw him there with his father and Lady Saeko. He never held me with his eyes, he did not even want to look at me, except out of curiosity maybe. No, I was nothing to him, and I felt nothing for him. But the visitor, he is different, I felt something for him. He did not force me. I let him come to me. I wanted him at that moment. I wanted to taste something even if it were only for the briefest moment in time, even if I knew in my heart it could not last for longer than it actually did. For the first time in my life I was making a choice for myself, it was what I wanted, for myself. I needed to taste that. He is a good man, I know that, I know that." Oyadori spoke without thinking what she was saying; the words, thoughts, and feelings poured out of her in an unstoppable flow.

"Pah, he is of the Imperial family, his brother is the Emperor. And you, what are you? Only a lowly maid, born into a low class *samurai* family, whose only task is to serve without question or even thought for ourselves. We are nothing compared to that man. He has greater authority in his fingertip than we will ever accumulate in a thousand generations. I have heard that part of the reason he is here is because of his ways back at the capital. Why do you think he was sent into exile? They wanted him out of the way. Someone, perhaps his brother the Emperor, may be it was the Shogun even, someone wanted him gone from there. He was trouble in some way, now he has come here, and has brought his karma with him. He has infected our family. Through your weakness, your foolishness, he has condemned us utterly. I have heard the rumours; you think I do not know what is being said about him. There were stories even before he arrived on our island. They always want to dump their trouble on us; it is a curse we have to bear for living here where we do. And you talk to me about his nice complexion? You know nothing and you understand even less."

"Mother, Oba-chan, listen to me. He is a good man, he has a heart, I felt it in him, I saw it in his eyes," Oyadori protested. "My child will be born, and he or she will have a chance to live." She lifted her head resolutely. Outside the light was beginning to fade, dusk was falling, she would have to return to her duties soon.

"No, no, what you felt, was not his heart, you fool." Oba-chan spat out the words. "If you do carry that child and it is born, it will be eternally cursed by this. Doubly cursed in fact, because it too will be nothing but a dreamer."

"I have to go back now. I will be missed if I don't get back soon. Kobuto san will get cross," said Oyadori softly as she stood up. Her mother remained motionless where she sat and her eyes saw nothing except the night rapidly descending.

❖ ❖ ❖

"Lady Saeko wishes to see you about something," said Kobuto. "Have you been up to something? You have been acting strangely these past few days. Are you in some kind of trouble? She is asking after you specifically."

"No," replied Oyadori. "It's nothing, nothing at all."

Kobuto looked across at her, her eyes trying to penetrate behind Oyadori's mask of a face, trying to divine the reason for the request from Lady Saeko.

"I'll find out you know. There is nothing that happens around here that I do not know about. So if there is something that you would rather share with me, well may be I could help you. Put in a good word for you with the lady." Kobuto spoke in a soft voice laced with sweet reasonableness, almost pity.

"Really, it's nothing. I have no idea why she wants to speak to me. Maybe it's something to do with this proposed marriage. I don't know, really I don't," said Oyadori.

"Humph. Why would she concern herself with something like that? After all it is a matter of little consequence to the likes of her," Kobuto snarled in frustration.

Oyadori left the room before the conversation could continue. She had never cared much for the acid tongue of Kobuto and now she cared even less. Though she was mildly surprised that little anger rose to the surface. It was as if the magnitude of the situation she was in pressed whatever feelings she may have toward her fellow maid into some distant corner of her mind. As she walked along the broad corridor to Lady Saeko's apartment she felt a great weight pressing down on her shoulders. Arriving outside the door to the room where Lady Saeko was waiting, she knelt on the smooth boards, straightened her back and took a deep breath or two.

Oyadori called from outside the door in a quiet voice, "Madam? Excuse me…"

There was a long silence, and Oyadori remained where she was kneeling on the dark polished timber floor.

"Enter."

Lady Saeko was sitting by herself at the far side of the room when Oyadori entered sliding the door closed behind her, closing out the outer world. She did not look toward Oyadori.

"Come. Sit over here."

"Ma'm… I…" Oyadori spoke as soon as she kneeled a few paces away from Lady Saeko, who remained looking out towards the garden, her face a mask of indifference.

Lady Saeko held one hand up to quieten Oyadori. Silence descended again, and fell across the two women as a shadow so dense that even the sound of the birds chasing through the garden could not penetrate it. Lady Saeko remained motionless for a long time, ignoring Oyadori's presence by staring out beyond the room. Oyadori could feel her heart beating out a steady excitable tattoo in her chest, the sound filled her head blocking out all else. She kept her hands in her lap with the fingers tightly entwined, knuckles bleached of colour, skin so stretched over bone that blood had no space to flow.

"So, Oyadori," finally Lady Saeko spoke.

'It's mother,' thought Oyadori. 'She is the only one who knows. She must have said something. Why? Why would she do that? She must know that it is for me to face the consequences of my own actions.' To Oyadori it felt like a betrayal, a severing of a bond between parent and child; she had been cast adrift to fate. Now she was on her own, as her mother had placed the welfare and concerns of the clan above and beyond her only child.

"So, Oyadori, certain matters have come to my attention. Grave matters have been raised which cannot be ignored, concerning your conduct," Lady Saeko's voice was icy calm, all the emotion locked in tight. "You are a maid servant to me, as such your behaviour is of direct concern to me. You understand that, do you not?"

"Ma'm..." Oyadori started to speak but the words caught in her throat and refused to emerge.

"You have been with a man, a man who is not the person chosen to be your husband. This is what I am told, is that right?" Still Lady Saeko looked away from Oyadori, her face turned towards the garden presented only a deep shadowed side to Oyadori. Her words seemed to be coming from beyond the room where they sat. The volume was so low, as if to guard them from any chance of being heard by eavesdroppers.

Oyadori bit down on her bottom lip, pincering the soft flesh between her teeth until her mouth filled with the warm salty taste of her blood. "Yes it is true. What my mother has told you," said Oyadori, she was staring at a spot on the floor halfway between them. Only then Lady Saeko turned to Oyadori and her eyes bore into her face. Oyadori felt the temperature in the room fall, and she shuddered involuntarily as if swept by a sudden chill draft.

"Who is the man?" Lady Saeko asked.

The question caught Oyadori by surprise and she looked up from the floor straight towards the grim mask-like look of her mistress. She tried to speak but the words could not get past her tight throat. The face of Hotaru swam before her eyes, his smiling face, his kindly face softened by a grin of satisfaction, the last image that she held in her memory of him.

"I... I thought my mother had spoken to you," said Oyadori at last, confused now by the question.

"It is of no consequence who has spoken what to me. I asked you a question, which remains unanswered."

"It was… was the distinguished visitor, Milady. I…he…" Oyadori's voice faded away into nothingness. She looked back down towards the floor as if she were preparing herself to receive the touch of the executioner's sword across the nape of her neck.

For a long moment nothing more was said between the two women. A gaggle of small birds suddenly descended on the garden; their raucous chatter filled the room for a moment or two, then with a flurry of beating wings they look off for some nearby trees taking their disputations with them. Quiet settled once more like a set of thin fingers being pulled into silk glove.

"I see," Lady Saeko said finally as if she were surprised by the news. "Lord Saeko knows nothing of this himself, as yet. So far as I am aware, no one has spoken to him concerning the matter. However because it involves the visitor staying under our roof he will have to be informed. I take it you know well enough of the position of the person of whom we are speaking? No doubt Kobuto has kept you informed regarding that, nothing much seems to escape her attention. His presence here is a delicate matter. Events that occur in the capital have all manner of consequences, their ripples can even reach here. There are sensitivities involved, that you would know nothing about." Her voice sounded wistful. "Then there is the question of the family of your husband-to-be. As I understand it arrangements concerning the union of the two families have been proceeding. You are aware of course that it was my husband, Lord Saeko himself, who sanctioned this marriage. It was his express wish for this… this union, to take place. He will view none of this with any pleasure."

"Ma'm, if I may be permitted to speak…" Oyadori spoke with a small voice.

"Oh, do you not think that you have caused enough trouble for all concerned already? I do not think that there is anything you could possibly say to redeem the situation. It is too late for that now. This is a serious matter, not something that may be brushed away and forgotten, there are far too many complications for that. Things that you could not possibly appreciate nor be expected understand." Lady Saeko spoke acidly. "And you are sure that you are with child?"

Oyadori merely nodded her head. 'I am trapped in this world,' she thought. 'Nothing is within my control or reach. These people, all of them, the Saeko family, Shigoto Kanyu and his father, my mother, even him, this distinguished visitor, they are all considering what is important to save their own face. None of them are concerned for what I am, who I am in this entire situation. I am nothing but an irritant to them all, some insignificant bug that causes an itch, something that can be squashed and flicked away out of sight. I mean nothing to them all.' She felt her fear turning to sour bitterness, hopeless, impotent anger that had no way to turn. 'But this child is mine, I will never allow them to take this child away from me. We will both die before that happens, we will die together, then we will be out of their reach, out of their control.'

"That will be all, for now." Lady Saeko spoke with a voice tinged by the weight of sadness. "You will continue with your duties for the time being. You are to speak to no one about your condition. No one, you understand," she spoke with determined emphasis. "Go now, I will see my husband and discuss the matter with him."

"Yes, Ma'm. I..." Oyadori started to speak, but still nothing would come out from her mouth. The words were there screaming in her mind, but nothing emerged. She raised her hands as if pleading, imploring to her mistress. But Lady Saeko had averted her gaze back towards the garden; she appeared to see nothing, her face set as if torn from a stone.

"Send Kobuto in to me," Lady Saeko said finally.

Oyadori backed out of the room. Before she slid the door to a close once more she looked back into the room to where the elder woman sat in solitude, immobilised by the weight of decisions. All she did was to raise one hand in a slow silent gesture of dismissal.

"So, what did she want? What did she say?" Kobuto whispered hoarsely, she could barely contain her curiosity. Despite her best efforts to overhear, she had not managed to decipher the conversation. "Is it bad news regarding the marriage? Has it been cancelled, or postponed?"

"She wants you to attend to her," said Oyadori, her mind was blank; her eyes did not seem to register either shadow or light.

Despite it being still warm in the early evening, Oyadori threw a thin shawl over her shoulders and went out of the room. She passed swiftly along the wide corridor outside Lady Saeko's apartments and continued walking, she did not have any particular idea where she was going, all she knew was that she had to get away, to go some place other, to be somewhere else. At the end of the women's apartments she turned a corner and continued walking, then she realised where she was headed. She stopped momentarily as if to gather her senses, but she felt a determination now. She knew what she had to do. It was, she felt, her only chance, her only hope for salvation. She rushed on now feet gliding over the polished boards.

At the end of another corridor she turned left, further along where two guards standing stock-still facing each other, in their hands short handled pikes held rigidly upright. They were talking softly to one another, but stopped, startled perhaps by her sudden appearance and looked up towards her. She saw their faces, which seemed hardened by the rigours of their training or perhaps it was the boredom of their duty. She slowed her pace a fraction, but she was so determined that she did not stop. As she drew nearer to the guards they looked across to one another, as if seeking to clarify the nature of their response to her unexpected presence. Oyadori saw their fingers tighten the grip on

The Gardener's Apprentice

the wooden stocks of the pikes. She carried on, slower now, moving more sedately, composing her face as if to show she offered no threat, no cause for alarm, one hand held onto the shawl she clasped tight over her shoulders and neck.

"Good evening," she said quietly, a wan smile trailing its way across her face. She looked neither of the guards in his face, but remained wholly focused on where she was headed. She passed between the men and continued to outside of the door of the apartment where Prince Hotaru was, then stopped. She knelt by the door in the corridor, the light was beginning to fade, the deepening shadows darkened by the rapidly fading light. She tried to compose herself as best she could, for her heart was beating wildly, pounding in her chest, her breath coming in short bursts. Oyadori realised that it was a sense of panic that had drawn her here to this place, this very door. Now she was here she felt only confusion over her motives, her expectations as to what she might achieve. Hotaru's face loomed up in her mind again: his face burnished golden by candle light, and smiling, smiling softly down at her with the tenderness that had overwhelmed any trace of fear she might have of felt that night. She raised her hand to knock against the wooden post at the side of the paper-covered door.

As she did so voices and laughter came from within, the deep toned voices of men, several of them; men who were enjoying a joke, a well placed witticism or a fine turn of phrase. She stayed her hand just before her knuckles struck against the wooden post, and she opened her hand and allowed her fingers to come to rest lightly on the cool smooth surface. There she stayed, kneeling on the floor, her head bowed deep as if in prayer or contemplation. Then she drew back her hand and rose slowly to her feet again. The two guards were staring in her direction, as if trying to decide the best course of action. Oyadori looked fleetingly at them, then stepping back a pace she bowed towards the room from where the sounds emanated. With a final lingering glance at the closed door she turned away and once more started moving smoothly along the corridor in the direction of the guards, whose attention was now wholly absorbed by her actions. When she drew near to them the smile was back again on her face.

"I did not want to disturb the gentlemen," she said in a low voice, looking into the hard, questioning eyes of the guards. "I can collect the items later," she lied fluently. "Tell me, can I fetch you a drink of water or something? It must be hard to stand here all the while."

"We are on duty, Miss. It is our job," one of the guards replied, his voice tinged by the confusion and suspicion brought about by her seemingly illogical actions.

"Very well then, I shall return later," she said and continued past them without further ado.

CHAPTER THIRTEEN

November 1587

There is a significant difference between standing at the bottom of a mountain looking up admiring the scenery, and being at the summit enjoying the view from on high. If Shigoto imagined that his call to begin work as a garden apprentice would herald the beginning of a new and glorious chapter to his life, then disappointment was to be a shadow trailing in his wake. For what he had not taken into account was the thousands of steps it takes to climb the mountain. His first day of work was followed by an evening of great excitement for him. He was hailed as a returning hero when he arrived home. His mother had found the time to prepare a special meal for him with several of his favourite dishes, and Shigoto for once found the relentless questioning of his grandmother a source of self pride, rather than an irritation. The pride and admiration of the women of the household, and the blessings of steamed eel on rice were in themselves sufficient compensation. As the stars flickered into life high above his head, he fell into an exhausted sleep, his night cushioned by grand dreams, of the young Shigoto achieving great honours and renown throughout the land as the 'greatest gardener Japan has ever known'.

The following day true to his word, Kamaboku arrived bright and early, and after accepting and drinking a cup of freshly made tea from Shigoto's mother, the pair set out to collect their tools and proceed to the Southern Courtyard, where Kamaboku had been instructed that he was to continue his work of the previous day. Kamaboku had between sips of the delicate tea informed Shigoto's mother that Maguro Sensei had decided in light of his youth, and his still developing body, Shigoto would begin by working three days and then be excused garden duties for the next two days. This pattern was to continue for the foreseeable future, as Sensei assessed Shigoto's progress and aptitude for the work. No promises were made concerning his future advancement.

"Maguro Sensei is a wise man, Shigoto, you will do well to remind yourself of this fact." Kamaboku said to Shigoto, when he saw the falling look on the young apprentice's face as he broke the news of the new routine to him. "Sensei sees things that the ordinary mortals such as you and I do not. He is our teacher after all, and it is most important to trust in the wisdom of our teacher, as then we too can absorb something of his wisdom for ourselves." While this placated Shigoto to some degree by at least momentarily feeling included in the same 'we' category as Kamaboku, he was still recalling dreamtime visions, which in his own eyes had elevated him to a status exceeding even that of his teacher. The present arrangement did not seem to him to quite take into account the prestige and honour that he had already garnered, if only in his dreams, following his first day as a garden apprentice.

"Is Sensei coming today to see my work, Kamaboku san?" Shigoto had picked up his rake and begun the task of tidying the gravel in the courtyard, the minute they arrived there.

"Well, we will have to see, eh," replied Kamaboku. "You have to understand Shigoto, Sensei is a man with many responsibilities, and he has many different things to do. He will come when the time is right, that you can be sure of. There is little that happens which Sensei does not know about, believe me, sometimes he sees more than you may wish."

As Shigoto looked about him and took in his surroundings, the courtyard did not appear quite as massive as he had remembered. It remained a dauntingly large space, but something of the edge of threat had diminished from the area. Even the imposing main hall did not seem to be quite so overwhelming. Its tone of authority remained, conferred upon it by the years it had been standing; that was something implacable and unquestionable. The veranda that ran across the front of the building ordinarily was out of bounds to anyone not of the immediate staff of the Lord Saeko and his family. Other members of the palace staff, such as the gardeners (with the exception of Maguro Sensei), townspeople or farmers, could only approach the bottom of the steps, in the line of duty or during one of the public festivals held to mark the passing of the seasons. To be caught transgressing this unwritten code would result in physical punishment, a severe beating and public humiliation. To do so whilst the Lord Saeko was on the veranda would result in the misguided transgressor being cut down in a flash of steel. The consequences were known to all, taken in with the nursing milk, and within living memory no one had ever tried.

"Come on, I shall work with you for a while, Shigoto. We can start over there. Step lively, eh."

Before arriving at the Southern Courtyard, Kamaboku and Shigoto had made their way to a building where the gardeners stored their tools and equipment. The palace complex was enclosed and protected on three sides by a boundary wall, almost twice the height of a man, and capped with a broad coping of dark silvery-grey tiles. It was pierced by three openings, the great North Gate, with its huge, heavy, studded timber gates and imposing roof, and lesser gates set into the eastern and western flanks. Beyond the Western Gate lay a small township, a sprawling and seemingly disconnected series of mainly single storey buildings and narrow lanes, all of which in some way served the needs of the Palace, and those who lived within its protective wall. It also housed storerooms, warehouses, offices of clerks, stabling yards, and beyond that a scattering of houses occupied by families of various members of staff. Shigoto's home was among the outer reaches of this melee of activity, among a group of other equally modest quarters housing members of the Palace staff.

To the rear of the stables, fronted by a small yard of beaten down earth, was a nondescript building, one of a row of such, all of which had seen better days. The slack hung doors were open, and the gaping mouth allowed the courtyard to flow seamlessly into the space within. On the walls inside were hung ropes and an array of equipment to dig and turn the earth, cut trees and branches, tools to lift and carry weights, brushes and rakes to tidy; winches, carts, and baskets of different sizes were lying on the floor. There was a precise and defined order to the place, as if every item there knew its place within the multitude. In one corner were two tatami covered benches, the weave of the matting surfaces worn and dark stained from use. On them lay several neat heaps of clothing and a few personal possessions, a respectful distance from its neighbour, waiting in readiness for their owners' return at the end of the day's work. The floor was swept clean. Shigoto had never seen the interior of such a place before. His eyes roamed the room looking from one place to the next, seeing much and hearing very little of Kamaboku's commentary relating to their use. They selected a brush, rake and basket each.

"They are all made of bamboo, you see?" pointed out Kamaboku with a certain pride, when they had made their selection from the array available. Shigoto had found a rake and brush with a handle of a more suitable length to the one he had the day before. He knelt down in front of the woven baskets, and after a few moments of silent contemplation, picked out one that seemed to silently draw itself to his attention. It felt comfortable in his hands.

"You like that one, eh? Then we will call it 'Shigoto's Basket', now you are a gardener, you must have your own tools. You can put your tools together here at the end of the day." Kamaboku pointed to a gap along the wall near one of the benches. Shigoto felt a growing sense of belonging and it warmed him from the inside. He said nothing, but a slight smile broke out on his face. Shigoto felt, more than heard, his name being spoken by the room, somewhere in the assemblage of tackle, his name was being called out. Fate had assigned a new, unfamiliar place to his acquaintance, and now he was being welcomed. It seemed to him he was being granted entry there. He had only been aware of the familiar before, his home and his mother, the constants in his life, which had always been there and required neither reasoning nor justification for their existence. His friends, the children of his acquaintance who lived near his home, they too had always been there. Alliances and friendships may have shifted, swung backwards and forwards over time, and bodies begun to fill out and mature, but the faces were still the same recognisable ones. This room, however was different, it spoke of the promise of a new world, a new order of things.

"On days when it rains heavily, we make new brushes and rakes, baskets too, repair the tools, that sort of thing. Kakugari san is skilled at basket making, he teaches us. Ah, Kamaboku is not good at that, a brush I can do, but basket making is not for me, too many bits to think about, eh. Anyway, now you have found your tools we had better get a move on. Leave your lunch here, just bring the water jar, you will be eating here now most days." Kamaboku pointed in the direction of the benches. "Come on, its going to be fine today, no rain, Kamaboku feels it in his bones, eh," he chuckled to himself.

As they left the room, clutching tools and with baskets slung in a workmanlike casual manner, Shigoto glanced back at the two benches. He thought he could vaguely make out the faintest of ghostly shadows of people sitting there, moving about slowly and lying back resting, with quiet meaningful small talk in the air. Another world, another time, a fork in the path, but where did his own path lead, and what was the emerging shape of things? On that the room was silent.

Following in Kamaboku's footsteps Shigoto crossed the Southern Courtyard. They left their water jars in the shade beneath the veranda, and then moved purposefully out into the open expanse of the yard. They set down their baskets and took up station within a few paces of one another, and began sweeping and raking the gravel to a smooth clean finish. They worked with few words said between them; the only sounds were the rustling, scurrying of the brushwood sweeps, and the gentle scratching of gravel running through the teeth of a bamboo rake. Every now and then Kamaboku would demonstrate how to swing the brush's tail across the loose surface in the most effective manner, or sometimes correct Shigoto's posture when drawing his rake. Shigoto would watch the light, economical strokes of Kamaboku's brush dancing over the gravel. He began to realise how clumsy his efforts were at this seemingly easy task. He had wielded a brush at home often enough, though more often straddling it, in imitation of some great warrior saddled on a fiery steed than as an effective means of sweeping the tatami mats. They worked on for an hour or more, making a slow dance backwards and forward across the courtyard, until Kamaboku called a brief halt. They then made their way across to their water pots in the shade of the veranda. Crouching down they drank a few sips. Kamaboku remained crouched, his sight drifting across the open space and out across the Great Dragon Pond beyond the sea of gravel. Shigoto watched Kamaboku's face for any sign of meaning behind that faraway gaze, but he could find none.

They worked together for the rest of the morning, making numberless sweeps of their arms as they traversed to and fro, leaving the gravel velvet smooth and glistening in the pale watery sunshine. Kamaboku stopped of a sudden, and looked up into the sky.

"Ah, I am sure it is time for our lunch. What do you think, eh?" he called to Shigoto.

Shigoto looked up from the ground and nodded. He had been waiting for this moment for what had seemed like an eternity. He felt as if burning currents were surging along his arms. His shoulders were stiff and sore, and he could not open the grip of his fingers clasped around the handle of his brush. His fingers had lost all feeling some time before, and now they felt numbed and claw-like. He had been keeping his back slightly turned toward his companion whilst they were working, so as not to reveal the growing grimace on his face. His early high spirits had dissipated in the hours of drudgery that the morning had become. Still, he would grit it out, it felt instinctively like the right thing to do. That was his way; joy was for sharing, pain and hurt were another matter all together.

Kamaboku led Shigoto back to the tool store. They passed the rear of the great hall, and skirting around the byways of the palace compound came to the East Gate. There was so much for Shigoto to take in. Everyday brought him to places he had not known existed before. Kamaboku clearly had an easy familiarity with the palace complex, as the gardeners were required to work in and maintain all the spaces between buildings around the palace buildings. Even, from time to time, they would work in the gardens attached to the rooms used by the ladies of the household over on the west side of the palace. Aside from the main *shinden* building itself, the remainder of the palace was made up of a series of interconnected, smaller timber buildings, each connected to another by a raised wooden walkway with a tiled roof. It was possible to move about the palace in its entirety without once stepping down on the ground. Inside the North Gate was a courtyard laid with a surface of tightly jointed flat stones of a dark grey hue, from which hooves of horses would strike sparks. Dismounting there, a visitor would take the two broad steps up into the Entrance Hall, a low building, with a floor of broad polished boards from some denizen of the forest that had relinquished its life for the very purpose. The polished floors flowed on to all parts of the palace. Between buildings the open sided walkways defined a variety of spaces, some of which had been developed as garden tableaux, others simply gravelled over, and some now simply used as open-air storage spaces. These little oases of life allowed light and air to penetrate into what otherwise would have been dark, damp, and gloomy spaces. By taking a circuitous route, which cut through several of these open spaces, and occasionally ducking under the walkways themselves, Kamaboku was able to navigate Shigoto swiftly back to the less imposing East Gate. Passing the guards stationed at the gate they were soon soon back at the gardener's store.

"You had better eat your lunch, Shigoto. We won't be staying too long you know, just to eat and rest a moment, eh." Kamaboku had sat down on one of the grubby tatami benches, and was already unwrapping a cloth bundle that contained his food.

Shigoto stood at the wide entrance absorbing the scene. Shafts of light slanted in towards the interior, illuminating the centre of the space with rectangle of light while shadows hugged the far walls. For a moment he forgot his physical aches and pains and as his eyes adjusted to the contrast of light he looked again at the array of tools and equipment set all about the interior. He had not said a word since the call to halt work. He had simply followed Kamaboku's snaking trail back to the storeroom. Shigoto looked toward the benches in the corner where Kamaboku was noisily eating. He saw the small heaps of belongings set out as territorial markers, claiming ownership of space in the absence of their owners. He was not sure where to sit down, mindful of the presence of others he had yet to come to meet and know. Kamaboku waved a pair of rice-encrusted chopsticks in his direction.

"Sit over there, at the end. It's fine there. That is nobody's place. Oh, you are a polite boy, eh, Shigoto. Well brought up, eh. Your father is strict I'll bet, no nonsense there. He is a personal retainer to Lord Saeko Machigai, eh?"

Shigoto was not sure whether this was a statement of fact or a question on Kamaboku's part. He sat down where directed and started opening his own cloth bundle containing his lunch that his mother had smilingly pressed into his hands earlier that morning. After a pause he spoke.

"Yes. He serves Lord Saeko. He is never at home. I live with my mother and grandmother, Obachan. I do not know where my father sleeps at night, maybe in the room next to Lord Saeko. That's what Obachan says anyway." Shigoto took a large bite out of the rice ball prepared and wrapped for him by his mother. Suddenly he was very hungry.

"He is an important person, your father, eh. Maybe one day you will be the same, "Kamaboku spoke though a mouthful of rice. Shigoto was shocked, at home his mother would not let him get away with anything like that. May be the world of adults had some compensations after all.

"We will head back to work shortly. But first Kamaboku will close his eyes for a moment of contemplation, eh."

It seemed to Shigoto, slowly chewing his way through a rice ball with some fish at its centre that no sooner had Kamaboku finished eating, than he was stretching himself out on the tatami bench on his back, eyes lightly closed, and sucking softly at a pickled plum stone. Both hands were loosely arranged over his flattened belly, one over the other and soon his chest was rising and falling with the gentle rhythms of sleep. One of his arms slid slowly down to his side, where it lay palm opened upward, with the wiry tanned fingers slightly curled on the tatami. Shigoto looked at the hand that seemed to be as fast asleep as the owner it was attached to, the fingers sporadically twitching as if trying to grasp at a passing dream. Shigoto looked down at is own small hands, which were blistering, pink and fleshy, not at all like the lean and weather-beaten hands of his companion.

Mindful not to make a sound, which might have disturbed the now gently snoring Kamaboku, Shigoto finished his lunch, and folded up his carrying cloth into a neat square. He took a sip of water. His shoulders ached, but sensation was coming back into his fingers again. He stood up in front of the bench and rolled his arms around in the air to loosen his stiff shoulder muscles. Kamaboku remained deep asleep caught in a web of private incommunicable dreams; soft peace descended with the dust inside the storeroom. From outside came the sounds and noises of unseen activity, voices calling out to one another, but the words had been heavily filtered by the time they reached Shigoto. Words bleached of meaning and context existed simply as sounds jostling for attention. He slipped off his sandals and sat back on the tatami bench, straightening his kimono, then leant his now gently aching shoulders against the wall, eyes wide open, tracking insatiably back and forwards across the room.

As his eyes adjusted to the soft luminescence of the interior; he leant back against the wall, as if to breathe too deeply might wake his sleeping companion. In the stillness of the moment, slipping in stealthily between the light and dark, wisps of the presence of the other gardeners returned to the room. The forms seemed to drift silently about the room, engaged in activities he could not quite make out the purpose of. A mouth seemed to open to speak, but from the dim hole that defined it, no sound emerged. An arm would rise and fall in slow motion. A body would appear to cross the room, and then simply dissolve, as if it were nothing more substantial than distant smoke. Shigoto knew they were gardeners; it was a set thought in his mind, as if he had to have an anchor on what could otherwise be taken for hallucinations or ghostly apparitions. This way any sense of threat was removed from the action, and he could sit and observe the ethereal forms coming together, dissolving then reforming somewhere else. He cast an occasional glance across at the sleeping form of Kamaboku, laid out insensible to what was taking place.

Shigoto relished the richness of imagination that allowed him to experience these apparitions as if they were real. When Maguro Sensei spoke about dragons and other matters connected with the garden, Shigoto was able to recreate in his own mind the visions that Sensei evoked; they were as real to him as his own hands, his own feet. He always enjoyed the unfettered imaginings of his own mind, it was something that had sustained him through many an hour of play. He often spent time on his own and had rarely felt the lack of companions or playmates. For what was missing from the world about him, he had found that he could amply compensate by the seemingly limitless wealth of his imagination. Indeed he sometimes found himself retreating into this world of his own, being a place that was more pliant and yielding to his own needs of the moment. Here he had control, he set the rules, and he laid out the boundaries for himself. In this way he was his own master.

What broke the momentary spell and dispersed the last traces of the ghostly forms, was a cough and splutter from the horizontal Kamaboku. The plum stone he had kept in his mouth as he slept threatened to choke him, and he awoke with a start. In less time taken to blink an eye, time and space rearranged themselves into a familiar manner, and Shigoto recognised himself as being back in the present.

"Back to work, eh, Shigoto," announced Kamaboku and he spat out into his hand the plum stone, which had been long since cleansed of any trace of the sharp-tasting pink flesh. "Cannot be sleeping the day away, eh. Not when there is work to be done. We'll go back to the Courtyard and continue. I will work with you for a short time, and then I have some other duties Sensei wants me to do. No peace, that's a gardener's life for you, eh. Did you know that, eh? Well, you do now. Take it from Kamaboku, he knows. I had many years as an apprentice too myself, many, many years. That was in the time before Maguro Sensei came here. There was only the four of us looking after the gardens then. Hikishio Sensei was the head gardener. Things changed when Maguro Sensei came, I suppose he brought his different ideas, having come all the way from Kyoto and all that. Still he knows about gardens, Shigoto. Oh, I tell you, if there is a man who knows about gardens, then that man is Maguro Sensei. Kamaboku cannot always see as quick or as far as he can, but I know the gardens here well enough. Hikishio Sensei was a Mikura man, born and bred, he never tasted the air of any place else, you know. Kamaboku too you know, never been nowhere but where I am now. Now that Maguro Sensei, they said he had been a priest at Daitoku-ji temple in Kyoto, many a fine gardener and tea master has come from there, they say. Different ideas he has, eh," and Kamaboku's voice trailed away, as he cleared his head of the last traces of memory and sleep. "Come on, Shigoto. Can't have two of Hirame's best gardeners sitting about chatting like elderly ladies all day." Kamaboku rose to his feet, chuckling at his own humour. Shigoto was already up and ready to move. They made their way through the maze of passages and shortcuts back to the Southern Courtyard, and were soon brushing and smoothing the gravel surface again.

"Is Sensei coming today?" asked Shigoto. The question was nagging at him. He felt it only right that Sensei should be there to see what he was doing, maybe even to offer a few words of praise and encouragement. It was important to him that Sensei should be aware of what a fine job he was making, and of the latent talent at his disposal.

"Coming to see us? Who knows, he may appear, then again he may not. That is Sensei's way. Some of the time you do not even know he is there, when he is there, if you see what I mean. Anyway, keep working, it is not a place to be seen standing around." Shigoto looked up at the veranda. It appeared to be empty, though some of the sliding doors of the *shinden* building had been opened up, so there must be people about. He for one certainly did not wish to have any inattention being drawn to Sensei's notice. Not now, not that he was at last a gardener, a real garden apprentice with jobs to be done.

CHAPTER FOURTEEN

June 1576

Kanyu was bored and distracted, and his mouth tasted of ashes. He glanced across at the other clerks sitting in the room and had to suppress his feeling of disgust with them.

"Hide your feelings, hide them well," his father had once said to him over some now long forgotten childhood explosion of anger and frustration. "A *samurai* does not show his feelings. It's a sign of weakness, and one that your enemy will exploit to his advantage. If you remember nothing else, remember that. Never forget who you are, and never show your true feelings regardless of the situation you may find yourself in." Kanyu had absorbed the lesson and held it closer to his heart than anything else in his life. In response to his father's words he had built a wall around himself, a finely wrought wall, that would in time become so well constructed that there were barely any gaps between the stones. Yet despite his best efforts there were always those who knew how to needle him, those who knew a way to insinuate a thin blade into that most vulnerable of places, his self-confidence. One of those people was his father.

"It's time you were married," his father had announced one day. "You are almost twenty-three years old. It's time you took on the responsibility of having a family of your own." (Kanyu was actually closer to twenty-four.) "I will find an opportunity to speak to Lord Saeko about the matter. Our family are owed a favour or two; he will give his attention to the matter I'm sure. Our stipend would be increased, it will be good for our family if you were married."

"I am not sure that it is really a matter for Lord Saeko's attention," said Kanyu quietly, already feeling chill fingers reaching into his chest at the thought of matrimony.

"Nonsense, what do you know at your age?" His father dismissed Kanyu's objections gruffly. "This family has served the Saeko clan for generations without blemish. Our record of service has been noted many times. Lord Saeko will heed my request for assistance in this matter. It is a way of bringing honour to our family. What do you expect me to do, call on the services of a matchmaker? Hah, not this family, we have shed blood for the Saeko clan, given our lives, it is the least they can do for us. Look at your brother, take him for your example of what can be achieved through noble service."

Kanyu shuddered at the remembrance of the conversation. He had other ideas, and following in the footsteps of his brother was not part of his plans. His brother, who had entered the world two years before him, was constantly held up as an example of what was expected of him. Kanyu hated his brother with a suppressed loathing, as a nocturnal animal detests and fears the coming of the light. Shigoto Kyōfu was a heavily built man, strong in arm and fleet of foot, apparently utterly fearless in physical confrontations, and he had risen rapidly in the martial ranks of the Saeko clan, many spoke of him as a future Captain of the Guard. No one really imagined that Kanyu would ever follow in his brother's footsteps, except perhaps his father, who seemed to stubbornly hold dear to the notion that one day both his sons would serve with distinction in some military capacity or other. In contrast to his brother, Kanyu was slightly built and had often been ill as a child. Every winter until the time of puberty he would be laid low with a bronchial complaint that saw him confined to the home. This he never minded as it gave him the opportunity to study. Kanyu, in contrast to his athletic brother, loved to read and had taken to it easily. He was given employment, not in the martial service of the clan, but as a clerk in the accounting office of the palace. His quick mind, fastidious nature and a facility with numbers made the work easy for him. These abilities were in truth a source of frustration to his father, and simply served to widen the gulf between the two brothers.

"Yes, I will speak to the Lord Saeko at the earliest opportunity. This matter can be agreed between the families in the shortest of time. It will be good for us, it will be good for our family." His father had said with a resolute firmness that left no room for argument, or further discussion. To him the decision was made, the matter settled.

Kanyu looked across at his father. He was a squat man, heavy across the shoulders with a large head that looked as if it were a growth. The older man was sitting cross-legged on the floor of the modest family home, beside him a small low table on which a ceramic bottle of *sake* sat next to a small cup. The table was delicate enough that Kanyu's father could have crushed it in one of his large powerful hands. 'I have no need for a wife,' thought Kanyu. 'there will be time enough for that. After all, heaven only knows what kind of woman they will find for me.' His thoughts drifted away from the immediate subject of conversation. 'Now if there were a woman I would choose to take as a wife it would be

Hanako'. Kanyu had met Hanako in the course of his duties stocktaking in the stores, she held a senior position in the kitchens and was regarded with a certain trepidation by most of the other staff because of her acidic manner. Strangely, Kanyu had not felt intimidated by her, rather the opposite. He had been immediately attracted by her haughty bearing, which he saw as a quality that he could admire in her. It was not long after they first met that they began a highly discreet affair. The improbability of that happening in the first place became their shield from the normally inquisitive and gossip prone world in which they existed.

A voice from behind Kanyu jerked him back to the present moment, breaking his reverie. "Hey, Kanyu, a few of us are going to a tea house for a drink or two, are you coming?" Kanyu knew full well what this implied. He shook his head by way of an answer.

"Come on, you who are always with your nose in the books. It'll do you good, we can find some women to join us."

"No," he answered firmly. "No."

"Suit yourself then," the voice was laced with cynicism, almost pity.

The day's work was coming to an end, the atmosphere in the large room that served as the clerk's office was jovial and lighthearted. Kanyu gathered together the papers scattered across his desk together and set them neatly into order, then put his writing brushes and ink stone back into their wooden box. His mood was sour and he felt as if there were dark clouds gathering over him. During the day a message had been put on his desk from his father telling him to come directly to the family home after his work had ended. It was less a request, more a formal order to attend. He had anticipated slipping away to meet with Hanako and steal a few hours in her company. There was now no way he could get a message to her to say that he would not be able to make the assignation. It was not that he hated to break off their meeting; that he could live with comfortably enough; rather, he detested the thought of something being disorderly or untidy. To Kanyu logic and order would always prevail over intuition or feeling.

"Kanyu isn't coming, he's practicing to be a priest," someone was saying rather too loudly behind him.

"Well, he is in the wrong company then, he should be coming with us. It's salvation we are looking for," another voice chirruped, and there was general laughter in the room. Kanyu shuffled the papers, once more trying to ignore the jibes.

'You'll see, you'll see, all of you. One day I'll rise above you all, and heads will roll. Then we'll see who's left laughing,' he thought with bitterness.

When Kanyu arrived at the house he still shared with his parents the rancour was still eating at him.

"Kanyu san, you look tired," his mother greeted him as he sat in the entry porch slowly removing his shoes. It was as if he were delaying the moment before he would have to enter the house and talk with his father.

"It's nothing," he muttered. "Is father here?"

"He is waiting for you," his mother answered. "Be forewarned, he's in a foul mood," she whispered to him.

This news somewhat cheered Kanyu. His mind instantly leapt to the thought that perhaps some news had been received in respect of the proposed wedding, a cancellation of the plans perhaps. His mood had been soured ever since the meeting that had been held at the apartments of Lady Saeko, when accompanied by his father he had been introduced to the girl who had been chosen as a wife for him. 'They want me to marry some chambermaid, barely even a woman,' he had thought with disgust. He had hardly been able to look at her. She seemed to cower in their presence, and his heart had turned to stone. He felt nothing but a mild disgust for her. 'So I suppose he is going to tell me it's all arranged, they all seem to be such a hurry to get this over with.'

His father was by himself in a room that was used to receive visitors to the house. Besides him was a small table with a few small plates of food and some *sake*. The food had not been touched and the cup empty. His father was looking out over a small garden carpeted with vividly green smooth moss, studded here and there with dark grey stones and a large stone lantern dominating one corner. The light was beginning to fade, and cicadas were making a deafening noise in the trees, the air was very warm and humid. Kanyu's father looked up when his son entered and greeted him. He did not reply to the greeting, only snapped open a fan in one of his heavy hands and with brisk agitated motions tried to stir the air about him into some kind of life. Kanyu noticed that there was sheen of sweat glazing his forehead. His father's mood looked as foul as Kanyu felt himself. He knelt down with a little distance between them and waited for his father to say something. 'Don't show your feelings,' he reminded himself. 'Remember to be patient, wait for him to reveal what it is that he has in his mind. Let him make the first move.' Kanyu wished he had brought a fan: the air was heavy and felt unyielding about him.

For a long moment his father said nothing. Kanyu could sense that he was holding himself back. It was as if his father was a storm brewing, the atmospheric pressure rising within him until it would became overwhelming enough to break open. He knew this characteristic of his father well enough from the past. All he needed to do was wait. 'Be patient and wait,' he repeated this over and over to himself as a mantra.

"The wedding plans are cancelled," finally the older man spat out the words as if they were too sour to be held in his mouth a moment longer. He offered no further explanation for the time being. Kanyu felt nothing but relief. It coursed through him like a sweet and satisfying draught, he struggled to keep his feelings in check, as all he wanted to do was smile. At that moment he cared nothing for an explanation of the sudden turn of events, he just felt like a condemned man given an unexpected pardon. The air in the room suddenly seemed to be lighter, fresher, to him.

"The other family..." Kanyu's father was struggling to find the words. Rage was boiling within him, his face colouring darkly, and he was clenching and unclenching his fists. "... They have called it off."

"Is that so," said Kanyu quietly, hoping that his father could not detect any trace of the feeling of elation that was sweeping through him.

"It's a damn mess, the whole situation. The girl in question has disgraced her family, and she is no longer fit to be a bride. Anyone's bride, come to that. The whole matter has become unacceptable to us," his father said. "I have to go and see Lord Saeko in the morning, and tell him the formal decision of our family that we are not prepared to proceed with the ceremony. The engagement gifts will have to be returned as soon as possible. It's an absolute scandal, we cannot accept it in the least. Another bride will have to be found for you. We are a proud family, we cannot accept this situation, and we deserve better than be treated like this." The older man turned and looked away towards the garden beyond the room.

"Can I pour you some *sake?*" said Kanyu. He noticed there was only one cup and wished there were two. He felt this was news that could be celebrated, not mourned. His father ignored the question. The two of them sat in silence for a long moment, each preoccupied with their own contrasting thoughts.

"Are you not interested in why the ceremony has been called off?" his father asked eventually.

"Yes, yes, of course," stammered Kanyu. "If there is some slur on our family, then we should seek retribution, compensation for the trouble we are put to."

Kanyu's father looked severely up at his son. His thick eyebrows were knotted together, and the lines across his forehead were deeply incised. He seemed to be weighing up his son.

"The girl has got herself pregnant it seems. She is with child. It's not even yours," Kanyu's father said. Kanyu started to colour, his own thoughts drifting away to his liaison with Hanako. Kanyu thought of the meeting when he had seen the girl who was being proposed as his bride, she had seemed very young, somehow too innocent, no more than a child in fact. It was something to remember for the future he thought, that people were not always to be judged at face value, for what they seemed to be. 'There is a lesson to be learned from this', he thought to himself, but the magnitude of what it might be eluded him for the moment.

"It's more of a complication than that," Kanyu's father continued. "I also hear that the father of this child is no less than the distinguished visitor to our shores. I suppose you understand to whom I am referring. Mind, this is not something for you to be prattling about to those other clowns you spend your time working with. This is not just a piece of gossip that can be bandied about. For one thing it involves our family, our name. It also involves a person of great distinction, regardless of the reason that he is staying among us for the time. You understand, I take it, you appreciate there are sensitivities involved here, and it's a matter of face, a matter of family pride." He sought to correct himself, to make his meaning clear. "Both to this family and also to the Saeko family. Of course in all matters we are here simply to serve the Saeko family, that is the way it has always been, and will always be. Even so…" his words trailed away and were lost in the background din of the cicadas, which to Kanyu seemed louder than ever, as if they were a ghostly, mocking chorus.

"Anyway, that is the reason I needed to speak with you. You understand you are not to speak to anyone about this matter," Kanyu's father spoke with great conviction and he looked directly at his son as he did so, something Kanyu found deeply unsettling. His father for all his limitations in Kanyu's eyes was a man with a powerful presence. He had distinguished himself in battle, he had blood on his hands and he had nothing to prove to anyone regarding physical strength and courage. "You can go now, I have said what it is you need to hear. Mark my words though, this is a matter of the greatest discretion. If you so much as breathe a single word of this to anyone at all, I will gladly snap your neck with my bare hands. I am telling you what you need to know, that is all." Kanyu's father looked away from his son sitting opposite him, his hands tightly clenched together as if he were crushing an orange between them. A curtain of silence descended between them. As Kanyu rose to take his leave, his father cracked the bones of his fingers and the sudden dry sound ricocheted loudly through the room. Kanyu felt as if ice cold water had been poured down the back of his neck, his legs almost gave away from under him.

"Yes father, I understand what you have said." The words barely escaped his lips. "I will never mention this to anyone, no one at all." Kanyu bowed towards his father and left as quickly as his legs could move. His father's gaze had returned to looking absently at the garden. Kanyu left the house as if he were on a cloud. He did not stop even though his mother implored him to have something to eat. He was too excited, and he felt he needed time to digest the import of what he had learned. He also wanted to see if there was a chance he could still keep his appointment with Hanako.

He would usually arrange to meet with Hanako in a distant part of the gardens of the palace, at a time and a place where they could be reasonably sure of being able to spend some uninterrupted time together. Over the year or so they had been meeting covertly they had evolved a complicated means of sending coded messages to one another, and Kanyu had sent such a message the day before arranging a tryst. As he rushed towards the meeting place he felt a giddy elation. It was not just delight in the anticipation of meeting with Hanako, but the sense that he had evaded the snake pit of fate. However illusory, it felt that he had been granted a kind of freedom for now. Though he recognised, and largely accepted, the constraints of clan and family obligations, he felt above all it was his most sacred duty to cling to his own emotional needs, to this end this he was prepared to take risks. By the time he was approaching the isolated pavilion where Hanako would hopefully be waiting for him, he was almost running along the path.

"Why Kanyu, it's you, you are sweating like a labourer."

"I had to meet with my father, that's why I am late. I was hoping that you would still be here," Kanyu panted out his explanation. He was not used to the exercise, and his heart was beating strongly in his chest. "I was looking forward to seeing you. I have something important to tell you."

"Not in that condition I hope." Hanako was a tall woman, a year or so older than Kanyu, she had a long thin nose, narrow shoulders and a bearing that most people found haughty, bordering on arrogant. She was dressed in a pale kimono that matched the pallor of her skin, and her black hair was immaculately combed back into a tight helmet.

"It's good news regarding the marriage."

"And is that why you come running up the path like some workman who has forgotten his tools? Look at the way you are dressed, your kimono is loose and your hair all over the place." Hanako regarded him with an apparent disdain. Kanyu stopped where he was, tried to straighten out his kimono, and ran a hand over his head, patting down unseen strands of unruly hair at the sides of his head.

"I was really hoping that you would still be here. I have found out some interesting information," Kanyu started to say.

"Yes, you said that already," replied Hanako. "So, what is this important news about your wedding that is so pressing that you do not even greet me politely?" She was looking at Kanyu as if from some great height.

Kanyu then began to relate to Hanako the conversation he had just had with his father. Hanako listened with an air of distracted indifference.

"So, if what you say is true, the little madam has more spirit than you gave her credit for," said Hanako with a mischievous smile spreading across her features.

Kanyu was shocked at her reaction to his news. His eyes were wide open and he was looking at her as if uncomprehending. "What, what do you mean by that? Surely you understand the importance of all this? My father is in a complete fury, he is beside himself with anger over it. The whole family name has been dragged into the mud with the shame of it. He is going to see Lord Saeko over the matter. After all, Lord Saeko himself sanctioned the marriage. It's his name too that has been besmirched by her outrageous behaviour."

"And surely by the behaviour of the distinguished guest too. After all Kanyu, do not forget that it takes two people, a man *and* a woman to make a child. Or have you forgotten that already in your state of alarm? Don't tell me you have forgotten how you have taken your pleasures with me? Or are you such a good actor?" Hanako was smiling openly now as she looked at Kanyu's face, which was twisted with impotent anger.

"Don't fool with me, woman," said Kanyu, the colour rising in his cheeks. He did not now look her in the face.

"Oh Kanyu, Kanyu, come here." Hanako held her arms out to him.

"It's a disaster for our family," he muttered and buried his face in her shoulder, Hanako held him lightly keeping her body slightly apart away from his. As she held him she was looking past his head, more concerned that they would not be overlooked.

"You don't understand," he said softly into her shoulder, his eyes closed.

Hanako pushed him back with her hands, her face hardened now, and her eyes glittering in the fading light. "Don't tell me what I understand, and what I don't understand," she said with a voice that cracked over his head like a whip. "I may be just a woman in your eyes Kanyu, but I understand far more than you ever will. You are just like your father in this matter. Is that what you wish to be? Another bone-headed *samurai*, all for spilling blood at the slightest trace of an insult? To think that I thought that you were somehow different! But you're just like all the rest of your kind." The contempt spilled out of her and showered over the form of her aspiring lover.

Kanyu stood before her, his mouth hanging slackly open. He was used to her abrupt manner of speaking when they were alone together. He was acutely aware of her attitudes to others, but in the circumstances he was shocked at her response. If he expected sympathy, he was receiving none.

"How can you say such things? How can you mean what you are saying? If my father knew what you just said, he would take his sword to your neck." He intoned, but the conviction was draining from his words. He was at a loss at what to make of the situation he now found himself in.

"Your father would do no such thing," she was now almost laughing at him. "You want to know why?" Kanyu looked at her in astonishment, he was alternately shaking his head and nodding.

"Do you see your father here? Is he standing here with us now? No, he's not, and you would never dare repeat what I said to his face."

Kanyu looked about with an almost wild terror in his eyes. Hanako was now laughing softly.

"Kanyu, Kanyu, you poor child. You just do not understand, do you? This could be your moment! Of course you must go ahead and marry her. You must not let your father carry out his threat."

Kanyu looked at Hanako with a glazed expression. He felt inconsolable at that moment.

"No? But I... I thought... that we..." he stammered.

"No, no, you must do everything in your power to persuade him otherwise. This could be your time, Kanyu, the occasion when you finally seize control of your life and take charge of events. Use this situation to your advantage, be smart, Kanyu; use that fine calculating mind of yours, think beyond the immediate circumstances. Be smarter than the others, you can take a step towards your dreams now. Do you want to be a clerk, a humble scribbler of lists for the rest of your days? That's not what you have spoken to me about. I thought I was dealing with a man cleverer than that. I thought you were a man of true ambition, Kanyu.

"What do you mean?" said Kanyu finally, as he struggled to bring his mind back into some kind of order again.

Hanako sighed as she looked at him. "Alright, I will spell it out to you in a way that even a farmer would understand. Though I should say, Kanyu, that I am disappointed that you have not grasped the real importance of this moment for yourself. I thought you were a bright one, someone of ambition, someone who was destined to go far in this sordid world."

"I am, I am, I mean, I will. Tell me though," he implored Hanako, he wanted to know, he wanted to be told what to do, his mind was such a whirl that he no longer trusted himself to know which was up and which was down.

"Now you listen well. Do exactly what I tell you, and things will work out just fine, just fine. You'll see right enough."

CHAPTER FIFTEEN

May 1588

On a day when he found himself alone in the Southern Courtyard, Shigoto decided to take a look over where a stream emerged from under the walkway leading to the 'Fishing Pavilion'. It ran down from the north-east side of the palace complex, then took a course that led past the women's apartments. The so-called 'Fishing Pavilion' lay at the end of an extended roofed corridor that projected out over the Great Dragon Pond. It was one of several such small streams that fed the large pond.

Shigoto dropped his basket by a small boulder that lay at the edge of the stream. The current brushed part of the dark stone, with a fine beard of brilliant green moss clinging to life just above the lapping water. The bed of the shallow stream would have taken him two or three strides to cross. On the far side a clump of iris rose from its pink-white tubers, anchoring the plants into the earth, diminishing the threat of erosion. The water ran crystal clear with a nervously excited energy. Shigoto knelt down and collected a few leaves that had gathered by the stone. The sight of the running water before him was intoxicating. The last of the day's direct light was falling over the roof of the walkway and glancing across the gently fractured surface, breaking up into ever shifting, yet constantly reforming patterns. Shigoto felt he was seeing something for the first time. Its very newness came to him with brilliant clarity. He felt utterly transfixed by the onward rush, the insistent running of the stream, ever renewing itself. He felt his whole being glow with the beauty of it all.

A rustling sound carried by the breeze caught his attention, and he looked up to see two women walking slowly along the veranda from the direction of the main hall. Shigoto did not recognise either of the figures, and he stayed kneeling where he was, seemingly pre-occupied with his cleaning tasks. Closer they came, with deliberate short steps that rustled the fabric of their bright *kimono*, until they stopped directly across from where he was crouching.

"You there, gardener. What are you doing?" Immaculately dressed in a pink *kimono* of a delicate shade, the older of the two addressed him.

"Working … er, Miss," Shigoto stammered.

"What is your name, I do not recognise you as being a gardener," the voice carried a haughty, almost condemning tone. It was a voice enmeshed in the projection of its owner's ego.

"I am fifteen grade Under Gardener Shigoto, M'am. Maguro Sensei is my teacher," he said slowly standing up where he was.

"Shigoto, eh. I am perfectly aware who Maguro Sensei is. You had better return to your tasks. I am sure your *sensei* would not wish to hear tell of one of his Under Gardeners not attending to his work in the correct spirit, would he?" She put the stress on the word '*under*', as if she did not wish to recognise the requirement for politeness, humility or even grace.

The Gardener's Apprentice

As he looked up at the two figures though, it was the second woman whom seemed to catch his attention. She was several years younger, perhaps even about the same age as himself. There was something about her that attracted him. She seemed to radiate an aura of calm that was in such a contrast to the spiky manner of the older woman. She stood a step or two behind the woman speaking to him, which allowed him to look in her direction without appearing to stare. She stood there demurely, her eyes cast down, as if she was patiently waiting. He could not tell what, if anything, she made of the performance of her companion. Shigoto stood there passively having to accept the admonition. For the briefest of moments he thought that she looked at him, giving him a glance that was so fleeting, so light and quick, he could not be certain that she had in fact even looked his way at all. It set his heart on fire, making blood suddenly race through his veins.

Having been berated by the sharp tongue of the older woman, Shigoto returned his attention to his work, somewhat bemused by the way in which he had been spoken to. 'After all, I was only getting on with my work. What is it to her anyway? Why did she have to stop here? They could have just carried on their way down the veranda and said nothing at all. But then if they had not stopped I would maybe not have noticed the girl. Now that was something, there was something special in that glance of hers. I'm sure she looked in my direction, looked me straight in the eyes. She was so beautiful, so very beautiful. She must live here in the palace, why have I not noticed her before? Surely she cannot be much older than me. Who is she, I wonder?'

Her face seemed to radiate a quality that was permeating deeper with every moment, sinking into his consciousness in a way he had never experienced before. He felt his face reddening, but it was not out of shame nor embarrassment resulting from the way the older woman had spoken to him. The two women stood where they were and watched him for a moment or two longer, before they resumed their passage along the veranda.

"Come on Nureba, we don't have the time to waste passing the day talking with mere under gardeners."

Shigoto continued what he had been doing, though he was not entirelusure what it was he had actually been doing. He knelt again and set about vigorously sweeping the water with his hand as if to catch imaginary leaves floating past. It was as if he needed something to do to cover the whirlwinds that were sweeping through his emotions at that moment.

'Nurema?' he thought, 'was that what her name was? Oh, I did not quite catch it, though it sounded something like that. Nurema? Oh no, what if I ever get the chance to speak to her again, and I do not know her name for sure? Then I will look a fool in her eyes.'

Cautiously Shigoto looked up from his activity at the backs of the retreating figures. The younger of the two, the girl who had so powerfully caught his attention was carrying a large bundle in her arms he had not noticed before. What it was he could not make out as it was wrapped in a splendidly coloured cloth. Out of the corner of his eye he continued to watch them make their way towards the pavilion.

He kept up the pretence of being busy, though he could not resist from taking surreptitious glances in the direction of two figures. When they reached the open sided pavilion they had stopped and knelt down on the wooden floor boards, then took from the cloth wrapping what looked like a slender necked, stringed musical instrument, which was now being held lightly in the hands of the young girl. She was evidently a pupil, or at least, was receiving instruction from the older woman in the pink *kimono*. He forced himself to continue with his tidying work, all the while as nonchalantly as possible making his way slightly closer to them, as close as he dared go. Neither of the two women looked his way. Soon the odd snatch of a musical phrase reached him:

"... deep in the mountains...
... the Ox roams...
... a lonely path to follow...
... the running stream..."

He could neither clearly make out the melody, nor did any of the snatches of words allow him much of a morsel of recognition to hold on to. They might equally have been leaves falling at random from a tree to the mossy ground below.

'Who is that girl?' thought Shigoto. 'I have not seen her about, I wonder who her family is. She's really pretty that's for sure. I would like to get to talk to her and get to know her more, but maybe she would not speak to me now, especially as that sour faced one will have said something rude about me. Why did she have to do that? It was as if she wanted to put me down in front of the girl and make me look small or stupid. What have I done to upset her? She is worse than a wasp that will not leave you alone until it has stung you somehow.' As he worked Shigoto would take sly glances towards the two women, but they were still a little distance from him and he could not readily make out the face of the young woman too clearly. 'I want to meet her again. I must find some way to meet with her. If I can talk to her then she will understand that I am not some bad person. I am going to be an important gardener like Maguro Sensei one day, I'll show all the sour faced people in this world just who I am one day, then they will be sorry for talking to me like that. I wonder if my mother would know who she is...?'

Later that afternoon when Kamaboku came by to see him and tell him the day's work was ended, he noticed that there were several almost bare patches of ground where the gravel had been over vigorously swept.

"Hey, Shigoto, you had better tidy up those patches, not leave them like this. What have you been doing here? Looks like you have been going a little crazy with the brush here, eh." Kamaboku laughed softly to himself pointing toward a section of gravel. "Here smooth out this area better at least, then you can finish for the day, otherwise it's not too bad, not too bad at all."

Shigoto was bursting to tell someone about his encounter earlier in the afternoon, but he checked himself in time. It would not look good he thought, to admit how the bare patches came to be formed. He liked Kamaboku, but even so, there were things that one could speak about, and there were things that were perhaps best kept to oneself.

"That's better," said Kamaboku when Shigoto had set things right. "Got to have the place looking smart, it's almost time for the Wisteria Festival. Sensei is driving the rest of us gardeners like crazy at the moment to get the whole place looking well for that." Kamaboku looked around at the courtyard with an approving glance. "You'll be working with the rest of us tomorrow."

"The other gardeners you mean?"

"Yes that's right, there is a lot of clearing up to do. You'll be helping us. Sensei will be there, so you had better look lively too. He's not in the mood for things being left undone."

"I haven't see much of Sensei lately," remarked Shigoto to Kamaboku with a sigh as they made their way from the courtyard. In fact he had hardly seen him at all, all his instructions for work being transmitted through Kamaboku. Of the other gardeners he barely saw them either. Kamaboku stopped and looked at Shigoto.

"Hey, let me tell you something. You may not see Sensei, but Sensei sees you. Sees what you do, and what you do not do, if you catch my meaning These Zen priests…. well, they are different to the rest of us somehow. Never forget that. Sensei can even read your soul in the way the gravel is swept, he can tell

The Gardener's Apprentice

everything about you from the merest glance." Kamaboku shook his head gravely, his eyes though were alight with a certain humour, but the look on his face said he meant what he was saying in all seriousness.

"Everything?" said Shigoto beginning to feel concerned.

"Yes, every thing," replied Kamaboku, carefully enunciating each syllable.

Shigoto was not sure how to take that last remark. He took one last look back over the expanse of the courtyard across to the now empty pavilion. Who knows what Sensei may read into what he had happened to him today.

The fifth day of the fifth month was the time of the Wisteria Festival. It signalled the beginning of the summer season. At this time many houses and shrines would be decorated with garlands of wisteria flowers. The participants of the various ceremonies adorned themselves with strands of flowering branches, women dressing in their finest kimono with the patterns and colours that reflected all the subtle shades of the flower. From early in the morning onwards crowds began to gather from far and wide to enjoy the dancing and musical performances to be staged in various places around the palace garden. The settings for those events were sited around the places where the wisteria was grown, scrambling over a series of raised bamboo frames, and in one particular location over a long narrow raised platform of polished boards. Thanks to skilled pruning at opportune moments, thick scented clusters flowers now hung down over the heads of any performers occupying the stage.

For the rest of the week leading up to the festival, Maguro Sensei, true to Kamaboku's words, drove the gardeners on in a frenzy of activity from early morning until the evening. His whiplash exhortations of, "Come on, come on. Get a move on," spurred on the gardeners in his charge, leaving them little time for rest. Shigoto felt happy enough, he was finally working as part of the team of gardeners under the direction of his enigmatic teacher. The principal concern was to be able to present the gardens to the visitors as a jewel shining in the sunshine of early summer. Shigoto had attended the festival once or twice before in the company of his mother, but he had never realised the work that went into the preparations beforehand. He was also happy because he was still carrying within him the image of the young woman he had met so briefly. Her face would loom into his mind from time to time, and it never failed to bring a quiet smile. He had held back from mentioning anything about the encounter to his mother, and Sensei had not remarked to him on having received any reports relating to his behaviour. As the days slipped by it was the face of the coy young woman that remained in his mind, haunting him in a most pleasant manner.

On the morning of the festival itself, Shigoto was up and ready for work by dawn.

"Will I get a chance to watch the festival with you this year?" Oyadori asked him, as Shigoto was bolting down some rice gruel for his breakfast.

"I don't know," he replied between swallows. "Sensei wants us gardeners to be on duty today. He asked me specially," he replied with a rising pride in his voice.

"Eat slowly please. You will make yourself ill, eating that fast."

"I have to get to work, there are things Sensei wants doing first thing this morning."

"Even so," said Oyadori sternly. Shigoto slowed down momentarily. "Maybe I will see you later," he said, putting down the empty bowl.

One of the popular highlights of the festival comes midway through the day, just as the sun begins to pass its zenith, when a troupe of dancers with slow, staccato movements counterpointed by a swelling accompaniment of flutes and drums begin

The Gardener's Apprentice

the Wisteria Dance. At this point, Shigoto had been given leave by Maguro Sensei to join the crowds gathered near the raised stage where the dance was held. Shigoto had looked about, but he couldn't see his mother in the throng of onlookers. He had managed to push his way to the front from where he could follow the action closely. He knew the story depicted in the dance well enough as his mother and grandmother had spoken of little else the previous evening.

The dance depicts a story as old as Japan itself: amid a stand of tall trees on the slopes of the sacred Mt. Fuji, a wisteria vine is carried high toward the heavens. At the critical moment of the unfolding of a new flower-bearing shoot, a hawk that happens to be crossing the sky catches the movement out of the corner of its eye. It swoops down at blinding speed under the cover of the brilliant light, and plucks the tender shoot with its talons before wheeling away back towards the sun clutching its prize. Out of a sense of sadness and loss, all subsequent shoots on the wisteria take a vow to the gods that they will never raise their heads towards the sun, lest they too be plucked before they are ready to display their beauty to the world. The vine then magically transforms itself into a writhing serpent in order to snare the hawk, should it ever dare to return from the sun.

The dance climaxes with a single dancer on the stage crouched low on all fours, whose torso is covered by a large fine silk square of cloth, the colour a vibrantly shimmering, yet delicate tone of green. As the figure begins to uncoil and rise from the ground, the drums settle into a steady insistent rhythm and the flutes running out soft rising scales. The dancer rises further, and as the cloth falls back to the ground, it is revealed that the dancer wears two face masks; a white mask with pursed red-painted mouth to the front, and a bright red mask with black open lips and a long protruding nose, to the rear. As the volume and pace of the music begins to build toward to a inexorable pitch of intensity, out of the intricate arrangement of the wisteria coloured *kimono* of the dancer, unfold two arms that are slowly raised heavenwards. Clasped in the dancer's hands, which become fully revealed, as the sleeves fall back, is a highly polished bronze disc. The music reaches its orgiastic climax as the dancer reaches up at full stretch, thrusting the disc skywards; all around the tumescent figure froths and cascades the billowing folds of cloth, and the sun glinting in blinding concentration from the highly polished surface held aloft. Few are the hearts that can bear witness to such a performance and not be moved to the very core, and the dance invariably concludes with a crescendo of applause from the audience.

Being so close to the stage Shigoto had been able to follow every action. The music intoxicated him, and the graceful, yet powerful movements of the dancer moved him more than ever. He was about to leave the stage and go in search of Maguro Sensei, when he caught sight of the dancer at the rear of the stage area, this time unadorned by a mask mask. Shigoto looked and then looked again. 'It's her,' he suddenly realised, and his heart leapt. The dancer was none other than the young woman who had caught his attention so powerfully a few days previously. He stood there open mouthed, not registering the dispersing crowd jostling him, but she did not seem to notice him standing there staring at her. Once more his heart went out to her, and this time he realised he was falling in love for the first time in his life. It was only the hand of his teacher shaking his shoulder that brought him back to earth.

"Ahh, Shigoto, there you are. I want you to check again that everything is in order along the route of the procession. Hurry now, and make sure it's absolutely perfect."

"Yes, Sensei." Reluctantly he dragged himself away from his reveries, and set off to attend to the task.

At the hour of the rabbit (3 o'clock) a grand colourful procession headed by white robed, chanting Shinto priests from the

Hatsukari Shrine, accompanied by the entire Saeko family, messengers from related clans and political allies, musicians bearing numerous instruments, loyal retainers with their flapping banners of rank, itinerant poets, painters and priests, craftsmen of wood, stone and clay, fishermen, farmers and shopkeepers, all would gather in a precisely ordained order to take a sacred mirror to the banks of the Great Dragon Pond. There, gifts of food, gold coins and jewels from the Palace are offered to the Mover Across the Endless Sky and esoteric ceremonies of purification and thanksgiving would be performed amid a welter of hand gestures, recitation of ancient prayers all amid rising clouds of fragrant incense. From there the assembly make their way to a part of the garden where there is a representation of a sacred mountain, a tall conically shaped grass covered hill encircled by a stepping stone path. Here more dances are performed, albeit in a lighter spirit, before the main party returns to the Great Hall for an extensive banquet. The crowd of extras, the curious, the hangers-on and the simply miscast, at that point begin to drift happily away to the makeshift stalls in the town for a cup or two of *sake*, thus as in other similar circumstances, what begins in great solemnity, draws to a close in a less than tidy and dignified manner for some.

As Shigoto was going about his last minute task he looked up and noticed that the thickly knotted branches of the ancient wisteria plants running over their supporting frames, would support the body of a young man of his height and build, while allowing him a good viewing position of the ceremony at the shore the Great Dragon pond. He was just registering this interesting information, when to his surprise he noticed leaning against a leg of a wisteria frame, a bamboo rake with its long curved teeth that had probably been used during the tidying work of the previous day. Thinking rapidly he snatched up the rake in one hand, and with a glance over his shoulder to check that he was not being observed, he nimbly sought out the sanctuary of the branches above, taking the rake with him. Spreading himself out among the branches Shigoto realised now he was out of view of the procession making its way towards him hidden by the bountiful foliage. He smiled to himself at his good luck and ingenuity.

The procession had arrived at the point where the leading priest bearing the sacred mirror in both hands above his head, was about take the final steps forward to the edge of the pond, his steely gaze fixed far in the distance. Here he would utter ancient and incomprehensible prayers and incantations, all the while the beating of the drummers and the shrill sounds of the flutes reaching toward an untidy crescendo. At this point of dramatic tension, a bee attracted by the scent of the flowers, landed on Shigoto's nose and without thinking he let go his grip on the rake, as he tried to swat away the source of the distraction. The rake slipped to the ground, gracefully and with barely a sound, it fell directly into the path of the oncoming priest. As his next footfall touched the ground, the handle of the rake leapt violently up and caught him utterly unaware between his eyes, fixed as they were on the far horizon. To Shigoto's horror everything seemed to happen in slow motion, he saw every moment of the crisis unfold from his hidden vantage place.

All that those in the procession saw, was the priest apparently stumble and the sacred mirror suddenly take on an unexpected upward trajectory. All time and motion came to a sudden and wholly unexpected standstill. With the exception of the mirror, which continued along its path eventually having described a graceful arc through space splashed through the limpid surface of the lake. The spreading rings forming an unspoken exclamation mark to a sentence that hung limply in the air.

In the seconds that followed there was only one man present who had sufficient speed of thought and insight to save the day from an even greater disaster. Maguro Sensei by virtue his

The Gardener's Apprentice

ordination as Zen priest was allowed to accompany the head of the parade. He had in an instant realised the cause of the sudden change of course of the mirror. As the eyes of the shocked and open-mouthed assembly followed the sacred object's flight, Maguro Sensei with the swift thinking response of a man absolutely alive to the moment, dashed towards to reach the tottering, star-dazzled priest, now further blessed with a rapidly rising aubergine coloured lump on his forehead. With one hand to the priest's back to steady him, Sensei reached out and with the other, swept up the rake from the ground and with a single fluid movement, thrust it back in the foliage whence it had come. The end of the handle caught Shigoto firmly amidships, momentarily knocking all trace of air from his lungs. The rake was swallowed whole by the mass of foliage and remained lodged out of sight of the assembly below, as did Shigoto.

The mirror flashed briefly as it fell through the layers of water before it disappeared entire into a dark cavern that was the mouth of Oguchi, an elderly koi carp which had been a wedding gift to Mameko Saeko, the dowager princess, some sixty-two years earlier. After a general recovery of their wits and the use of their tongues among those at the head of the procession, discussion arose as to how the situation could be recovered. The debates were long and intense, but in the end, the resolve of the company was unanimous. The ceremony had to be concluded and the mirror restored to its proper resting place at the Hatsukari Shrine, dire misfortune would surely otherwise befall all of Mikura. A party of farmers were dispatched into the lake armed with sections of hastily constructed bamboo fencing in an attempt to herd the fish into a shallow bay. The plan called for Oguchi to be cornered and somehow persuaded to relinquish his prize, thereby allowing the formalities to be drawn to their proper conclusion. The unfamiliarity of farmers becoming hunter-gatherers in their attempt to corner a slippery quarry in an unfamiliar environment, gave the excited and boisterous crowd on the shore cause for comment (not always complimentary at that) and needless to say, much amusement. It was rumoured for months after that fortunes were won and lost that day in wagers as to which of the non-swimming farmers would be the next to be completely immersed.

The atmosphere among the onlookers traversed the complete cycle from ceremony to carnival. Eventually the reluctant fish was cornered between the knees of a half drowned member of the chasing party long enough for a number of his colleagues to fall bodily on it. Despite their every effort though, the mirror remained stubbornly lodged in the body of the long-suffering Oguchi. To conclude the ceremony without creating offence to any of the deities, the utterly confused fish was placed in a temporary wooden holding tank, and in due course after much persuasion and prodding which provoked a bout of indigestion, the mirror was ejected from its gullet and fell to the floor of its container. Now the mirror could be restored its more natural place in the hands of the still bemused priest, and all was well with the world again, as the natural order of things was set back on a steady course. The priest though was to wear a distinct bump in the shape of a fish on his forehead for the rest of his days, and Shigoto was destined to spend many long months consigned to sweeping leaves and other such menial tasks under the stern watchful instruction of Maguro Sensei.

CHAPTER SIXTEEN

June 1576

Kanyu was nervous about having to go back to his father to set out the plan of action that Hanako had outlined to him. Once it had been explained fully he grasped its audacity and saw its advantages. In his initial reaction though he had been reluctant to accept that it might work, let alone that he wanted any part in it all. But the more he considered it, the more that he saw the potential advantages involved. Above all, it chimed with his deeply held ambitions; a part of him that only Hanako was privy to. He knew that he was taking a huge risk, but as Hanako explained to him, "without risk, there was little chance of gain in the long term". Despite having considered all these aspects over and over, he remained unsettled in his mind. He felt as if he was standing at the edge of a whirlpool.

"You know me, Hanako, I am not a natural risk taker. I despise gambling in all forms," he was wavering. "We must think more about this very carefully."

Hanako looked at him with barely disguised contempt. "Bah, you are as bad as the rest," she snorted her derision. Kanyu winced.

"Look, all I said was that we must think about this."

"No, you must *act* on this, Kanyu. If you are the man that you have lead me to believe you are, then you *will* act on it. It's the only way. You are being presented with an opportunity here. The only question is: are you going to grasp it, or not."

"I need to think, that's all," said Kanyu. He looked out at the trees that surrounded them. The light was fading and night approaching rapidly. The choice was his alone he knew that. "What if my father will not accept this idea?"

"He will," Hanako said simply.

"You seem very sure of yourself in all this. There is the family name to consider, the truth will come out in the end, then what happens? People talk you know."

"People talk about many things, but know very little," observed Hanako, she was regarding Kanyu sternly. "It is those who know the most that prevail in the end. Knowledge is real power, Kanyu san. Consider that. That's what you want, isn't it, what you crave, you dream about? You have told me that often enough in the past. You are a smart man, Kanyu san, you have been gifted with a mind of a strategist, a leader of men, yet what are you now? What will you be in the years ahead? Merely a stick in someone else's hands, that's all."

Kanyu felt pride swelling in his breast. He knew that Hanako spoke the truth, she of all people understood him, sometimes better than he did himself. It was glaringly obvious to him now. The plan she had laid out was so simple, and that was its strength.

"You are right. I will speak to him in the morning, now is not the best time. He was in such a fury when I left that he would never listen to anything. Better to catch him after he has had a chance to rest."

Kanyu looked over at Hanako, she was smiling at him, that sweet beguiling smile which he could never resist, or at least not for long. He laid his hand in hers. "Perhaps, then…" he began to say.

"It's the wrong time of the month for that," said Hanako, withdrawing her hand from under his. "Besides you will need all your strength my dear, don't forget that." Again a smile grazed her lips.

"Well, we had better get back," said Kanyu with insincere conviction. "It's getting dark already, and there is plenty to think about as it is." Kanyu hated the dark. It made him feel uneasy, and they were out without any kind of lantern.

"We will be fine, Kanyu," said Hanako. "Here take my arm, I know the way well enough."

That night Kanyu hardly slept at all, his mind a whirl of activity. He recognised the gravity of what lay before him, Hanako's words revolved through his mind, and he turned them over this way and that, until he felt that he had thought through the whole process from every potentiality. A vague image of Oyadori came to him and he shuddered at the thought of her. She had seemed so innocent and compliant, and yet she was also an ill defined component in the whole scheme. He liked to deal with certainties, he felt secure with numbers and lists as they were things that could be predictably manipulated, tabulated and ordered. People were unpredictable; things happened that could not always be controlled. Against this he weighed the situation of his life. As the younger son he had always felt of less importance thN his brother in the eyes of his father. The martial life held no thrill for him, it never had, and he remembered with a burning sense of injustice the bullying he had received when he was younger. Hanako was right, this could be an opportunity chance to improve his station in life, to act for himself, to make his mark. Yet he had to shift his father's thinking and probably work to persuade the Saeko family. If he acted on this scheme, then he had to act with the full force of his being, put everything he had into this plan. If he hesitated, then everything would be surely lost. He had to be ready for everything and anything. Kanyu realised he had to act as if he were a *samurai* going into battle. But he had Hanako on his side and she would stand by him and support him. She was the one he felt love for, the one he wanted, and she had made it clear to him that it was more than a humble clerk that she wanted for herself. As the first traces of light began to seep into his room, he felt now all issues were resolved in his mind, and he was ready to act.

"Father, I wish to speak to you. There is something we need to discuss. I have been thinking, thinking about our family, and this situation regarding the family's honour. I have found a way to resolve things to our advantage."

His father was sitting alone eating breakfast. Beside him on a tray was a bowl of soup, rice, a small plate of tiny cooked fish and a cup of green tea. He barely looked up when Kanyu came in and knelt down by the door. He just grunted something, and waved the chopsticks he was holding vaguely in Kanyu's direction. His mother had implored him to leave his father be, warning him that he was in a foul mood, but Kanyu had pressed on.

"I am sorry to disturb you at this hour, but it is a matter of importance. I need to speak to you, before you go to see Lord Saeko. About the matter of the marriage, my marriage, that is." Though he had rehearsed in his mind what he would say over and over again, the words came haltingly now that he was in his father's presence.

This time his father looked up at his younger son, but still he said nothing. Kanyu took this as a sign of assent. His father looked older, the lines etched across his forehead were deep, and the corners of his mouth were turned down. The food beside him barely touched.

"What is it?" he asked after a pause.

"I have been giving much thought to what has happened. In respect to how our family will lose face over this matter, and…"

"I do not wish to hear anything. The matter has been decided," his father said with a low voice. Kanyu had rarely seen him like this, usually his father was a man of great vigour, "the warrior spirit", and he was constantly reminded that was the very quality that he himself lacked.

"I think that there is a way we can profit from the situation," Kanyu began again. His father said nothing, he stabbed the chopsticks into the bowl of rice and took a mouthful. "We must urge Lord Saeko to proceed as if nothing has happened."

At this his father coughed violently, grains of rice flew from his mouth, and his face turned an angry red colour. His eyes were wide open now, staring at his son. With great effort he swallowed the rice, and took a sip of the tea. His countenance was stormy when he addressed his son.

"Fool, idiot, are you completely insane? Whatever did I do to anger the gods to have produced a son as stupid as you. Get out of my sight, you arrogant imbecile. How dare you even enter this house with such thoughts in your mind, let alone come into this room and tell me what your dumb thoughts are. Do I have a son, or a barbarian lunatic? Where is my sword?" He was shouting loudly now, and in a moment Kanyu's mother appeared at the doorway.

"Goodness, whatever is the matter?" she said, then addressing Kanyu directly, "I told you not to disturb your father, he hardly slept last night for worry. Are you trying to make him ill? And please no shouting, the neighbours will hear, everyone will hear if you raise your voice like that."

"Get out," shouted his father.

"Father please forgive me for my impudence, but I beg you at least listen to what I have to say. At least consider my words, then if you are still angry with me, I shall leave this house never to return again."

"Oh, my, what madness has sprung upon us this morning," wailed his mother, burying her face in her hands. "I will call a priest, and have this house cleansed, there must be evil spirits haunting us."

"Get out," shouted his father again, "and take your priests with you. I will listen to this madman, because rumour has it he is my son, then I will remove his head from his shoulders. I am a fair man, and let no one say otherwise. Leave us woman. You can come back later and clear the blood off the walls and ceiling."

"Oh, what a way to speak, such words." Kanyu's mother withdrew from the doorway sliding the door closed behind her. Kanyu clenched his hands together until his knuckles shone white. He was glad he was kneeling on the floor, it would have been obvious to all that his legs would not have kept him upright for long.

Silence filled the room. Kanyu wanted to say something to fill the dread quiet that had descended, but his tongue felt as if it were stuck to the roof of his mouth. His father picked up the bowl of soup and slurped noisily at it, then set it down again. He seemed to have recovered some sort of equilibrium, but his neck and cheeks remained flushed.

"So, you wanted to tell me of some crazed dream of yours. Some mad scheme, which evil spirits have poured into your ears whilst you slept no doubt? This is not talk for women to hear. In fact it's not talk that anyone should have to hear, I must have been infected by your craziness to permit you to speak at all. So, what is it that you have to say?"

"It's just that, I... I think that the marriage should proceed. We should accept the marriage as it is, that is." Kanyu started to speak, but he had not yet regained his confidence before his father.

"Speak straight, no fancy talk. Just spit out whatever you have to say," his father growled.

"Yes, of course, I have been thinking that we should agree to the marriage, there are advantages in doing so for the family, our family that is. We will be doing them, that is, the Saeko family a great favour by doing so. Surely there will be some sort of reward in that for us." The words poured out of Kanyu, not in the elegant and controlled manner he had imagined but at least now that he had started he was emboldened to continue. "It is not just our family that stand to loss face over this matter. It is the Saeko family too. The girl has been made pregnant by the visitor, a member of the Imperial family no less. If he were anyone else it would be an entirely different matter, and this situation would never arise. This dilemma, that is. I do not know why she was chosen by Lord Saeko in the first place to be my wife, but the fact remains that she was. I am sure there are many things that I do not understand in this matter, but by agreeing to proceed with the marriage at least we can save the face of the Saeko family. A scandal can be averted, and a lid put on the whole thing. No one knows she is pregnant apart from the girl's mother, and I am sure she will be embarrassed with the whole situation as we are. She would want to find some way of averting the shame I am sure. I am prepared to act to protect the honour of our family. That is something you father have always been strong to teach us about, family honour. And to be of service to the Saeko family, that's true isn't it? Surely Lord Saeko will understand the trouble that this family is going to for his benefit, and there may be some reward in all this for you, an increase in the allowance perhaps, a promotion for you even. No, I have given the matter serious consideration and I am willing to proceed as if everything is in order. As to the child I am sure some suitable accommodation can be reached in due course. If it turns out to be a girl it will be little consequence, another nun for the world."

Kanyu's father took a drink of the tea, then continued to cradle the cup in his two large worn hands. He said nothing for a long time. Kanyu waited for him to respond. He had spoken out probably for the first time in the presence of his father, and he was not sure how his father might react. Though he felt pleased he had made his point, and he had taken in all that Hanako had outlined to him. He had taken it all in, weighed it carefully. Ultimately it came to a matter of his father accepting the advantages inherent in the proposal. Hanako had outlined to him various reasons why the Saeko family were bound to be grateful for being offered a way of avoiding the loss of face that the situation had created. There were risks, he knew that, but the rewards were there for the taking; as Hanako had emphasised, there was in fact little for him to lose. It was after all one way he could continue his liaison with her. He felt pleased with himself.

"Has someone put you up to this? Have you spoken about this matter with anyone?" His father suddenly asked.

Kanyu felt the room turn cold even though it was quite warm. He could feel the blush rising in his cheeks. Yet he had come so far, there was no turning back now. "Never, no, that is unthinkable. I would never do that. You commanded me not to, after all. This is a matter that affects our family. No, no, I have spoken to no one about this. These are my thoughts. I speak to you in confidence, I swear on that." Kanyu hoped that attack would be his best defence, and he hoped that his voice carried a sufficient tone of injured pride. Heaven only knows what his father would make of him consorting with Hanako; that was *his* secret.

His father continued to cradle the cup, while he looked across at Kanyu. He set the cup down, and picked up the lacquered chop sticks from the tray, pincering a few of the tiny fish he put them into his mouth and chewed on them reflectively. Now Kanyu felt he was moving onto safer ground. Hanako had

The Gardener's Apprentice

explained to him that if his father were horrified by the suggestion he would likely reject it out of hand. Kanyu began to relax a little.

"For if I find out that you have spoken to anyone about this…" said his father in a low growling voice, he gestured with the chopsticks drawing them slowly across his throat. Kanyu swallowed hard, and tried not to allow his inner feelings surface. He just shook his head.

"Lord Saeko has granted me an audience later today, I will raise this matter with him. There is one complication though, the child will bear our family name, if it's a boy." Then slowly Kanyu's father resumed eating once more.

Kanyu felt elated as he left the room. He wanted to rush off to tell Hanako how his father had received the news, but he knew that was not possible, and after all, the plan was only half sprung. His father still had to sell the whole idea to Lord Saeko, and that was beyond his control. No, he thought to himself, he had achieved his part, he had acquitted himself well and he felt a flush of pride. Life was good; he was taking control of his destiny, making his move. He would show them all just what he was made of. 'Let no one misjudge me', he thought. Of Oyadori he gave no thought at all, after all she was merely a pawn in the whole process, a piece of the puzzle that the gods had set in his hands to use and then disregard according to his will. To Kanyu she was merely a steppingstone set there for him to tread on. Hanako, well, she was different, from her he could learn things. She had pointed him in a certain direction, but it was up to him to take the advantage from it all. Her time would come too, she was proving useful to him now, and perhaps there would be a future for them. "Be patient and bide your time", was that not what the sages advised? As he passed his mother on his way out of the house he stopped and turned. She still wore an anxious look. "I think father will want some more tea," he said.

All through the day Kanyu experienced a mixture of excitement and apprehension. He could not help but wonder how the meeting would go between his father and Lord Saeko. Would his father explain things clearly, had he really grasped the plan entirely? How would Lord Saeko react to the proposition? Would he relent and agree? What would be his reward? It was hard for Kanyu to concentrate on his work. He almost made several errors, but fortunately he detected them before they came to light, and no one questioned him. For once he was happy to ignore the occasional jibes coming from his fellow clerks. He felt that he was above them, as they would remain toiling with the daily tasks. He was headed for something better, something grander. When the time was right he would show them who the master was when he rose above their world, then it would be time enough for him to repay their sharp-tongued comments. He could almost taste the power coming to him, it would be his by right.

That evening when the administrative tasks had been completed, he hurried home to see if his father was there. He was anxious for news of the meeting with Lord Saeko.

"Is father home?" he asked the minute he entered the house.

"Is that how you greet your mother now?"

"I am sorry, I have urgent things to talk over with him. Good evening mother."

"No, he's not back. He went to see Lord Saeko, and has not returned yet. There is food ready for you when you wish."

"I'll take a bath, then eat," said Kanyu.

Later that evening Kanyu heard his father return to the house, and he had to restrain himself from rushing to see him straightaway. He convinced himself that his father would call for him soon enough, and he paced about his room waiting for a summons. Eventually he could wait no longer, and he went to find his father.

"Better not interrupt him just now," said his mother when he bumped into her. "He is talking with your elder brother. He sent me away as they are discussing '"important matters" and did not want to be disturbed." His mother quizzically looked at him.

"But then I should be there," protested Kanyu waving his arms helplessly at his sides.

"He just asked for *sake* and said that he did not wish to be interrupted. That's all I know. You men are all the same," said his mother as she moved off to her room.

"Damn, damn them all," muttered Kanyu to himself.

CHAPTER SEVENTEEN

October 1592

On a day after the other gardeners had moved on leaving him to the work of clearing up the pruned branches and fallen pine needles, Shigoto was crouching on his haunches by one of the pine trees growing out from bank of the Great Dragon Pond. He mused to himself, 'If I had been born a fish, how different life would be. My home is an island and my place of work and learning surrounds the Great Dragon Pond of the Hirame Palace gardens. Is this what people refer to as fate I wonder?'

He was looking down into the water, where a bustling shoal of carp attracted by his presence had gathered in anticipation of being fed. The fish both fascinated and repelled him. He disliked their lazy corpulence, those thick-lipped swallow-it-all mouths and small black beady eyes; yet he had come to love the iridescent colours splashed across their flanks, and he envied the effortless mastery of their environment. Not to mention that they seemed to be able to do whatever they chose to do in the moment. The contrast with his own situation was all too apparent to him.

"Shigoto, haven't you finished yet?" That familiar voice with its quality of a partly unsheathed blade cut across his thoughts, bringing him suddenly back to earth.

"Nearly Sensei, I..." he choked off the sentence as he hurried to return to his task.

"Nearly! Nearly never saddled a runaway horse, Shigoto." The voice of the unbidden, unseen Sensei was tracking his steps.

He considered for a moment asking Sensei what he meant, but just managed to stop himself before the question emerged as words in the air. Knowing Maguro Sensei as he did, the answer would as likely leave him as confused as enlightened. He had become well used by now to his teacher's strange elliptical way with words. Maguro Sensei, his teacher, mentor, and sometime nemesis. The willowy figure, who was strong enough in limb to shift and arrange boulders, yet also loving enough to collect up and reassemble fallen pieces, was someone Shigoto had come to know as a person he could rely upon, if not always in the way he expected.

Shigoto doubled his efforts to clear up the twigs and pine needles pruned from one of the trees bordering the shoreline, gathering up the last of the waste into a neat heap he pincered them between the short handled bamboo rake and his hand, then dropped them into a basket of woven bamboo.

"There Sensei, done," he said with not a little relief colouring his voice.

"Right then, gather up your things and catch up with the others." It was a consisely given order.

Shigoto collected his basket and bowed toward his Sensei who was standing a few paces back gazing intently at the tree that had just been pruned, checking that the work had been done to his satisfaction, that there was a clear separation between the pads of foliage to allow light and air to reach all parts of the tree, whilst still allowing a degree of expression that was graceful and natural.

"Hurry along now Shigoto, you are the last to leave and a meal has been arranged for the gardeners tonight. It would be most impolite to be late."

A meal, Sensei had said. This was news to Shigoto, no one had mentioned anything about this before, and none of the other gardeners had spoken a word to him about it. It was a certain tradition among the gardeners that when there was some particular reason to celebrate they would get together as a group. Food would be brought from the kitchens and a flask or two of rice wine would be discretely circulated. Maguro Sensei being abstemious never indulged himself, though he would turn a blind eye to others indulging. It had become one way for the gardeners to strengthen the bonds that held them together as a group, confirming their identity and status. Shigoto ran along the path bordering the pond. A capricious breeze had risen which sporadically animated a few crisp leaves that lay along his way. He imagined he had a sword in his hand instead of a rake, with which he thrust and parried at the dancing leaves and the clipped mounds of azalea bushes as he passed by. Coming near the gardener's store he slowed his pace to a more sedate pace. He was after all, he reminded himself, a man about his business, not just the child he once was.

He passed the stables which always announced their presence before one came upon them, then left his basket and rake in the building used by the gardeners. Unencumbered now he ran the short distance with increasingly light steps to where his quarters were. He was now living away from his family home, living in shared space with the other gardeners. Sensei had decided that he was now strong enough to work full time with the other gardeners, and in recognition of this he was given a place to sleep in what was known between them as the House of Gardeners. Occasionally, he would go and visit his family home, to regale his mother and grandmother in particular with tales relating to his work and duties, embellishing his tales with rich details as he saw fit to enliven the telling.

He stepped into the entry porch of the modest building, and with an unconscious fluidity shook off his sandals and slipped inside the gloomy interior. As he reached the door to his room his whole world appeared to stop in its tracks. The sliding screen which acted as a partition was slightly ajar, something that he was always most careful to avoid. He stood listening for any sound within, not daring to release the breath in his lungs. The light in the room was too dim to see far inside, he hesitated before gently sliding the door open a little further. No sound emerged. As silently as he could, with all his senses on full alert he slipped inside.

Shigoto stood stock-still, his back pressing against the paper covered door. Something was not right, this space as familiar to him now as his own skin was sending him an urgent warning, but one that he could not immediately decipher. His eyes strained to reach through the gloom to locate whatever intrusion it was he was being warned against. If he moved forward or retreated he would advertise his presence for sure. He was trapped between the comfort of familiarity and the disquiet of change.

Forcing himself to move away from the door, to penetrate deeper into the suddenly alien stillness, he crossed the room drawn onward by pure instinct. Reaching the shutter of the small window on the far side he slid it open enough to allow in more of the day's last remaining light. He turned to face the centre of the room his heart pounding wildly in his chest. His eyes scanned the room registering the forms of his meagre belongings, until his intense gaze came to rest on something unexpected, something out of place. There against the wall to his left was a large flat black lacquered box.

Shigoto knelt down in front of the box, and then ran his hands across its smooth cold surface. With a hundred questions running through his mind he raised the lid and placed it gently on the floor to one side. Peering over the edge he softly exhaled. Lying on top of what appeared to be a fresh tunic was a pair of gardener's scissors partially in the cloth that they had been wrapped in. He reached out and picked up the bundle. The dull grey metal felt heavy in his hand. Shigoto understood well enough their significance. "Now I am a proper gardener," he said to himself softly. It had seemed an interminable time to him since he had been assigned the position of apprentice gardener, and while at first it had seemed to promise so much, over the intervening period he could not disguise a growing feeling within himself that in practice it seemed to amount to little. He had assumed that some degree of responsibility would have come with his position, yet that had not been the case. Apart from his mother and grandmother no one had seemed to recognise and appreciate his trajectory into this world. Certainly not in the way that he had hoped for, nor if he were to be completely honest, in the way he had assumed and expected. Even moving his belongings, such as they were, into the House of Gardeners, had turned out to be a disappointment.

Kamaboku remained the person he seemed to have most contact with. The five other occupants of the House of Gardeners were barely respectful of his presence and by and large ignored him. Shigoto reconciled this to himself by accepting that the difference in their respective ages set them apart. He was after all much younger than his fellow gardeners, they were familiar with the work, and seemed to have an unspoken bond that somehow sidelined or excluded him from most of their activities. This he felt he could accept, but beneath it all it was the lack of contact and communication with Sensei that nagged away at his confidence. Shigoto felt as if he had slipped from the position of closeness to his mentor, whom he now rarely saw, and even more rarely was addressed directly by. Somehow Sensei had become a peripheral figure to him, whereas he has expected the opposite.

When Kamaboku announced to him that Sensei had decided it was time for Shigoto to live as part of the community in the House of Gardeners, he had felt both elation and trepidation. His mother had smiled and cried a tear of pride on receiving the news. Just as he was feeling that his trepidation was in the ascendant and things were slipping once again out of his control, it seemed that Maguro Sensei had conjured a way to draw him back. He lifted the scissors, and felt how they fitted his hand. Slowly he opened and closed the blades, captivated by the way one blade slid so smoothly over the other. Opening, and closing, opening and closing. How good it was to feel their weight in his hand. Now he could begin to practise his craft, now he could really begin to be a gardener, one who climbed nimbly into trees and pruned things. Maybe there was something to celebrate after all.

The meal that evening was to be a celebration of his coming of age as a gardener, a mark of acceptance of his arrival finally into the fold. Food had been delivered from the kitchens and the full crew of six gardeners in the company of Maguro Sensei sat around in a relaxed fashion, eating, drinking in moderation, and swapping stories.

"Well, Shigoto, now that you have your own pair of scissors you can now begin to practise the art of gardening. This is another beginning, as all life is but a series of circles." Maguro Sensei raised his cup of tea to toast his arrival at this crucial point in his career. The other gardeners all did the same, though they raised the small cups that were filed with *sake*.

"Hey, you are a man now, eh, Shigoto-san," added Kamaboku, a wide grin splitting his face. "But mind, no going to sleep tonight with the scissors, I would hate to think of you having some kind of accident." The room dissolved into laughter, even Sensei laughed at this remark. "Besides which it may ruin your prospects of marriage, at least of having children." Again the room rocked with laughter, and Shigoto's face blushed crimson.

"We all hear the rustling at night, eh. We know it's no mouse creeping about," Konnyaku, one of the gardeners added, which set the room blazing with ribald amusement once more. Plainly the *sake* was having an effect on the company. Maguro Sensei who was sat with a ramrod straight back, looked across at Shigoto.

"Pay no heed, they may be gardeners, but they all have rough edges yet," he said smiling.

"It's true we may have rough edges Sensei, compared to the family in the palace, and your good self of course. But scissors are sharp, no matter where you come from," Ekichū, another of the gardeners, added for effect and once more the company convulsed into merriment.

"Enough, enough,' said Maguro Sensei. "I shall leave you gentlemen to your conversations. I trust you will not corrupt this young man utterly by the morning. Kamaboku I hold you responsible for what happens, and I expect you all clear eyed in the morning, is that understood?"

'Yes, Sensei, and thank you," replied Kamaboku waving his hands over the now empty dishes, still grinning from ear to ear. The others put down their cups and bowed respectfully in the direction of the now standing Maguro Sensei, and they chorused their thanks and appreciation.

"Good night now," said Maguro Sensei, and he slipped out of the room and disappeared into the night.

"Ahh, that was a good meal, eh," said Kamaboku when they had all sat down again. "He's a good man, that Sensei, treats us like human beings at least, which is more than can be said by some folks, eh?"

The Gardener's Apprentice

That night Shigoto fell asleep with the sense that he was finally beginning to belong someplace, and for the first time since he had moved to the House of Gardeners he did not miss his mother and his home. His future seemed stretched out before him into some kind of infinity. There was a direction, a path before him to follow, where it led he could not tell, but for the moment he felt content in the unknowable.

"Oku-chan, it is coming up to your birth date soon." Shigoto's mother instinctively adding the suffix –*chan* to his name, something he always found comforting. "We should go to visit the temple, and offer prayers for you. Would you like to do that?"

"I am not sure." he replied hesitantly. "That is, if Sensei will give me the time to go. He is keeping me very busy. He is always finding new work for me, no sooner have I nearly finished one job, and then there are ten more to be done. And he says I am slow, and then he points out something is wrong, or this or that could be done better. It's not right. I think that just because I am the youngest, everyone picks on me."

Shigoto was alone with his mother; he had finished work in the garden for the day, finally having completed the jobs allotted to him, and rather than spend the evening at the House of Gardeners, he had decided to visit his home. He had settled in well enough with the others, though the comfort of home still drew him back. At the end of that day's work, as they were gathering up their tools, Sensei had come to him and instructed that branches of various foliage plants were needed at the Palace to make up flower arrangements. Sensei showed him which were the required plants, and gave him detailed instructions as to the number, lengths of branches, the proper way to cut them from the source, and how to tie them together for presentation at the Palace. It was typical of the chores that Sensei had been finding for him at the end of the day, obligations that Shigoto felt perhaps were in some way a means of testing his spirit, his willingness to learn. At least there was one side benefit to this particular request. Shigoto realised that he would have to deliver the bundles of foliage to the kitchen area of the Palace, and if the fates were on his side, there was always the chance he might catch a glimpse of a young household maid. If he still was not sure of her name, the image of her face remained burned into his memory. If he was particularly in luck, it may even be to her that he would deliver the bundles of foliage, which would allow him to linger in her presence and perhaps even exchange a few words.

His luck was not running for him that evening. Having left the bundles at the kitchen, he made his way to his family home. On his way he hoped that his father would not be there, as he had increasingly come to recognise a feeling of estrangement from him. The chances were good that his father would not be there, in truth, he rarely was, it seemed that his duties at the Palace absorbed most of his time. By and large it was no longer something that unduly concerned him, though from time to time his conscience was pricked at the gulf that yawned between father and son. 'Most of the time, he behaves as if he would rather not have a son at all. He seems to hate me, as if I have done something to hurt him', he thought to himself, then turned a corner into the familiar alley, where he knew his mother and grandmother would at least be happy to see him again.

Oyadori was predictably delighted to see her son and she greeted him warmly at the door.

"Ah, Oku-chan, come in, come in. Oh, what have you there? Have you brought some of your work with you?"

"No, this is just some foliage that they did not want at the kitchen. I thought you might want them instead. I have been to take a delivery there," he explained.

"That's kind of you. Oba-chan, look it's Shigoto, come to see us." She called over her shoulder whilst fussily ushering him in. "My, you are growing big and strong too. Soon I will not be able

The Gardener's Apprentice

to recognise the young boy who became a garden apprentice. The work seems to suit you. Are you getting enough to eat where you live?"

"Yes, yes, there is enough. And you keep sending parcels of food as well. I share them with the others, otherwise they would get jealous. Sometimes I am not always sure if they like me."

"Oh, Oku-chan, I am sure that's not the case at all."

"You don't know the others, they always give me the worst jobs to do, and they are happy to spend time in each other's company. They like to drink rice wine you know, and get drunk and fall asleep, snoring like wild boars."

"Okugi! That is no way to speak of your comrades, I am sure that does not happen at all. That man Kamaboku, he is always so nice, and polite. I am sure the others are too. Maguro Sensei would not have it any other way. What a way to speak about your colleagues, I hope that you do not tell such tales to anyone else."

"It's true, I don't know where they get the wine from, but when they do, you should see them."

"Well, I hope that you do not drink too," his mother turned to him with a look that brooked no argument.

"I tried some one time, but it made me feel bad afterwards. I don't know what they see in it."

"Oh, listen to him, drinking now, is he?" Shigoto's grandmother came into the room, catching the tail end of the conversation. "Mind you do not turn out like the rest of them then. There will be no hope for us all if you do."

Shigoto was just about to launch into a more detailed elaboration for the benefit of his grandmother, but a single look from his mother as she left to make food ready for him, helped him realise the wisdom of not doing so. "How are you Oba-chan?"

"Oh my, how this young one is growing, must be all that fresh air." She came and tousled his hair. He felt his cheeks suddenly heating up.

"Now mother, leave the boy alone while he is about to eat something." Oyadori cheerfully called from the kitchen area.

"That's all he does when he comes here. It's not really to see his ageing grandmother at all, he just comes here to eat," the older woman harrumphed grumpily.

"Why don't you have some tea, mother? Come and sit here for a while, it's not that often now that Shigoto-chan gets to visit us."

"Like his father in that respect at least," she snorted crossly. "He's never here either. He is still only of a junior rank, but with all the airs and graces he puts on, you would think he is the right hand man of Lord Saeko himself. Huh, if that were the case, he could have found his son a better position than being a garden apprentice, don't you think? What does that say for the future, eh?" The elderly woman laced her words with sarcasm.

"Oba-chan, enough, enough. You know my husband has a very busy life, and has many responsibilities," replied Oyadori returning with a small tray of food. Shigoto wondered if this was a subject that they touched on when he was not there. He guessed it probably was. When he looked across at his mother there was no trace in her face of what she was thinking, what she was feeling. Her face was now wholly passive, like the surface of a lake. You could read what you wanted into its reflective surface, and know absolutely nothing of what lay just below the surface.

"Huh, I am sure you are right," the older woman said, though she clearly did not entirely believe it herself. "Anyway, you had better eat your food Oku-chan. He looks as if he needs a good meal inside him," she said to no one in particular.

CHAPTER EIGHTEEN

July 1576

The first that Oyadori heard of her fate was when her Lady Saeko called her into her chambers early one morning. "I wish to speak to you regarding this matter," she said in a voice that was flat and unemotional. "First you must answer me truthfully though." She paused for a moment, as if to gather her thoughts. "Who have you revealed your... shall we say, personal situation with? Think carefully before you reply, as it may have some bearing on what I am about to tell you."

Oyadori knew immediately to what she was referring, and she answered in all honesty. "No one, that is, apart from my mother. She is the only person who knows, and that is the whole truth." Suddenly she felt very concerned and afraid. Had someone spoken out of turn? Were rumours floating about already? Kobuto had been intensely curious as to what had been the nature of the personal discussions that had taken place between Oyadori and Lady Saeko, but Oyadori had brushed off her none too subtle queries, as being "merely family matters". It had become a matter of contention between the two, and Kobuto had become even more critical of Oyadori in respect of her tasks. First there had been a question of Oyadori having been selected before her to serve the distinguished visitor, Prince Hotaru, and then to compound Kobuto's wounded pride at knowing all that went on at the palace, "secret talks" as she expressed it, were now being held between Oyadori and Lady Saeko.

"They are not secret in that way, it's just that it's a family matter." Oyadori had tried to explain, but she knew Kobuto well enough by now to realise that this was not enough to satisfy her. The pressure she was feeling was intense and Kobuto's constant sniping and carping only made matters worse. Even her mother was unsympathetic when Oyadori had complained to her.

"You only have yourself to blame. Just look at the condition you are in. If you had not thrown yourself at him, none of this would have happened. You would have been married in due course, and had children the proper way, and our family would not have been damned. I hate to think what they have planned for our fate, and your father is not here to help us. Well, maybe that is for the best. We are done for, that's for sure."

"My baby will be born," Oyadori had said. "And I did not 'throw myself' at him as you put it."

"You are stubborn. Stubborn and stupid. Those are not a good traits in a woman," her mother had replied bitterly, and so the conversation had ended.

As Oyadori waited to receive her final sentence from Lady Saeko, she recalled that conversation with her mother. It was the last time they had spoken, and it deepened her sense of gloom to think that perhaps it might possibly be the last conversation she might have had with the person who had delivered her into this world. She felt that her fate was not in her hands, that not even her breath was her own at this moment. She actually felt deeply attached to the notion that there was a new life growing inside of her, she felt it was the fulfilment in some way of her being a woman. Ever since she realised that she was pregnant, she had felt an inner satisfaction, as if she had achieved a part of her destiny. She understood that the social consequences were potentially disastrous for her and her mother, but beyond that, in a part of her mind that she could never share with anyone, not even her mother, she felt pleased. She had felt nothing but dread at the thought of bearing the children of Kanyu, there was something in the look of his face that revealed he detested her. If she had detected even a glimmer of kindness in his attitude, possibly she may have felt differently. But she had sensed only disappointment and her heart had turned against him.

"So, Oyadori, your situation has caused great consternation to my husband, to say nothing of myself. Perhaps if you had shown some little restraint in the face of, shall we say the charms of our visitor, then this trouble would never have arisen in the first place."

"I am sorry, Madam, I am truly sorry," said Oyadori, and she bowed so low to the floor that her forehead touched the *tatami* mat she was kneeling on. She stayed where she was; it was as if the foreboding she felt held her locked down in that position, with the full weight of the shame now being heaped upon her shoulders. "Please do not punish my mother for this. It is me who must bear the blame for the trouble caused to you and the great Lord Saeko. My mother is entirely innocent. Please do not punish her. Since my father died she was been grieving for him, and now I have shamed the family name too," she said quietly without raising herself from the floor.

"Your father was a good man, he served this family well," said Lady Saeko with severity, as if she too was touched by concern for his name, and took offence at the apparent violation of his reputation. Slowly Oyadori straightened her back again, but her eyes, full with tears, remained downcast. Lady Saeko looked away towards garden beyond her chambers. The maples were in full glorious leaf, azalea bushes were glimmering a vivid green in the intensifying morning light, and the cicadas and grasshoppers were winding up their sawing, grinding noise. A small cluster of sparrows suddenly descended into the garden, landing on the deep green moss, where they pecked before rising as one and flying noisily off again. Just then a discreet knock came from outside the closed door. Lady Saeko looked around, her face twisted in annoyance at the interruption.

"Who is it?" she called out abruptly.

The door slid ajar a handbreadth. "Madam, I am sorry to interrupt, but there is a message from Lord Saeko's quarters. He asks if you will be joining him later this afternoon. I…" It was Kobuto kneeling outside the doorway.

"Kobuto, I wish no interruptions. Fetch me some tea from the kitchen will you."

"Yes, Ma'm, I will send Oyadori, as soon as you have spoken with her. The message…"

"No, go now, attend to it personally. The answer for my husband can wait." Lady Saeko took no pains to disguise her impatience. The door slid silently shut again.

"Damn woman," said Lady Saeko after a few moments. "She is always listening at the door. I suppose you have noticed that." But she was not really addressing Oyadori. "Have you spoken to her? Does she know anything at all? If she does, then it will be all over this island in moments."

"No, Ma'm. I have only spoken about this matter with my mother, as I said. That is the truth." Oyadori repeated. Lady Saeko grunted softly, her lips curling upward, twisting her face in an expression of disgust. Oyadori shook her head and said nothing. She was still waiting for her fate to be declared, and she sat unmoving her hands folded over her belly, as if to protect from harm the growing seed hidden there.

For a long time nothing further was said. Lady Saeko went back to looking at the garden. Oyadori tried to weigh up whether she should say anything, or should she just remain passive and accept the fate thrust upon her, whatever that may be.

'In all this matter', she thought, 'one thing is certain, I can never imagine finding love with Kanyu. I am not sure he has it in him, particularly not for me anyway. Perhaps that is what I felt a glimmer of in the manner of Prince Hotaru. Not that I believe he loves me, but that somehow he is capable of loving, of caring enough to love someone. That man Kanyu is as cold as a stone, and no more capable of feeling love. The only thing I felt from him was complete indifference. If I am to bear the child of someone, then, along with that seed there must be some love, some kindness. Otherwise, what kind of a world will that child know? There is too much sadness in this world, everything is so transitory, so fragile, fleeting, and our lives are nothing more than blossom that falls from the tree with the rain. Is that not what the poets say? If we cannot even carry a glimpse of love within us, what else is there to make our lives worthwhile? Men only consider fighting, it seems as if they even happily seek out death sometimes, as if that will some how vindicate their existence. No, my child will know love, even if it is only the love of its mother, but it will know love. That's why they cannot kill me over this, because this child *must* be born, so that it will realise love. Even if I have to leave this island, and have to make my own way in the world doing the most disgusting things to survive. I will live for my child, I have to live for my child, there is no other path to follow now, then perhaps one day....'

"Oyadori!" the voice snapped her back into the present moment so sharply her head jerked backwards. "Have you taken in what I just said?" Lady Saeko was looking at her with furious burning eyes.

"I am so sorry Madam, I was just thinking of the child," said Oyadori, her voice small and quiet, her eyes dropped to look towards the empty space between them once more. Lady Saeko continued to stare at her, then resumed what she had started to say.

"The decision that has been reached has been influenced by an intervention of the family that you had been chosen to be married into. Lord Saeko has considered their request and has decided to grant it in this case. Because of my personal intervention in the first place in selecting you, he asked me to inform you of the decision that has been made."

'I must have not heard something,' thought Oyadori. She was stunned and felt a chill numbness creeping through her body. 'What have they decided?'

"So in order that things be settled as soon as possible, the marriage will take place before the month is out. The other family have been informed and are in accord with this. Everything will proceed as before, except there is to be no particular ceremony to mark the event. A priest from the Hatsukari shrine will conduct the service, in private, that is all. You will be found alternative employment until the child is born, and then you will live in the house of your husband. Do you understand me?"

Oyadori was trying to make sense of the words: on the one hand Lady Saeko seemed to be offering her a reprieve, and on the other she felt as if she were being condemned to a fate that seemed worse than anything else. She shook her head to try and clear the dense fog that was obscuring her ability to take in what had been said to her.

"I asked if you understood," said Lady Saeko, "not if you agreed to it. What you may think is of no concern at all at this moment. If the father of the child had been anyone other than who he is, then matters will probably have been very different. That is all, you may leave now."

"So I am to marry Kanyu after all?" Oyadori was still struggling to take it in. "But…"

"You heard what I had to say, that is the decision of Lord Saeko, he has granted the wish of the other family. There are aspects to this matter that will be beyond your understanding, but that is of no consequence, and all that is important is that you carry out the word of Lord Saeko. And you are never to reveal the content of this discussion to anyone, do you understand? If word was to get out about this then…" Lady Saeko paused, her eyes never shifting from Oyadori's face, "Then the child will not see the light of day. That is the order from Lord Saeko himself."

Oyadori was utterly numb. If she had tried to stand at that moment her legs would not have supported her, her face had turned ashen. She gripped her belly tightly, as if she were holding on to the one and only thing that was a reality to her, the only thing that made any sense at all. She looked across towards the opening in which the garden was captured but it was swimming before her, spinning round in a daze of smeared colours, so that the sky seemed to be somehow below the earth. She could hear nothing but the rushing, pounding of blood in her ears, and her heart beating wildly in her chest. With a low groaning sound she collapsed to the floor.

When she came to she was in the dark, its velvet comfort enclosing her. When she heard the sound of someone moving, a door sliding back, and a shaft of light suddenly arrowing its way toward her, she gasped in surprise.

"Ah, you are awake?" It was her mother's voice. Oyadori relaxed her body as if she was a child once more, shielded and protected from the harsh realities that lay beyond. Her mother came over and knelt down beside her.

"Where am I?" she asked.

"At home," replied her mother as if surprised by the question. "Are you alright now? No pains anywhere? In your belly, perhaps?"

Oyadori considered this for a moment before replying, "No, no. I am fine, really." She tried to sit up.

"Stay where you are a little longer, I will fetch some soup."

"What happened? How did I get here?" she asked when her mother returned with a small tray bearing a steaming bowl.

"You were brought here from Lady Saeko's apartments. You fainted there and they could not wake you."

"Oh," said Oyadori, she was still trying to piece together her memory, but her mind was in a dense fog and the shape of meaning was hard to distinguish.

"What's going to happen now?" asked Oyadori.

"We'll speak later, in the morning, it's late now."

"I need to know," said Oyadori struggling to sit up. Her mother sighed and pushed the tray with the soup across within reach.

"Here, drink this. I'll go and get a light." When she returned with a small hand lamp and set it down on the floor, her mother went over what Oyadori had been told by Lady Saeko earlier. Oyadori drank the soup and took in her mother's account of events.

"So why did they change their minds?" she asked, putting the bowl back onto the tray. But her mother only shrugged wearily. Her face bore the weight of her concerns, and she looked much older.

"Who is to say? It's the ways of men, perhaps they know things that we do not. May be it is better that way, "she said, and shrugged again before lapsing into silence.

"Are there things you are not telling me?" Oyadori asked. Her mother looked across at her, half of her face in deep shadow and a stray lock of hair hung down over her forehead.

"Such as what?"

"I don't know," said Oyadori weakly, she lay back down again. "I don't know."

"Try and sleep now, we can talk more in the morning."

Oyadori's mother got up slowly. She went and picked up the lamp and started to move towards the door.

"Mother," said Oyadori. "I still have my child don't I?"

For a long moment her mother stood in the doorway looking at her daughter. "Yes, you still have the child," she said finally. Then she moved out of the room and slid the door closed. Darkness returned to the room once more, there was no moon that night.

Oyadori lay a long while without sleeping. She reviewed the events of the last few months in her mind. At one point while she lay there, Kanyu's stern face loomed out of the darkness, an apparition that frightened her and she pulled the cover up and hid her eyes until it dissolved again. 'I will know you well enough for real,' she thought. 'I do not need you as a ghost to haunt my waking hours too'. She tried to recall Prince Hotaru's image but it refused to come into her mind. 'So, you are hiding from me are you? Are you too so ashamed that you cannot visit me at all? And what happens to you now? I suppose you will just carry on with your grand life as before, perhaps you do not even know that there is life planted within me. Maybe you would not even care if you did. But that's all right; I do not need you and your finery. Somehow I will get by, my child will be born and grow up, perhaps never to know its true father. But it is better that than to be born a child without love. That would be the worst kind of fate of all. My child will never suffer that, he or she, whichever it is, will always have love as long as there is breath in my body.' She slid her hands under the layers of clothing until her palms lay flat and warm on her lower belly. 'Whoever you are, whether you are a boy or a girl, whatever happens in our lives, you will always have love, that is my promise to you. You will be born, and you will do good things in your life.' She pressed her fingers down into the soft flesh as if she were trying to reach the unborn child within her. 'Please if there are gods in heaven, let this seed become a boy, so that he may become strong in limb, and that one day, one day, he may leave this place. Let him break free of the ties that bind him to this place, so that his spirit may soar in the sky. That is my earnest wish, my sincere request to all you gods and spirits that watch over our foolish lives. And if it is a girl, may she find it in her heart to forgive me one day.' As she thought that, the bare traces of a new day began to spread soft light in the room through the paper-covered window.

PART II

CHAPTER NINETEEN

October 1593

"Hey Shigoto, it's time to... oh you are up and awake already, eh?' It was the ever-friendly, cheerful voice of Kamaboku come to rouse him, to reel in him back in from the freedom of his dreams, back to the world of work, responsibilities and expectations. "Come on there is tea ready, and some breakfast too. Today is a busy day, you are to be with us today. Sensei's instructions."

In the gloom of the main room of the House of Gardeners, assorted figures their outlines softened by half formed light, were either moving slowly about the business of rousing themselves, or sitting still sipping tea in silence. In all five people shared the space, four other gardeners and Shigoto. The four older men slept on tatami mats in the main room, while Shigoto had been assigned a sleeping space in a small room of his own, its bare dark plastered walls punctured only by a small window set high in the wall. Set into the floor of the main space was a hearth with a hook hung down from a blackened beam on which a large kettle was suspended. A few wisps of smoke lazily roused themselves from the bed of ashes. Maguro Sensei himself lived apart. It was said he had shunned accommodation near the main palace buildings, and had chosen instead to renovate an old teahouse in the grounds of the gardens where he lived a solitary life. The few callers to that out of the way place were met by Sensei at the simple wicker gate set in a low, open bamboo-work fence. Between the gate and the entry porch to the building were a scattering of flat topped stepping-stones, almost invariably Sensei would be standing there waiting, even before the visitor had a chance of calling out a greeting.

"Here, have some tea, and some food," Kamaboku indicated a vacant space by the hearth to Shigoto and pushed a warm cup and a plate over the mat toward him. Shigoto was wide awake.

"So, what are we doing today?" he asked to no one in particular.

"Huh, work, that's what we are doing today," the silent figure next to him suddenly became vaguely animated. "What else do we do, every day it's the same thing. Go here, go there, dig this, move that, cut this, lift that. Listen to him chatter on! Give him a job, and all of a sudden he is chirping like a sparrow in a tree. You are too young to know anything. You think life is one big adventure, eh? Well, when you finally grow up is when you realise that it's not. It's just hard work, that's all, just hard work."

"Pay no attention Shigoto. Konnyaku san had a belly full of *sake* last night and bad dreams to follow no doubt." Kamaboku intervened.

Konnyaku was sitting cross-legged by the hearth, holding a plain ceramic cup between his hands, his barely open eyes looking into the ashes. The dullness of his expression contrasted with the rather delicately defined set of his round face. Konnyaku had never shown any great openness or particular warmth to Shigoto. It was more as if he was another obstacle to be manoeuvred around. Konnyaku was a puzzle to Shigoto, there was something in the way he did things that Shigoto could not quite reconcile. It was as if there was something of an air of fussiness about him, which somehow reminded Shigoto of his father. Though it came without the latter's stern forbidding silences, as Konnyaku was invariably free with his opinions.

It always came as a surprise to Shigoto to hear a tone of complaint or dissent from any of the gardeners; before he came to live in the gardeners' lodging, he had heard none, and never suspected anyone could harbour ill feelings toward their work or even Maguro Sensei. There were occasions, after he had been told he was moving into the House of Gardeners, when there had been whispered conversations which had not included him, or sentences broken off and left hanging in the air as he entered the main room. At first he imagined he had probably been the subject of conversation. This he had expected, after all it was he who was the novelty. It was he who wished to gain acceptance into their world. After he had been there a few months and the novelty of his presence had begun to wear off, he would catch an occasional intemperate remark coming from one or other of the gardeners, and Shigoto began to realise that the gardeners saw themselves as being a breed apart. They held little or no status in society, yet they clearly considered themselves more as artisans than common labourers. For himself, Shigoto had always taken great care in respect of venturing an opinion, in particular in making judgements concerning other people. It was instinctive to him, one that had not required particular schooling to reinforce. It was just part of his natural caution.

"So what are we doing today?" Shigoto asked again, this time directing his question specifically at Kamaboku who had taken his place on the opposite side of the hearth.

"We are moving stones. Sensei said he wanted the whole crew there. He specifically said you were to be there to help out. We should get going soon, there is equipment to collect first, and Sensei will be waiting for us no doubt." Kamaboku took one last sup of the tea, and rose to his feet. "Are we going then?" he said to rest of the room. "Let's get going, eh."

Having selected from the gardeners' store what they might need for the day, Shigoto along with Ekichū pulled on the handle of a handcart. He had carefully stowed his scissors still wrapped in cloth along with the other equipment. Yadokari, a quiet and retiring presence, pushed the cart from the rear. Kamaboku, relishing as always his role as team leader had issued instructions as to precisely where they were to go, and had gone ahead with Konnyaku to meet Sensei. Laden with equipment the wooden cart was heavy and ponderous to move. They took a broad gravelled path that skirted around the Great Dragon Pond, and then took a smaller path that threaded its way between the trees further into the depths of the garden.

"Are you sure you know where we are supposed to be? It seems so far," said Shigoto to Ekichū, his arms were aching from pulling on the handle, and several times he had nearly slipped.

"Keep going, and don't talk so much will you. Hey, Yadokari, are you pushing this thing, or just leaning on it for a rest?" There was no reply from the rear of the cart, but Shigoto could see that Yadokari's cheeks were bright red with effort. They trundled on pulling and pushing their burden. Sometimes Shigoto pulled on the cart whilst walking backwards, and then he would change over and pull on the handle facing forwards. He recognised the part of the garden they were entering. It was an area where many maple trees grew, and the ground undulated with a series of small hills and hidden hollows. It was quiet with branches of trees arching over their heads and birdsong filling the air. Shigoto remembered the area as being a place that Sensei and he had walked through many times, during the period when he had accompanied his teacher on those lengthy walkabouts through the garden. They stopped briefly to catch their breath having taken an incline in the path, Shigoto glad for the opportunity to ease his aching arms and legs.

"They are supposed to be around here somewhere, I am sure we have taken the right path. Hey, Kamaboku. Kamaboku san." Ekichuu called out loudly. He then put his fingers to his mouth and let out a shrill sound like the call of a bird. The result of this was a clattering sound high above their heads as several birds took umbrage at being disturbed on a peaceful morning. Just as a silence began to settle about them again Kamaboku's voice came from between the trees:

"Where have you been? Did you stop for a nap on the way? Come on. Sensei is waiting for you. Hurry up, will you!"

"Oh, he is a fine one that Kamaboku. He says that nice and loud just because Sensei is there." It was the first words Yadokari had uttered since they had left the store, though he was discreet enough to mutter them under his breath. They left the cart on the path having wedged a couple of stones under the wheels and headed in the direction from where Kamaboku's voice had come.

"The trees which have been marked can all come down. The roots will need to be dug up too. Shigoto, fetch a saw." Sensei's voice crackled through the air. The gardeners set about the instructions that Maguro Sensei issued in rapid-fire succession and within minutes the area was feverish with activity. By the end of the morning they had cleared sufficient vegetation to reveal numerous stones. The trees that had been cut down had been reduced to heaps of neatly stacked branches, with Shigoto and Yadokari bundling the branches into bound stacks to be used as firewood, nothing was to be wasted. As he worked Shigoto kept an eye on Maguro Sensei as he wandered from stone to stone inspecting each one in great detail, sometimes running his hands over their exposed surfaces, revealing none of his thoughts except to continue to issue further instructions.

For Shigoto, the morning passed quickly as he leapt nimbly and enthusiastically from task to task. It was he realised, one of the few times that he had worked with the other gardeners when they were engaged together on the same task. Though the work was at times heavy and unrelenting, he felt content. When the last of the cords of firewood had been carried out of the area and stacked by the side of the path, Sensei turned to Kamaboku. "That will do for now Kamaboku, the men can rest a moment and take some food and water."

Most of the men turned and went back to the path, where they sat together to eat their lunch. Maguro Sensei sat himself down on a broad flat-topped stone elbows resting on his knees, a far away look in his eyes. Kamaboku made himself comfortable a little distance away. Shigoto was unsure where to place himself. He wanted to find a place near his teacher, so that he could continue to study the man, to try and further understand his way of working, his way of seeing. Shigoto started to eat the lunch he had brought with him. He wondered if it would be polite to addresses questions to Sensei directly. Enlivened by the pleasure of being part of the garden crew wanted to convey his pleasure to his teacher.

"Well Shigoto, you are a gardener now, what are your ideas of what do with these stones?" The question caught him by surprise and he dropped a piece of fish that he was about to raise to his mouth into the grass beside him.

"Sensei, I…" he stammered.

"You what, I wonder?" Sensei's voice had softened into a more teasing, amicable tone, lacking the usual stern edge.

"Sensei, forgive me for not mentioning it before, but I wanted to thank you for the opportunity to learn from you…" he looked across to Kamaboku as if he may expect some support from that direction. He could feel his face reddening. Kamaboku smiled back at him mutely, an amused air playing about his eyes, which only made Shigoto feel his embarrassment more keenly. "Excuse my rudeness, Sensei, I have felt there has not been much opportunity to thank you before now, and I am most grateful indeed. To be learning from you, that is."

Maguro Sensei looked across at Shigoto, one eyebrow cocked upwards, pricking Shigoto's embarrassment, and inflating Kamaboku's amusement.

"I wanted to thank you before, but you are always busy, and I.... I.... that is...." Shigoto began to utter out the words. He had planned and rehearsed a speech of thanks in his mind that morning as they worked. He had gone over and over the words in his mind, except now when the opportunity arose, the words seemingly vanished into the air about him, leaving him floundering like a fish out of water. Kamaboku laughed aloud, and slapped his thigh.

Sensei said nothing for a moment, his attention still seemingly somewhere else, as he gazed absently about him. "Something amuses you, Kamaboku?"

"Oh no, Sensei, I, I was merely coughing ... some rice went down the wrong way that's all." Kamaboku tried unsuccessfully to cover the grin smeared across his face.

"I see," said Maguro Sensei, and then he looked away, as if some other more pressing matter had caught his attention. "Anyway," he said directing his attention again to Shigoto again. "Think nothing of it Shigoto. You are a gardener now, and now you have your scissors too. You live with the other gardeners in the House of Gardeners, and I am merely fulfilling the orders that were given to me that's all. No more, no less. Is that not true?"

"Yes, Sensei, but I wanted to thank..."

"So, to answer the question I asked you in the first place, what would you do with these stones?" Maguro Sensei pressed on ignoring all that had passed on a moment ago. "You have seen them before, several times I believe, were you not curious about them? Why are these stones lying here, who placed them, did anyone place them, or did they arrive borne by the gods, do you think?"

Shigoto had no answer, he looked again across at Kamaboku, who was so wrapped up in his amusement of the conversation between master and pupil, that he was clearly to be of no help whatsoever.

"I... I don't know Sensei," he managed eventually to blurt out. "That is to say, I am not sure."

Sensei's look came to settle on the young man sitting near him, his eyes regarded Shigoto as if he were seeing him beyond time and space. There was no trace of condescension in the look, perhaps more a question of mild curiosity; it was as if some part of him was trying to envisage where his student was headed, what he might be truly capable of.

"No, I don't suppose you do just now. Why would you know? after all the path a gardener follows is long and has many twists and turns, and not all " he eventually said after a long pause, ".... more than even Kamaboku here knows himself." The latter part of his remark removed the last traces of a smile from Kamaboku's face. Silence descended between them, the only sounds remaining were distant calls of the birds, as they made their busy way invisibly among the trees.

CHAPTER TWENTY

October 1593

"Raising and setting stones is the most important art that a gardener can learn, and the highest art he practices. The very first gardens were created for the gods, you know. The ancients created gardens as a place for the gods to be, a place where they may feel comfortable. Is that not right, Kamaboku?"

"I have heard that said before, Sensei." Kamaboku leaned forward entranced by the direction the conversation was heading. He found it slightly odd that Maguro Sensei, a monk of the Zen sect, should mention the gods in this way. This was something he would have expected to hear more from a Shinto priest. Though in truth his grasp of the detail of religion was sketchy to say the least. It was something he was happy to pay respect to, but it was his work as a gardener that really provided meaning to his life.

"That is history, legends and stories of the ancients, I could not say whether it is really true or not. What I do know though is that the setting of stones is the greatest art of all. There are many ways of doing this, ways that men of knowledge have studied, practiced and handed down from one generation to the next. It is part of the secret teachings passed from generation to generation, as from the setting of stones all other things spring." Now both Shigoto and Kamaboku were leaning forward towards Maguro Sensei. At the mention of secret teachings Shigoto had felt the hair on the back of his neck stand upright, for him nothing else now existed except the voice, the words of his teacher. His scissors lay idly at his side along with the remains of his lunch.

"But what of this secret teaching, Sensei?" Shigoto felt a rising pressure, a tide that he could not hold back and the question came bursting out of him. Maguro Sensei ignored the question as if he had not heard it; his attention was far away, far from this place, perhaps even far beyond this time. Finally a long sigh came from him and he gently patted the surface of the stone on which he was sitting.

"You know, Shigoto, it used to be said that if you placed stones in the incorrect place, in the incorrect manner, you would bring disease and disaster down on to the household. I have heard it said that the Heike clan were brought down because of just these sorts of matters, and that it was the true source of all their misfortunes. But for that, they might still to this day be the rulers of Japan from some great palace in Kyoto, ruling the land as far as the sun reaches. Can you believe that, Shigoto? Do you believe that we, as mere gardeners, have the power to sway the movements of history? To bring even the mightiest of men to their knees, and turn them into dust? Is that what you want to learn?"

Shigoto opened his mouth to speak, but nothing emerged.

"I don't believe in such things myself," Sensei continued after a pause. "Men are men, and we have follies enough of our own, sufficient to bring even the mightiest rulers tumbling from their horses. Ambition, greed, spite and jealousy are enough on their own to bring such people down. We don't need divine intervention to achieve our own downfall Shigoto. We are quite capable of doing that for ourselves, without the help of any 'gods' we love to surround ourselves with. These stones were not placed here by the 'gods', they were placed by people, people such as yourselves. What I have learned is that the placement of stones can have a power, evoke an energy that we do not always appreciate. That much is clear at least." Then Sensei paused again, he was trying to bring up some kind of explanation for things that perhaps had no explanation, at least not in any rational sense, even to him. Another language was required, words that were not words, images that were not images, thoughts that were not thoughts, as we know them.

"Who knows when this work was done? These stones have been lying here a long while, that much we can be sure. Many of these stones are no longer in the positions where they were originally placed, some have fallen over, probably when the earth trembles and shakes itself, as if it were a dog trying to rid itself of fleas. It is our task to put these stones back in their rightful place, to re-set them, so they may have the opportunity once more to speak to those who are capable of hearing what they are saying. Should it be that good people with eyes to see happen to pass this way again." Sensei slowly got to his feet. The faraway look had returned. He turned away from the two sets of eyes, wide with amazement following every word and gesture he made. "Come, it is time to get back to work, and Shigoto, don't leave those scissors on the ground there, you will forget them. It would not do for a gardener to be without his scissors, would you not agree? Call the rest of the men back, Kamaboku. There is much yet to be done."

Some of the stones were taller than a full-grown man. Shigoto wondered how these stones had been brought to the garden in the first instance. Even dragging them with teams of oxen they must have taken a great effort. Did the setters of these stones have access to the secret knowledge Sensei had hinted at; did they really know and understand just what they were doing? Did they know the power the stones might hold? Sensei's words, or rather what he had intimated, in that brief conversation had lit up Shigoto's mind, and he had to keep reminding himself that Sensei had not actually revealed anything of what the secret teaching was, merely hinted at its existence. In doing so he had confirmed to Shigoto its potential, which was sufficient for the moment. Now he could realise for himself that there was more to this whole business than simply the "hard work and nothing but hard work"{, of which Konnyaku frequently complained.

For the rest of the day the gardeners under the close direction of Maguro Sensei continued resetting the stones. Some which Sensei decided had fallen over were lifted back upright, others were moved a fractionally in one direction or another. Before they tackled a stone, Sensei would look intently at it for a few moments running his hands over its surface, sometimes stepping back a few paces to look at the stone from a variety of positions, before finally coming to a decision as to how the stone was to be re-positioned. He worked with the air of someone deep in concentration, straining all his being to make a profound connection with the materials, to find some certain space in which he could hear what the materials demanded of him, and not just to impose his will on them. There was no conversation or banter between the gardeners as they worked; it was as if Sensei's concentration had infected them all. If there was logic or system to what Sensei was doing or trying to achieve, then he revealed little or nothing of it to the rest of the crew. Shigoto became aware that they were expected to work to a degree of precision, the significance of which often passed him by. "Lift that corner a little more, the height of three fingers," he would say, and they would push a long wooden pole under the stone, and bear down on the end of the lever to force the stone upward a few degrees, then Sensei would step back, eyes never straying one moment from the stone. Having checked on the effect achieved, fresh instructions would come. "Lift a little more... no, too much, let it fall back again. Now twist it this way a little, no not quite so far... there, hold that position. Don't let it move." When the stone was in exactly the position Sensei required, they would force earth under the stone, pounding it again and again with the blunt end of a shorter pole to pack it in tight and hard. Once this was done Sensei would step back again, moving his position this way and that, eyes always fixed on the object before him, his brow furrowed, until finally he would let them know that he was satisfied. He would with a gesture of the hand or an approving grunt signal his approval, and the earth would be smoothed and tidied around the stone. Once he was satisfied they had achieved the best they were able, they moved on to the next piece. Occasionally when they had fixed a stone in a revised position and moved on to the next, Sensei would revert back to a stone they had shifted previously to make yet another fine adjustment. Sometimes these further corrections were barely perceptible to the gardeners themselves.

There was one boulder that seemed to resist the efforts of the gardeners to move to Sensei's satisfaction. No matter how they pushed, pulled, levered, or dug about it, the stone defied their efforts. It was the piece that Sensei had been sitting on earlier, it was a very large stone, probably weighing far more than the weight of all the gardeners together, and Sensei was intent on setting it absolutely upright. Despite the combined efforts of the gardeners to raise it, it seemed to be fixed to its resting place at the top of a rise. For over an hour they applied their labour to manoeuvre the stone into a position that Sensei could be entirely satisfied with. They pushed it again and again, heaved, pulled on levers and ropes, but every time Sensei stepped back to look at the progress they had made, one glance at his expression was sufficient to convey that they had not succeeded.

"Stop lifting, Kamaboku, prop the stone where it is, don't let it slip back any further. Keep it where it is." The gardeners did as they were bidden, and fell back in a group, bruised, tired and beginning to feel that they were attempting something beyond their powers. Sensei looked at the stone first from one position then another. He was clearly dissatisfied. Shigoto could see that there was not too much wrong, after all they had finally managed to get the stone more or less upright, a few degrees this way or that would have made not a jot of difference. After all, who will ever know that the stone was intended to be any other way? If, as Sensei had said himself, the stones had been placed here many years ago, perhaps the people who set them were satisfied with what they had achieved. His arms ached terribly now, and weariness was spreading through his body. He just wanted someone, Sensei in particular, to call the day to an end, so that they could gather up their tools and equipment scattered about, load up the handcart and head back to the House of Gardeners, and he could finally sink into the comforting embrace of a tub of hot water. There was always another day, and what did it really matter if it was not perfect? Would it really be so tragic a misfortune that the stone was a few degrees out of an alignment that only Sensei himself could see? Would that really condemn the house of the Saeko clan to some grievous misfortune? He was coming to doubt it.

The gardeners had gathered together watching Maguro Sensei making his continuous inspection, each one silently praying that an end to the day would be called. Even the normally irrepressible Kamaboku stood looking down at the ground, lost in his own thoughts and shuffling his feet.

"It is still not right," Sensei spoke at last, finally letting out the fateful words that the gardeners were dreading to hear. The light was now beginning to fall. It had been a long day and above their heads the birds were gathering to roost.

"Kamaboku, "Sensei spoke in a firm voice, his eyes never leaving the stone before him, even though he was constantly shifting his position.

"Yes, Sensei." Kamaboku looked towards where the others were standing, their eyes avoiding his.

"It is still not right yet, we need to do more with it. It cannot be left like this."

Kamaboku looked at the weary group of gardeners about him. "Perhaps tomorrow we can bring a few more people with us, Sensei, and extra rope and levers," he said tentatively, more in hope than expectation.

Maguro Sensei pursed his lips and a frown deepening across his forehead, in the gathering gloom. "No, it would be better to get things right now while we are here. Tomorrow there will be enough work to be done to tidy up the area around the stones. You can bring a couple of the others, Shigoto and Konnyaku, and lift some of the moss from deeper in the woodland and re-plant it about the stones."

"Yes, Sensei. We can do that tomorrow, as you wish." Kamaboku's voice betrayed the sense of resignation and weariness that they were all feeling.

It then occurred to Shigoto that there were three separate and seemingly irreconcilable forces in opposition to one another: Maguro Sensei, who was clearly unhappy with the finished effect; the group of gardeners under his command, all of whom who were more than willing to call an end to the day; and then there was the stone itself. Who, apart from maybe Maguro Sensei knew what the stone was thinking? If thinking was what a stone was capable of. A stalemate existed. How much more sensible to call a halt to the day and return the following morning, refreshed, and maybe reinforced by additional helpers, to make whatever fine adjustments that needed to be made. After all nothing would change before then. Shigoto was just coming to the conclusion that seemed to him to be a sensible compromise, when Maguro Sensei once began to once more circle the stone. Then, standing a few paces away from the stone, which reached higher than his head, he seemed to lean almost imperceptibly to one side, as if he himself was the stone, and he was indicating the direction in which he wanted it to move. He then took a half dozen steps backwards, all the while fixing his complete attention on the stone, as if his eyes were boring into the rock itself, seemingly challenging the stone, pitting his will against that of several tons of stubborn, mute, rock. Then he loudly clapped his hands together three times, and closing his eyes extended one arm straight out, his finger pointing to a spot just off centre of the stone. There was a low groaning, grinding sound which seemed to spring from the earth. With that, the stone shifted on its axis, bringing the head of the stone precisely up to a vertical alignment.

The gardeners looked on in disbelief and astonishment. Kakugari, who was holding a long wooden pole, which had been used to lever stones, let go of it as he took a few involuntary steps backwards. The pole, as it fell caught Ekichū a glancing blow on the shoulder, making him to stagger back in surprise, and with a loud crash it fell to the ground causing several birds to take noisily to the air. In the silence that followed a thin shower of light grey feathers and a few leaves fluttered to the ground.

Kamaboku was the first of the gardeners to react as an uneasy peace settled again about them. "But... but... Sensei, what happened there? The stone seemed to move itself!" His voice, high pitched, quivering in shock and astonishment, eyes wide and disbelieving of the evidence before him. They all turned toward the figure of Maguro Sensei who had not moved an inch, except now his face had a serene expression.

"Pack the earth around the base of the stone, before it decides to move again. Now we have the stone as it should be, we can finish our work for today," his voice was barely audible. None of the gardeners moved. They were staring at Maguro Sensei expecting some kind of explanation for what they had apparently witnessed, held motionless by the disbelief of what their eyes were telling them.

"Why the look of surprise? When the stone is as empty as the mind, then there is no hindrance in its passage from earth to heaven. Did you think that creating gardens is simply a matter of planting trees and placing stones here and there? The garden has no beginning and no end. As for the gardener, even with his strength of arms and legs, he is no more than the sound of wind through the leaves of the tree. Do not waste your time on seeking after that which you are standing upon." With that he turned on his heels and set off through the trees leaving the gardeners to complete the task at hand.

It took a few moments before the group of disbelieving gardeners collected enough of their wits together to begin to move again. Gingerly, Kamaboku was the first to approach the stone, his heart still beating wildly, and ready to flee at a split second's notice in case the stone was tempted to shift again. Picking up a digging tool that had been abandoned nearby he warily began to throw soil around the base of the monolith.

"Come on, you heard Sensei, let's get the job finished. Kakugari, Shigoto, tamp down the earth around the stone, pack it down hard. The rest of you gather up the tools and clear up. I think it's time we got out of here. Where's Yadokari gone?"

The still disbelieving band of gardeners now burst into life, and the scene suddenly became one of frenzied activity. In a few moments the base of the stone had been packed around with earth and the tools and stray equipment had been collected and returned to the handcart. By the time they had finished the gloom of early evening was settling about them. Kamaboku was the last to leave the site. Before he did he once more approached the stone, and gently touched it with his outstretched hand, it felt solid enough, as if rooted to the very centre of the earth. Shaking his head, as if waking from a peculiar dream, he walked back to the path where the handcart stood loaded and ready to return to the store. Around it stood the other gardeners, silent and only too ready to get away.

"Where's Yadokari?" he repeated when he rejoined his comrades, but the others just shrugged their shoulders. No one had seen Yadokari since the moment the stone had moved. "Never mind, he will find his way back, let's get out of here. I don't know about anyone else but I could down a flask of *sake* myself tonight."

Shigoto and Konnyaku picked up the draw handle of the cart, and with the others leading the way they started back down the path. The cart lurched forward leaving the huddled, foetal and still quivering form of Yadokari exposed in the middle of the path.

"Don't leave me here. Hey, don't leave me here." He leapt up and ran as if his clothes were on fire, rushing to catch up with the others.

That evening back at the House of Gardeners several flasks of rice wine made an appearance, and in due course the sounds of laughter and merriment were to be heard coming from within. As he fell asleep that night Shigoto thought about Maguro Sensei, and he decided that though a strange and unfathomable man he may be, he was beginning to admire him above all others.

CHAPTER TWENTY-ONE

May 1594

Shigoto was making his way though the gardens at the end of the day's work. It had rained on and off throughout the day, and he was soaked. He was looking forward to a hot bath and a change of clothes, and had decided he would go and visit his mother. He planned on eating his main meal of the day with her and his grandmother, rather than spending the entire evening in the company of the other gardeners.

As he made his way, he stopped every now and then to look again at certain features in the gardens; the rocks and their placement had become of particular interest to him since his last conversation with Maguro Sensei. Now at every opportunity he would stop and look at the stones, to see them in the context of their arrangements, and try to understand why the rocks had been placed in just that particular position. He would walk about the stones, scrutinizing them with a close interest, and had taken to running his hands over there surfaces, as he had seen Sensei do many times. He realised that he was seeing the stones and their arrangements in a different, a new way. Previously they had for him simply existed where they were. He never questioned the whether there may have been a particular logic to their being where they were. Sensei had at times made comments as to the nature of stone arrangements, but he had not sufficiently made connections between ideas being expressed and the stones' placements. Now he felt he was beginning to see something of what had been veiled from him before. As a result when he looked at the stones now, it was with an awakened critical eye, and an expectancy that they might yield up secrets. Now the garden was beginning to evolve in his mind's eye into something far deeper than he had imagined. He loved to stop sometimes and just stand where he was, close his eyes and listen, just listen. He could hear his own heartbeat, and the sound of his own breath, he could also hear the complex tapestry of the garden's soundscape too. When it all fused within himself it seemed as if the garden, the earth, the wind, trees, and birds… creation itself were speaking directly to him, calling to him.

He had stopped to examine a rock set to the side of the path, and was now standing quite alone with eyes closed to better absorb the sounds of the garden. He became aware of the water dripping from the trees. So distracted was he by this melody, that he failed to hear the gentle crunching sounds of feet walking along the path behind him. By the time he had registered the sound, and turned around eyes now wide open, it was too late. Coming up the path were two women from the household with short stabbing steps in their tight kimono and hands clasped in front of them. One had a flat basket hanging on her arm. With a sense of surprise Shigoto saw that one of the figures was the girl he had seen dancing the Wisteria dance. Her face, her poise was unmistakeable, he had been living with her image in his mind ever since, and now here she was before him. A previous chance meeting in the garden so brief though it was had at least yielded the opportunity to discover her name, Nureba. He had clung to that fragment as if it were something precious.

"Ahh…" managed Shigoto, as he attempted to recover from his surprise.

"Well, we were just wondering who this figure might be, looking lost in the garden. Not that we expected it to be one of the gardeners, did we, Meikin-chan?" The speaker's companion shook her head lightly.

Shigoto gathered his scattered senses the best he could, but his mouth was dry, and it felt as if his tongue was stuck to his palate. One part of his mind was screaming out a thousand questions he wanted to put to this girl, yet somehow there was nothing but confusion in his mind.

"Nureba san," he at last managed to stammer out her name. "What are you doing here? I mean, is there something that you need, something I can fetch for you? There were no instructions to bring foliage to the kitchens. Nobody said anything to me." He waved his arms in a vague gesture.

"We were just taking advantage of a break in the weather. We had a few moments to ourselves, that's all," said Nureba confidently. "We thought we would take a stroll through the gardens, didn't we, Meikin-chan?" Nureba's companion nodded silently, her eyes remaining on Shigoto as if assessing and recording his reaction to this chance meeting, in order that the information may examined in greater depth at some later time.

"Oh," said Shigoto, his mind blank, unsure of the protocol of the moment. Nothing so far had prepared him for a moment such as this.

There was a quietly defiant, even challenging quality to the way Nureba looked straight into Shigoto's face. It was as if she realised the social and moral obstacles standing between them, but was prepared to take the risk and ignore all injunctions as to what was 'proper and right'. It was an unwritten but widely accepted rule that fraternisation between classes was discouraged outside of formal relationships. Not that relationships did not occur: the laws of attraction and repulsion do not always accord or align themselves with social convention. Shigoto returned the look directed toward him: he looked into the lacquer-coloured glowing eyes of Nureba and he was aware of an overriding sense of beauty. All about lay the garden and they were but actors treading its stage. After a short brutish downpour so typical of the season, the sun was making vain attempts to break through cloud cover. The ground was still absorbing the moisture and it yielded a complex, almost sweet scent. The leaves of the trees shone brilliant green, their surfaces coated wet and glistening when the sun's rays found a gap in the clouds, and from far off came the distant sound of water falling which fused with the calling of birds in the verdant canopy above them.

"Oh well..." he tried his best to recover his balance. "Well, if there's anything I can fetch for you. I mean, anything I can find for you, just ask. I know the gardens well, you know. I have known the gardens all my life. I was just... just, standing here looking at the stones. There is meaning to how they are placed, you know. The stones are very carefully set. It's the sort of thing that you learn as a gardener, you know."

Shigoto racked his memory to try and find some neat phrase that Maguro Sensei had said. Nothing at all came to mind, and all he really wanted of this moment of his life was to suspend time itself, so he could remain wholly immersed in the beauty that he felt about him, to stay as he was, caught in the web of swirling sensations and delicious emotions.

"Well, you are I'm sure, a font of knowledge concerning the gardens. But really we should not take up your precious time. I am sure you are a busy man with many responsibilities, and we are but like two butterflies. You must forgive us for holding you up. Meikin-chan, we must be on our way, how foolish and selfish we are to keep the gardener from his duties. Come, we should proceed with our walk, besides we have to be back at the apartments soon enough." Nureba broke off from looking at Shigoto and addressed her companion, who was simply nodding and smiling.

"No, I mean, it's all right. I have finished work for the day, I just have some chores to do, then I was going to see my mother," blurted out Shigoto. Already he missed having those eyes looking at him; he felt a surge of anxiety, a fear of impending separation and loss.

"No, we must be on our way. It was a pleasure and a surprise meeting you. Please accept our apologies for taking up your time." Nureba was looking his way again with her eyes that seemed to have the capacity to melt him, then turned back again to her companion. "Come, Meikin-chan, we should be on our way."

With that the two women continued moved on with short stuttering, yet flowing steps in their wooden sandals, the gravel crunching beneath their tread. Shigoto turned to watch the two figures retreat down the path, heading deeper into the gardens. His mouth hung slack, and he felt that he had been disconnected from the facility of motion or purpose. The two kimono clad women gradually dissolving into the scenery, sometimes their heads would incline toward one another as if sharing some deep secret, and they left a trail of soft laughter in their wake.

For several minutes he stood still just watching the two forms, until they disappeared from sight around a curve in the path and were swallowed by the garden. Part of him ached just to take flight and run down the path after them, but his legs would not move. His feet seemed to be rooted to the ground, as if he had now become one of the taciturn rocks he had been until so recently absorbed in. He was just about to turn away and resume whatever it was he had been intent on when something lying on the ground in front of him caught his eye. He dropped down and reached to pick up a small piece of silk. It was of the palest green with a cluster of tiny yellow flowers stitched into one corner. The handkerchief had been folded over several times, and tucked away into the folds lay a tiny sprig of grey-green foliage with a delicate citrus-like scent. Shigoto slowly stood and looked up the path in the direction that Nureba and her companion (whose name now escaped him) had gone. He wondered if it he should run to catch them up so he could return the handkerchief. But with a smile to himself, he carefully and deliberately re-folded the thin layers of cloth and tucked it away into the sleeve of his kimono. Then with light seeming to flood into his heart he resumed his way to complete the last of his chores.

When he eventually arrived back at the House of Gardeners the others were sat eating contentedly, a little banter being passed from one to another. Shigoto sat silently eating, lost among the thoughts running through his mind, not tasting the food at all.

"Hey, Shigoto," Konnyaku san called out to him, after he had emptied his bowl. "You know, if it's you who ends up with dirt stains on your kimono, and not your lady friend, then maybe you need some lessons." The room collapsed into laughter, as Shigoto's face reddened and glowed bright.

"I don't have a girlfriend, "he said defiantly.

"Then maybe it's time you quit practicing, and got yourself one." Once more the room rocked with good-humoured laughter.

Shigoto had joined a small group that would meet from time to time with Maguro Sensei to study the Tea Ceremony and also practice meditation. It gave him the chance to spend more time with his enigmatic teacher, and he never missed an opportunity to slake his thirst for knowledge. Many of the others who had come in the beginning found that their interest had gradually waned and one by one they fell away. Another of the other

The Gardener's Apprentice

regular attendees was Konnyaku san, whose presence was both a surprise and a matter of slightly jealous concern to Shigoto. Konnyaku was several years older than Shigoto, with a well-built, even brawny physique that gave him a strong physical presence. Shigoto would look across at his fellow gardener as they sat listening to Sensei elucidate some point or other. Konnyaku would be leaning forward, elbows resting on his solid thighs, face dissolved into a frown as he strove to take in the significance of what was being explained. Seeing Konnyaku out of the corner of his eye would always spur Shigoto on to make more of an effort, to renew his own determination.

One difference between the fellow gardeners began to emerge when Sensei guided them through the practical aspects of the ritual of preparing tea. A contrast would show between the intense concentration of Konnyaku, which was revealed by a certain lack of fluidity of one action flowing into the next. Shigoto's movements were lighter and easier, though he would often stumble over a detail in the order of which each aspect of the ceremony was carried. He would forget to fold the square of silk cloth in the prescribed manner before brushing it over the tea caddy, or he would forget to rotate the bowl before presenting it, and therefore not position the front of the bowl towards the guest. Sensei watched them intently as they ran through the motions, leaning forward to touch an arm or shoulder, to remind the student of his posture, or issuing a quiet word here or there by way of brief, concise instruction whenever a student lost his way. He would watch, correct, remind and encourage, but never once did he compare or contrast one student against another.

"Sensei, do you know my father well?" Shigoto and Maguro Sensei were sitting on the veranda of Kokiburi-an after an evening lesson in Tea, and the other students had left. There had been a lull in the conversation when Shigoto raised his question.

The question caught Sensei by surprise and he stiffened slightly before replying.

"Your father? No, no, I do not know him well. I see him from time to time when I have to report to the Palace. I did ask him once about teaching you the Chinese Classics, as I do for all the children there, but he was adamant I was not to. It would be true to say, Shigoto, your father and I are not close friends. Why do you ask?"

"No reason really," said Shigoto distractedly. "Well, it's just that we do not get on well. We never have really. I find my father... I find him a difficult person to understand, that's all I suppose. He is so rarely at home, it's difficult to remember the last time he was there. When I visit it's always my mother I see. Well, and my grandmother, but she is different, she's old and talks to the neighbours."

"I'll remember that, thank you for the warning," said Sensei slowly, all the while looking at Shigoto, as if he was trying to divine the meaning and intention behind the words.

Another silence wrapped around the two figures sitting on the edge of the veranda, their legs dropping down into the garden, which neither of them was really looking at.

"Did you know your father well, Sensei?" immediately Shigoto checked himself. "I'm sorry that was a rude question. Forgive me. I should not have been so personal. Excuse me." Shigoto stammered, realizing his mistake of over-familiarity with his teacher.

"That's alright. The answer to your question is, no. Since we are speaking openly to one another, I will tell you this, which may surprise you to hear. My father, I never knew, nor even my mother, I was left at a temple in Kyoto to be brought up by monks. Though when I was older, I did become curious as to whom my parents were. I wanted to find them, to know at least who they were, to be able speak to them perhaps. Don't get me wrong, by then I had learned to be content with my life. My 'family' was the temple where I lived. I had become content with that."

The honesty of the reply emboldened Shigoto to ask another question.

"Did you find out who your parents were?"

Maguro Sensei paused before he replied. "No, not exactly. But it seems my father may have had some connection with Mikura. That's partly the reason why I came here. When Lord Saeko offered me the post of Head Gardener, I accepted, hoping perhaps to find some clearer answer."

"So your father was from Mikura?" Shigoto was shocked at the intimacy and honesty of the confession.

"Not necessarily, but there seems to be a connection I have yet to make clear. May be I never will," he said with a slight smile. "Anyway, from what I know of your father, who we were talking about, he is a busy man these days with many duties attending to Lord Saeko. I do hear he advises the Lord in private. He seems to be an important man, Shigoto. Never forget that. He chose a different way for you, that is something you have accepted, so now it is your duty to follow your father's wishes to the best of your ability."

"I love my work. I love being a gardener. I will never do anything else. I want to learn Sensei, I want to learn what you know, to be able to do what you do." There was a fierce pride and determination in his tone when he spoke.

"I know that Shigoto. I have seen what you have to offer." Sensei paused and smiled again. "You know when I was studying to be a gardener myself, my Sensei said that not all those who studied would become gardeners. He would say that many people try, many people can learn how to do this job or that, but few have the ability to go beyond that. To be gardeners who really create as an artist, to really understand how to set stones, compose and create. Like the carver who can look up at a tree in the forest and see a statue of the Buddha, or the artist who can make the wind blow simply by drawing a pine branch with a few strokes on paper. There are those who can, and those who never will."

"Is Konnyaku a real gardener, Sensei?" Shigoto interjected fiercely, letting out more emotion than he had intended to do.

"Worry not about Konnyaku, Shigoto. Measure yourself against those whose work has endured from the past, that is the important thing to know. Understand their work, follow the paths where they point to. Konnyaku is Konnyaku, he is making his own way in this life."

"Sometimes I hate him," said Shigoto bluntly.

"I thought you meant your father for a moment there," and Sensei laughed lightly, trying to break through the mood of impenetrability and anger that Shigoto seemed to be clutching like a shield to his chest. "Cultivate No-Mind Shigoto. Cultivate No-Mind, leave that monkey mind of yours behind."

"What do you mean 'no-mind'? It does not make any sense. How can you have no mind? There is always something in your mind. Except when you are asleep maybe, but then there are dreams sometimes," Shigoto said.

"Here let me explain." Then Maguro Sensei stood up, and slipping into his sandals he walked over to a bamboo plant nearby. With a few short twists, he snapped off a thin cane then resumed his seat on the veranda. With his foot he smoothed out the sand on the ground in front of him. He snapped off the very end of the cane. When he was ready he turned to Shigoto again.

"Do you know the Chinese characters '*mu*' and '*shin*'?"

"No, no not really. My mother has taught me to write and read a few characters, but I don't know that many yet."

"*Mu* is like this," said Sensei, and with the end of the stick he scratched out a Chinese character 無 in the fine gravel before them. "*Shin*, is like this, 心. We also read that as *kokoro*, you know that word, do you not?" and again he wrote with a free flowing hand in the sand before them. The two characters were side by side on the ground in front of them." *Mu*, we understand the meaning of as being 'nothing', literally 'no-thing'. '*Shin*' has the meaning of 'heart' or 'spirit'. We can also read those characters together as one word, '*mushin*'. It literally means 'No Heart' or 'Empty Heart'. We can also write '*Mu*' like this. "Then Sensei drew a circle around the two characters sketched in the sand. He paused, as they both gazed at the ground in front of them. Shigoto trying desperately to puzzle out the meaning of what Sensei was trying to teach him.

"In the practice of Zen, '*mushin*' is the body and the heart together as one. That is why you have the circle. The circle is empty, it contains 'no-thing', and therefore it is empty. We can also understand that being empty, it is also empty of emptiness itself. Therefore the empty circle contains everything we need to know within it. If you look at the circle and see nothing, then you are still only seeing a part. Not the whole. Our task as students is to try and grasp the whole, and not be distracted by our monkey minds into thinking about this and that, high and low, big and small, nice and horrible, good and bad. Do you measure the depth of a pond by the height of the sky? Of course not, the pond is the pond, and the sky the sky. So do not chase after demons, which are, after all, only in your mind. Do not be distracted by Konnyaku, he is Konnyaku, not you. Konnyaku has to learn what he has to learn, and you will learn what you need to learn. It is only that which is important. Think, Shigoto, when next time you are looking at a rock arrangement, ask yourself the question: 'where is the heart of the stone?' When you want to find the heart of the stone, you must first acknowledge the heart of the stone. When a man of Zen strikes the rock with his stick, there is no sound coming from the rock, or entering into the rock. There, it's simple, is it not?"

Then Maguro Sensei leaned back and a deep laughter welled up from inside him, the spilling out into the evening. Soon Shigoto could not stop himself laughing as well.

"Hey, Shigoto, I have kept you here late. It was time you were heading back, is it not? That is more than enough for the moment."

Shigoto slipped down from the veranda and pushed his feet into the rice straw sandals waiting there for him. He stood looking down at the characters written in the sand, before extending a foot and rubbing them thoughtfully out.

"Do you wish to become my successor, Shigoto?" Sensei was looking directly at him now, those hawk-like eyes boring into him, as if he were trying to read his soul, or maybe even write something there for the future, when Shigoto would be able to read the signs more clearly.

"Successor? Successor to what? You don't mean as Head Gardener?" Shigoto was taken aback.

"Yes."

"But Sensei, that will never happen. You will have to… to… not be the Head of Gardens, how could that be? … It's not possible."

"Shigoto, even the last of the mountain flows into the sea one day as a grain of sand. If you do wish to be my successor, Shigoto, you will have to learn so much more, so much more about so many things. But do not spend too much time thinking these things over. Our fates are already spoken for; the fine cords have already been spun. Here, take this with you." Sensei pointed the bamboo cane toward him, only to pull it back swiftly as Shigoto's fingers were about to grasp it. "Hurry now, and do not be late in the morning." Maguro Sensei carefully watched as Shigoto bowed politely to him, and with a final nod of the head dismissed him. His features were expressionless, unreadable.

The Gardener's Apprentice

Slowly Shigoto made his way back to the House of Gardeners. Night had fallen and the sky was overcast with no moon showing. He knew the way back well enough, and the dark did not hold any terrors for him. He was passing a tree of considerable girth, whose branches reached far into the dark sky, his mind still turning over thoughts of his father, Maguro Sensei, and Konnyaku, trying to piece it all together in the light of Sensei's teaching. Suddenly something grabbed him by the shoulder and pulled him back. He was wrenched back into the present, his heart beating wildly.

"So, what a good student we have been, eh. Stopping over late with teacher. Think that impresses any one, do you?" The voice was oily and laden with sarcasm.

"Konnyaku, what the hell are you playing at. Let go, you idiot." Shigoto flung out an arm at the hand that held him tight; he missed, and flailed at the air.

"Nobody is impressed by that. That would not even knock a firefly from the air, "taunted Konnyaku, who was managing to stay behind Shigoto, as they manoeuvred about.

"Let me go. What are you doing, jumping out on people anyway? Have you been drinking again?"

"Drinking. No, I have not been drinking," sneered Konnyaku. "I suppose you have been sucking up to Sensei. Telling Sensei stories about that mean person Konnyaku, I suppose? Sensei, Konnyaku does not care much for me," he sneered in a mean spirited, child-like voice.

"No, I haven't. Let go, you idiot."

"Idiot, eh. Idiot, am I? Well, I have something for you, young Shigoto. Young mister garden apprentice." And with that Konnyaku let go of the grip he had on Shigoto's shoulder and grabbed him by one ear, twisted it painfully, then landed a foot on Shigoto's backside, sending him sprawling in the dirt.

He landed heavily, the air gone from his lungs momentarily. When he looked up Konnyaku was standing over him, his face looming out of the blackness, a satisfied grin across his face.

"Idiot, am I? That requires an apology, Shigoto. A face in the dirt kind of apology."

"Never, go to hell with you," Shigoto spat out, his ear aching from being twisted so violently, and his breathing fast and laboured. Konnyaku's foot loomed out of the darkness. Shigoto just managed to dodge the blow to his head at the very last moment. He felt the wind of it pass his stinging ear. He scrambled to his feet, before Konnyaku could launch another kick in his direction, then stood and faced his opponent.

"You know what they say about you, don't you Shigoto. You know what everyone says behind your back?" Again, the sneering, almost pitying voice.

They were moving slowly about one another, as if locked in some ancient, ritual dance, each waiting for the other to present an opportunity to strike, or to offer a sign of acquiescence. In the dark all that could be heard was their heavy breathing, the soft shuffle of their feet over the ground.

"You know what they say," Konnyaku repeated. "You're a bastard. The person who calls himself your father, he isn't that at all. He never lies with your mother, that's why. You're a bastard. Cursed. And now you are trying to get on the good side of Sensei. Hah."

Shigoto no longer saw the world with reason, the pent up fury, anger, and bitter thoughts he had tried to speak of to Sensei, all exploded in his mind. He hurled himself at the taller man in front of him, quite without any regard for risk of injury to himself. Konnyaku brought his arms up to fend off Shigoto, and tried to dodge out of the way, but Shigoto caught him a glancing blow to the side of his body which it was enough to push him off balance. He stumbled down onto one knee. As he pushed himself up again, still confident in his ability to fight an opponent a good head shorter and several years younger, Shigoto came at him again. This time Konnyaku did not have his feet well planted on the ground; as he brought his arms up to meet the onrushing Shigoto he was slightly off balance, and the speed of Shigoto's approach surprised him. As Konnyaku rose up, Shigoto with a wild haymaker swing, caught him hard on the side of the head, The sound reverberated through the darkness, and several crows roosting in the tree above began squawking and beating their wings. Konnyaku went down with a heavy thud, and stayed there.

He lay on the ground shaking his head to clear it, to bring himself back to this world. When his vision cleared Shigoto was standing above him chest heaving and fists still tight clenched out in front.

"Stand up," he ordered to his prostrated foe, "Stand up, will you!"

"Whoa, slow down Shigoto. Hey, take it easy."

"Get up, or I'll kick you right there."

"Alright, alright, I'm sorry. I apologise. I said something out of order, I apologise." Konnyaku's voice was almost pleading now. Shigoto knew he would not have to hit him again. As his breathing quietened, so the red mist that had filled his sight, slowly started to dissolve. He shook his head, and when he looked down again, there was only the blackness around, and Konnyaku lying in front of him, propped on one elbow whilst he gingerly feeling his jaw with the other hand.

"You've got quite something of a punch, did you know? Where did you learn that from, eh? Don't tell me Maguro Sensei taught you that too." Konnyaku's voice had lost all the bitter taste.

"Why did you call me a bastard? What do you mean people talk behind my back?"

"Listen, it's just the way folks are. They love to talk, any gossip goes round and round, somebody picks up one thing, adds a few juicy details here and there, and then passes it on. You know how it is. This is a small place we live in after all. Everybody knows everybody's business. People do love to gossip. It's like that. Hardly anything is true anyway. I hate to think what they say about me, when I'm not around."

"I don't know about any of that," said Shigoto. "I am only trying to be a gardener, to learn what I can."

"Hey, give me a hand. Help me up will you. You know, that was quite something of a punch. You are a surprise, Shigoto." There were the beginnings of a tone of admiration coming into Konnyaku's voice.

Shigoto hesitated a moment, half expecting some new trick from his opponent, then held out his hand and pulled him up. When they were both standing up facing each other, Konnyaku was smiling, a lopsided smile and rubbing his jaw still.

"Listen, I am sorry. I mean it, I apologise. Tell you what, let's go find some rice wine, eh. I think we both could do with a drink or two. When we get back to the house, we will just give them a story. I shall tell them a girl smacked me in the face. They'll like that. That will get their tongues wagging, eh. Come on."

"You will have a bruise there, on your face I mean. I am sorry too."

"Forget it. It's my fault. I spoke out of turn. I didn't take you too seriously before. I promise I won't make that mistake again. Come on let's find something to drink, I need it."

CHAPTER TWENTY-TWO

May 1594

The following day the gardeners had divided into two groups to attend to a variety of tasks around the grounds. Shigoto was with Kamaboku in a corner of the gardens that had been set aside as a nursery and storage area for plants. Here were gathered plants and trees of many different kinds and sizes, many of which were being pruned, shaped and developed until they were deemed ready to be placed into the gardens. Some trees were the height of a man on horseback, and they shared the space with a varied collection of principally evergreen shrubs, some barely tall enough to reach Shigoto's knee. There were many pines, which were in the process of being trained into a variety of forms. The long stiff needles had been plucked from the stems, leaving only clumps of the dark green foliage clinging to ends of nascent branches and side shoots. Kamaboku and Shigoto were clearing the ground around the base of the trees and shrubs of weeds, with one hand pulling a small, hand-sized, curved and serrated blade through the crust of soil to loosen the roots, the other hand pulling out the unwanted plant by its stem. They were crouched on their haunches working methodically through one patch of ground before shuffling on to the next.

Hearing Sensei's voice call out, Shigoto took the opportunity to stand up and stretch his sore limbs, and straighten his back.

"Good morning Sensei."

"Good morning Shigoto. Good morning Kamaboku san."

"Morning Sensei, I trust you are well yourself."

"Indeed, I am, Kamaboku," replied Sensei amiably. "I have come to tell you that an important tea ceremony is being spoken about. The tea garden will need particular attention to make sure that all is in order."

"Ahh, will there be many guests Sensei?" asked Kamaboku with a smile.

"Invitations are being sent out now. Maybe a half dozen at the most will come, no, not a big gathering. But they will be people of the highest rank, friends of Lord Saeko himself."

"Indeed, the tea garden will need to be tidied before then." Kamaboku rubbed his chin.

"Of course, I was heading over that way myself now to see what will need doing. You can join me there in a while, and we can go over what jobs will need to be completed. There will be some pruning and cleaning to do before, and some of the azaleas may need replacing by better, fuller plants. What azaleas are there here ready to be moved?" Maguro Sensei looked around the area at the array of plants available.

"There are some over there which were moved from the Winding Stream garden about a year or so ago. They have good shapes, now they have filled out a lot." Kamaboku pointed towards a group of shrubs.

"Good, then you can come over before the end of the morning." Sensei turned to go. "Oh, and bring Shigoto along with you too."

"Yes, Sensei. We will be there." He returned to a crouch, his eyes followed the retreating back of Sensei, and then Kamaboku turned back to Shigoto.

"Hear that? A tea ceremony, eh. Must be some big deal, eh. Do you think we will get an invitation to be there too?" Kamaboku's eyes lit up with amusement.

The two gardeners resumed their work. Above them the tall crowns of trees sporadically broke into waves of motion, before settling once more into their preordained shapes. Eventually it was Shigoto who broke the silence.

"Have you ever been to a tea ceremony, Kamaboku san? I mean a proper tea ceremony, with guests and everything." Shigoto asked.

"No, now you don't really think the likes of me would be invited, do you, eh?' He chuckled at the thought of the possibility. "No, they will all be fine men who come. Men of good standing all of them, and with fine manners to match, no doubt. They would not want the likes of me, a simple clumsy gardener there. No, I have had tea with Sensei, though, a few times. Sensei does not mind, he loves his tea and will drink with anyone."

"I know. I go sometimes to study Tea with Sensei. I enjoy it," said Shigoto.

"That's good, drinking tea in that way is something that gentlemen do. Sensei likes you, you know. I can see it in him. He will teach you whatever you ask. Sensei knows a lot of things, you know, he is a cultivated man is Maguro Sensei. You can trust old Kamaboku's eyes on that one, Shigoto."

"He came from Kyoto didn't he? He told me that one time." Shigoto sensed the conversation heading into areas of great interest to him.

"Yes, so they say, a Zen priest and all. Fancy that. Makes you wonder sometimes how we end up as we do, doesn't it? There he was, a priest in the capital, at some big monastery or temple the one moment, and then Lord Saeko brings him to Mikura to be Head Gardener. Hey, Shigoto, do you think that I will end up in a temple in Kyoto sometime, eh? An inexpensive geisha house would do, I dare say." With that Kamaboku rocked with laughter at his own humour so much that he over-balanced and landed on his back, among the desiccating weeds and seedlings they had recently torn from their fragile hold to the soil. When he had recovered his poise sufficiently he asked Shigoto, "You ever think of those sorts of things?"

"No, not really. Have you been to different places in Japan, Kamaboku san?"

"Oh no, you must be joking. When would the likes of me get the chance to travel? Not that I would even if I had the chance. Though I have ventured all over this island. When I was an apprentice in the times before Maguro Sensei. We travelled all over the island collecting plants for the garden. Hikishio Sensei, the Head Gardener then, was especially keen on that. Sometimes we would be away for days at a time, sleeping out in the open, rain, sun, and frost, whatever. We would collect trees and plants from the wild, from nearly every part of Mikura. Sometimes we had to go backwards and forwards many times to bring back the things we found, and even sent word to the farmers to come and help gather things in and bring it back to Hirame. What wonderful times those were. I was about your age, I suppose, when I went the first time. Could not believe how big this island was myself."

"You brought back trees for the gardens?"

"How do you suppose these things got here in the first place? They did not just spring out of the ground by magic, you know. Sometimes rocks too, then we would have to send for oxen and timber sledges to drag pieces back. One time Lord Saeko, when he was younger was out with his falcon hunting and he saw a stone he wanted brought back. It took us a week to get it here. But we did it. It's on the shore of the lake now."

The Gardener's Apprentice

"A week? To bring one stone back?" Said Shigoto incredulously.

"Sure. It's the tall, square looking one, with red markings on one side. The colour is supposed to bring good luck, wealth, that sort of thing. There are no really good trees left on Mikura, not one's you can get at anyway. Sometimes the farmers bring trees in, but all the best ones have probably gone by now. We had the last of them, they are all here in the gardens now. You look next time, I mean really look at what is about, and think how all these things got where they are. The gardeners of Hirame have been building this garden since... well, a long time anyway."

Kamaboku had settled on the ground his legs now drawn up under him in a comfortable manner. His weeding tool lying idle at his side.

"Oh yes, we travelled all over this place in those times, you know. On the other side of the mountains there's a place where the earth looks as is has been ripped apart. Imagine that, it looks as if a giant being came along and tore at the earth with his bare hands, bursting it open like flesh slashed open by a sword. You are walking along one minute, and then the ground just drops away, straight down." He motioned with his hand, the fingers plummeting downwards. "Down where, who knows? "

"What's down there?" said Shigoto, becoming intrigued at the prospect of a story developing.

"Well ... There's a stream that falls into it at one end, you can hear the water running, but you cannot see it. We tried to enter the gorge from below but the passage became blocked with huge boulders and there was no way through. The sides are sheets of bare rock, but in the cracks there are trees and other plants that have grown there from seed. Because the roots cannot run far, the plants stay small and have twisted shapes from growing out towards the light. Some of the best pines in the gardens came from there. But those trees came at some price, they were hard to get at you know."

"How do you mean?" said Shigoto encouraging his companion to elaborate.

Kamaboku looked across at him a moment before continuing. "There are the bones of someone in that gorge to this day, unless the foxes have carried them away and buried them by now." He paused, as if to invite the inevitable question.

"Bones, whose bones?"

"There was one tree Hikishio Sensei was especially keen to get at. A pine, a real beauty, may be seventy, eighty years old, older perhaps, who knows. The branches were short and stubby, and shaped like perfect clouds. You would not have had to do a single piece of pruning to it. Not like these," he gesticulated at the trees in the ground about them. "It was the sort of tree that you dream of finding, and may be you do, but only once or twice in your life. The trouble was it was growing high in a crack in the rock face, there were no ledges nearby, and the rock fell straight down, below it there was nothing, a sheer drop. There was no way to climb down to it. It was near the waterfall, so there was always a mist, you can imagine how slippery that rock face was. The only way to get at it was to suspend someone down on a rope while they tried to dig the tree with as much root as possible out of that crack. Hell of a job, just like hanging off the end of a rope in a rainstorm. Sometimes you would have to hack away at the rock first to get at the tree roots, they would be so wedged in there. We had done it before, going down a rock face on ropes, I had done it myself and got some decent trees that way. I had no fear in those days, climb anything, go anywhere. I was young then. Bit older than you but not much probably. We would be paid a reward when we managed to bring particularly good trees back."

"Did you get the pine then?" Shigoto was eager to get to the climax, and could vividly picture Kamaboku hanging perilously over a yawning chasm.

"I did not go down, someone else did. Then the rope snapped." Kamaboku paused in his narrative.

"The rope broke? Did you get the tree though? Is it here in the garden still?" Shigoto was impatient to get to the climax of the story.

"The rope broke." Kamaboku quietly repeated. "The tree is probably still there. A bit older now no doubt, but still there."

"What happened to the gardener?"

"Still there too, I guess. As I say, unless the foxes have stolen his bones."

"Who was it, the gardener, I mean?"

"Oh, just someone I knew. That's all, just someone I once knew very well." He spoke in a far-away tone. A gust of wind caught the trees above their heads again, and the crowns swayed and rocked drunkenly. "Hey, we should get moving. Sensei wanted us to meet him at the Shikiami-an teahouse didn't he? We can leave the tools here, we'll be coming back later."

The modest building was set within its own garden: with mud plastered walls, and an overhanging roof of deep thatch, the elegant curves of which were designed to resemble a fisherman's net. It became the focus of intense activity in the days leading up to the tea ceremony. Its two rooms were swept and cleaned meticulously in preparation, the main room with its *tatami* mat covered floor, a small alcove built into one corner. Set into the floor was a square hearth with a deep polished wooden frame. The interior walls were a dark coloured plaster flecked with short pieces of straw. The windows were covered with opaque white paper, which let in a soft light. One sliding door led to smaller room at the rear, where the tea utensils were stored. Another small square sliding door, the formal entry point, was set into the opposite corner from the alcove, its size so constrained, a grown man would have to enter the room on all fours. To the front of the building was a small, but immaculately groomed garden. The whole scene gave the impression of a bucolic retreat.

The date of the tea ceremony had been set for the tenth day of Fourth month, and at the appointed hour a small group of Lord Saeko's oldest friends gathered at Hirame Palace, each in his own way was a distinguished member of Mikura society. Isogashii Okane, a well provisioned merchant from Mikura, with a round ruddy face, whose wife had recently retired from this world to take vows and enter a nunnery. Cruel tongues dared to suggest it was because of her short-fused husband's habit of loudly whistling traditional tunes to overcome his fear of sleeping. Yukuri Kani, a nature poet, whose diminutive, wind-blown figure, reminded some folk of an abandoned scarecrow, but he was a writer with a reputation that had reached far beyond the confines of the island of Mikura. Kirifuda Shiku, a venerable retainer of Lord Saeko's, who had a particular skill with poetry and painting, and had a encyclopaedic knowledge of herbal plants and their uses. Kutsushita no Keita, a willowy tea master, the oldest of the group, who sported a large curved whalebone hearing-trumpet hung by a lanyard about his neck.

The teahouse sat in isolation, well away from the main Palace buildings, surrounded by clumps of tall maple trees, with their silvery grey trunks and branches that stretched up to suspend a filigree of gleaming green leaves above the scene. The guests passed through a simple arched gateway made of logs the thickness of a man's forearm, the surfaces of which had been scorched black to preserve the timber. Then they followed a newly wetted-down stepping stone path, which led to an open-sided waiting arbour with a bench seat and thin cryptomeria shingles for a roof. When all the final preparations had been completed Lord Saeko himself emerged from the building. He walked towards the group gathered in muted conversation at the arbour.

"My dear friends," he greeted them in a firm voice. "Please excuse the tardiness of an old man. The tearoom is ready to receive you. Please step forward." Then he left them and re-entered the teahouse from the rear of the building.

The four men filed forward encouraging the other to take the lead toward the building. They took a stepping stone path across a carpet of deep, rich textured moss, and at a junction in the path they crouched down in turn at a low stone water basin, and lifting the bamboo ladle to take fresh cold water from the basin poured it deliberately over their fingers and refreshed their mouths, and then in a mood of contemplative quiet resumed their way, which concluded at a large raised flat stone lying beneath the open small square doorway. One by one they removed their shoes and crawled inside. The last guest to enter slid the door closed behind him.

As an expectant hush settled on the dim lit interior, the door at the rear of the room slid back and Lord Saeko entered. With arthritic care he knelt at the open doorway and bowed stiffly towards the four guests kneeling around the room. Then Lord Saeko came forward and slowly settled himself on to the host's mat in front of the alcove, next to the hearth, where a black, heavy metal kettle gently sighed. Behind him in the alcove a long scroll painting depicting a spring scene hung down, and set below it a sparse flower arrangement of young maple leaves floating in a black bowl. Despite the social ranking of company, the atmosphere was one of humility, restraint and conviviality.

With deliberate movements Lord Saeko served each guest with three small sweet cakes, and then prepared a bowl of lightly whipped, thick emerald green tea for every person present. Each man drank his tea by raising the bowl to his lips three times. After they had drunk the tea each bowl was inspected, admired and briefly commented on. Each guest was served a different bowl which in some subtle way reflected the season. After the bowls had been admired and had been put away, the host signalled to the assembled company with a slow gesture of his fan that the ceremony was over. The host was the first to break the intense stillness that followed.

"Dear friends, please sit comfortably. The tea bowls are finished with and now it is time to talk." He paused as the men relaxed their postures. "Each one of you is a follower of the way of Tea, and you are also my oldest friends. You Kutsushita san, you and I are the same age, we even knew each other as children. Kirifuda san, before you retired from the world to follow the path of Tea and prayer, we hunted with falcons and hawks together many times. Yukkuri san, Mikura's finest poet and native son, are you not? Okane Isogashii san, you became a wealthy man through the sharpness of your instincts. We have been linked with one another over the years, is that not so?"

The guests all murmured their assent. Lord Saeko waited for the sound to settle, then continued: "As you may have heard, this winter I have been ill, and it came to remind me I am no longer a young man, as none of us are any longer." He held up a hand to stall any protest. "It has brought me to consider privately the question of my succession as lord of the clan of Saeko. I am strong enough yet to hold onto the reins, but in my heart I think about nothing more than spending more time drinking tea with my friends, writing poems, and talking about past times. Therein lies my dilemma."

"But Lord Saeko, we are amazed how you speak." The first to reply was Yukkuri, the anxious faced nature poet, who was dressed as was his wont in a worn kimono that had seen far better days. "Why, you are the very picture of health and vigour. We were expecting to hear an announcement of a new born son, not such a sad speech!" At this remark the men relaxed into convivial laughter.

"You poets are all the same, silver-tongued and worse, flatterers," grumbled Lord Saeko, and they all laughed again. "In all seriousness, please hear me out. I already have two healthy sons to consider, and that is enough. The eldest, Kezure, a fearless warrior in a time of crisis, but not someone who cares for the details of peace; and Ito, his younger brother who has rapidly acquired the silky skills of an administrator beyond his years, but he would faint before a sword can be lifted from its scabbard. In the natural course of events, Kezure, the eldest, would be my named successor. Can I trust the fate of this family and Mikura itself, to a hothead who would love nothing better than to single-handedly invade the Middle Kingdom itself, simply out of boredom? Or, do I choose a son, who spends his days in the treasury with an abacus, and his nights there too, no doubt? I have asked you here my friends to hear your words of counsel and listen to your sage advice. I am sure I need not remind you, that anything discussed between us in this room will remain behind when we leave. Already I have to keep the two sons well apart and well occupied. Mikura cannot afford to have them locking antlers, there would be too much at stake for us all in our own different ways."

All afternoon the meeting continued, each man spoke, giving his opinion in respect of the topic raised by the host. When all had spoken their view, conversation drifted towards the arts, a field the guests were much more comfortable with. Finally, accompanied by generously taken sips of rice wine, the group set about the pleasures of mutually composing poems, with verses linked by subject and subtle word play. The wine mellowed their senses noticeably, and by the time the meeting broke up the tone of their voices was easy, intimate and rising in volume. On leaving the teahouse the host reluctantly and a little wearily, bade his dear friends farewell. The group of old friends, their spirits buoyed by companionship and fuelled by *sake* lingered on by the slim gateway once more, taking leave of one another and offering thanks for the pleasure of each other's company reluctant to break the renewed bonds of companionship that had prevailed throughout the day.

One evening a few days later, an altogether more modest group gathered about Maguro Sensei to study Tea broke up from their session. As they did so Sensei took Shigoto to one side.

"Shigoto, a word please, before you leave." He turned his thin face and shaven head toward his apprentice. "You seem to be making good progress with Tea. You enjoy it do you not?"

"Oh yes, Sensei. I find it all so interesting, and I especially enjoy the stories you tell," said Shigoto.

"Good. I'm glad you find something in all this, Shigoto. It's good, very good. That's the way it should be. Listen, I want you to go across to the Shikiami-an teahouse on your way back to the House of Gardeners. Keita no Kutsushita san is using it again tomorrow. Please check that everything is in order, and that it has been cleaned well. Go now before it gets dark, please."

Shigoto left his teacher's modest dwelling beaming to himself. Not only had he been personally singled out for praise and encouragement that evening, but Sensei had also entrusted him to a task bearing some responsibility. With head held high and shoulders drawn back, he made his way swiftly to the teahouse.

When he arrived at the gateway that marked the rear entrance to the tea garden, he stopped and briefly looked around. Nothing much had changed from the time when the garden and building had been spring-cleaned in anticipation of Lord Saeko's Tea meeting with his friends. Shigoto pressed on towards the building. As he approached, coming out of the now deepening shadows, he halted in his tracks. He thought he could hear the sound of voices; he proceeded carefully around the building to see if any one was there. The teahouse was used by a variety of members of the family, and he certainly did not wish to disturb any one who may be using the room. The paper-covered sliding doors were shut at the front, as were the windows and there were

The Gardener's Apprentice

no shoes to be seen at the entrance. There could not be anyone inside. Looking across the front garden he could see no one there either. He was just about to move again, when the sound of voices came again. This time with surprise he thought he could hear the voices coming from the interior of the building. These were not the voices of friends enjoying the gentle pursuit of Tea, but the sound of passionate argument. Unsure as to the best course to take, Shigoto decided to edge closer to the building and try and establish who was there. He crept up to a deep shadowed side of the teahouse, and crouched down below a window.

"... Anyway it is for you to say. You have heard the facts, and it is for you to choose which side you're on. The time is coming for action. I for one am not prepared to sit on my hands for much longer. It is up to you, to decide where you stand on these matters. I need not remind you that you are already a long way down this particular road. Everybody will have the final choice to make when the time comes to act. Believe me that time is coming soon. " The voice growled with an impatient authority.

"Sire, you have only ever received the best of my advice on these matters. You know where I stand. If we rise, then we rise as one."

"Good, you are a man who ... What was that? There was a noise. Listen!"

In shuffling forward a little to strain to hear what was being said, Shigoto's shoulder scraped across the rough plastered wall of outside of the teahouse making a dull noise. As the voices suddenly halted inside, he froze in panic. He heard rapid footsteps, as the occupants rushed to their feet to investigate. The door to the kitchen was roughly slid back, and then slammed shut again. The sliding doors at the front of the building were hastily pushed open.

"Check outside the front, look in the garden, go around the building, hurry. Look everywhere." There was tense apprehension and urgency in the instructions. Quickly and silently as he could Shigoto slipped into the narrow space between the underside of the floor of the teahouse and the ground. It was as dark as the thickest night under there. He lay flat out, not daring to move a muscle, hugging the dry earth, and silently praying it would swallow him whole, wishing his heart would stop pounding so noisily. As he lay there, he watched through one open eye, as a pair of sandaled feet rushed past the spot where a moment or two before he had been crouching. Dull thuds of footsteps pacing on the floor inches above him resounded through the dusty cavity.

"I cannot see any one." The sandals had returned to the front of the building.

"Are you sure? You looked everywhere?"

"Yes, I would have seen anyone about. It must have been a mouse or animal of some sort."

By craning his neck Shigoto could see a second pair of feet, unusually shod in leather shoes appearing on the ground near the first, at the front of the building. The two sets of feet were pointing towards one another. Shigoto held his breath. His head was beginning to spin, and his lungs were burning. He tried to pretend he was meditating.

"We had better go. Take different ways back though. Damn! I wish I had a sword with me, but it would arouse suspicion in here. So, we know where we stand anyway. You are with us now." Then the feet were gone.

How long he lay there after the unexpected visitors to the teahouse had gone, Shigoto did not know. The teahouse and garden had fallen silent, apart from the wind moving stealthily through the trees. The last of the light had been wholly consumed by the night. He remained there until he felt he could slowly open his hands and relinquish his grip on the earth beneath him. His body began to relax, and gradually he brought his breathing under some degree of control again. As his head cleared of anxiety and fear, he crawled out from his hiding place, stopping every few moments to check and check again that he was truly alone. When he was sure, he finally emerged and ran out of the garden through the rear gateway, only halting when he was well clear. As he hurriedly brushed down the front of his tunic with his hands, there was one consideration that kept reverberating though his mind. At first it had seemed so illogical a notion that it had barely warranted any attention at all, but the thought stubbornly persisted, orbiting insistently in his mind. Of the two voices of the unseen and unexpected occupants of the teahouse, one he did not recognise at all, the other was all too familiar. So recognizable in fact, that to somehow link its presence with the scraps of conversation he had overheard seemed foolish and absurd at best. All the while as he cautiously made his way back to the House of Gardeners, two questions spun through his mind. 'What was my father doing there? Who was he speaking to?'

That night Shigoto dreamt a mouse was tearing frenziedly with its teeth at a bulging sack, until the coarse material gave away and the grain spewed out across a highly polished floor of a dark and locked room. As it did, someone came into the room and walked across the floor crushing the seeds with the soles of a pair of leather shoes.

CHAPTER TWENTY-THREE

June 1594

One evening when the gardeners were settling down for another sultry night at the House of Gardeners, Kamaboku san arrived bustling with energy. Even before he had quite removed his sandals in the entryway and stepped up into the main room, he shouted out his news.

"There is a new gardener starting tomorrow, what do you think of that, eh? Sensei just told me, I have just come from talking to him. He was telling me about the work for the morning, and then casual as you like, he drops in that there is a new man starting."

"Fine. That's all we need, another kid, who does not know what to do!" was Konnyaku's gloomy assessment of the situation.

"No, no. He's a man," said Kamaboku. "Not a young one. Anyway, Shigoto is coming on fine, he's learning well enough, eh. No it's a man. Heaven knows where he's come from. He's not a Mikura man, Sensei did say that at least. Next time anyone goes

The Gardener's Apprentice

by the kitchens, ask around there, someone may have picked up some news."

Kamaboku came and sat down by the hearth, the other gardeners closed in around him for further gossip. Even Shigoto was intrigued enough to ignore the slight directed towards him and pull forward to hear more.

"So, who is he? Where is he from?" asked Yadokari.

"That's a queer thing," Kamaboku left the rest of the sentence hanging in the air.

"What's a queer thing? Get on with it. Who is he?"

"Sensei did not say. He seemed angry about the whole thing, if you ask me. Strange, eh? Just said it was of no importance. Boom, and that was the end of it. You know how Sensei can be sometimes, eh." Kamaboku shook his head and wiped the sweat from the top of his head.

They did, they all knew how Sensei could be sometimes.

"Oh, well, we will all find out tomorrow soon enough I guess. There is a lot of work to be done. I am not so sure that it can all get done, even with this new person... even if he is any good at all. Oh well, eh. Anything to drink about?"

"I thought it was going to be good news," whined Konnyaku, as he made his way back to his sleeping place.

"Why do you assume the worst? May be he will be a nice person." Shigoto felt the need for someone to speak up for the unknown quantity.

"Sure, sure, Shigoto. Everything will be wonderful, eh." Kamaboku turned to him with a mild smile. "It's funny, Sensei was definitely cross about the whole thing, though. One thing I have learned for sure about that man, is that the time to duck out the way, is when he says nothing, eh. Oh well, perhaps tomorrow will shed some light on the matter for sure."

Shigoto could only mutely concur.

The following morning the gardeners were hard at work at the edge of the Great Dragon Pond. Their task was to lift up all the pebbles of a section of beach, sweep away any leaves, pine needles or other detritus and then replace the pebbles in as natural a manner as possible. It was slow tedious work. Nothing further had been said about the imminent arrival of the "new man", and by the time they started work, there had been no sign either. Kakugari and Ekichū were pruning some of the upper branches of a pine tree growing above the beach, which the others were engaged with cleaning and making good. All of a sudden there was the sound of a bird calling, and the sound came from the pine tree above.

The Mikura gardeners had developed a system of communicating with one another whilst working in the extensive gardens. They would not have been allowed to shout instructions or exchange banter among themselves. There was a code of conduct they were expected to follow, part of which followed along the lines, that gardeners should work, and not be heard. The human is a resourceful creature, and in response to this condition, the gardeners had over many years developed a vocabulary of birdcalls. Between them developed an understanding as to how these coded signals could be interpreted. It had the additional benefit of providing them with a shared, hidden language which contributed in no small way to drawing them closer as a group. It was always a contention of Konnyaku's, that Shigoto was not a fully accepted member of their inner circle, precisely because Shigoto had not mastered complete fluency with these signals. Indeed it was only a couple of years previously that Shigoto realised that not all the bird sounds he heard about him actually came from the feathered variety. He had been learning through the good offices of Kamaboku, but had trouble mastering the various ways of shaping his tongue to get the appropriate effects. The other gardeners refused to countenance anyone using this hidden means of communication until they had proved an ability to pull off the trick with fluidity. Their feeling was that if any one tried and failed, it may lead to their "secret tongue" becoming common knowledge, and this would scupper the whole process.

On hearing the urgent sounding mating call of the Green Insect Catcher, all the gardeners looked up. It was warning note that a person, or persons unknown were approaching, and generally served to quickly refocus everyone's attention to the work in hand.

"Hello, I am Tanuki. The Head of Gardens, Maguro san sent me here. He said you would be here, and I was to help you. Which one of you is Kamaboku san?"

They all looked up to see a tall, well-built figure standing on the bank above where they were working amongst the rounded pebbles at the water's edge. He had a friendly open smile playing about his lightly bearded face.

"I am," replied Kamaboku, bowing with a nod of the head, unsure as how to address the stranger, of whom Sensei had forewarned, but sadly not furnished him with any further details of.

"Oh, pleased to meet you," said Tanuki, as he jumped down to join them, in the process absently kicking over a pile of rubbish, which had been swept into a neat heap. "Maguro san asked me to tell you I was to join in with the work you are doing. I am a gardener too, you know. Been a gardener for many a year. Lovely work being outside all the time and all that. Still hot though, eh? The weather I mean, guess the rainy season will be here soon enough, eh?"

"Well, you had better start by knowing, it's 'Maguro *Sensei*', or '*Sensei*'," corrected Kamaboku, speaking with his foreman tones.

"Oh sure. Maguro Sensei sent me. What do you want me to do?" The stranger again beamed a broad smile at them all standing before him. Then noticing two heads staring down at him from the pine tree, he said, "Oh hello, did not see you up there. I am Tanuki. The new gardener." Again the winning smile was flashed. The two heads silently withdrew, and moments later a thin trickle of pieces of pruned branches and dead pine needles recommenced to shower down around the base of the tree.

"I am Shigoto. Shigoto, Under Gardener here at Hirame Palace, and apprentice to Maguro Sensei. Pleased to meet you," said Shigoto, and he bowed politely, though not excessively.

Later that evening mother and son were sitting alone together in the waiting arbour near the Plum Field, it looked out toward the western sky, and had become a favourite place for them to walk to on a fine evening. Nobody ventured there much out of season so they would have no other company on their walks.

"Oh, you know your father, always engaged with the service of the Lord Saeko. He is a busy man Shigoto. Such a busy man these days."

"So, what has that to do with anything? Too busy for his family to be a father. I am busy, as a gardener too, you know. I have duties and responsibilities. Does he not want to be a father for some reason? Is that what it is?" He stood up suddenly and paced the floor of the shelter. He felt a hot pang of anger suddenly well up, and tears began to prick his eyes. Shigoto's mother looked across at her son, her hurting son. As ever she wrapped him in the open smile of a mother, compassion unequivocally dispensed, all without a word. Shigoto was disarmed and his gaze fell from her face to the floor, and he probed no further, preferring to remain in a place that he recognised all too well. He sat back down beside his mother who had remained seated. "Anyway, I am busy with my life. Sensei is teaching me things. I go and sit for meditation most mornings, at first light. I also visit in the evening. Other people go sometimes too, different people, even Konnyaku. Though he is rarely there in the morning. He likes his sleep too much. Sensei can do this magic stuff with rocks, it's very strange you know. You know he can make stones move by themselves and things like that. I want to learn to do that. "

"It's good, Shigoto-chan," his mother remarked. "He is a good man, a man of religion. Yes, you learn from him. And what about the others, how are you getting on with them now." She spoke tenderly aware she was holding a string attached to his heart.

"We have this new person started today. He's called Tanuki san. I liked him, the others didn't, I could see that straight away," he laughed to himself. "They are suspicious of him for some reason. I saw that. They are like that, it's like they are part of a gang and they... they are suspicious of anyone not in their gang. I am not really in that 'gang' either. They are all older than me, they like to drink sometimes when they can."

"I trust you don't drink with them," his mother's face remained calm.

"No, I have had some *sake*, but it's not nice stuff they get. Yadokari gets some from some friend of his who makes it. Nobody minds much. No, they just seem to kind of stick together. Kamaboku is fine with me, and we always get on well. He's a nice guy, he's always showing me things, how to do this and that. The others don't much, they just criticise when you do something wrong. Make comments for ages, you know. Kamaboku is great, we talk when we are working, well, sometimes, you know. When it's just the two of us. He tells me about things in the garden. He really loves the garden, he was an apprentice like me once. He's a funny guy, he's got wonderful stories about what happened long ago." Shigoto's face relaxed into a smile. "No, I liked this new guy, he seems alright. I could show him stuff, you know. I know how to tie the various branches together now. When we take branches and foliage to the kitchens, they have to be tied certain ways, depending on what they are. It's complicated; there are at least four different ways of tying them. Bet you didn't know that."

"No, I did not. Now I have learned something too," and they both laughed this time. Then there was a long pause. It was still pretty warm in the evening, but the clouds were building with the promise of relieving rain not too far away, Shigoto's mother took a handkerchief from her broad cloth belt and dabbed her forehead before carefully tucking it away again.

"I hit Konnyaku. We had a fight, a while ago."

"Shigoto-chan, you didn't tell me. When did this happen?" His mother was now paying full attention to him.

"I hit him in the face, knocked him down, and he had a lump on the side of the face the following morning. He has been all right with me since. It's funny, we have got on better since that happened," he felt defensively defiant, but also a relief came with finally letting something out.

"But Shigoto-chan, do the others know? What has Sensei had to say? He would not approve of such a carry on, I'm sure. What was the cause of this?" His mother had not expected this. "Sensei is a man of religion, he would not approve at all," she repeated as if to herself this time.

"Nobody knows, well I don't suppose so. Konnyaku made light of it when we got back to the House of Gardeners. Just made some crack or other to the others, didn't even mention anything about me. I think he was embarrassed to say anything. He was teasing me, as he does sometimes. It just made me angry and I flew at him, just like that. He said... I, well, I just sort of threw myself at him, we grappled a bit and I hit him" Shigoto's mother looked down at his hands lying in his lap trying to imagine them balled into a hard fist. "He said... he said I was a bastard, and that father was not my real father, and that everyone knew it." He spat out the last words, as if to clear a bad taste.

"I see," said his mother at last. They had both turned to look toward the sky, both absorbed in their own thoughts, watching the clouds massing in the west. Rain would come, the iron embrace of high summer temperatures would be broken, and life would move on. The rain would come and wash over everything, soon.

"Well, is it true? Is that what people say? Is it true?" Their eyes never touched or even shifted a degree toward one another. As he asked the question that had been haunting him, as he finally found the air, and the voice to let it out, he felt calm and in control.

"Is that what people say?" repeated his mother to herself, her voice barely registering. "Is that what people say? It's a cruel thing that people say, if that is so."

To anyone passing by they would have appeared as a mother and son enjoying a few quiet, intimate moments, just looking over the field of low spreading trees, taking in the view, just seeking a breath of fresh air. No one came by. They both fell into a trance of their own private space, where thought, feelings, memory and experience mingled. Shigoto at last glanced toward his mother. Her face was set and impassive. He recognised his unconditional love for this woman, and knew she accepted what he had to offer; it never had been any different. There was a wedge of light falling across her rounded face, as she sat without moving, her eyes wide open, the colour of a deep pitch pool. She was looking far into the distance, looking out towards the sky, may be even further than that, looking back into the past. Looking at his mother's face, he saw an impassive mask that he could not see behind.

"The world can be a cruel place, Shigoto-chan. People say things without substance." Finally she spoke to her son, looking straight back at him. "Very little is as it seems to be, when you really look at things. Your father is an important man now; you know he has many duties, which tie him to position. Many responsibilities, there are all manner of matters we know nothing off, so we should not comment on what we do not know about. Your father wants the best for you, I am sure he does."

"Is my father in some kind of trouble?" He was not sure why he phrased the question in this particular way, he had not intended it to come out as that.

"Trouble? Why do you say trouble," the light shifted in his mother's eyes. "What other things have you been told?"

Then Shigoto told his mother in full of the incident that ended with Konnyaku being hit in the face by her son. About unexpectedly overhearing voices in the teahouse, his father's voice seemingly plotting something with someone. Even about the dream with the mouse that ate into a sack, and the shoes, the shoes walking across the polished floor crushing the grains underfoot. It all poured out, the flow unstoppable. He even told her about Nureba. She was the one who had released the final impediment in his mind, pulled the stopper from the jar. After the chance meeting with her, he had felt himself soar from the sticky dark depths of despair, to feeling a supreme lightness. Shigoto found himself floating in a sea of love, and then the realisation came to him suddenly. From his father he had never felt any such sense of warmth or love. He had no memory or recollection stored away, even in the most secret and inaccessible reaches of his maps, of any place marked with a sense of affection coming from his father. It had always been his mother: she had been the generous, never stinting font of all that was good and nourishing. Nureba and he had but exchanged glances, but in that one split second, he felt as if they had told each other their life stories. He had sung her name to himself to himself a thousand times. If there was a song for his father, then it had neither words nor music.

"I see," his mother said. "Shigoto-chan you should have come and spoken to me earlier, and not carried all this inside. Listen, I do not know what you father's business is. I do not know what he knows, or anything about what he has to do. He does not share that with me, it is his right. I accepted that long ago. Your father has always provided for us both, always, even in the days when there was not much to be had. We have never gone without, Shigoto, even when others have. That is worth considering too. Your father is not without honour, and he has his principles too. I am sure he is loyal to Lord Saeko. The honour of his name stands on that, and ours too. People will always make out bad things, whatever your father is doing, and I am sure his honour is there with him, wherever he goes. You must not speak to anyone about this. It is important for your father's sake not to speak a word about this to anyone. You do understand that don't you?"

"I have never said a word to anyone. Not even Sensei."

"Good. Then it's best to keep it that way, Shigoto-chan. All I know is that sometimes there are things that can be spoken about, and there are those things not. Perhaps who we are is the sum of those things we cannot speak about. The world is too cruel to be too open. I'm sorry I wish that it were otherwise. I pray to the shrine gods for us all. I ask assistance of the Buddha of Salvation that some good comes out of this life. Sometimes it is all we can do. Even if everything else were spoken for we can still pray, pray for better times, pray for better understanding. But understanding means standing out in the open sometimes. It's best to be prepared. I do not know what you father is doing, I swear. He confides nothing to me." His mother's mask was now set back in place. "Something is happening though, I know that, my son, but I do not know what. As for the rest, people will always have things to say, pay no heed to idle gossip, it's tongues wagging that's all. Be sure this new friend of yours does not carry you away with his stories. At the end of the day it is not important. What is important to you, and important to me, is for you to be a good apprentice. Learn well, he is a good man that Maguro Sensei, he will teach you well I'm sure. He is a man of religion. I trust him. Your time will come, it always does. Make yourself ready for when it does."

The spell was broken; the tension that had held them bound by time and space released them again back into the everyday world once more. From the crouching plum trees laid out in their rows there came the distinct scent of dry earth mixed with the metallic taste of high summer.

"We had better get a move on, I had not realised that it was getting so late." As she stood and brushed her hands down her kimono, she sniffed the air coming into the open sided pavilion. "It's going to rain soon. We had better hurry now." She took Shigoto's arm in hers.

"It's alright," he said, "I know my way around the gardens, even in the dark."

"Well, what an advantage to be walking with a gardener," her laughter spilled gaily out. Now they could both smell the unmistakable sweet scent of rain borne on a strengthening breeze.

CHAPTER TWENTY-FOUR

September 1594

"I believe you like horses, Shigoto," came Maguro Sensei's voice. Shigoto was bending over collecting up the last pieces of pruned branches from between some bushes.

"Pardon, Sensei. Horses?" Once again the apprentice had been thrown off balance, that if he had been by an edge of the pond, he might well have fallen in.

"Umm, horses, Shigoto. Horses. The four legged variety that some warriors strut about on. They come in various colours I believe." The smile, if Shigoto could have seen Sensei's face from where he stood, now stretched across his face, and the eyes had a definite twinkle of mischief about them.

"Well, Sensei, I do not really know anything about horses at all. I have seen one or two about. I watched the horses and riders out on the big grass field one day. They were practicing firing arrows while riding at full speed. Most missed the target, but there was one warrior who did not miss any."

"Ahh, yes, that would be Kezure Saeko, the eldest son of Lord Saeko. They say he can ride his horse, the one that is the colour of freshly ground ink, as fast as a typhoon wind. Must be an experience to travel like that, don't you think? Anyway, come and sit down here. I did not come over here to spend the afternoon engaged in chit chat over horses."

"Sit down, Sensei?"

"Yes, yes, sit down Shigoto. Sit and let's talk like men together."

Shigoto came forward, and sat down cross-legged near his teacher. He was still quite wary of what the purpose of this visit from Sensei might be. His mind raced over the past few days trying to find if there was any particular incident or misdemeanour of his that may have been brought to Sensei's attention. Then it struck him with grim clarity. Of course, the kitchens! He had delivered foliage for flower arrangements recently: someone must have noticed him asking after Nureba and had reported him to Sensei. He sighed to himself, 'was there nothing that one could do in this life that would not attract the interest and attention of somebody? If people were not gossiping about others then they were usually only too willing to try and get them into some kind of trouble.' Shigoto glanced across towards Maguro Sensei, but his brow was not furrowed, and as far as Shigoto could make out he still had a cheerful expression on his face. Still, he knew from both his own experience and that of others that Sensei was at his most "dangerous" when you least expected it of him. That you could reasonably expect.

"So, tell me about horses then."

""As I say Sensei, I know nothing about horses."

"But I hear you dream about horses. Surely that indicates some sort of interest in the beasts, does it not?" The smile broadened across Sensei's face, clearly amused by the way the conversation was turning out.

"Oh that, it was just a dream, that's all. Konnyaku told me after that I had probably been possessed by the spirits, and transformed into a horse in my sleep." Shigoto felt his face colouring suddenly at the memory.

A couple of weeks earlier the gardeners had been asked to join a party of people to help in cutting and gathering miscanthus grasses. The long grassy stems were used to thatch roofs, and repairs were to be carried out to some of the buildings scattered about the garden. Far from being a pleasant day away from the gardens, as Shigoto had anticipated, the work had been monotonous and tiring in the extreme, and the grasses readily cut his hands. During a break for lunch he fell asleep and was visited by a strong dream in which he found himself riding a wild and powerful horse. The animal of his dreams was sleek, its dark flanks glistening with sweat and was swift as a lizard across the ground. In the dream Shigoto rode the beast without fear or effort, and was able to be free for those brief moments of the burden of being Shigoto, apprentice gardener. It was with some difficulty that the reed-cutting party managed to wake him when the time came to recommence work, and for some time after it was the cause of much amusement to the others. He had for a while become attached to this dream, and looked forward to every opportunity to fall asleep, in order that he could set about finding again the horse. Inevitably, word of his sleeping must have reached the sensitive ears of Sensei.

"Certainly, it is often enough said that we can become spirits in our dreams. Myself, I am not so sure about that. Though the ways of the world are strange, so we must anticipate that any thing is possible. Anyway, I did not raise the subject to chatter about dreams and spirits. I was wondering if you would like the opportunity to travel on a horse." Sensei looked straight at Shigoto as he made his proposal, and as far as Shigoto could tell he was utterly serious about it.

"Really, that would be wonderful Sensei, do you think that it may be possible? I am not a *samurai*, would I have to learn how to fire arrows whilst I was riding? And what about being a garden apprentice? I would not wish to be anything other than a gardener like you."

Maguro Sensei rocked back and roared with laughter at this.

"Oh, Shigoto, you do amuse me sometimes. Listen, I know that your father is now an advisor to Lord Saeko, and yes, he has permission to carry a sword, but you for whatever reason were fated to carry scissors not a sword. In my estimation a noble enough calling, and I will hear from no man that it is inferior. You know, in that time when the courtiers were the rulers of the land, many of them were also garden-builders. It was deemed to be the mark of a gentleman. Knowledge of the Classics and an ability to create gardens, these were abilities which lifted men above others. That is where the tradition we follow to this day really began. Have you heard of a story called the Tale of Genji? No? Well, a lady wrote it a very long time ago. The hero of the story, Prince Genji, was a great leader of men, and also a builder of great gardens. So do not let anyone tell you that gardeners are anything but noble people. There is so much more in a garden than most people could even dream about, greater riches, more strength and power, not to mention beauty. Beauty speaks across the ages, it has been said that beauty is the very voice of the gods themselves. No, Shigoto, do not underestimate the power of a garden, that would be a grave error indeed."

"Excuse me Sensei, but what has all this to do with horses, and what does it have to do with me? If it is the matter of falling asleep, then I apologise for that."

Again the roar of laughter came from Maguro Sensei.

"What it has to do with you, dear Shigoto, is that if you are interested, I am willing to arrange for you to be able to ride a horse. That's all."

"You mean it? Oh, Sensei, that is wonderful news. I will go and tell my mother tonight. That's wonderful news. Thank you.

My mother did mention that you had come to visit, but she said it was to ask about going to visit somebody, nothing about a horse."

"Well, it's true, I did ask her about taking you to visit someone, maybe it slipped my mind about the horse. So you agree then do you? In that case I will finalise the arrangements. But in the mean time there is work to be done. An idle gardener will not get his tasks completed, eh?"

Shigoto leapt to his feet borne on a wave of excitement. A horse! He could hardly contain himself, he was going to ride on a horse, travel faster than the wind itself.

"Thank you Sensei, that is wonderful news indeed, just wonderful news. Thank you so much. You said about going to meet someone, who is that? Does he have a horse too?"

Maguro Sensei rocked backwards and forwards with laughter that boomed out across the pond that they were sat beside.

"It is a friend of mine, Shigoto. That's all, a friend of mine. Kirifuda san is his name. He lives here on Mikura, but no, he does not have a horse. He is a Buddhist priest, a painter and a Tea man."

As he returned light-headedly to resume his tasks, Shigoto realised not only was Sensei offering him the chance of travel, and travel by horseback at that, but he was also doing something out of kindness for him. He was not used to that, from his mother certainly, but not especially from the man he respected, admired and feared in equal measure.

True to his word a few days later Shigoto was told by Maguro Sensei that he was to undertake a journey to a distant part of Mikura to visit a small temple where Sensei's friend lived. They would be gone for two or three days, and they would be taking various supplies with them, both for the journey and also as gifts. He could barely sleep for excitement and anticipation of what the day would bring.

On the appointed day Shigoto was awake early. He dressed in a fresh tunic that his mother had provided, collected up a small bag of provisions she had also prepared, and on a last minute whim picked up his gardener's scissors and pushed them into his bag too. In the half-light of the dawn he stepped carefully across the main room of the house of Gardeners, trying his best to avoid the sleeping forms of his fellow gardeners. As he was standing in the entry area tying his rice straw sandals, Kamaboku rolled over where he was lying.

"Hey, Shigoto, is that you, eh?" he whispered in a low voice.

"Yes, I am about leave, Sorry to wake you."

"No, it's alright. I was awake, anyway it will be time to get up soon enough." Kamaboku was lying on his side, his head propped up by a thin arm. "Big day, eh."

"Umm, yes. I suppose so." Shigoto was trying vainly to contain his growing excitement, wanting to appear casual to the outside world, as if what he was about to do was nothing out of the ordinary. He struggled to keep his voice down to a whisper. He just wanted avoid the conversation and to set off on this epic adventure. The previous evening, the other gardeners, who thought the idea of going anywhere on horseback strange and even unnatural, had teased him, and he wanted to get away before they had an opportunity to resume their amusement.

As he left, Kamaboku called out. "Hey, Shigoto, good luck, eh. Don't come back with bandy legs, eh."

As he slid the outer door closed behind him, Kamaboku's chuckling laughter followed him out into the cool, still air of a brand new day.

He made his way to the stables where he had arranged to meet Sensei, and his new companion for the journey. When he saw the beast that was to be his escort in this new adventure, he had to admit to a certain sense of disappointment. The animal was clearly elderly, and far from the sleek, lithe beast of his dreams. Still, when it came to it, a horse was a horse. Maguro Sensei explained that as the journey was far, it would take them the best part of the day to get there, also the path not always easy, but this only served to replenish the tide of excitement rising within him. Master and pupil set off, leading the horse by a rope that had been slung around the animal's neck. Tied down on its back were two sacks containing their supplies and gifts. Shigoto took hold of the rope and walked nervously alongside the animal. He half expected that the beast would take off at a gallop, and he was uncertain how he would react in that eventuality. He also wondered where he would sit, there hardly seemed to be room for him, even though the horse had a broad back. The horse gave off a warm, friendly smell, and the travellers were soon clear of the Palace grounds, and heading across the open, rolling country. Shigoto soon realised the pace they would be able to travel at would be dictated in a large measure by that of the horse, so he fell into rhythm with it: listening to the hooves clattering over the dry, hard ground, and trying to make sure that those large feet did not step on his by mistake.

They walked in a convivial silence for several hours, the travellers wrapped in their own private thoughts. The sun was beginning its ascent into the sky and any early chill in the air seeping out of the day. After having left Hirame Palace behind, Shigoto looked back several times the way they had come. He was surprised at how small the world they were leaving behind looked from here. He could now just about make out a cluster of trees and the outlines of the roofs of the Hirame Palace that were beginning to fade into the distance. He had never been so far away from the place of his birth that to him had always seemed so large. Now it began to appear small enough that it could all fit into one of the sacks the horse was carrying. Far away beyond the Hirame Palace, the township of Mikura was barely a smudge of smoke, beyond that the sea gleaming and shimmering silvery.

They continued their way over open ground studded with small groups of trees, then swung towards the east and started to climb into the foothills ranged around the mountains that rose in the centre of the island. Reaching a small stream Sensei called a halt. Shigoto stood holding on to the rope lest the horse decided to continue, not that it showed any inclination to do so.

"It's alright, Shigoto, you can let go of the rope now. The horse will not go far, even if it does wander. We can stop here for a moment to rest and drink. From here we will make our way over the side of the mountain there." Sensei pointed in the direction he meant. "We will travel over that shoulder, then down the other side."

After they had rested for a short while they were ready set off again. This time Sensei suggested the Shigoto might like to ride on the back of the horse. It required unloading the sacks and retying them again in such a way that allowed room for him to be able to sit straddling the broad back with his legs hanging freely. Sitting up there, Shigoto felt suddenly detached from the earth, something that was both exhilarating and also nerve wracking. There was nothing to hold on to, and when the horse snorted suddenly sending a shiver through its flanks, he nearly leapt off in surprise.

"What do I hold onto, Sensei?"

"Just keep hold of the rope, and don't fidget about. You will be fine."

When all was ready Sensei gave the horse a light slap across its rear quarters, and the animal lurched forward before it settled back into its lumbering walk. Shigoto nearly pitched off, with only the sacks stopping him falling off completely.

"There we go Shigoto, sit up straight and relax, just follow the rhythm of the horse. You look a natural rider up there. No taking off in a gallop, mind."

After a few minutes to adjust to the new sensations, a feeling of pride and unadulterated happiness began to spread through

Shigoto. He consoled himself with the fact that he was more than content with the elderly beast, though he remained apprehensive that the animal should decide to break into anything more than a steady walking pace.

The journey seemed to stretch on and on, his legs were beginning to be very uncomfortable, and his back and hips scarcely less so. The pleasure of horse riding was beginning to wear very thin indeed, and still they travelled on. They made their way through a forest of stunted oak trees, climbing all the while, and kept climbing past the point where the last stragglers of the scrubby oaks gave out and only a sparse covering of pine trees grew. The air was noticeably cooler and it chilled his cheeks. Sensei walked on alone a little way in front of the horse that appeared content to follow after the man. They lapsed into silence again. Eventually they went over a crest of the side of the mountain, and now Shigoto could see the sea again, but this time from a direction he had never set eyes on it before. He marvelled at the range of silvery grey tones, the immensity of the sea reaching right out to the flat horizon, and the vast expanse of sky above it all. He realised that he had never been as high in all his life, and had never before been able to see so far. "The world is so very different from here", he murmured to the horse beneath him.

By the time Sensei called a halt by another small stream tumbling down the flank of the mountain eager to rejoin the sea, Shigoto's legs had gone numb and his back was aching. He slid down from the horse but had to stay leaning against its dark sweat streaked flanks until he was able to get sufficient sensation back into his own legs to be able to stand by himself. They removed the sacks from the back of the horse, and it wandered to the stream where Shigoto watched in fascination as it drank splay-legged with its nose thrust into the cold rushing water. Sensei built a small fire, and soon he had some water warming to make tea. It was the nicest tea that Shigoto could ever remember drinking. When they had rested, eaten and slaked their thirst, the bags were slung over the back of the horse, and with still stiff legs, Shigoto clambered up. He adjusted to the movements beneath him now, and he was beginning to lose his fear of falling off, or the animal suddenly taking off at speed. He sensed that the horse had no inclination to do so anyway, and somewhat doubted that it could, even if encouraged to do so. They continued their winding descent, always heading toward the sea.

"How far is it from here, Sensei?"

"Not so very far now."

Shigoto gradually lost track of time, as his attention became trapped between the steady rocking of the horse beneath him and his increasing physical discomfort. Sensei turned back to him without breaking stride and announced that they were near the end of the journey. By this time his legs were numb again, his feet had lost any feeling and his back was rigid as a plank of wood. Shigoto could even detect a sense of resigned dejection in the dull rhythm of the horse beneath him. All he could think of now was parting company with the beast. When they finally stopped he slid from the back of the horse and found that his legs would not respond to his desire to stand. He collapsed into an untidy heap beside the horse, which turned to give him a baleful look. From his position on the ground he tried to take in the destination of what seemed to be an epic journey.

It seemed more of a remote hermitage than temple. The entry gate with its remnants of bark shingles for a roof and drunken timbers had seen better days, one good gust of wind might have sent it to the ground. Beyond it, to his despair, the path seemed to twist and climb up a steep slope towards a small thatched building. Maguro Sensei untied the sacks from the horse's back, and leaving the animal to graze and water by a thin brook nearby, led the way upward toward a trace of smoke, seemingly unaffected by the long journey. Shigoto struggled along trying to lift one foot then the other, a sack in either hand. A twisting worn track skirted around a few large scattered stones. Growing out from a crack in one large rock a pine clung on for its life, silently observing his unsteady progress. Occasionally, between the stones and plants the view stretched away: in the far distance was the sea again. Shigoto was relieved to see a simple cottage appearing in front of him. He remarked cheerfully to Sensei that they had finally reached their journey's end. Sensei chuckled softly and turned to his young companion.

"Ahh, Shigoto, even before you take the first step, the journey is complete; and yet even as the journey is completed, it is time to take the first step. Fullness is the empty circle. The staff you carry for support, break it over your knee. You will know all this, one day."

No one appeared at the entrance to greet them; even so Sensei bowed deep and offered a short prayer of thanks for their safe arrival. Shigoto was tired and somewhat disorientated, his throat was dry, his stomach empty, and legs stiff and aching. "Shigoto, do you forget your manners, do you not bow to greet our kind host?" He bowed toward the empty porch out of a sense of duty, as he straightened up there in the entrance way stood a figure of an elderly man dressed in a simple kimono of dark blue. Looking Shigoto directly in the eye, his voice soft yet firm he welcomed his guests. 'Greetings young man, so kind of you to bring this rascal to visit. Please forgive the humbleness of this abode." Before he had time to reply, Maguro Sensei had slipped off his sandals and entered the cottage leaving him standing outside. Gingerly picking up the two sacks and pushing his aching limbs into action once more, he followed the two men inside.

Leaving his sandals neatly next to Sensei's he entered the dark interior, following the sound of voices toward the back of the building. There he found the two men comfortably settled on thin cushions, an iron kettle suspended over a few coals sighing softly to itself. He carefully lowered the two sacks to the bare wooden floor, and took a place slightly to one side and behind Sensei; at last he could rest his limbs. The two men seemed to be already deep in conversation. Creeping tiredness washed over Shigoto's body and he was pleased he was not required to make conversation. The room was as simple as could be, bare polished wooden floor, a low writing desk with ink stone and a ceramic pot with a few hair brushes of different sizes were the only pieces of furniture. The paper screens had been opened completely to allow an unobstructed view of the landscape beyond. Mountain after mountain stretched as far as the eye could see. The valleys plunged steep sided, the bottom of the valleys filled with shades of soft verdant greens. The house seemed to be perched at the very edge of the world; the sound of running water in the distance was both refreshing and calming.

The two older men's conversation seemed to merge with the warming kettle. Tiredness was now dragging heavily at his limbs and his eyes. On one side of the room the wall was lined with shelves; crowded onto the shelves were lidded ceramic jars of myriad colours and shapes. Though he looked carefully, he could not find two the same. There was an atmosphere of deep rural peacefulness and tranquillity. As Shigoto took in the space where they sat, he was aware that the whole room was pervaded by a scent he could not quite trace the origin of. There was an earthiness, a faintly sweet fragrance that reminded him of plants and flowers, without bringing a clear recognition of either the source or the precise constituents of the scent. In one corner of the room was a *tokonoma*, a shallow alcove in which a piece of calligraphy composed of a few dynamic strokes was hung, and below it was a small vase with a simple handful of leaves with a shower of tiny white flowers held aloft by the thinnest of stems.

His attention drifted away from the alcove toward the paper-covered screens that made up the remaining interior walls of the room. At first glance he thought the paper was streaked with age or stains, then as he peered closer he realised that in fact they had been painted with thin pale ink. In some parts the ink so barely stained the water the paper, the ghostly shapes that existed only at the fringes of perception. Yet, the more he looked, the more he began to see. The screens had been decorated with paintings of landscapes of mountains, streams, forest and mists. A small bowl of tea had been placed in front of him, the vapours from which rose up to him and brought to mind the scent of spring moss after a shower of rain. His eyes roamed from the paintings to the scenery beyond the veranda and then back to the paintings. There hardly seemed to be any difference between the one and the other. Perhaps Kirifuda had made the painting by looking out onto that very same view, he wondered? Without having to move a muscle, Shigoto found himself travelling effortlessly through the landscape before him, from mountain peak to mountain peak, roaming the thickly forested valley sides, seeing the fish beneath the rushing water of the streams. It was as if he was a bird, completely free to go wherever he choose. High or low, it was all the same somehow. First he drifted up one valley, its sides thickly crowded with trees, and the sound of the hurrying river below no more than the sighing of a kettle. Then he turned about and followed the flow downstream, where the river joined with another and the valley broadened out. If he glanced upwards he could see the mountains rising way above him, their peaks garlanded with clouds.

"So, young Shigoto, I hear that you wish to become a garden maker following the path of your Sensei." Kirifuda spoke in a quiet voice that held its knowledge and authority in reserve. The words of their host brought him back to the room.

"Tell me, what do you think of my efforts then?" The older man was sitting cross-legged on a thin cushion, comfortably cradling a small rough ceramic bowl in both hands, his quiet eyes looking toward Shigoto.

Shigoto did not know quite how to reply. Did he mean the paintings? But Kirifuda's thin arm stretched out to indicate the space beyond the veranda. As he looked again Shigoto realised just beyond lay a small carefully tended garden only a matter of a few paces deep. In his shock and confusion Shigoto mumbled something indistinct, and Maguro Sensei straightened his posture as he sat, a smile playing about his lips.

"Kirifuda *san*, forgive us, this young man has made a long journey. Finish up your tea Shigoto, your horse will be pining for company. Then perhaps when you have checked on the beast, you had better get some rest yourself."

"Yes, Sensei." Still uncertain as to where he really was and what he had really been looking at, Shigoto swallowed the now cold tea in one awkward gulp, and then hurried out to see to the horse.

Awakening with the dawning light, Shigoto stretched out his stiff limbs out before clambering to his feet. Memories of the journey the previous day were fresh and vital in his mind, as if during the night he had retraced his steps. As he stepped into the main room he could see Maguro Sensei sitting framed by the open window. Sensei was sitting still as a rock, still as a mountain, and Shigoto realised that he must have been awake early and he was now meditating. Of Kirifuda, there was no sign. Silently as he could, he stepped across the room and stopping only to slip on his sandals in the tiny entry porch, he emerged into the cool air and early morning mist that clung to the ground around the house.

Shigoto wanted to see the horse, to check that it was all right, but first he went in the direction of the sound of running water. The stream that ran near the house was narrow enough for him to jump over. The banks had been lined with small boulders, and here and there clumps of plants clung to the border between soil and water. Crouching down on a flat-topped stone that partly projected into the stream he knelt and cupping his hand raised a draught of water to his mouth. It was delicious, even if the coldness set his teeth on edge. Once again he leaned forward and raised a handful of water with which he splashed over his face. There were no sounds but the running stream nothing disturbed the serenity of the moment. Shigoto realised once again how far he had journeyed from the place of his birth. Hirame Palace and his fellow gardeners seemed to belong to another world, and he wondered why it was Sensei had brought him to this place. Was it just so that he could ride a horse? That seemed unlikely, Maguro Sensei was not someone given to acting on a whim. Still, here he was, and he felt a determination to enjoy every moment of this time. Perhaps the moment may never come around again? As he crouched on the flat stone with the stream bustling past, he looked up at the mountains shrouded by mist, and he felt that he had travelled a very long way, into another world. 'Will I ever get back again?'

As those words formed in his mind he could feel a prickling sensation in his eyes, and tears began to form. Not only was he now fully aware of being separated from Hirame Palace, and the life he knew there, the only life he had known, but he felt a chilling sensation of being separated from his mother. He shivered, but it was not because of the cool air that hung over the rushing water. As the image of his mother began to form in his mind there came the sound of the horse neighing. He could not see it, as it must have wandered away during the night, and was now swallowed by the blanket of mist. Shigoto rose to his feet and with a leap made it across the stream and headed in the direction of the sound. Stepping carefully across the uneven ground he could now hear the sound of grass being torn from the turf, and soon came across the horse, head contentedly down pulling on clumps of grasses.

Shigoto approached the horse quietly as he could. He did not wish to alarm the animal, give it cause to run off into the white clouds that covered the ground. But the horse had no thought to do anything other than continue to feed. It looked up at Shigoto with its huge dark soft eyes and its jaws working to mash a mouthful of vegetation. From its neck the halter rope dangled loose and Shigoto realised that the animal could have easily taken off at any point in the night. He came right up to it his arm outstretched bearing a gift of grasses. The animal turned its long head toward him, sniffed at the proffered handful, and returned to tear at another clump of grass at its feet. Shigoto touched the side of its face, and ran his hand along the coat of its flank; his hand came away damp with dew. Then he pressed himself into the side of the horse, enveloped himself in its quivering warmth, and the tears finally flowed freely down his cheeks.

"Ahh, young Shigoto, you are there. You found the horse." The voice of Kirifuda came out of the early morning light that was still to find its strength and purpose.

Shigoto brushed a hand across his face. "Yes, the horse is here. He is eating, that's all."

"Good, good. I didn't think he would have wandered far, but you never know. It's hard to see far this morning. Rather beautiful though isn't it?" Kirifuda came and picked up the trailing end of the halter rope. They both stood there a moment looking at the horse, which seemed entirely unconcerned at the attention it was receiving.

"Have you had some tea, or something to eat yet?" Kirifuda asked.

"Er, no, no, not yet. Sensei was still meditating, I did not want to disturb him. I… I came to see if the horse was alright."

"Quite right too. He will lead you home again. Always look after those that look after you," Kirifuda's voice was friendly and had a welcoming tone.

"Come, bring the horse, you can tie him to a post over there. When the sun gets up a bit higher it will burn off the mist. If he can see a bit further, he may be inclined to wander." Kirifuda handed the rope to Shigoto, and they together walked to where a stake had been driven into the ground, about halfway up its length there hung a large metal ring. "Tie the rope to the ring. There is plenty for the horse to eat here, not that he looks underfed. Then we can go and get some food ourselves, eh."

By the time they had all finished eating the sun had risen fully, and the mist was retreating up the sides of the mountain. As he sat and finished his food, Shigoto's eyes were drawn back to the tiny garden just beyond the shutters that were now slid fully back. A low hedge of evergreen bushes framed the garden, Shigoto vaguely recognised the plants from the Hirame gardens, he had been allowed to prune some a little while back. The space between the hedge and the building was a matter of a few feet, and as the floor of the room where they were sitting was raised above the ground, Shigoto felt as if he was at some high point looking down at a landscape arranged below him. There were perhaps a dozen rocks scattered across the space, carefully chosen for their shapes, any one of them could have been a mountain in miniature. At the base of some of the groups of stones small dark pebbles had been laid which could have been winding stream courses. Once more he felt as if he were soaring above the scene, liberated from all earthly concerns, his spirit lighter than the clouds. He felt deeply drawn toward the garden, as if it were in direct communication with him, speaking straight to his heart, sidestepping the use of words. Shigoto turned towards Kirifuda.

"Your garden is wonderful. It makes me think of the mountains. Did Sensei build it for you?"

Kirifuda laughed heartily. "No, no, I am afraid it is only the work of an old man, such as I am. I am glad you like it though.

We can draw a deep strength from being near mountains and water, don't you think?"

"Today we will go up into the mountains," said Maguro Sensei, who had been watching Shigoto carefully.

"Are we taking the horse for a walk?" Shigoto asked.

Sensei laughed. "No, no, we shall leave the horse here. We are going with Kirifuda *san* to collect some herbs. A good walk will get the knots out of your legs, I dare say."

"Herbs," said Shigoto, as it dawned on him what the scent was that hung about in the house, drying herbs. Then he looked at all the jars set neatly on the shelves of the room where they sat. "Ah, are those all herbs in the jars, then?"

"Kirifuda san is not just a man of Tea, a poet, and a painter, Shigoto. He is also very knowledgeable about plants and their uses. Keep your wits about you today and you may learn some new things."

Once again Kirifuda san laughed. "Now, now, do not fill the young man's head with silly notions. We all have a lot to learn, isn't that right? We are all apprentices, even you Maguro Sensei. We all have so much to learn in this life, and it's all we have time for. "Then both the older men laughed together, and this time Shigoto joined them.

By late morning with the mountains now sharp and clear, the two men and the young boy set off armed with a couple of empty sacks. Kirifuda also brought a crude looking short curved knife attached to a wooden handle.

"What's that for?" asked Shigoto, when he saw the blade in Kirifuda's hand, just before they set off.

"This?" Kirifuda san handed the blade over to Shigoto. "You are a gardener, are you not, you should know what this is." Shigoto took the proffered tool, and turned it over in his hands before handing it back.

"No, I've never seen anything quite like that," he said.

"It's for digging up roots. Sometimes that is the part of the plant that you want. Sometimes the essence is stored in the leaves and sometimes in the roots," Kirifuda explained. "Here I'll bring one for you too."

The three made their way up the flank of the mountain. As they climbed higher Shigoto was able to look down on the now tiny cottage that was Kirifuda's house. For a time he was able to make out the horse still contently tethered to the stake, but after a while he could no longer make out its form. Above him rose the peak of the mountain, its top occasionally catching and holding onto a passing cloud. Beyond where he could now just make out the house they had left behind, he could look out over the immense stretch of the sea.

'I am bigger than the horse which is but a speck of dust now', he thought to himself. The immensity and grandeur of the world struck him with a force that made him giddy. A huge smile spread across his face and he felt as if he wanted to dance all the way down the mountainside to the sea. As he looked out he could understand the vision of Kirifuda's tiny garden, back at the house, which was so small he could not make it out anymore. 'His garden has captured this mountain,' he thought to himself, 'all this scene is in there somehow.' The revelation came to him with great force and meaning: it lifted him, as the wind was tugging now at his kimono, not that he cared about that. Here he was at the top of a mountain looking out across the world spread out before him, and now he began to understand for the first time in his life the power and majesty of a garden that was in many ways so easy to overlook.

"Sensei, I can see it all now," Shigoto with infectious excitement shouted. "I can see Kirifuda san's garden. I can see what he was doing with his garden." The force of revelation was overwhelming. It excited him in a way he had not realised possible, and showed him something that he had not realised could be done. In that moment, more than ever, he wanted to create gardens, work with rocks, and create worlds of his own imagining. "Sensei, I can see it all now." But Maguro Sensei was too far away for his words to carry to him before the increasingly strong wind whipped his words away and carried them far, far over the landscape, over the sea towards the distant horizon. Now he ran to catch up with the two men ranging ahead of him, prowling the slopes of the mountain, eyes down looking intently at the ground searching for something other.

"Kirifuda *san*," Shigoto blurted out when he caught up with the diminutive figure of his host. "I can see the landscape from here, the whole world, it looks just like your garden, we must be on top of the world itself."

Kirifuda turned from where he was kneeling on the soft ground, digging furiously at an insignificant looking plant growing in a crease of the mountainside. The older man looked up at the young boy rushing towards him a smile beaming across his youthful face, and he smiled back at Shigoto. He understood his joy.

"You like it here, eh?"

"I have never seen anything like it before," Shigoto was almost breathless.

"Yes, it is beautiful, isn't it?" he replied as his eyes swept across the scenery that lay before them. In that moment there was a unity of vision between the two of them, they were looking at the same scene, feeling the same deep excitement. "And you know, Shigoto, so very few people ever get to see this, so very few. That's why you must learn well from Maguro Sensei, and then you will maybe build fine gardens in your time. This is the kind of place where gardens arose from and return to. It is what garden creators such as your teacher try to capture in their works," and he waved his digging tool out before him. "It all starts here, but first you have to see it. Without that…" the words trailed away into the breeze.

"It's something I never really understood before," said Shigoto. He was unwilling to allow the moment to pass. He wanted it to last forever, to somehow seal it inside of himself.

"Yes, it's very beautiful indeed," repeated Kirifuda. This time he was addressing the landscape itself. "I tell you what is also interesting, that plant you are almost standing on. Do me a favour and dig it up for me, make sure you get the roots too, it is good for fevers."

The three of them spent several more hours on the mountain, filling the two sacks they brought with them with a variety of plants. Shigoto remained at the side of Kirifuda as the older man pointed out various plants and elicited for the young gardener their medicinal benefits. Finally with the strength of the wind increasing all the while, they decided to call a halt to their foraging and began a slow steady descent back down the slope.

"The young man seems happy with his day, Maguro Sensei," Kirifuda said as they descended. Maguro Sensei merely smiled.

The air had the limpid softness of early morning as they took their leave of Kirifuda the following day. As they took the path back to the sagging gateway, Kirifuda's fond farewells went with them, Shigoto's mind was still going over the sights and sounds of what he had experienced the day before. He asked Sensei if it would be all right to walk alongside the horse.

"Do not concern yourself with the journey, Shigoto, for how could one ever leave the place where one already is? Coming and going, they are the same thing."

Shigoto did not have the mind to question or argue. Perhaps it was because of all the unanswered questions revolving like fireflies in his head, the journey back seemed to pass quickly, and it was with a sense of relief that he saw the familiar outlines of places that he recognised.

The journey by horseback had cured Shigoto of whatever desire he had to ride a horse again. Though what he had seen of

Kirifuda's garden, and the vision of the world spread out from the mountainside stayed in his mind. It confirmed his desire to be a gardener, to be able to create something so enchanting, so simple that a viewer could be transported away into another space, another time altogether. When he remarked upon this to Maguro Sensei, after they had left the horse at the stables, Sensei simply replied, "Ahh, Shigoto, the Universe is boundless indeed, yet everything is contained within a circle. I have told you before, the empty circle contains everything. Now you know for yourself. You have seen it for yourself. You have breathed in beauty. What remains is to complete the task of breathing it out again. "

CHAPTER TWENTY-FIVE

October 1594

The late heat of the Indian summer held out for a few days more, before as spectacular lightning storm announced the arrival of a change in the season which came a sudden downpour. It was still raining relentlessly the following morning and water poured off the roof of the House of Gardeners directly into the roadway outside. Konnyaku sat by the entrance of the building looking out at the roadway that resembled a broad, shallow river in spate.

"There'll be no garden work today. What do you think, Kamaboku *san*? Did Sensei say anything about rain to you last night? There will be enough work to do to tidy up after the storms that's for sure."

Kamaboku had come and knelt by Konnyaku, and the pair of them silently contemplated the rain continuing to pour down in bleak heavy sheets. Kamaboku blew the air out of his cheeks in one long slow exhalation.

"It's a shame, it means we can't get on with that job in the woodland. I was enjoying it, it was getting interesting, eh. We have made good progress the past few days with the new man working." He paused. "Funny character, what do you think? He can talk though, eh. He can talk the stars to sleep, the trees to flower. Aiieeee yah! Does he ever shut up, do you think?" He spoke low into the space immediately before them, the volume of the rain giving them a shield of privacy.

"Talks too damn much, if you ask me. Mr Been-Everywhere-Done-Everything. Mind you, some of the stories are funny you have to say, but … why not send him along to Sensei? To get a message to Sensei asking if we are working today or not. Otherwise we could be cooped up in here with him all day. Imagine that. Non-stop stories all day. At least when we are working he gets on with it, even if he doesn't really have a clue. He's nothing more than a clumsy dolt that man. He's never a gardener. Come on, Kamaboku, you are not trying to tell me he is a gardener. A Kyoto gardener at that! You must be kidding me."

Kamaboku looked over his shoulder as he knelt; glanced towards the main room, then back out again towards the water sluicing noisily past the door.

"He'll just get lost somewhere," he sighed.

"Well, send Shigoto then. He knows the way well enough. He goes there often enough. I see he didn't go for meditation this morning though. Didn't fancy getting wet, no doubt," scoffed Konnyaku. "God knows what we are going to do cooped up with Tanuki all day though. Drive you crazy he will."

"You have got long legs, and you know the way well enough yourself," said Kamaboku. "Someone will end up with Tanuki, unless he falls asleep. Mind, he'll just talk in his dreams anyway." He laughed lightly at his own joke. He was silent awhile as he considered the options, then he turned around and firmly addressed the varied postures of the other gardeners in the main room. "Right, this is what we will do today. Outdoor work, apart from any essential things, are not possible with this rain. Shigoto, you will go to Maguro Sensei and tell him what my instructions to the others are. Yadokari, you and Ekichū, go to the Gardeners' store. There will be tool repairs to do; you can meet Kakugari there. He will make his own way there. Take the new man, Tanuki with you. Konnyaku, you will go to make sure all is well at the North Gate area. Then check on the Southern Courtyard. I will go to the kitchen to wait for any messages there. I will let you know by midday if there are other tasks. If not then, we will take the rest of time for ourselves. Shigoto will return to me with any instructions from Sensei. That's settled then."

"I will need an umbrella. It's pouring down out there, I'll get soaked putting one foot in front of the other," wailed Konnyaku. "I'll go when it slackens off a bit. Crazy to go out in this."

"Have some rice and tea first. It'll make you feel better. I am taking the umbrella myself. Use a rain cape like everyone else," said Kamaboku as he rose and was swallowed by the gloomily lit interior. Konnyaku sat in the entrance on his own a little longer before slowly getting to his feet.

By the time Shigoto got to Maguro Sensei's house he was soaked to the skin. He had waited until the rain relented some, then with a growing sense of impatience he decided to make a dash for it. It was not cold at all; the rain was quite warm, and the air still sultry. Not even tucking his kimono up into his waist belt and running along barefoot with a rain cape held over his head prevented him from a mud splattered soaking. Paths in the garden were running with soil-stained water as puddles quickly coalesced, and raindrops bounced up past shin high when they struck the ground. When he arrived at the Kokiburi-an he was utterly wet through and mud streaked his legs, he clutched a pair of sandals in his hand, having found running barefoot more pleasant. Shigoto ran through the rudimentary gateway that marked the entry to Kokiburi-an, then skipped over the glistening stepping stone path that lead toward the main entrance, to the relative shelter of the overhanging eaves to get out of the rain at last.

The house was silent, and seemed unbowed by the weather, the peak of its thick thatched roof lost in the grey murk. Under the shelter of the eaves Shigoto had not yet shouted out a greeting as he would have normally done from the gateway. He shrugged off the rain cape, and left it leaning against the front wall from where the water leaked out and ran in thin rivulets. Then he stood with one hand to balance and projected a bare leg out into the force of the rain beyond the dripping eaves. He twisted himself one way and another to wash off the mud, then hopped onto the opposite leg and did the same with that. He smoothed down his dripping tunic, and turned toward the entry door, hoping he did not look too disrespectful to present himself to his teacher. He opened his mouth to call out, when he realised that Sensei was kneeling there in the doorway, his legs folded neatly underneath him, a cloth in his hands.

"Oh, Sensei. Good morning, excuse me. I did not see you there. It was dark. I was about …" Shigoto was shocked to see Sensei's figure calmly sitting there, silently watching him. He bowed toward Maguro Sensei. "Good morning Sensei. Kamaboku asked me to come to you for instructions for the men for the day. On account of the monsoon rain it not being suitable for working outside, that is." Shigoto conveyed to Sensei the content of the instructions that Kamaboku had issued earlier. He stood up to his full height as he spoke and at his feet a puddle formed from the water dripping off him. After Shigoto had delivered his message he waited arms down at his side for Maguro Sensei's answer. Sensei's attention was on the ever-widening puddle spreading out from where Shigoto stood, then he set the cloth down in front of him and rose easily to his feet.

"Use the cloth to dry yourself off with. I will fetch some dry clothes for you." Then he disappeared inside. Shigoto came forward and took up the cloth and wiped his face and hands. In a moment Sensei was back at the doorway with a dry robe in his hands. "When you are dried off, and changed out of that soaking tunic. Come in, I will make some tea ready."

As Shigoto slipped the sodden garment off his shoulders, and dropped it to the ground, he realised those were the first and only words Sensei had spoken. Having quickly rubbed himself down with the cloth provided, he dressed again. Sensei had left a white length of cloth for a loincloth, and an old robe that may once have been dark blue. He called out, "Excuse me," as he stepped up into the tiny entry hall. He left his wet clothes where they were and stepped inside.

Beyond the entry hall was another open doorway and then the main room, at first the room seemed dark, as his eyes adjusted to the gloom, Shigoto saw Sensei in the small side room where they often sat after meditation sessions.

"Excuse me," he called out again, and went through to join Maguro Sensei who was sitting by an open doorway that gave way to a narrow veranda, and then onto a tiny courtyard garden now cut off by the sheets of rain. All the doors and windows in the building were open wide but the light inside remained dim as in a cave. Only at the periphery was there any natural light available, however strained it may be. Sensei motioned for Shigoto to take a flat square cushion that lay on the polished floor beside him. Between them sat two small tea bowls on a thin bamboo lattice tray, on a low open metalwork stand sat a pale green teapot. Shigoto came forward and bowed again to Sensei.

"Well, Shigoto, you look quite like a wandering poet this morning. Come, come and have some tea, it is good for the body.

The Chinese knew about that you know. Before tea became all the rage and a fashion, as it is today, tea was a medicine; we should never forget its origins. Come, drink, the tea is waiting for you."

Shigoto sat crossed legged on the cushion, and having made himself comfortable, accepted the cup, into which Sensei poured a thin stream of tea. They drank in silence. When he had finished the first cup he reached over and took the teapot and poured Sensei's tea before replenishing his own cup. Then they both sat and sipped. Shigoto felt a lightness of mood, even a sense of excitement about Sensei. The coming of the rain would be a relief to anyone after the fierce dry heat of summer. Sensei's close shaved head bobbed up and down as he sipped his tea, smiling to himself at some private amusement.

"It looked as if you had swum through the mud to get here, Shigoto," he said after they had both drained the cups. "I did not expect anyone to come up through that. Kamaboku knows how to arrange things; I have no doubts over his ability and strengths at all. It's good to see the rain, don't you think? It's a time for poets. I love a good storm, there is great beauty in a storm. I always felt that, even as a child. If I could I would lie in the open window and watch the lightning fighting across the sky," he chuckled to himself and gave Shigoto a warm look.

"Kamaboku will be at the kitchens, waiting for an answer." Shigoto replied.

"Well, at least he will be out of the rain there, and have plenty of company, no doubt." Maguro Sensei knew well the value of a place such as the kitchen courtyard as a hub of communication. "No, it's a good storm this one, we should enjoy it while it lasts. Each in his own way, don't you think, Shigoto?"

"I suppose so, I hadn't thought about it really," replied Shigoto returning his cup to the tray next to where Sense had placed his. They sat for a while watching the rain pour down. Then Sensei slapped his knee and replied with a firm intention.

"We should sit first for a little while, then we can talk about gardens. Maybe the rain will ease for a while later. Kamaboku has everything under control, I am sure. If there is anything urgent someone will come. There is no hurry for you to go back yet. If that's agreeable to you, unless you are keen to go swimming in the mud again that is?"

"Of course, that would be wonderful, thank you. That's if you have the time, Sensei, "Shigoto's eyes sparkled in the gloom.

They retired to the small room where they normally meditated in the mornings, Sensei lit an incense stick, then having assumed their positions they sat in the gloom, with the rain pounding down onto the thick thatch above their heads. As he sat all manner of images and thoughts cut across Shigoto's mind. A manically jagged procession of random events, facts, fantasy, people's faces, places, seemingly every facet of his memory was available to be dipped into, juxtaposed in a tangle of meaning. He felt anything but serene. Maguro Sensei had spoken to him about his "monkey mind" before, and had explained how at those times not to consciously attempt to prevent the flow of images, but to try and detach oneself from it and concentrate on breathing, following the breath in and out of the body. Shigoto tried the breathing exercises he had been taught, but he could not halt the flow of images that were flooding through his mind. His attention seemed to be scattered all over; he did not feel centred, grounded and certainly not in control. Nureba's face sprang into his mind's eye, a floating transparent image of her face loomed up into vast proportions, she was smiling an inscrutable smile to him and him alone. Then her lips moved, as if speaking, but the voice in his head was his mother's. Then Nureba's face dissolved and revealed images of mountains, horses, cloud, and sky, all crazily cutting into one another at high speed. He heard his father's voice somewhere in the mix, and then it was the sound of running water that washed everything else into oblivion. After only a few minutes had seemed to pass, Sensei bowed and clapped to signal the end of the sitting time. He rose and left the room as usual. Shigoto remained where he sat as he tried to get himself back to some kind of equilibrium before he stood up. He felt guilty as the thought occurred to him that perhaps Sensei had brought the session to an abrupt ending having somehow sensed the turmoil in Shigoto's mind. But when he looked across at the bowl where the incense had been burning, there was only the last of the ash lying in a crumpled heap, and its lingering scent hanging thinly in the still damp air of the room.

"Come and sit," said Sensei as Shigoto came into the room. He waved a hand toward the empty cushion beside him. There was a smile playing about his face, and if there was any trace of irritation about Sensei, then it certainly did not show. Shigoto knew that Sensei was not a man to hide his feelings. Especially if he felt someone was coming up short of the standard he demanded. Failure he would tolerate, as long as if it was accompanied by sincere effort. As Shigoto sat down and made himself comfortable, he surveyed his teacher's face, but detected no ill will. "So, Shigoto, tell me, how is it with the garden?"

Shigoto paused to collect his thoughts, "It's fine, I mean, it's well. I am enjoying work." He was unsure where to begin, as of late his mind had been such a swirl of different emotions, often contradictory and always deeply questioning. He did not feel he had really been always connected to his work. It was something he did because it gave him a stanchion to hold on to. What he actually did had not mattered so much as the discipline of the doing itself. "Actually I have been enjoying clearing that old piece of woodland, uncovering the stones. At first, I could not see anything much there, but now I can see that there seem to be connections between the stones, and I wonder about the people who put them there, what they were thinking about." He hoped he was giving something of the right answer. Sensei's eyes were gazing intently at him as he spoke, weighing, measuring, and

The Gardener's Apprentice

always looking beneath the skin, beyond flesh and bone. The rain continued to fall heavily outside.

"The work's been going well, since Tanuki *san*, has been with us. I like him," Shigoto said, only for Sensei's eyes to narrow sharply at Tanuki's name being brought into the conversation. Seeing the shift in his teacher's look, Shigoto remembered a comment Kamaboku had made when he first broke the news of a new gardener starting.

"Anyway, I was interested to overhear something of what you were talking to Kamaboku about, about stones having 'faces', sides they were intended to be seen from. I had not thought of looking at them in that way, they have always just seemed to be there. I had not thought about stones having...." he paused, searching for the right words. "Of stones, well, if they have 'faces', then they must have 'bodies' too. Oh, I don't know. It's if they are like people, like us; then, do they think too, feel things like we do too?"

Maguro Sensei's face softened in the half-light, as he leant back in his posture, though his eyes never left Shigoto's face. He held out a hand with the fingers slightly cupped, palm upward as if he were offering his pupil an object. It was probably a completely unconscious movement, a simple gesture, but it caught Shigoto's attention, and he felt his eyes drawn towards the long thin fingers clustered together in mid-air.

"It is true, we do speak about the 'face' of a stone. There are many qualities on which a stone is assessed, but that is an important consideration. We also speak of the stone having a 'root', that is the part buried into the ground. That's also very important." He paused momentarily. "You know the term *ishigumi*, meaning 'rock arrangement', yes?"

Shigoto nodded. Sensei's other hand, which had been lying in his lap, now joined the raised one, the two palms pressed together.

"There are two parts connected with *ishigumi*; first, there is the technique, and in second place, there is following the correct spirit of placement. The first is easier to describe than the second, as in truth there are few rules to follow. Always compose your arrangement according to the old laws of placement by triangles, in this way you will never go far wrong. Set one stone first, as the 'Quickest to the Eye Stone' or the 'Master Stone'. This is the principal, the ruler, now all the other stones can then take their rightful place, according to the requesting mood of each one in turn. We should understand that the arrangement of stones forms the skeleton of the garden; therefore a strong arrangement will give a strong feeling. But a weak arrangement will give a feeling of bad fortune and decay; it will be unsettling to someone looking at the stones. Do not be in too great a rush to place the stones, allow the garden to show you where the stones need to be placed. Let the ground speak for itself, the rocks too. Let them talk. They will, you know, they can have a great deal to tell us, if we can bear to listen. Nature may be wholly indifferent to your existence, but it will always have a tale to tell about itself. If you listen and observe what the stone is telling you, you will know how and where to place it. The stone will tell you. This is the way that has been passed on from one generation to then next. When we are arranging stones today, it is because of the understanding all those who have done it before us. This is following a tradition."

Sensei's hands dropped back onto his thighs. His eyes were still focused on Shigoto, who had been absorbed in the explanation. It felt as if he were being presented with information that was precious, privileged. In his mind's eye he could begin to picture the area where they had been clearing undergrowth and revealed many stones. He also recalled the strange incident at Kirifuda san's house, where he had made a connection between the screen paintings and the small rock arrangement outside in

The Gardener's Apprentice

the garden. He could vividly recall how he felt as if he were able to float freely through that landscape.

"Would you like more tea, Shigoto?" Sensei asked. Shigoto picked up his cup and held it forward without thinking. They sat without speaking for a few moments. The rain had eased and the light had strengthened marginally, overflowing puddles were scattered across the ground everywhere. To one side of the veranda a banana tree grew, its flapping leaves had caught the corner of Shigoto's eye from time to time, as Sensei had been speaking. He leaned forward a little and looked over towards the tree. Its long bright green leaves had been battered down by the weight of the driving rain; some of them torn to thin shreds. Where the leaves were more or less intact, they were shedding water from their waxy surface in hundreds of minor torrents. Shigoto straighten his back again.

"But how do you do that magic with the stones, Sensei? Making stones move without even touching them. I want to be able to set stones like that."

"Then you need to pay attention, Shigoto," Sensei chuckled. "Do you assume that this knowledge is just given to anyone, just because he demands it? It does not work like that, even if Lord Saeko entreated me here and now to bestow that knowledge on him. I could not."

"But, you would have to. If the demand came from Lord Saeko, there would be no choice in the matter, "said Shigoto indignant at the thought of refusal of such a command.

But Sensei merely rocked his head from side to side. "No, not for Lord Saeko, not for the Emperor, not for any soul. These ways are taught and learned through experience, you follow the hands and eyes and heart of the teacher, observing and trying to follow every movement. The student must find a way to see through the teacher's eyes. You must learn to see through my eyes, see what I see. When you start to do that, then you begin to learn, but only then. It has always been in our tradition that the student steals from the Master. That's as it should be, as the Master can only point this way or that. It is for the student to look that way too. Then, when he sees, when he *really* sees, when he sees as the Master does, then there is no more the teacher and the student. I can only reveal myself through your eyes. I only become myself as Sensei, through you. These are important things to consider, Shigoto. Never underestimate what it is you have set out to learn, you are dealing with Nature and the power of *Tao* itself."

Shigoto had gone back in his mind again to the rocks they had uncovered, emerging into the light again. He began now to see how the stones were linked, their relative positions one to another were not random as he had first assumed. Rather some invisible force had carefully placed each and every stone, one set to another. In this way he began to see the whole arrangement, over forty large stones in all, all as one coherent unit. He was thunderstruck at the thought.

"So all those stones there were placed exactly according to those principles? But why? Why do we go to all the trouble? Look what happened, everything got grown over, and it disappeared, and was was lost. No one now knows who placed those stones, or what was their thinking."

"We are not always the greater force in this matter, bearing in mind the energies that the gardener creates with. Far from it, we compose according to the needs of the land and in particular to the voice of the stones themselves. The garden master becomes as a servant to stones and trees. The required attitude of humility is the biggest mountain to climb, greater than any cloud-scraping peak, even in the Buddha's homeland. This is the reason why we must observe carefully the way in which a stone desires to be placed, and set it according to what it tells us. Remember the rock draws its strength not only from its size or weight, but also from being deeply connected to the earth. From which it one day rose, and one day beyond time it will return."

To Shigoto it seemed that each piece of information Sensei spoke about was opening new avenues for him. It dawned on him that the garden was far from just a nice place to be, he was seeing it more and more as a place of mystery, deep secrets and powers beyond his raw conception. He no longer heard the falling curtains of rain and no longer saw the raindrops exploding into the puddles of water. Realising now that he was a part of a process so awesome, and would be in a position to add to and influence its course, excited him more than anything else he had known before. It seemed to Shigoto that Sensei had taken a key and opened a door in his understanding; light was flooding into his mind.

For a long time they sat together, barely a word passed between teacher and pupil, until finally Sensei spoke, his voice calm and measured again.

"Shigoto, I hate to disturb your reveries, but perhaps it is time for you to return. We must not forget Kamaboku. He'll be waiting for some instruction from me. Perhaps we had better put him at his ease, eh? Tell him to organise the men's time as he sees fit to do for the rest of the day. There will always be another day for the garden." He leaned forward and craned up to look towards the sky. "It's still raining I'm afraid, but not as heavily now. Keep the robe."

"But Sensei, thank you, but I could not. After all you have given me today," protested Shigoto, as he stood back under the eaves by the front door, his damp clothing bundled under his arm. He felt so elated that "thank you'" seemed too inadequate an offering, but he had nothing else to give.

"Go quick and safe, Shigoto. Your time will come, and yes, I believe one day you too will call yourself a gardener. It all starts and ends with the heart, you understand that now." He beamed a last smile at Shigoto. "Now, be gone for the moment."

Shigoto danced away, not a care for the rain that continued to tumble out of the sky. He was riding an ox, a huge, ancient beast that lumbered on regardless of the terrain, its broad hips rocking him in a soothing rhythm. He saw himself on the back of the ox, sitting backwards the rear, a bamboo flute in his hands as he picked out a genial melody, the trees and plants were swaying, the waters danced, and the rocks were singing. Singing to his tune.

CHAPTER TWENTY-SIX

November 1594

Having finished his chores for the day, Shigoto went to visit the bathhouse the gardeners used. When he arrived there he found Kamaboku had beaten him to it. They chatted of inconsequential matters as he washed himself thoroughly, and rinsed by pouring cold water over himself with a large bamboo ladle. When Kamaboku had vacated the large tub of water Shigoto stepped into to soak for a few minutes. After he rose from the tub, he dried himself and slipped into the blue dyed kimono that Sensei had given him. Shigoto had tried to return the kimono but Sensei had refused to accept it, and instead insisted that Shigoto should keep it. Shigoto was vaguely aware of the privilege of wearing the garment bestowed on him by his teacher, but had taken it as a gesture of amicability and goodwill. The other gardeners were quick to notice the symbolism involved, and it had created some annoyance and comment, and did little to further endear Shigoto to some of his fellow gardeners. Kamaboku, typically, was the one who came quickest to accept the situation. As he rubbed himself dry with a cloth before dressing, he saw the *kimono* folded and waiting to be put on.

"Sensei has bestowed a great honour on you Shigoto, in giving you that garment. It is an act of favour to you personally. It is also a burden, you know."

"How's that? He didn't want it back. It's just a *kimono*, an old one at that." said Shigoto slightly puzzled by the comment.

"Sensei is indicating his preference by his generosity. So today he gives you a *kimono*, maybe tomorrow he gives you the seal of his teaching." Though Kamaboku's face never shed its usual smiling façade, the tone he used was serious and grave. "That is something to think about."

"He told me to wear it. Not to put it away."

"Then wear it, and be proud too. It suits you. But be aware that not everybody will see with the same eyes as old Kamaboku here, eh," and he laughed softly, his tanned face creasing in amusement.

"You are not so old," protested Shigoto.

"Oh, old enough, eh? Old enough, to be able to see some things. I am just a simple gardener, Shigoto; my father was a gardener here, and his father too. For myself, I am content with my life. The garden and my ancestors have taught me much, that's for sure. Just as every plant, every rock in the garden has its own life, its own spirit, so every person is different too, eh? Listen. I am not smart a man like Sensei; I know my limitations, even if I do not always understand his ways. But…" he paused searching for just the right words, "…well, Sensei is a gardener, a fine gardener too, and he does love this garden, I see that." Then he broke off as if the correct words would not quite gel in his mind sufficently to express his thoughts clearly. "Anyway, enough of this serious talk, eh. Tell me, are you going to see your mother, eh?"

"Yes, after my bath, when I am cleaned up. I was going to eat with her tonight. Why?"

"Oh, no reason," and Kamaboku pursed his lips theatrically, a look of delight dancing in the light in his eyes.

"No, why do you ask? Do you have a message for her?" persisted Shigoto.

"Nooo," drawled Kamaboku, stretching out the syllables.

"Oh come on Kamaboku *san*, spit it out. There is something on your mind, I can tell." insisted Shigoto.

"Oh, I just wondered if you were dressing up in your finery, 'cause you were going to meet someone, eh?"

"I am, my mother," said Shigoto firmly, suddenly catching the drift of the conversation. He was getting irritated at the teasing tone Kamaboku had adopted, and was not in the mood.

"It's just that… it's just that there is talk around the kitchen area, that's all, eh." Kamaboku looked towards Shigoto gauging the effect of his words.

"There always is, isn't there. That's why you like hanging around there so much, isn't it?" Shigoto's face was beginning to redden despite his best efforts not to be provoked by his companion. Nureba's image danced up before his eyes. He hurried to finish dressing before the gentle ribbing could go any further. "Anyway, I must be going, Kamaboku *san*, I will give my mother your best regards."

"Yes, give your mother my regards. Any woman could not help but be impressed by you in that kimono, eh," was his parting shot as Shigoto bundled his belongings together under his arm and rushed out into the evening light.

He ran over to his parents' house, the place he still thought of as his home, all the while his steps lightened by the thought of Nureba. In his mind she was running gaily along beside him. They were running through a landscape, weaving in among the trees, dodging between shrubs, and all he could hear was the sound of her laughter, her voice as sweet as a running stream. 'Nureba, Nureba,' he wanted to shout her name out aloud, and let his voice fill the air with her name. He was still running when he arrived at the front of the house where his mother was waiting for him.

"Well, Shigoto-chan, you seem to be in a good mood. You must have got wet today, it rained heavily, no? I was thinking of you." His mother greeted him as he shed his sandals and stepped up into the house. "Come and eat, sit down and have some food."

He sat on the floor and his mother brought several dishes set on a tray to him. She poured tea from a small pot into a simple white porcelain bowl.

"Well, Shigoto-*chan*, are you not going to say 'Good evening', to your grandmother before starting to eat. How like your father to are sometimes." From the gloom at the rear of the room his grandmother spoke up. Shigoto had not noticed her sitting there.

"Oh, Oba-*chan*, good evening. I'm sorry," he said his mouth already full of rice.

"And you are wearing that old kimono too."

"Sensei gave it to me," he said, his chopsticks pincering a piece of fish and lifting it up to his mouth. Remembering the teasing he had received from Kamaboku, he felt his cheeks beginning to warm.

"Well, there's a thing, then," said his grandmother still sat in the gloom of the rear of the room. "I still sew things for your mother, my eyes are not bad yet, you know."

"Mmm, thanks, "he mumbled, wishing the elderly woman would not speak to him when he was eating, he did not want to be rude but he was hungry, and occupying himself with eating helped to disguise any trace of embarrassment he might reveal.

"Just like his father," said his grandmother to no one in particular.

"Now, Oba-*chan*. Let the boy eat in peace, he'll get indigestion," interjected his mother. "Shigoto-chan eat more slowly, and sip the tea. Oh sometimes, your manners! You may work as a gardener, but that does stop you from having good manners." Shigoto ate more slowly.

"So, tell us Shigoto-*chan* what you have been doing of late?" asked his Grandmother ignoring her daughter

"Oh, not that much really.' Shigoto tried to think of something to say that would be neutral, and not involve him being drawn into a discussion of what the thoughts were actually streaming through his mind. "Work, really. That's about all." He resumed his meal.

"Not very talkative is he?" said his grandmother, after a moment.

"Now, give him a chance, Oba-*chan*."

Shigoto tried to concentrate on eating, despite the pressures of his mother and grandmother watching every move he made. He held a last piece of fish clamped between the slender chopsticks, poised between bowl and mouth. He tried to think of something interesting to say, some anecdote to occupy and amuse them. But all he could bring to mind were images of Nureba walking along a path, softly dissolving into the trees. He finished the last mouthful and laid his chopsticks across a small plate, and pushed the tray gently away from him. His mother rose and cleared it away.

She was returning to the room where they sat, when the sound of men's voices entered the room from outside. The three figures were silent, their attention drawn towards the open doorway, as Shigoto's father appeared in the entry hall. There was immediate consternation in the room as clearly he had not been expected.

"Ah, welcome back," Shigoto's mother was the first to react and went towards the entry porch where she knelt to wait to greet her husband. Shigoto Kanyu looked into the room and noticed his son sitting there.

"Oh, the boy is here," he said as he slipped off his shoes before stepping up into the room.

Instantly on seeing his father standing in the doorway Shigoto felt the hairs on the back of his neck rise. It was the last person he wanted to see. He glanced across at his mother but her face was impassive, submissive even. He had not seen, let alone spoken to his father for some time and hearing his voice again, that clipped, abrupt voice, he felt himself transported back in time to hearing the two voices within the teahouse, before he had made a noise and disturbed them plotting. He vividly remembered hiding in the narrow space under the teahouse as the unexpected occupants searched for him in vain. Had his father noticed him?

"Come in, come in, husband. Shigoto-*chan* is here, let me make some tea, while you make yourself comfortable." Her voice was calm and in control. "Shigoto-*chan*, make room for your father."

His father strode into the room and he sat on a cushion.

"I trust you are well." He greeted his wife with no particular enthusiasm, and then turned toward his son. "So son, you are here?"

"Yes, father, I came by to see mother and Oba-*chan*."

"Umm, I see, "again the familiar clipped tone, It seemed his father had not expected to find his son here, and had been momentarily thrown off balance. "I see," he repeated.

Shigoto's mother appeared with another tray bearing a small tea bowl, which she set down beside her husband. "Are you hungry, husband, there is food I can bring if you wish."

"No, I have eaten. The tea will do." He made no move to drink.

An awkward silence fell on the company.

"So husband, to what do we owe this pleasure," said Shigoto's mother as if she were addressing a rarely seen guest.

Kanyu started to say something, but before the words could form he closed his mouth again. His presence had brought a tension into the room. Shigoto was wondering how he could make his excuses to leave. He felt trapped in a place where he really did not want to be, with a person he had neither expected, nor wished to see. He had hoped that there might have been a few moments when he could have spoken to his mother regarding a subject that was burning in his mind. Now all he wanted was to flee as far as possible. He hardly dared look toward his father. He stared at the floor in front of him. Toward the rear of the room Oyadori's mother rose unsteadily to her feet.

"A nice greeting for his mother-in-law, wouldn't you say?" she said to no one in particular, but her voice dripping with sarcasm in its politeness.

"Forgive me, mother-in-law, I had not seen you there. I trust you are in good health."

"Thank you, I am fine, my eyesight particularly," said the elderly woman. "Now if you will excuse me, I have things to do. I was just heading for a bath. I am sure you will wish to speak to your family." She bowed slightly toward her son-in-law, and left the room.

"Hasn't the rain been heavy of late?" Shigoto's mother spoke to break the silence before it could become entrenched between them.

"Eh? The rain? It's the rainy season, what did you expect?"

Shigoto looked across at his father sitting cross-legged on a cushion a few feet away from him. He seemed older than he remembered, his face more lined and care worn. Kanyu sat holding the teacup in both hands in his lap. He still had not drunk from it. He was shorter in stature than his son; he had the frame of someone who had devoted his time to administration rather than physical work or action. His hands were soft and pink, his kimono of fine quality. As he sat his back was slightly rounded.

"So, to what do we owe the pleasure of your visit?" Oyadori said again, and even Shigoto felt moved by the irony, of someone being greeted like a guest in his own home. He almost smiled, but a lingering fear of the man before him held any expression of emotion in check.

Kanyu looked over toward his son before speaking. For someone who obviously desired to project an aura of authority he seemed uncertain of himself. He looked towards his wife kneeling beside Shigoto. "Well, I came to speak to you as it happens."

"Then maybe I should take my leave, if you will excuse me. Mother, thank you for the meal. There are things I must do, and the others are expecting me back at the House of Gardeners." Shigoto felt an opening, a means of escaping the presence of the man in whose company he felt distinctly uncomfortable. He did not feel as capable of projecting a sense of calm as his mother. He started to rise to his feet.

"Sit down," his father barked, then realising that he had spoken harshly, he repeated more softly this time, "Sit! Sit down. This concerns you. As you are here, you may as well hear what I have to say."

Shigoto sank back onto the cushion a feeling of dread spreading through him. No one else spoke, mother and son waited for Kanyu to resume, to unburden himself of his thoughts.

"I came here to speak of the boy," he said, not looking at Shigoto. "Word has reached me of him, that is of a relationship he has entered into, and I as his father do not approve. There is a time and place for such things, and it is not now, not here." Shigoto felt an icy feeling came over him. As his father paused before continuing, he knew what it was he was about to say and already tentacles of hatred were spreading and poisoning his system.

"The boy..." every time his father employed that expression it was as if a nail was being driven in. "It seems the boy has being talking to one of the serving maids. It is causing comment. It has to stop, it cannot continue. I will not have this family subject to gossip like that. It does my position no good, these are difficult times, it is nothing that needs to concern or interest you, but I cannot condone such actions on behalf of... the... my son. In due course these matters will be taken care of in accordance with the proper way of acting. He is far too young for one thing. As his father I cannot allow the matter to continue. It's far better to nip it in the bud now, before it gets any further. That's the end of it."

Shigoto's mother turned to look at her son who was staring intently at the patch of floor in front of him as his father spoke. Her expression had not changed or altered as she took in the words Kanyu spoke. For himself, Shigoto was incensed. He felt nothing but cold anger toward the man who referred to himself as his father, but acted as his tormentor. He wanted to shout at, even to reach across and strike at this man with his fists, he was physically much bigger and better built, the years of garden work had seen to that. He wanted to confront his father with the knowledge that he had overheard him plotting in the teahouse, what he had no idea. But he knew the air of tension surrounding that occasion indicated something important and secret, though what he could not begin to guess at.

"Perhaps this is a matter we can speak about..." began his mother with an even tone of voice.

"No, no. I will not hear of it. The matter is closed, finished, ended. Perhaps it is fortuitous that he is here, then, he hears it from me. Do you understand? The matter is ended, here and now."

Relieved of the burden of his words Kanyu raised the cup to his mouth to drink. As he did so, Shigoto jumped to his feet and made for the door. Kanyu was startled by the sudden movement and instinctively raised an arm as if to protect himself, but Shigoto rushed by. As he reached the doorway leading out to the entry porch, he stopped and turned around.

"What right do you have to say this? What do you know, what do you care anyway? It's not a matter that concerns you in the least. What do you care? For all I know it's probably true what others say. What right do you have? You don't care one bit for us." He shouted at the two figures still sitting there in astonishment.

He jumped down the step into the porch, and without even stopping to find his sandals ran barefoot into the lane. He was blind to where he ran, cared not where he was headed, only to get away as fast as he could from the figure of his father.

Shigoto ran and ran, until he felt his lungs bursting, and there were stars before his eyes. He stopped by a large oak and leaned with his back against the rough bark of the tree. His chest was heaving and breath came in jagged draughts, tears rolling down his face. Burning tears not of sorrow or even sadness, but simply hatred. As he slowly began to calm his pounding chest, he realised it had gone quite dark. He was somewhere in the gardens, but he had no idea where. He had not noticed anything of which direction he had taken, he had just run. Run and run until his legs had given out. Out of the darkness that now enveloped him, Nureba's face loomed bright as a star and as large as the autumn moon, but this time it brought him no joy or comfort. He turned around and letting his forehead touch the coarse bark, he flailed at the trunk with his fists and wept openly.

There was no moon and the cloud cover was thick. The air carried the sweet scent of more rain. Shigoto slumped down at the base of the tree and hugged his knees to his chest. The wind was picking up, a strong gust caught the dark branches above him and he could feel the subtle straining movement of the trunk against his back. He pushed his legs out in front of him and closed his eyes. Before him floated Nureba and her smiling face, the one that he had seen the last time they had met so unexpectedly in the garden. That time he had felt great joy surging through his body and his heart. Now not even the sight of her face, so clear in his mind's eye that he felt he could reach out and run his fingers across her cheek, could bring him any solace. He felt torn from his being. Then Nureba's face dissolved and he could see Maguro Sensei's image looming in front of him, looking down at him lying there at the base of the great tree.

"Sensei, why? Why this? Why does my father hate me so? What have I done to make him hate me so? Why is life so cruel?" He cried into the black inky night, but there was no one to hear, all that came back was the cry of a bird, calling out a warning perhaps. The wind continued to come in gusts, stronger now, until it seemed as if it were tearing into the fabric of the night. Then the rain started to fall, at first a few heavy drops rattling the leaves of the tree above him, then to fall more evenly onto the ground beyond the canopy of the oak. Shigoto barely registered that it was raining until it began to fall heavily enough to penetrate even the canopy of leaves and to run in thin rivulets down the craggy bark. Even then he didn't care. It seemed to him that he been torn from that which he most cared about, the person he cared most for, even if he had exchanged but half dozen words with her. All he knew was the emptiness of loss mingled with a growing loathing for his cold and heartless father.

"What is the point of all this? Tell me. What is the point of it all?" he wailed into the inky night around him, but there was no answer. The rain only fell with an increasing intensity driven by an ever strengthening wind.

Shigoto could not move, or rather he had seemingly lost all will or motivation to move from where he was. He sensed the blackness swirling around him as if it were a fog stealthily creeping across low ground. In what remained of his rational, conscious mind he recognised that he was about to be swallowed whole. Even if he had wanted to get up, to escape, he could not; he was skewered by inertia and indifference. He heard Sensei's voice, coming from some distant place: 'Nature is indifferent to who you are'. Then waves of dark clouds swept over him, and took him whole as he was. Then there was nothing, no sound, no light, nothing.

"Nureba? Nureba, is that you?" She was wearing a robe of pure white luminescent cloth, which seemed to flow about her. She was alone, with nothing about her that was recognisable, to fix her in a familiar space. She turned her face to him and seemed to be speaking yet there were no words to be heard, just the slow opening and closing of her mouth. "Speak, speak to me. It's all right I am alone, there is no one here to listen, you can say what ever you wish. You can tell the truth." When he could hear the sounds coming from her it was not with Nureba's gently teasing tone, but the gruff, strained voice of his father: "There is nothing to be done here. Everything has been thought of, every contingency covered. I have waited long enough, suffered enough for this. Everything has been prepared, put into place, now it's too late to hold back any more. We must strike, and strike hard. Now is the time to move."

"Shigoto, hey, Shigoto, you there?"

Nureba's image faded, dissolved into the mire, and all he could see was a field of flowers, tiny white flowers stretching out into the distance, each one sparkling, and dazzling so bright that he had to shield his eyes from the intense light. Yet it remained dark, not even the light thrown by the iridescent jewels scattered across a mountainside could penetrate the dark. Both dark and light, so dark that he could not see a hand he raised up to his face, yet light enough to be able to sweep his eyes across a mountainside. The ground swept up to his left, rising steeply and evenly, covered in low grasses that caught the wind

The Gardener's Apprentice

that swept across the open space creating alternating waves of shimmering silver and cool greens. Everywhere the flowers, or were they flowers? They were so small, mere pinpricks, yet so intensely bright and dazzling that the source of their light became obscured. Then clouds swept in off a distant sea, carrying the scent of salt and seaweed, billowing, piling in on one another. White opalescent mounds in which he thought he could recognise faces for which he had no names. "We are waiting for you, but you have to reach the mountaintop first. No, keep walking; there is nothing here to detain you. You need to keep moving, continue to the top and keep on, just do not look to either side, there's nothing there. Nothing to hold onto."

"Shigoto, hey, Shigoto, you with us yet?"

He felt a rocking motion, he was swaying first one way then another, sometimes it seemed as if he were being spun about in complete circles. Birds had gathered somewhere near for he could hear their incessant chatter against a sawing, mechanical background noise that was difficult to ascribe to anything. It made him feel ill at ease, all the suppleness had left his body, and everything was now angles and sharp corners, pieces that did not seem to fit together one way or another but had been placed in a haphazard, illogical manner. "Nothing makes any sense anymore", he heard his voice say, but it did not seem to come from within him.

"He's waking up, look."

Shigoto blinked several times and finally managed to get his eyes to stay open long enough to begin to focus on what was about him. He felt disorientated as if he were emerging from a long troubled sleep, his head ached and pounded.

"Hey there, Shigoto, so you are with us after all." It was Kamaboku's voice, and his kindly face looking down at him. Shigoto tried to move, but his body was as heavy as lead and reluctant to stir. "No, stay still. Don't move. Here, drink some of this, it's tea made from herbs, it will make you feel better. Here sip some."

Kamaboku held the wide bowl to Shigoto's mouth and tipped a little of the greenish watery liquid between his lips. Shigoto took in a little of the potion, it was bitter tasting and he momentarily gagged as he swallowed.

"That's it, swallow, Here take a little more, eh." Kamaboku held the bowl to Shigoto's lips again and tilted it to pour a little liquid into his mouth.

Shigoto tried to get up, but Kamaboku pushed him back down, and gathered the futon over his shoulders.

"Hey, Shigoto, you had us worried for a minute there." Then he turned to address someone behind him, "Go and tell his mother he is awake, go on, run."

Gradually Shigoto's senses began to fall back into some order, and he began to take in where he was. He could hardly move his limbs, but his vision was beginning to clear sufficiently for the room that he lay in to begin to come into focus. He recognised that he was back in his room at the House of Gardeners, in a familiar space again. Kamaboku was kneeling beside him looking part anxious and part greatly relieved to see him regain consciousness again.

"Kamaboku, what happened, where have I been?" He slurred, his throat felt dry and constricted, and his tongue seemed to be swollen.

"You were found in the garden, soaking wet. Seems you had passed out. Nobody knows how long you had been lying there. You've had a fever. Anyway you will be all right now. Your mother was here until a short time ago and she will be back in a while. I asked Ekichū to go and fetch her. Hey, you had us all worried you know. You had some fever, that and ranting and raving away, we thought you were going crazy for a while there." Kamaboku laughed.

"Sensei ..." Shigoto stammered out.

"I'll get word to him soon as your mother gets here. He has been here too. Tell you, you had us all worried for a moment there, eh. Anyway you are going to be fine now, just get some rest, eh. Everything's fine, just fine."

"Is it..." said Shigoto as he allowed his eyes to close again, and slipped into a deep and dreamless sleep.

In a few days Shigoto was back on his feet again, a little unsteady at first. As soon as he was fit enough he was moved to his family home, and there his mother and grandmother brought him back to full health again.

"What happened? Why was I ill?" he asked his mother one time when they were alone. She looked toward him and began to say something but decided against it.

"You caught a chill, then a fever, "she said simply. "In a few days you will be fit enough to start work again. Sensei is coming over later. He said you were to be brought back to full strength before you start work again. So rest and food, that's all you need for now."

As his mother had predicted, in a few days he was feeling able to venture out into the fresh air. At first his legs felt weak, and the activity tired him easily, but he recovered his strength soon enough. He never spoke to his mother about the cause of his collapse and illness. He had recovered some memory of an argument with his father and the bitter aftertaste that it left in him and he did not wish to pursue the matter. He felt resigned to the situation: no matter how he may protest, it would be to no avail. His father's word was there to be obeyed, he knew to go against that now would cause untold trouble for others. As he gathered his strength again he silently dwelt on the matter and in time came to his own resolution. He would obey his father for now, but his time would come, and when it did he would act for himself; then, nobody would stop him, no one would hinder him. It felt as if it were a resolution that had been carved in stone, implacable and unchangeable. He would learn to bide his time.

When he resumed his garden duties again everyone seemed pleased to see him, especially Kamaboku and Tanuki, the two people he felt closest to among his colleagues. He received a thorough ribbing for taking such a long 'holiday', but they were pleased to have him back. Even Konnyaku welcomed him back again.

"Eh, Shigoto, it's a good job you are back. That Tanuki, he drives me crazy with his incessant talking, that and the sleep-walking. It's enough to send any one off for a holiday." Konyaku was grinning at him.

"I have not been on holiday, "said Shigoto flatly, though there was a hint of a smile.

"I know, I know, but please, can't you have a word with him? Least when you are about he mainly talks to you, gives me a break, eh. The man gives me a headache. He's nothing but trouble," said Konnyaku firmly.

CHAPTER TWENTY-SEVEN

January 1595

After the early morning haze had cleared, a weak sun appeared for the first time in several days. Shigoto and Tanuki had been assigned to cleaning duties in the Southern courtyard. The high winds and storms of late had blown debris to all corners of the garden, and pairs of gardeners were assigned different areas to tidy. Shigoto was content to be spending time with Tanuki. If no one else did he enjoyed the wholehearted company of the stranger from Kyoto. It also allowed Shigoto the opportunity to take charge of certain operations, for it was evident even to Shigoto that Tanuki's skills as a gardener did not come naturally to him. He frequently needed reminding of the ways "things are done round here", a role Shigoto was happy to take on, and Tanuki seemed happy enough to oblige him in.

For a couple of hours they had worked silently with their brushes and rakes sweeping across the ground in unison. Each lost in their own efforts and thoughts as they worked. It was Tanuki who broke the spell between them with a grunt.

"I need a sup of water," he said and set off across a patch of gravel they had just raked spotless, and ducked into the shade of the veranda that ran along one side of the great expanse. They had left a water flask there and Tanuki pressed himself into the deep shade to raise it to his lips. Shigoto watched him walk away, then with barely a grimace made his way toward Tanuki, sweeping away any scuffed prints as he went. Tanuki held out the flask toward Shigoto as he approached, his arm and the flask bordering the light, his face and torso in shadow. As he came near and was about to drop his brush and join Tanuki, he noticed a group of well-dressed people walking along the veranda in his direction. They were too close to him to call a warning to Tanuki, as it would be obvious to the approaching figures, but Tanuki must have of picked up the sounds of their feet on the boards above his head and he dissolved further into the gloom. Shigoto continued sweeping, keeping his eyes trained on the ground, ears keenly alert to the oncoming party.

There were three men heading the entourage, walking swiftly and engaged in deep conversation. As the men swept imperiously past, Shigoto recognised the imposing figure of his lord and master, Lord Saeko himself and one of the figures accompanying him was his father, Kanyu. If ever there was a time when he wanted the earth to swallow him whole, then it was right now, but the men swept past along the wide boarded veranda without stopping or even breaking their concentration. After they passed Shigoto looked up long enough to briefly watch the retreating backs move away along the veranda. He was about to smile in relief when he noticed two women making their way after the men. They were walking at a much more leisurely pace, and had fallen several paces behind. One of them carried a pale wooden box,

The Gardener's Apprentice

the other, free of any burden, spotted Shigoto and looked coldly down at him. They stopped opposite him.

"Are gardeners not supposed to show respect and bow to superior ranks?" The taller of the two women spoke, her voice chilly and tunelessly devoid of any feminine warmth.

"Ma'm." Shigoto bowed toward the figures above him.

The tall woman with the hard, pinched face and hair pulled back continued to look towards Shigoto. Her eyes bristled with arrogance, as she looked down on the world set out below her. Shigoto was racking his memory to place his interrogator. Lingering in his mind was a memory shard tantalisingly just out of his grasp. The woman appeared to Shigoto to be in her middle years, somewhat older than the silent companion who stood beside her. Her eyes that were looking away across the garden, avoiding the scene before her as if it were not to her taste at all.

"Don't I know you?"

"I have worked in the East garden (the garden facing onto the women's apartments) Ma'm. I was there a few weeks ago, tidying up, with Kamaboku *san*."

"What's your name?" she stabbed out.

Shigoto shuffled his feet, his mouth felt dry. He prayed that Tanuki would not do anything sudden or to reveal himself, as he was crouched directly under the boards on which the women stood. He looked up to see the group of men disappearing down to the far end of the open gallery and desperately hoped that the women would rush off to catch up with the main party and, thereby resolving the immediate problem of the hidden Tanuki, whose brush, rake and basket were still lying out in the open for anyone to see.

"Under Gardener Shigoto. Apprentice to Maguro Sensei," he bowed formally. Holding the bow longer than he really needed to. At the mention of his name the older woman whose gaze had remained pinned on him, stiffened noticeably, and she jerked her head back.

"Ah, yes, "she said slowly. "Under Gardener Shigoto, I remember you now. That was your father who just passed you know, with Lord Saeko himself." The voice had lost none of its haughty cold indifference.

"I bowed to them too," Shigoto lied defiantly.

The woman's focus on him had shifted, as if she were re-evaluating him. Reconsidering her strategy in the light of what she now knew.

"It strikes me there is a lot of work to be done here," she threw up a hand in the direction of the expanse of courtyard behind Shigoto. "There's debris all over the place. You gardeners are struggling to cope, that's clear to anyone. You'll have to put in more effort, waste less time when you work. Your father's an important man, you know, you are letting him down with your slack attitude to your work in my opinion."

Before he had time to react to her unjustified condemnation, Tanuki burst out of his hiding place. It so surprised Shigoto that he reacted as if a firecracker had exploded at his feet. The women were equally startled by Tanuki's sudden and unannounced arrival in their midst. The starchy woman took a step back, whilst her companion gasped and clutched the wooden box tighter to her chest. Both the women looked up in the direction where their male companions had gone.

"Excuse me butting in on someone's conversation. Here we go, Shigoto, the water flask, I found it at last, I knew it was under there somewhere." He held out the vessel towards Shigoto, a beaming smile playing across his face. Shigoto suddenly had a vision of Tanuki generously inviting the ladies for a drink of water, and why not a stroll around the gardens too? The smile was that dazzling. "As I say, excuse me for butting in and all. Tanuki is the name. Tanuki, the gardener."

All Shigoto could do was stand there and watch with a mixture of horror and fascination, this display of outrageous bravado by Tanuki. He himself would never have of dared to speak so informally to someone one of a higher rank. Even with Kamaboku, he was aware of how far he could take a sense of light-hearted camaraderie and joshing. One of the ways of negotiating the world was to play by the rules, do what was expected of you; it was part of the invisible web that held everything together. At least Tanuki's arrival had shifted the centre of attention away from himself, though he was already beginning to dread the retribution that was sure to follow if a complaint were to be made. Insubordination always extracted a price.

"Ahh," the outspoken woman finally managed to choke out. With releasing some sound she managed to regain something of her station again. "Well, I was just saying the place needs tidying. It shows," she said firmly, this time addressing the bobbing dark head of Tanuki.

"Oh yes Ma'm. That's what we are about, that's just what we're about. Shigoto and I are sweeping the place clean enough for Lord Saeko himself to dine off. Should his Lordship so wish to do so, that is." The radiant smile so brilliant and convincing, though who could remotely consider the absurdity of such a claim?

"Well I suggest you get on with it then." It was a weak parting shot, that of an aggressor who having bitten once, decides the taste is too bitter to continue. The two women turned on their heels and started after the men, never once turning their heads to look back. If they had done, they would have seen Tanuki bent over slapping his thigh, as he tried to hold himself back from bursting into laughter. And Shigoto standing there dumbfounded by the whole episode.

"What did you say that for? Why did you leap out like that? You idiot, she'll make some sort of comment now. Then we'll be in trouble, for what...?"

But all Tanuki could do was to hold in his good humour. "Eh, see her face? The old crow. She nearly fell over when I jumped out! Ha, ha, hah," and again he slapped his thigh. "Come on, we had better make it look as if we are doing something." Still chuckling to himself he put the flask down on the ground and wandered back to where he had abandoned his tools.

"You mad man!" Shigoto ran to catch up with Tanuki, and began to sweep at the gravel with agitated, jerky strokes, whilst a smile played across his companion's countenance. "We're going to be for it. They'll find something to come up with. What possessed you to leap out like that, you could have stayed where you were. She had no idea you were there. They would have gone any moment, you just had to stay where you were," Shigoto protested. "And that idiot grin! We're sunk. Even my father was there," as the full horror of the situation enveloped him like ice cold water surging over a drowning man. He redoubled his effort with the brush.

"Hey, relax. She won't say a thing to anyone, nor the young one. Forget it. No problem with women. Just give them a smile and there you go, charmed off their feet. Thought you had a lady friend anyway. You'll know all about that kind of thing by now," Tanuki continued to chuckle away to himself. "Learnt a thing about women over the years. Easy as hell to charm, except the ones that aren't. Then you are in trouble. No doubt about that. Something happens when they get to a certain age I reckon. Did I ever tell you about the geisha of the One Lotus House? Must have told you that. Now there was a woman to be reckoned with. Oh, I stepped out with her. Me, Tanuki! I was but a decoy in some romantic plotting it was true, a background actor. But, hey, you know, I was there, even if it was only a walk-on part. The One Lotus Teahouse, that's what it was called, in Shimabara."

"Look now's not the time for stories. She will tell. She is just the sort to make trouble. Some of them are so struck up, they treat you like a bad smell sometimes. Believe me, I know what it's like round here. Most people are fine if you don't cross them, they don't say much, don't bother you. But there are always a few who want to be nasty somehow. Anyway, she'll say something for sure."

"Nah, doubt it," said Tanuki, and he spat into the gravel he was idly sweeping at. "Nah, I know all about women, she won't say a word. That type, they're all puffed up, full of themselves. It's all feathers in the air, that's all. Quite fancied her companion myself, how about you?"

"You are crazy, "said Shigoto and he instinctively moved away a pace or two. They talked as they worked, gradually making their way out toward the centre, well out of earshot.

"Fancy her with those airs and graces, she's a dry stick if I ever saw one. Now, the younger one, she was all right. She's pretty enough to interest Tanuki. No, you can keep the older sourpuss, I'll have the younger one, she's real cute." Tanuki had been buoyed by the whole experience; he was like a cork bobbing on the waves. He was flurry of words and activity, none of which seemed to be getting anywhere. "Reminds me of one time, I think it was when I was in Osaka, at the castle. Nah, listen, forget it, believe me she won't say a thing. I know her, she won't whisper a note."

Shigoto stopped what he was doing. "What do you mean you know her? Don't tell me you know her. She's…"

"She's no one very important." Tanuki cut him off. "It's too late now anyway," he said absently as he looked over to where the women had rejoined the men. They were all sitting on the floor together in a pavilion at the end of the walkway. Writing brushes, ink and paper set out on the floor between them, presumably they were composing poetry: that's what people from the House often did when they sat there perched over the Great Dragon Pond. For the first time since he had emerged into the light, Tanuki did not have the smile about him.

That evening as Shigoto settled into the folds of his bedding, he wondered again about his friend Tanuki. He had laughed off the incident with the women that afternoon with such a certainty, that rather than being mollified by the outcome, Shigoto felt even more uneasy. He wondered if he should raise the matter with Sensei if they happened to be alone after meditation. It was clear to him that Sensei too regarded Tanuki with some suspicion. Should he fan those flames, or would this be another matter that he would put away in some accessible only to him part of his memory? He was tired, it had been a long and busy day and for now he just wanted to sink into the balm of sleep. Tomorrow would bring whatever it would bring, regardless. As he lay there, he pulled the cover tight in around his neck, and drew up his knees and let go of the world.

As sleep came, so did the dreams that meandered in the infinite space behind his eyes. First came a line of five rocks rising from the water's rippled and teased surface, labouring to rise from some great depth, reaching up toward the sun for air and light. The rocks become mountains, then islands with rocky coasts with sea birds taking off and landing from sheer cliff sides. White capped waves broke and glistened, and looking up from the restless sea one lost sight of the tops of the mountains among the clouds that both hid and revealed their sharp outlines. The islands shifted and adjusted their positions one to another, as if in some slow and stately dance to an eternal rhythm. At some points coming so close that they almost touched, other times seemingly bent on a collision course, until they would veer off in perfect synchronicity. In certain motions, the mountain islands would sink deep into the briny wash, 'til they were but pinpricks breaking the surface, before slowly rising again, their flanks sparkling and glistening as the heaving waters fell back.

The islands were supported on the backs of giant turtles, their burden an encrustation so tall and far reaching, the upper slopes and gullies supported teeming hordes of life forms. Birds constantly rose and settled from the cliffs and the thick-forested precipitous sides. Even above the sound of wind and water avian cries pierced the air. Many of the trees bore fruits soaked with dew, so they appeared as jewels hung from the branches. Here and there among the clouds that wrapped tight as an underskirt, darker shapes could be made out that bore a resemblance to the outlines of roofs and walls. Then a net fell onto the surface of the sea as soft and as stealthily as a rain shower caressing into the earth.

Two of the islands seceded from the group, slowly but surely they drifted away from the others. First they became hard to pick out in the glare across the distance that separates them, then becoming finally lost altogether in the mists of distance and time. The three remaining continued with their slow dance, pirouetting, dipping, shifting and endlessly tacking. Nothing halted the process. All trace was wiped clean, even memory expunged and made again, reinvented from the future, rather than the past. Then he was diving deeper into the sea heading for the depths where no light existed, way beyond the fealty of dreams. At last all fell into silence and dreamless sleep.

When the dreams returned they had him rushing back toward the surface, if that is what it was. He was in a tube of space barely wider than he was, outstretched with hands out before him and his feet trailing behind. He was moving, possibly at great speed, but with nothing to guide him it was impossible to tell. He felt as if he were ascending, but there was nothing to confirm that either, until he noticed that it was getting lighter, far ahead between his outstretched fingers. He was moving there, this he could tell as his hands were painstakingly slowly filling with light, as he felt strength pouring into his arms. As the intensity of the luminescence increased so he felt himself wanting to speak out, but he was still too deep for that to happen. Indistinct objects came and observed him from the other side of the tube's transparent wall. Sometimes it seemed as if they would break through and invade his already narrow and constricted space, but they never did. They remained on the outside swimming free, at liberty to come and go as they may.

Just before he was about to break through into the light, into the air, that he could use some of it to speak, to call out, he became aware of a sound. Barely perceptible at first the sonic waves rolled in so gently they barely disturbed anything at all. There was something indistinct that may have been the soft beating wings of birds, it was more as if they were coated with thick carapaces, not feathers. The noise reverberated and was amplified in his hollow space, gradually ratcheting up in pitch and intensity, until it was an insistent call, buzzing loudly in his ears, drowning all other considerations, thoughts and feelings.

Shigoto suddenly woke up lying on the floor in the same foetal position he had adopted when he fell asleep, the covering over him still drawn tightly around his neck. It was pitch black at first, until his eyes adjusted from the brilliance of the dream to reality. He breathed softly and evenly. The dream sank back, receding slowly as if a tide were slowly emptying an estuary. Then it came again, a muffled rustling sound. Someone was moving in the room next door. It was still night, he knew instinctively it was not time to rise, it was too dark, the light was wrong. One of the gardeners sleeping next door must be shifting in their sleep. 'Maybe they are dreaming too.'

He edged forward and was able to peer through the open doorway that separated his small space from the main room. It was too dark to see anything. He had just laid his head back on the futon, to try and slide back into sleep, when a momentary shift in the shades of grey gloom caught his attention. Immediately he sprang back into attention, holding his gaze on the spot where he thought he saw something. Then there was distinct the sound of someone moving in the room. Shigoto inched himself forward to see who it was who had to get up in the night. He could not tell at all but there were movements he could just make out, and then a figure slipped out and was gone. Tanuki, he realised, and then threw back his cover and as delicately as he could he crossed the floor and made for the doorway too.

When he emerged from the House of Gardeners into the night, he looked up and down the narrow lane that ran across the front of the row of buildings; on the opposite side of the lane were the bland walls of storehouses set pushed up to one another. Nothing appeared to move, and there were no sounds, then in the deep gloom at the end of the lane where it turned a sharp left hand corner Shigoto was just able to make out the dim figure crouched over tying on a pair of sandals. Then it was gone around the corner. Shigoto slipped out of the doorway of the House of Gardeners and started up the lane toward the corner, one hand running along the wall beside him as he cautiously moved forward. At the corner he peered around keeping flat to the wall. There was nobody to be seen. He turned the corner and pushed on, quiet as he could.

The lane ran on for about another block of buildings then it crossed a small patch of open ground before heading back between buildings again. At this juncture he stopped again to reconsider. There was no trace of Tanuki, and he was sure it was Tanuki he was following, even though he had never clearly made out the figure in the dark. He was sleepwalking he told himself, Shigoto was curious to see where his friend went; maybe he could even prevent some sort of accident happening. He faced a choice; either he could continue on the lane in the general direction of the gardeners' store, or he could cut across the open ground. He knew that he could slip through the thin band of trees and tall shrubs easily enough, and would emerge in the garden. It was a way the gardeners knew and used on occasion. There was no way of telling which direction Tanuki had taken. He may have been aware of the shortcut into the gardens, Shigoto did not know. Where was Tanuki going anyway?

   A decision had to be made, thinking that if he had lost track of Tanuki, nothing more could be done, and he would have to go back to bed none the wiser. Nothing much would have changed after all. He strained to pick up the slightest sound, but there was nothing out of the ordinary to notice. He made up his mind and cut directly across the open space. When he stopped again he had wormed his way into a gap that he knew was there. Carefully and silently he parted enough of the branches in front of his face to allow a view through. He could see into the gardens; the moon was quarter full and there was high cloud cover, but there was some weak light coming from the sky.

   The garden, in so far as he could make out any features at all, was depicted in dull monochrome. If he looked across the surface of the Great Dragon Pond, there were patches of faint steely light across the water's surface. He could make out one or two of the pruned pines along the bank closest to him, and was able to orientate himself by memory as much as by sight. Across to his left there was a gravel path with grassy banks that swung in a lazy loop around one side of the pond. It lead towards a boathouse, then turned away from the pond linking up with another path, eventually to make its way past two huge oaks to the exercise field. Shigoto scanned the direction of the path for any movement or sound. Seeing nothing to alarm, he was about to step forward when the distinctive figure of Tanuki came hurrying along from his right side. It was as if he had made a false turn, realised it, and then turned on his heel to resume the correct direction of travel. Except that he was no longer alone; there was someone running along beside him. Shigoto could not make out who it was. It was someone smaller than Tanuki in build and whoever it was, was having to hurry to keep up with Tanuki's long strides. It was a man for sure, but he was on the far side of Tanuki, and they were soon past Shigoto's concealed station and cutting across a grassed area making towards the gravel path. When they got to the path Shigoto could just about make them out, dropping down on one knee and looking about. Tanuki got up and tugging the other man's sleeve started to move again, except he kept to the quieter grass verge and pulled his companion in behind him to do the same and they were soon swallowed up by the blackness of chimerical shadows.

All of a sudden Shigoto knew where they were headed, it came to him in a flash, without being able to explain logically why, he knew they were aiming for the two large oaks. He was so sure that he decided to take another route that would bring him there. He could visualise a place that would give him a clear view across towards the trees yet furnish cover too. That way there would be no chance that he might come across Tanuki by surprise. In fact if he found his directions easily, he reckoned that he would be in position before they arrived in the area. The bearing he was intending to take skirted close to where Sensei lived at Kokiburi-an. He considered waking Sensei, but then realised he was sure of nothing. It could all be a wild goose chase, and he was potentially in line for a reprimand anyway, if the vindictive woman who spoke to him yesterday in the courtyard had made some comment. They were in potential trouble as it was, why stir the pot even harder? He pressed on deeper into the garden, skilfully making his way, his senses on full alert.

He arrived at the spot and it did indeed give him a clear view across towards the oaks. The nearest of which stood about thirty paces from where he crouched low amid thick foliage. Very soon after his arrival he made out two figures coming slowly along from the direction of the pathway. He had anticipated correctly, which pleased and calmed him; he felt very clear in his mind. Shigoto realised that if Tanuki went for the deep shadow of the oaks themselves he would be invisible, and there would be no safe way to get any closer than where he was now. He was content to watch and observe if anything happened, and allow Tanuki to make the next move. First they made for the tree nearest Shigoto, then after a brief interval they crossed over to the other tree, where they were lost to sight. He strained to hear any sound, and he thought he caught a trace of voices, but it was so faint and indistinct he could not be sure.

The pressure was building in his tensed muscles as he watched the area of the tree for movement, then to his complete surprise three figures, not just the two he had followed, broke from out of the dense shadow of the tree and headed towards the woodland further along to his right. It was the area where the gardeners had spent time before the onset of the monsoon rains, and had uncovered the presence of an extensive rock arrangement. Shigoto cursed to himself as he knew that the cover was dense in there and the ground contours highly irregular, there would be very little chance of finding anyone in there at night. The light was poor and there was some distance between him and the three stooped figures, but it was obvious enough to Shigoto that they were struggling to carry what appeared to be a large box between them. It must have been heavy, as they made slow and halting progress until they were swallowed by dense shadows once again.

Shigoto was caught between apprehension and curiosity. Whatever it was that Tanuki was involved with was highly irregular, and moreover he had clearly being spinning tales to Shigoto. Suddenly it occurred to him that the stakes had been raised, also that whatever was happening here was beyond his reckoning. There was also a certain sense of anger too, as he felt that his friend Tanuki had been misleading him. He had taken to the new man and tried to defend him from the jibes of the other gardeners. Now there was a nagging feeling of betrayal growing within him. Had the other gardeners, even Sensei, been correct all along in being suspicious of Tanuki? Was there no one that could be trusted after all?

Shigoto decided that discretion was the better path to follow: in truth he felt out of his depth. There were things happening he had no understanding of, though it seemed clear enough that trouble was afoot. So he melted back into the shadows and turned to make his way back to the House of Gardeners. He had not been gone long, but the tension of following and staking out Tanuki had made time seem to crawl past. He crept back into the comforting dark of the room where the gardeners remained asleep and oblivious to the drama. They slept on protected by their innocence. He reached the sanctuary of his own space and had not long lain down before he heard the furtive rustling of someone moving in the room next door. This time he did not even strain to listen. He knew it was Tanuki returning from whatever secret assignation he had been engaged with.

As dawn broke and the curtain of night stealthily slipped back, Shigoto awoke and got up. He had but one thought and that was to head for Kokiburi-an and Sensei. He was resolved to tell his teacher all that he had experienced last night. Sensei would know what best to do. Above all Shigoto felt he could be absolutely trusted. The other gardeners were still asleep as he slipped out. He knew they would be stirring soon, and he wanted to be away before they awoke. He glanced across the room as he left, and saw Tanuki curled up, mouth hanging slightly open, deep asleep, a look of complete innocence and peace across his face. He did not even stop to put the kettle over the coals for tea.

As he made his way through the garden towards Kokiburi-an, light was beginning to flood into the garden, seeping into every corner and crevice. Shigoto loved this time when the place was invariably empty of people. He took the path that ran near the Great Dragon Pond, the very same path along which he had tracked Tanuki in the dead of night, and he marvelled at how different it all looked now. An order, a sensibility had been re-established once more, the scene did not inspire the heart to pump stronger, fuelled by adrenalin and fear; it was calming, gracious and welcoming. The birds were rousing themselves, gathering their voices, re-establishing primacy to territory; a light mist hung over the glassy mirror that was the water, only disturbed here and there by the edge of a fish's fin, slicing through the surface film as if it barely existed at all.

As he pressed on Shigoto rehearsed the words he would say to Sensei, how he would introduce the subject of the happenings of the night. His mind ran over and over the scenes, trying to recall every last detail, to shake reality out of what may as easily been a dream. When he reached a point in the path when he needed to bear to the right towards Kokiburi-an, he hesitated; he knew he was not far from the twin oaks. He debated whether to take the path to the left and head in the direction of the woodland into which the load bearing figures had disappeared. It was not far away. He was curious as to what had gone on there, it might provide proof, but proof of what? Treachery or simply a misunderstanding? As he stood at the point of making his decision a crow passed overhead, lazily flapping its wings, the harsh toned plaintive cry seemed suddenly sad, as if the bird was in mourning, keening for some irredeemable loss.

Shigoto approached the rustic entry gate to the entry path that led to Kokiburi-an, the building was thickly shrouded by planting that hid most of it from view, only a section of the thatch roof could be glimpsed. The whole place seemed to be caught in a web of stillness. He slowed his pace and stepped through the gateway. Straight away as he did he realised that Sensei was not there. It was not the quiet that told him, but a rounded fist-sized stone had been set on one of the stepping-stones leading to the main entry door. It was Sensei's signal to forewarn visitors that he was not in. Sensei had once explained the origin of the stone sign, but he had not retained every detail except that it was a device used by Tea masters. The stone was usually tied with a black dyed cord, and it had a name that escaped him now, as he stood deflated looking at the mute stone. He glanced up towards the building and was ready to call out a greeting, but he knew that only Sensei would have taken the trouble to place the stone there. It could only mean one thing. There would be no meditation this morning.

He made his way back out and then stopped to consider his next move. He could simply head back to the House of Gardeners and some breakfast and tea, or he could head off towards the woods and see if there were any visible signs or clues of the activity during the night. His skin prickled with a vague sense of fear when he thought about plunging into the woodland, looking for of who knows what. Then out of the blue, the image of Nureba's face sprang up in his mind, so clear, so well defined she may as well have been standing beside him looking straight into his eyes. Nureba, he jolted at the guilty realisation he had that he had somehow managed to push her to the back of his mind. Now here she was as clear as the light rising in the sky. He had tried to get a message through to her via Kamaboku, but there had never come any kind of reply or acknowledgement. He knew that one day he would have to confront his father head on, and probably the issue to spark such a conflict would be Nureba, or at least his feeling towards her. He did not relish the occasion, but neither was he prepared to back away when the moment did come. He might have of decided to stay his hand for now, but that was more out of respect to his mother, than any particular affection held for his father.

As he stood there caught between the two courses of action, the tiredness he had been fending off seeped back into his body. He felt heaviness creep back into his legs and his spirits sinking into a quagmire of disappointment and bitterness. He had so hoped that Sensei would have been home, so that he could at least relieved himself of the burden of the secret knowledge he now have to carry with him all day. He would also have to face Tanuki and listen to the thin chirruping voice spinning those tales, so enticing and believable, which would now only seem hollow and false. Nureba's image had now faded from his mind, and Sensei was not home, therefore he would go back to the House of Gardeners, collect himself for whatever lay ahead for the day, put away the tiredness, the dark thoughts and feelings that were haunting him. He would fix his mask into place, the mask worn by Shigoto, garden apprentice; fix it on real tight so that the light of the day could not penetrate the façade.

When he got back to the lodgings he joined in the others in eating a breakfast of soup, cold cooked vegetable shoots, a small piece of grilled fish with rice and tea. Shigoto ate in self-absorbed silence. It took him until he had eaten to realise the difference in the atmosphere in the room: it was quiet, with only the shuffling early morning movements of the gardeners to break the peace. There was no Tanuki, nor his voice that usually started up soon after waking. Shigoto looked across to the sleeping space normally occupied by Tanuki, but there was only a rough blanket folded against the wall. He felt a relief flooding into him with the realisation of not having to look at his 'friend', at not having to be the undoubted audience for one of his monologues. Not this morning. He could not have faced it this morning. Yet Tanuki's absence only prickled his suspicions.

"Where's Tanuki?" he turned to Konnyaku, who was stuffing his mouth full of rice. Konnyaku impotently waved a pair of chopsticks he was holding.

"Gone…" he said as he cleared his lips of the last grains of rice. "Gone out early. Thankfully, quiet, isn't it? Like it used to be before that clown arrived in our midst. Yap, yap, yap." Konnyaku took a long swallow of tea and stretched his arms out in front of him.

"Gone where?" Shigoto wanted to press Konnyaku.

"Give up. Gone I said, can't say I care where. Gone, that's it. I didn't ask, and he didn't say." Konnyaku gave Shigoto a look of disgust, as if to imply disdain at the thought of wanting to know any more. "Just be grateful for small mercies," and he laughed at the thought.

"Sure." Shigoto had learnt when to withdraw.

"Anyway, who cares, there are more interesting stories about. You know what I heard last night? I got it on good authority." Konnyaku's eyes were smiling from his still sleep-dusted face.

"What's that then? What stories did you get back with last night?"

"Hey Kamaboku *san*," Konnyaku called across the room ignoring Shigoto completely. "Kamaboku *san*. "Did you hear about the ships yesterday? You know the people in the kitchen well, you must have of picked up some talk."

"I did hear something, yes." Kamaboku looked serious and continued to eat.

"Told you, eh," Konnyaku swung his attention back on to Shigoto. "Ships were spotted yesterday afternoon. Black ships, off the coast to the north. Nobody knows if they landed, there have been no reports of trouble yet. The guard is on alert in case. It's probably nothing. Some farmer got bored, or drunk, and started a rumour for the hell of it. Everybody will get excited for a day or two and then they will go back to sleep again, eh. We won't be getting the day off work, put it that way, eh, Kamaboku *san*?"

CHAPTER TWENTY-EIGHT

February 1595

When Shigoto awoke it was still wholly dark, there were no remnants of dreams tailing lazily away into wakefulness. There was shouting and sudden noises that did not belong, the rolling boom of thunderclap explosions, and in the distance what sounded like crackling sound of dry twigs being broken. He was suddenly awake, eyes wide and senses on full alert, without the luxury of a slow re-emergence. As he sat up he recognised the scent of smoke, thick and oily and hanging there as a threat in the air, an unmistakeably malevolent sign of something out of place.

"Get out quick, there's fire. Fire, get out!" Someone was shouting in the main room, which was instantly alive with bodies which seconds before had been asleep and were now milling about, uncomprehending, blindly reaching out for the bare essentials in the blackness. Shigoto's heart started pounding. Fire! It was everyone's nightmare, but the air in the room was relatively cool, the smoke and the sounds had clearly drifted in from outside. They were not in immediate danger, still, someone someplace was. The gardeners made for the door, delayed by the short step down into the entryway where various pairs of shoes lay waiting. There was a dull sound and a curse as someone kicked over a bucket of water in their haste to evacuate the room.

"Shigoto, are you there?" It was Kamaboku's voice.

"Yes, yes, I'm here. I'm coming," though in the surreality of the moment he could not tell if he had whispered or shouted a response, it was as if all of a sudden his voice no longer belonged to him. There was a level of terror that felt icy cold, it was not quite on him, but within easy reach, staring right at him

"Get out, every one get out, Leave everything and get out. Fire. Get out quick," Kamaboku's voice cut through the dark confusion, and the thickening smoke that had now infiltrated every corner of the room. "Leave everything, just get out."

Bodies stumbled out of the main entrance of the House of Gardeners, pitched out randomly into the dirt lane that ran across the front of the building. Kamaboku was standing in the entry porch and had pushed Shigoto out before he even had time to find his sandals. He stumbled out into the open, into the distinctly smoke-stained night air, straight into the back of Yadokari who was standing lost and disoriented looking up the lane to the left. The sky, in most part inky black and punctuated by a smear of pinprick stars, was beginning to lighten in an easterly direction. But it was not heralding the coming of dawn, it was a blaze of fire that lit up that quarter. Above the warehouse building opposite they could see flames and showers of sparks leaping high into the sky, as if desperate to escape the mayhem of conflagration below. For a few moments the gardeners stood shocked into indecision by the thickening smoke, then a shift in the wind brought the sounds of people shouting interspersed with dull booms and thuds. They looked to Kamaboku for guidance and direction, but he too seemed momentarily thrown by the situation. As they stood there in a huddled group, a small party of Hirame guards came running up the thin ribbon of the lane armed with spears, their faces streaked with sweat and eyes wild with what may have been excitement, but was probably fear.

"Get out of the road!" the leading soldier shouted as they drew towards to the gardeners. "Get out of the road. The palace is under attack. Get out of the road. Take cover, get out of the road!"

"What's happening?" yelled Kamaboku. "What do you mean under attack? Where is the fire? We can help. Where is it?"

One of the guards came to a halt in front of them. A young man dressed in a tunic that was torn, dark patches staining the cloth and hands streaked with some thin dark colour. He was panting heavily from running hard, eyes unsteady. "The palace is under attack, you had better get out of the way. There are fires all over. People have been killed already." His words came in staccato bursts as he dragged air into his lungs. "I killed two of the raiders myself. They are everywhere. Heavily armed. It's chaos. Get out of the road. It's not safe anywhere right now." He started back up the lane after the others who had simply pushed the gardeners aside in their determination to get to wherever they were going.

"Let's go to the Gardener's store, there are tools in there we can use to protect ourselves." Konnyaku was the first to speak up. He was pumped, primed ready for action. "There's nothing here. I'll bust a few heads if anyone comes after my money purse. They'll get one hell of a crack, I'll tell you."

"Calm down you idiot. And keep your voice down. You'll be the one with the head cracked open like a nut, if you go looking for trouble. They've got soldiers for that business. We've got to get out of the way, that's what we've got to do. No point getting in deep." Kamaboku wanted to maintain his authority and he felt he held a duty to lead the others. He was after all the most senior gardener among them, and had earned his status without question, even if it was only recognised among his fellows.

"We can't stay here. There's fire over in the palace buildings somewhere. That's the kitchen area, isn't it? Come on, we've got to move from here. You heard what the soldier said. I need something to protect myself with. We all do. It's got to be the store, there's plenty of stuff there." Konnyaku was fixed and insistent.

"We can't stay here for sure. Alright let's get to the store. Keep together, keep quiet, and keep your ears and eyes wide open. The shit pot has been kicked over, don't step in it, eh." Kamaboku said in a low voice that was not prepared to accept questions. He grabbed Shigoto and Ekichū by the shoulder and propelled them along with him as he started to move quickly in the direction that the soldiers had taken minutes earlier. He looked back to see that Yadokari and Konnyaku were close behind. As they ran together the occasional burst of sound came over the roofs to them: the crack of muskets being discharged, dull thuds and snatches of indistinguishable voices, all mashed together, then torn apart and thrown back again into the air in disjointed fragments. They reached the end of the lane where open ground loomed in front of them, dark and vacant. To their left, lay the night-swallowed outlines of vegetation beyond which was a route out into the garden. To their right was another lane that ran parallel with the one on which stood the House of Gardeners, and ahead of them lay the mouth to the beginning of another narrow way that cut between more storerooms and warehouses. In that direction lay their intended goal.

Kamaboku knew that to turn left and head for the vague forms bloated with the night's cover, they would be on familiar ground, their territory. Each of the gardeners would have known their way even blindfolded by the dark; they could easily seek out safe haven on instinct alone. Keep their heads low, keep their wits about them, and stay out of sight and wait things out. A restoration or imposition of order would come eventually and normality of some kind would be restored. What was uncertain was how the table would be laid for the restoration of peace. It was as if all their beliefs in the future had been shifted and they were now treading along a very narrow blade edge, every step taking them perhaps deeper into, closer to the unknown and the unknowable. That was at the heart of it, nothing was certain anymore, the past had collided with the future and fallen through the cracks in the present. Kamaboku gave a brief glance to the left and edged out further. He stopped and looked toward the right: in the deep gloom of the distance were the muffled sounds of shuffling, voices locked together and the clash of steel against steel. The only light came from a sky stained now by the pale glow of flames from several locations about them.

He paused for a few seconds in the lee of a wall, the others pressing up against him. He caught his breath, and could feel their collective urgency pushing against his back. Nothing untoward came from the mouth of the passage in front of them. It was Kamaboku's choice; whichever way he stepped the others would follow. His mind was surprisingly calm, as if he had been somehow emptied, as if the power of decision had been delicately removed. All he had to do was trust in his own instincts to lead his companions to a temporary place of safety. He looked back briefly then with one hand held trailing back he ran crouching forward, beckoning the others to follow him. In a moment the mouth of the opening had swallowed them whole. They carried on along the deep-shadowed lane. Kamaboku knew that they had to reach one further corner,, and then take a right turn and the gardeners' store would be thirty or forty paces further on. It was inky black ahead, and for the moment at least, there were no sounds to alarm them and set them back in flight the way they had come.

The Gardener's Apprentice

"It's not far," he turned and whispered to the huddled mass behind him. It was not as if they did not know well enough for themselves; it was a route they had walked at least hundreds, if not thousands of times over the years. He was not expecting an answer, it was for comfort only and it bound them ever closer. It was to let them know they were committed now, all of them together. They edged on behind Kamaboku. Shigoto found he had been holding his breath as they had halted; someone's elbow was pressing into his side, but he didn't even looked to see who it was, least of all complain or try and move away. He felt better when they moved. He could breathe normally then, and the motion, the effort of running brushed the hovering fear to one side for the moment. Time appeared be both compressed and also spinning on an endless loop where no moment is ever closed down. You were just held waiting for it to come to its own conclusion. They pushed on trying to make as little sound as possible, Shigoto was bare footed and though the soles of his feet were hardened and well used to contact with the earth, from time to time as he inched forward received a sharp stab in one foot or the other. At the next corner they stopped again while first Kamaboku peered around the corner, then Konnyaku slipped round and joined himself to Kamaboku's shoulder. They leaned together weighing up options, trying to read the signs.

Konnyaku nodded at Kamaboku and they moved on, the others following without being told, as if they were welded together in their collective need. They ran fast for the door of the gardeners' store. Kamaboku halted momentarily before sliding back the door on its runners just enough to admit one person at a time. He pushed them all though ahead of him, and then stopping only to listen again, he slipped in and drew the door back but did not fully close it. The palest light defined the opening from the inside, but stood no chance of shedding any illumination as far as the interior of the storeroom. As each gardener moved inside the room the space appeared to have lost any defined shape. Shigoto just stopped where he stood, holding his balance, whilst his eyes adjusted to the lack of light, and gradually he made out the indistinct forms of his companions. Kamaboku had remained posted at the doorway and Konnyaku stood there with him. Nothing disturbed the quiet of the store or the lane outside. Nobody made a move to do anything. It was, they realised after all, simply a temporary goal attained. Now they had to pause and consider which path to chose from here. The real choices, hard choices would need to be made from here on in, even if they did not know what all the options were.

Kamaboku's mind was now racing as he kept watch from the gap in the doorway. He was acutely aware of the pulse racing in his neck, veins throbbing as if the blood could not squeeze past the constriction of his tight shoulders from his heart to his brain fast enough. He was thinking of his parents, both of whom had passed away peacefully in their sleep of old age, poor yet contented. He had been there at the bedside as they drew their last breath and moved on, without a struggle, without fear or fright. It was not a sudden conclusion, but the end of a logical progression; they had simply run out of time. The spectre, the possibility of his own death, a sudden, messy unheroic death haunted him. That was not what he wanted; he felt that to give his life would also in some way diminish the chances of his comrades, and he clung to a desire for life through them, through his sense of duty to protect them by all his means, to lead them away somewhere safe, out of harm's reach. They had to reach the gardens, as it was their only refuge in face of the madness they stood at the very edge of. They had to get as far away from the palace as they could. What could they do? There were only a few of them, and they did not even know who the enemy was.

Kamaboku felt no call to be a hero, to win plaudits on the battlefield, commendations or honours meant nothing to him.

He was a gardener he reminded himself, someone who had dedicated himself to maintaining and encouraging things to develop. He knew he was part of a process that was greater than his own self. He acknowledged life and death in his own way, keenly aware of the whole cycle: after all he worked with it every day. More than most of the others Kamaboku took great pride in his recognition that he was but a link in chain that stretched back in time, and would carry on after he too passed away. He was making his mark now on the garden, making his contribution that history would never formally record, but he knew he was keeping the work of other generations before him alive too. That feeling filled him with a satisfaction that had penetrated into his bones; it had come to shape him into the person he was. He was no one of any particular consequence, yet somehow vital to the greater process.

"Find something to protect yourselves with," he whispered into the darkness. "You all know where the various tools are, pick something you can carry easily. Just be quick and above all, don't make a sound. Don't knock things over, and move slowly. Help each other. No talking, we cannot afford to give ourselves away. But be quick about it, there's no time, no time to waste at all." He had no real idea what constituted a good weapon, or something useful in the circumstances. That would be for each person to decide for himself. How could you, when the circumstances you were about to meet were so completely shrouded in uncertainty? They had neither food nor water with them, it came to him as he tried to swallow, his mouth parched and his throat dry. With a struggle he raised a speck of saliva, rolled it round his mouth with his tongue and swallowed. It eased the tension he felt.

Kamaboku decided that there was no other way than to take the gardeners as a group and head into the garden, then to pick their way carefully around potential perils until they passed into the wider landscape beyond. They needed to get well away from the palace, and give wide berth to the town area: those would be the seats of most danger, the most chance of running into trouble. He knew the countryside beyond the gardens and the ways to get there, he was confident in finding his way. It came to him as a solution, clear and uncomplicated. There were a thousand places they could hide, to wait it out. Wait out this storm of humanity, this madness. He pictured himself drinking the water of the spring by the ancient pine they knew as the Ketsudan pine. They could stop there briefly to regroup, catch their breath and then simply melt away into the landscape and safety. There were villagers out there insulated from the maelstrom breaking about the palace that could shelter, even feed them if necessary. The landscape itself would protect them. His confidence soared as these thoughts dripped down into his mind, his own confidence in the land was his choice of their means of protection.

Ekichū reached out both hands and stole forward into the deeper recess of the storeroom. He had regained his equilibrium and now his only desire was to get out of the store. To run, run as far away as he could, further if necessary, escape to a place beyond this time, where he would be invulnerable. His family were farmers who scratched a living some distance away from Hirame palace, beyond the mountain that rose in the centre of the island. His thoughts raced there, as his hands closed around a short wooden shaft leaning against the back wall of the room. He heard the dull thud of someone near him push over what was probably a stack of baskets. There was a low oath and suddenly all was still as everyone froze. Ekichū relaxed his grip on the shaft slightly. When he turned about face, his eyes could just make out where the gap in the door was. Silently he moved in that direction, shuffling his feet over the ground one after the other never losing contact with the earthen floor. About him in his peripheral sensory field he was aware of other figures moving, searching out their weapon of choice.

Yadokari also knew the interior of the room well enough. He had been a gardener here for nearly thirty years of his life. He had never worked anywhere else, knew no other place than Hirame palace and its gardens. It had framed his entire existence. Both his parents had served as low-grade domestic staff. His father had died several years previously, passing on to his son the right to a life of service in exchange for food and shelter. Yadokari had fallen in love in his early twenties, but the girl in question had died one winter of the fevers. He had been heartbroken for a long while, though he kept his grief locked away in a place so deep that no one else had access to. Time built a carapace around his feelings and he never set any store on the future again. Work in the gardens was his only reason to remain in contact with other people at all. Left to his own unspoken desires, he would have shunned all company. Light or no light was no real hindrance, as the room like a second skin to him. He moved noiselessly across to where the saws were kept. Despite the intense black in the further reaches of the room, he found and pulled out a long curved handsaw with a wooden handle. He reckoned the strong blade and the coarse cut teeth would make a fearsome weapon. He weighed the implement in his hand. He was ready to do what ever he was asked now, whatever was required of him. That was enough for the moment, no other distracting thoughts cluttered his mind. Despite the chill of fear that had kept him company ever since he had roughly woken, he had no doubts, no thoughts as to possible consequences. Whether it was to run or fight, it was all the same now.

For Konnyaku, there would never be any doubt in his mind as to the right course of action. The call to action was surging through his body in an irresistible flowing, which gave him additional strength and added extra steel to his already poised and tensed muscles. His first concern from the moment of sudden waking, of being dragged reluctantly away from his dreams, was to protect the contents of the cloth pouch tucked into the folds of a broad cloth belt he tied around his waist. He thought about his family too, uncomplicated folk who made a living by taking to the sea in a small boat to snare its rich bounty, or would work their way along a stretch of shoreline collecting seaweeds and shellfish, instinctively knowing how to seek out the hidden places most likely to yield a harvest according to the season. He had always known that nothing, nothing at all could be taken for granted. It always came down to a question of relying on oneself. Rules and orders had to be obeyed to conform to social demands, but ultimately it was one's own strength and guile that kept one alive and living into the next day.

When he was very young, before he had become a garden apprentice he had been propelled by the wishes of his parents away from the sea, after he had nearly drowned in an accident. He had been out with his father in a skiff. They were prospecting new fishing grounds, bobbing like a cork along the base of tall cliffs, his father's eyes searching the surface of the waters for some indication as to the potential of what lay below them. Their narrow flanked craft had been hit broadside by a wave that seemed to have arisen from nowhere out of sequence with the rest, and they had both been pitched over the side into the depths. Konnyaku had felt the hand of death reach towards him, a fact that was distinct even to his child's mind. A clear recognition of the inevitable cascaded into his mind whilst he struggled and kicked out in desperation with arms and feet, as if trying to escape the attentions of some sea borne predator lurking below, bidding its time to drag him down into its world. His father had managed to get a grip on his sodden clothing and pulled him in with one hand as he made contact with part of the upturned boat with the other. The experience had frightened and shocked the family, and his mother and father had thereafter sought out an opportunity for their son, their only son, to be raised, educated and trained for a life safe from the clutches of the sea. Their reasoning was simple: the boy had been given back to them, but with a warning.

Konnyaku pressed himself against Kamaboku who had remained at the gap in the doorway after all the other gardeners had slipped into the store. Together they listened to the darkness. Any sounds drifting over were deeply muffled and distant, they knew that they were safe for the moment, though they both also recognised that the situation could change without warning.

"It's quiet out there for now," he whispered in a barely audible tone. His mouth pressing so close to Kamaboku's ear that he inhaled the scent of his hair. Kamaboku's head dipped slowly, though his attention never wavered one iota from the world beyond the door. "Do you have a plan? We can't stay here. Stuff is going on all over the place it seems."

"Fire is a bad sign." Kamaboku slightly turned his head, as if preparing to embrace Konnyaku. He spoke in a voice so soft it hardly required breath. "Get yourself something to carry, your strength may yet be needed tonight. We have got to get out through the gardens. It'll be our best chance to reach somewhere safe. We know the places to go. We have got to get clear of anywhere near the palace ground. What ever is happening we have to get away."

"Do you know what's going on? Who's attacking the palace, attacking us?" Konnyaku whispered under his breath, eyes fixed on the opening.

"For now it doesn't matter. Who cares, eh? We have got to get out, get away safe. The garden will protect us. Now go, like the others, get yourself something to carry, hurry. We are not safe until we get to the garden." Kamaboku repeated and pushed back at Konnyaku, urging him away. Not because he did not want him near, rather he realised that he needed him now more than ever.

With the sound of baskets falling inside both men looked out and listened with greater attention. The air outside was ever more stained by drifting smoke, it was being carried to them more strongly now and at more frequent intervals. Still there were no sounds of people moving, no sounds of footfall in the lane. When Konnyaku moved away from the door, he was surprised just how dark it was facing the interior of the storeroom; he needed a few moments to adjust his senses. He thought carefully about a weapon; for him it needed be a weapon and not just something to carry in his hand. He wanted a tool of aggression. He felt more thrill than fear with the adrenaline coursing through his body, he knew it was a time of danger, but he realised it also represented a time of opportunity. As he made his way deeper into the room one hand clutched at the lump at his waist, the other held out in front of him lost in the dark. He knew what he wanted to feel in his hand and he made his way directly there.

As he had slipped through the partially opened door, the images that flashed through Shigoto's mind were of people. He was alive to the fact that they would be safer in the gardens, and that was inevitability where Kamaboku would decide to lead them. He trusted Kamaboku's judgements entirely. The garden represented the most obvious escape route, he was keenly aware that heading for the storeroom had taken them closer to danger. He had half expected Kakugari, the only married gardener, who did not live with them at the House of Gardeners to be there, to hear his familiar voice. He crowded forward with the others into the silent void darker and thicker than any night. Within him he carried a series fractured images, a projection of his racing imagination merging with shapeless space where light and sense had all but been extinguished; images of Tanuki, his father, mother, Maguro Sensei, the lop-sided roof of Kokiburi-an, Kakugari, glimpses of flashing lights in the sky, and Nureba. He saw them all now as ghostly forms without any more actual substance than heated air billowing upwards from the flames. In such a rapidly changing picture, it seemed as if these images were all crowding the scene at once, all clamouring after his attention.

He had no idea what to reach out for and it made him feel more disorientated in the room. He pushed out his hands in front of him as much to keep balance as to search out something solid. 'To protect myself from what?' he wondered, but there could not be an answer. Outside there was terror raging, that was all too painfully obvious. It seemed that panic and fear spreading like a contagion through the world. He was breathing it in, stinging his nostrils as much as the smoke, such a contrast to the cool quiet of the storeroom. Now and then he detected the presence of the others moving about around him. Once his hand brushed against something, maybe someone's shoulder or back and he jerked his arm away so fast it sent shock waves through his elbow and along his forearm. Then he stumbled into a stack of baskets knocking some of them over, involuntarily his face reddened as he froze. When he sensed movement beginning again he tried to move cautiously onward hopefully steering clear of anything on the floor that might have tripped him. He was not really sure where he was in the space, his mental, intuitive map of the interior of the storeroom had not yet had a chance to become as automatic as that borne by the others. He groped his way through the darkness inch by inch.

"Hurry up," Kamaboku's voice came sotto voce out of the total gloom. "We've got to get moving again. Bring whatever you have found."

Shigoto had nothing in his hands. Feeling out for anything in front of him, most of the time there was nothing there, his hands brushed against objects that seemed not fit for any purpose he could recognise. He had stumbled into a stack of brushes, some thin stakes used for tying down branches when training trees and shrubs, the handle of the handcart caught him a sharp blow in the side. Urgently now he pushed his hands out as if he were fishing in the sea with just his bare hands desperate to contact anything. Then he felt the cool touch of a wooden shaft of what might be a digging instrument. His fingers eagerly closed around the shaft and he lifted the satisfying weight of the tool towards him, and turned to try to make his way towards the door.

The gardeners re-emerged from the deep darkness of the store and gathered by Kamaboku near the door again. Konnyaku had regained his position and stood coiled but motionless, the blade of the saw reflecting dully in the fraction of light that came through the barely opened door. Kamaboku was about to speak when there came the unmistakable sound of multiple feet rushing down the lane in their direction. They all froze as one. Konnyaku tried to slip the door shut the final few inches, but Kamaboku caught his wrist in steely fingers. The sounds were getting louder as voices came closer; they shrank back into the encompassing dark of the interior, what ever means of attack or defence they had in hand raised. Konnyaku alone stayed by the doorway ready to slash with his crude blade at anyone attempting to enter, be they friend or foe.

The feet came to a ragged halt a little way from the door, but far enough to be beyond any possible line of vision.

"They didn't come this way, I told you, idiot," a hot and hoarse voice was screaming in the shadows. "Take three men and head round the building in that direction, we'll go back the other way. That way we can trap them somewhere. Come on, this sword is anxious for wetting again."

A rush of feet came past and even Konnyaku flinched back as the ragged sound hurried past the door, behind which a fearsome though wholly untested reception committee stood. The feet did not stop but hurtled on into the inky shadows, and then it was still again.

"That was not the palace guard," Kamaboku was back at Konnyaku's side as the younger man whispered under his breath. "They've gone for now."

"I know. I think we may have stepped right into the shit pot though." Kamaboku was plotting in his imagination a way to the gardens. Normally they would have stepped out to the left, continued to the end of the row of buildings, taken a left turn, and followed the path between some more building a short distance before cutting into the garden. In normal times it was the journey of a few minutes, four or five at the most. Kamaboku ran through all the possible permutations of route to get into the gardens at a point that offered the least chance of getting caught in the open. Every which way that he could imagine held potential for trouble. "Which way do you think we should take to the garden, eh?"

"I know, I have been asking myself the same thing. Those dogs have gone both ways now, they've split up, there's more chance of bumping into someone. Who knows how many of them there are anyway. This is no rice throwing festival, that's for sure. I think we have to just make a dash for it, fast as we can, direct, the fastest way." Konnyaku was willing to run at the risk head on, his gambler's instincts aroused.

"I'm not sure. We may run right into the back of that lot that just went past."

"Then I'll have some heads to crack open, all to the good," Konnyaku hefted the saw in his hand. "Look, everyone can run. If we get split up there are always the secret call signs we can use, nobody will know it's us. We need a place where we can all meet up."

"We all go together. It's the only way we can do it. We have to stay together. When we go we go together. That way if we hit trouble at least we all have each other. Everyone will fight if it comes to that. We'll be all right when we get to the gardens.

There is nothing to attack there. We'll stick together at least till we get to the garden. Then we can to divide into smaller groups, we can split in two groups there," insisted Kamaboku. "You take one, and I can look after the others. Where can we meet up? Somewhere deep in the gardens, well away from here."

"The gardens may not be so safe." Shigoto had pushed his way forward and had caught the drift of the whispered conversation between Kamaboku and Konnyaku.

"Shut up, Konnyaku and I decide what we do," Kamaboku wanted to slap down Shigoto. His mind was moving more slowly than he wished. He was grimly aware that Konnyaku was quicker at coming to a decision than he was, and it made him aware of being the older man, less agile in thought than the hard to contain young buck.

"No, I mean Tanuki met some people in the gardens the other night. They were carrying something."

"What the hell are you talking about? Listen this is no time for stories." Kamaboku turned sharply toward Shigoto.

"Tanuki, eh? I knew he was up to no good," Konnyaku joined in the whispered debate. "Where, where did you see them?"

Shigoto briefly outlined what he had seen the previous night when he had followed Tanuki into the garden, about how he had met up with some others and the heavy box they carried.

"Why didn't you say anything before now?" Kamaboku was astonished.

"I was going to tell Sensei in the morning, but he wasn't at home. I had no idea what he was doing there. He just met up with a couple of other people. It could have been anyone really. I had no idea what it all meant," Shigoto explained. Konnyaku and Kamaboku looked at each other without saying a thing.

"There's only one thing for it, we head for the gardens and then get out far away as quick as possible." Konnyaku was the first to whisper again.

"Then we go together as far as the garden, then we split in two. Meet up at the Ketsudan Pine. There is the spring there and we can get water at least. Regroup there, then away into the countryside. That's the plan, that's what we'll do." Kamaboku had come to a conclusion.

Kamaboku whispered again to all the others what had been decided on for a course of action. Everyone understood and no one asked any questions or sought clarification. Kamaboku edged the doorway open a crack more until he was able to peer into the lane in so far as he could. The sky had taken on a deeper, brighter stain of red since he had last been aware of it. The muffled sounds of explosions continued, seeming to build toward a crescendo of activity, before falling away once again.

Shigoto stood with the others. He was holding tight on to the shaft of the digging tool he had found, holding it up in front of him. He felt deeply ashamed now that he had not ventured to say anything to any of the other gardeners about his experience of having followed Tanuki into the gardens. He had had opportunity to confide in Konnyaku and Kamaboku. He could have taken either one of them to one side and divulged what he knew. He could have of told them a lot more besides. But he had not, not even Sensei knew everything. Where was he in all this chaos, Shigoto wondered? Perhaps he could have of halted all this madness before it started. Instead it had all remained locked inside him, such a burden to carry that he could not even share it, and now they were all in real peril. Perhaps people had already been killed, and there was fire and destruction raging somewhere in the direction of the palace buildings. Had he in some way caused all this to happen?

Then he thought of the safety of his mother, he could clearly see her at home, and his grandmother ensconced in one corner sewing cloth. As the image flashed through his mind he knew that whatever else he did, he had to go to their aid. The house where he had been brought up was not too far from where he was. Except that it was not in the direction of the gardens. Whatever ties bound his fate together with his fellow gardeners, the ties that bound him to his mother were more powerful. Thinking of her, he also thought of Nureba, where would she be? Likely in the palace buildings, in the very centre of the maelstrom exploding around all of them now. How would she fare, who would be watching after her? He shivered in frustration.

The door slid open a little more and this time Kamaboku squeezed through the opening into the lane. He looked both ways with great care and beckoned the others to join him. When they were all together they set off at fast pace hugging the shadows, each one praying and hoping. They reached the end of the lane safely, stopped at the corner with Kamaboku at the front of the group and Konnyaku bringing up the rear. Shigoto was just in front of Konnyaku, he could hear the tread of his feet right behind him as they ran, and occasionally a hand descended on his back urging him forward.

Kamaboku leaned back from the corner. "There are two men down there, in our path," he whispered feverishly. He had been hoping against hope that they would be able to make a dash for the gardens and just melt away into the night and safer surroundings. Their way now seemed blocked with no way of returning the way they had just come. That would lead them directly into the jaws of danger.

"Are they palace guards?" someone whispered hopefully from the huddle.

"We've just got to make a run for it. Whoever is in the path, then… too bad! Go, run," Konnyaku's frustration with Kamaboku was threatening to spill over. This was neither the time nor the place for strategy discussions. It was a time for action, pure uncompromised action, delay would carry a price, and it was not a chance he was willing to take.

"Get ready," Kamaboku was suddenly aware that of all the group of gardeners he alone had not picked out any kind of weapon, his hands were empty. As they broke around the corner and began to sprint down the lane towards the two raiders, Shigoto broke away from the group and clutching his pick he made a dash in the direction of his mother's house, the place that was home to him. It was clear now in his mind, somehow he was complicit in the destruction that had been unleashed. He had put them all in danger and he had to at least act to protect his family. It was the only way he could redeem himself, even if it meant putting himself into greater danger.

"Hey…" Konnyaku cried out as he saw Shigoto slip away from the group and run across the road, but there was nothing he could do, it happened too fast.

Shigoto ran as fast as he could down the lane. The air felt sweeter to him now he was on his own, the stench of collective fear had receded, though it was still heavy with the smell of burning. He ran on with only one goal in mind, one thought. He had no idea what he would find, nor even what he would do when he got to his mother's house. Beyond that nothing existed, for now there was only the pounding in his chest and the will to close the distance between him and where he wanted to be. There were confused noises ahead of him. He could now hear voices raised, shouting, and the grim sounds of steel on steel; he was running straight into trouble. This time there would be no chance of avoiding it. He gripped more tightly to the handle of the digging pick, its flat broad blade raised high in the air.

"Look out there's another!" The warning shout came from somewhere in front of him.

As he descended onto the group of people ahead of him, he recognised the uniforms of guards attached to the Hirame palace locked in combat with an overwhelming number of attackers. Raising the pick above his head Shigoto charged at full speed into the midst of the melee. Something, or somebody reared up, looming like a giant in front of his eyes. Without thought, he swung the pick with all the force he could manage. For a spilt second all time seemed to be compressed into a silence, then there was an explosive thud as if a hand had smacked against a firm wet object. The pick shuddered in his hands and he almost lost his grip on it. Whoever or whatever was in front of him, now fell in an untidy heap pole axed by his blow. From somewhere he could hear a crying, a keening moaning voice, but the red mist had descended on him, and he was only consciously connected with time and space as through a lens that made time seem to stand still, and everything else was detached, distant from him. Another figure rose up as a huge dark shadow, blocking off all light and he swung again. This time his feet were well planted on the ground and he swung the pick with all the strength with his legs and torso. The heavy blade made contact with a substance that had no chance of resisting its momentum; the shadow fell away as if dissolved into air.

Space seemed to open up before him and without thinking Shigoto plunged into it and ran again without any thought for who or what he left behind. There was nobody ahead of him now, the way was clear and he sprinted in a lung-bursting effort. Wildly unshackled now by any consideration apart from the one burning in his mind, to reach home. A fire was burning in the road ahead, debris scattered across the lane, but there were no figures to bar his way. It was as if the storm had passed this way but had since moved on to bring devastation elsewhere. There was a body, a torso, lying across his path, its limbs stretched at unnatural angles, and dark thick liquid pooled where a head would be expected to be. At last he burst into a narrow track running between simple shingle-roofed houses and board fences, at the end of which he hoped his mother and grandmother would be waiting for him. A building further along was burning, the flames reaching out as insatiable hot tongues eating ravenously into the roof.

"Mother," the word was forming in his mouth, when out of the house he was about to enter three heavily armed men stumbled. Shigoto simply pitched his head down and raising the pick, with its handle now smeared with wet blood, high above his head and charged blindly into their midst. The first man went down with a crash that filled his ears with noise. There were sounds of someone shouting, yelling in a hoarse voice, the words indistinct and meaning lost. Shigoto felt a piercing pain in his left shoulder as something struck him there, and shocks of pain jagged and convulsed along his forearm, his fingers numbed. Yet he managed to cling on to the pick handle. He swung again wildly at another dark figure looming up before him, but it was moving quickly, and there was only the sensation of a glancing blow being landed, though there was a howl of pain from somewhere. Then suddenly everything changed in an instant, a heavy blow caught him at the back of the head, it seemed as if any light that existed was sucked into a vacuum. Now not even his imagination could function any more. He felt himself free falling, gliding smoothly through space, diving freefall in a graceful arc without impediment into a void, without light, without past, present or future.

"Leave him. Take what you have. We've got to get out, back to the boats," a voice called hoarsely, but Shigoto heard nothing at all.

CHAPTER TWENTY-NINE

February 1595

When Shigoto suddenly broke away from the group of gardeners, Konnyaku's first instinct was to grab hold of him and haul him back, but he had missed and his outstretched fingers had merely grazed Shigoto. Konnyaku was holding tight and tense on to the hand saw in his right hand, which meant he had to reach across himself with his left hand to grab hold of him. It was sufficient an obstacle that he missed his target. In the next moment Shigoto was gone, racing across the lane and disappeared into in the opposite direction. He thought briefly about chasing after Shigoto, but it would have meant abandoning the others. He was not sure that anyone else had even seen him go, everything had happened so fast. Konnyaku cursed to himself, if it came to a fight they would need everyone to be together: that is how they would survive this madness. Even the hot headed Konnyaku knew that their main strength lay in their being together, looking out for each other, covering each other's backs. Now they were one less, weakened.

Kamaboku was on the move up ahead, running crouched over keeping as low as possible to the ground, hugging any shadows he could find. He knew they could not stop now. Konnyaku had to put Shigoto out of his mind, though it raised a deeply disturbing thought in his mind. Was Shigoto in some way connected with the forces attacking the palace? He alone of all the gardeners had forged a friendship with Tanuki. It had been apparent from the beginning, from when Tanuki had materialised out of nowhere among them, it was only Shigoto who was seemingly willing to befriend and defend him. Konnyaku spat into the ground as they sped along towards the sanctuary of the garden at the mere recollection of Tanuki's name. Surely Shigoto could not be in league with the raiders?

Equally he felt frustrated acting as a shepherd to the group of gardeners, when what he really wanted to be doing was to insinuate himself into the thick of any action; be in there swinging with his saw, cleaving heads or limbs, not scurrying through the night away from the main focus of activity like a frightened rodent. He surprised even himself how calm he felt inside, boiling with anger maybe, shocked and surprised by the intensity of the moment certainly, but deep inside calm as ice. He had only to look towards Kamaboku to get a measure of that. Kamaboku was afraid, frightened by the whole experience. All he seemed to want to do was to put as much ground between them and potential trouble. All this was clear to Konnyaku, who was seeing things now with a detachment and certainty, which pleased him immensely. He could appreciate Kamaboku's concern; he was after all their 'leader', by virtue of his seniority among the gardeners. Everyone accepted that. He recognised that Kamaboku has responsibilities to the others, but once they reached the gardens then he would make his move. No one could criticise him for that. He would have fulfilled his duty to the others, and then he would be free to make his own moves. There must be opportunities out there for him to profit by: part of the anger he felt was that of someone missing out on opportunity to make gains. To gamble, put his stake on the table, challenge anyone else who felt brave enough to come up to confront him, now that could make things very interesting indeed.

Twice they were almost caught, as they moved from point to point, zigzagging their way through the area known as the palace township. The narrow lanes were potential death traps: it would have taken but a handful of men to ambush them. Then they would have had to face another kind of test together. Moments after Shigoto had scurried off into the night, they had seen actual fighting taking place, hand to hand, but it was a little distance away, and no one had noticed them to raise the alarm as they slipped past the confused melee. Konnyaku's eyes though had been drawn toward the sight of real action, and he felt a pang of regret that he could not bound in there with arms flailing. The second time they were spotted, shouts and threats were raised against them. It was just as they were making the final sprint for the garden itself, running at full speed for the reassuring comfort of the cover of the deep shadowed spaces that they knew so well. They were at the point of slipping the leash, getting that final liberation from the clutches of pure terror, horror and fear. Perhaps for the first time during that brutal night, when time had been compressed into itself so hard, that but a minute's passing was in itself almost an unbearable strain on each one of them, they almost lost the protection of being together as a group. Sensing the garden so close now, they began to move for themselves, each man knowing exactly where he was and where he wanted to be, darkness or no darkness. They lost the cloak of cohesion and caught the attention of a band of men bearing arms and looted goods. In the space of time it takes to blink and clear one's vision from the sting of smoke-stained air, the gardeners were gone. It was as if they were rabbits or gophers disappearing into their private world at the first warning sight of a predatory kite wheeling and patrolling overhead.

They all made it to relative safety, without a closer brush with the physical violence that had erupted like some virulent rash breaking out randomly across the palace grounds. The gardens opened her arms wide to her favourite sons and gathered them in, as a mother hen drawing her straggling, frightened brood under her feathers. Almost immediately the night air was punctuated by new sounds, more subtle and understated than the explosions that continued to rent the night. Using their secret system of calling using the voices of birds the gardeners were able to keep in contact with one another as they fled, now at last on their own, and masters of their own destiny in their domain.

Hearing the calls ring through the night of the garden, Konnyaku was aware that everyone had escaped the immediate danger, he was tempted to stop and turn back. Now, surely this could be his time, a time to make a stand, pitch himself into the very face of danger. He licked his dry, hard lips, and let out the call of green-backed finch, a common sight darting in among the branches of the trees around Hirame palace, if not much known to fly at night. An answering call came from over to his right side, and he knew where Kamaboku had taken shelter, over the far side of the Great Dragon Pond.

Within in a few minutes, guided by the same 'finch's' calls, he dropped down beside Kamaboku who was nestled in by a large upright boulder set near the pond shore. As they silently looked back towards the palace township, the spluttering lights of the fires were reflected in the surface of the pond, which withheld its counsel on the tragedy of mankind.

"It's not even dawn yet. There must be a couple of hours of darkness yet," Kamaboku whispered. His voice flat and drained, the strain of tiredness hitting him.

"It all happened so fast. I cannot believe that not so long ago I was in bed, asleep, dreaming of some lady, then…" Konnyaku let out a breath. "What do you think is happening?"

"It's so hard to tell. The palace has taken an attack that's for sure, eh. Fighting is still going on, though I think there may be less of it now."

"Less? Less fighting?" Konnyaku tensed again, his eyes trying to scan the darkness trying to read the unreadable.

"I don't know, maybe." Kamaboku continued to watch. "Hey, you know where Shigoto got to? I cannot hear his whistle, his call." There was a note of anxiety in his low whisper.

Konnyaku turned slowly towards Kamaboku. He could just about make out his creased and worn face, his eyes wide open, the whites of his eyes very white. "He slipped off, just as we made off for the garden. Don't know where he went, or why. Bastard, cheated on me there. It could have been me to slip off but I stayed with the others. Bastard. He just took off someplace."

"Shigoto?" Kamaboku was disbelieving, this could not be right somehow.

"Bastard, went off on his own, some kind of pick in his hands. I'll strangle him with my bare hands if I ever see him again." Konnyaku's ire was building with every passing moment. Kamaboku said nothing; he needed some time to take this information in, digest it properly. An image of Maguro Sensei loomed up in his mind looking at him with a penetrating stare accusing him personally of having 'lost' apprentice gardener Shigoto, and he felt an sense of despair rising in his throat, making all but breathing difficult.

"Konnyaku, you'll have to go after him."

"Did you think I wouldn't? Have you any idea where he might be heading for?" Konnyaku wiped his chin with the back of his hand. He was weighing up the prospects, weighing up the odds.

"His mother's house, I guess. It's the only place he would go. It's where any of us would've gone, eh?" Deep weariness, a fatigue tinged by sadness, crept into Kamaboku's voice.

Konnyaku barely registered the tone of the older man's voice. He was primed now, rising on a tide of adrenaline. He picked up the saw, his improvised weapon, then he turned once again to Kamaboku. "You don't suppose he had anything to do with this do you?"

Kamaboku shook his head, "No, not Shigoto. Not him," he said simply.

"I hope you are correct in that, though it would save me the job of killing him myself, eh." He was smiling now, then he was up and running towards the township under the cover of the dying hour of the night sky.

Konnyaku ran in the direction of the gardeners' storehouse, the same route by which they had so recently made their escape. Now he was heading in there of his own volition, hackles raised. As he scampered besides a wall, staying as low to the ground to keep in the shadows, his eyes scanned fore and back, senses constantly on the alert. "Don't rush," he said to himself. 'Don't rush, and take your time. You are the hunter now.' That thought had a good clean edge to it. He made it to the store without meeting any opposition; it hardly took him any time at all. He pushed back the door and slid inside for the second time that night. When he remerged he had two lengths of rope, one slung over his shoulders and one crossing over his chest and back. The heavy handsaw was still in his hand. Having quickly looked up and down the empty lane, he slipped out and made his way in the direction of Shigoto's family home. The path was littered with a variety of the detritus of combat, a storehouse had had its doors ripped off and thrown down in an apparently random act of vandalism. Here and there bodies were scattered along the paths, victims abandoned without hope or care. Konnyaku came across the body of a palace guard whose chest had been carved open by a spear, the jagged stub of its broken shaft pointing accusingly into the night sky.

There was an explosion nearby and he dived headlong for cover at the base of the nearest wall. He felt the ground shake momentarily and there was a heavy crashing sound, followed by shouting and the clash of steel on steel. Konnyaku picked himself up, shook his head to clear his ears, readjusted the ropes and gathered up his weapon. He saw lying in the lane an abandoned spear which had been broken just above the grip, the broken end of the shaft a frozen shower of splinters, but there remained six feet of wooden shaft attached to a wicked looking heavy blade slick with someone's life blood. He threw the handsaw aside and rushed for the prize lying waiting for him to take possession. With a grim satisfaction, he thought of it as his first acquisition, a handsome one at that, but surely only the first.

He had run on a little way when he saw a group of four men approaching. He crouched in the lee of an open doorway. They were all dressed in fine kimono, with swords in their hands, two men were occupied with carrying a large wooden box that was clearly not light. Konnyaku weighed up the situation in an instant; they were running, not fighting. He instantly sensed fear about them, and something in the way they moved with lumpen, clumsy strides that they were men who were more used to giving orders rather than responding to them. Despite the odds of numbers being against him, he felt that he held the better ground and surprise was on his side. He had seen them and they had not yet noticed him, preoccupied as they apparently were arguing amongst themselves. He slipped back into the doorway and waited, waited for his quarry to come to him.

"I tell you, we have got to get out while we can." The voice was hoarse and almost pleading, barely making any real attempt to keep the volume down.

"This has become a night of..." the sentence was choked off as Konnyaku burst onto them from his lair.

Swinging the spear at shoulder level as he charged forward, a scream coming from his lips, he must have appeared in the split second, if they had opportunity to see anything clearly, as a demon coming up at them from the chambers of Hell itself. The blade cut an arc through the air and sliced into the chest of one of the men who dropped to the ground without making a sound, the box he was carrying almost fell with to the ground. Two armed men confronted Konnyaku, and the fourth still clutching the box's carrying straps with both hands hovered behind the cover of his comrades, his sword hanging in a scabbard from his waist. Konnyaku watched the one still clutching the box, his eyes now round with terror. He made no attempt to run on his own as he could have done, leaving his companions to deal with Konnyaku. 'Rich pickings, eh,' Konnyaku thought, and his eyes gleamed bright.

The two men facing him moved apart, until they were almost diametrically opposite to him. Konnyaku knew he had to induce one of them to step in and to make a move. The man to his right was sweating heavily and the tip of his tongue was working round and round his lips. He was heavily built, with the figure of a man whose lifestyle had been sedentary until this moment. He held a sword but the tip wavered fretfully, shifting from side to side as if it were drunk and the blade gleamed clean The other man to his left side was of a leaner, harder build, he was staying just out of striking range and held his sword in both hands. The blade was steadier, its point shifting to cover the movements of Konnyaku's head. Konnyaku feinted to the right and that bought him a fraction of space as the man on that side shifted back momentarily. Konnyaku had brought his weight forward onto his right foot. The man to his left choose this moment to attack and lurched forward with sword raised above his head. He never had a chance to strike, as he came forward Konnyaku shifted his weight to his left foot and holding the spear out from his waist drove the spear blade into the oncoming attacker's throat. Blood ejaculated from the swordsman's mouth. Konnyaku's mind was shrieking in victory even as he reversed his thrust by simply swinging the spear shaft and caught the other man holding a sword a fearsome blow across the top of his head. He too went down his knees collapsing under him, his sword clattering noisily to the ground. The fourth man, who had just witnessed the entire scene was aghast, ignoring the weapon at his side he shrieked in terror and attempted to throw the box at Konnyaku, then in sheer terror turned on his heels and sprinted away.

The box collapsed to the ground in what seemed like slow motion. Konnyaku almost had time to think of laying down the spear and attempting to catch it before it hit the ground. It landed with a dull thud almost at his feet. He stood with his chest heaving, his lungs now desperate to draw in as much air as possible. His ears ringing loudly with the sound of his heart beating like a large drum being struck with particular venom. Shouting from further down the lane dragged him back into the moment. It was a small detachment of palace guards; they had cornered the man who had let go of the box. Now facing overwhelming odds alone with only his still sheathed blade for protection he thrust both arms towards the sky screaming as he did so. Konnyaku nursed the spear in his hands a moment and then swinging it once more brought the gory blade down on the side of the wooden box. The timber, stout as it was, held no chance and burst open, spewing silver coins over the lane.

Konnyaku knelt down on one knee as if he were about to pray. The palace guards had made short work of the box-carrier, and they left his pierced body in an untidy heap, its essence soaking into the dirt. Konnyaku reached down with his blood-smeared fingers and dipped them into the pool of silver.

"Hey, you, don't move. Lay down your weapons or you are a dead man like your friend there."

As he looked up into the faces of the onrushing guards, faces streaked with sweat, dirt and blood lust. Konnyaku was bristling with steel and malice, yet his heart still and quiet, his head clearer than it had ever been. Even when he had looked into the vortex of death as a child he had not been as clear in his mind as this, all he saw about him was a powerful beauty, a magnificence, and majesty. He knew all danger was past, the the storm had abated, blown itself out, nothing could touch him in this moment.

"Where have you lads been hiding? It takes a simple gardener to sort out the mess you got yourselves in, eh." Konnyaku pulled himself up to his full height, threw back his head and laughed, letting his voice rise into the dying moments of a dark, dark night, and so to greet the first moments of the birth of the new dawn. The guards stopped in astonishment to take in this madman, lunatic or trickster, standing in the middle of the lane. Around them were the bodies of three men, three of the bodies limp corpses, the fourth body, more that of an administrator than a warrior, twitching, spluttering back into a state of semi-consciousness.

"I know him. It's one of the gardeners. What in heaven are you doing here, in the midst of all this mess?" One of the guards, his eyes rimmed red by exhaustion, only held at bay by tapping into the collective frenzy, thin streaks of dried blood clinging as war paint to one side of his face, recognised who was standing in front of them. "Konnyaku *san*?"

"Don't tell me, you are looking for a game of dice? Not the best time for me, I'm looking for someone. Here you had better look after this," Konnyaku pushed his foot into the pool of silver coins that had spilt from the shattered box. As he did, he straightened and tightened the cloth belt around his waist. "This lot must belong to someone important I guess. More important than a mere gardener, anyway," he said laughing again.

"It's the traitor, Saeko Kezure, look!" One of the more inquisitive guards had pushed forward and was staring down at the prostrated form of the eldest son of Lord Saeko, a livid welt raised across his forehead where Konnyaku's spear shaft had dealt him a vicious blow. Another guard broke away from the gang and came over to look. He stared down at the figure, groaning, and then he spat and kicked the twitching form in the midriff as hard as he could. The corpse-like figure grunted in pain, but barely moved.

"That's for all the people who have died and suffered because of you, and the scum like you. They are the lucky one, you have to die yet." He spat again.

"Isn't he dead too?" asked Konnyaku with a note of regret; a heroic tale of him taking on four men at once and leaving them all dead and mangled at his feet, was shaping in his mind, and he could now see his kill rate falling. "Thought I had killed him too."

All the guards crowded round to see Lord Saeko's son themselves, to confirm the truth of the matter with their own eyes. So, the would-be-king had fallen.

Konnyaku left the ropes he had slung over his shoulders and the guards to their prize and their post battle weariness. He dismissed with a noncommittal shrug the half-hearted cries of palace guards to beware of any stragglers among the insurgents who may still be hiding out. The general consensus was the danger and threat from the attack had passed, the tide had been turned. Konnyaku reminded himself of the principal reason he had set off back into the township. Shigoto, he was supposed to be looking for him. He had taken a few paces down the lane when he turned around and called out to them:

"Hey, have you come across another of the gardeners? A young man, Shigoto by name? You may have seen him about, eh."

But the soldiers were more concerned with their task of clearing up the detritus of war, and being positioned to claim capture of the biggest prize, one of the largest fish that swam in the small pool that was Mikura. There were the bodies of several fighters who had fallen, and by and large the broken corpses, and the mortally wounded still lay in disarray where they had fallen. There was much work to be done to repair the physical scars; the mental scars would heal or not accordingly. He moved freely now. As light was seeping into a fresh day and the terror of the dark was lifting. It was as if a curtain had been swept back to fully expose the consequences of the mayhem of those few hours of night. When under the cover of the hours of darkness, violence had spread as a virulent, mutating contagion, affecting all that it touched, drawing out heroism and cowardice, joy, despair and loss in unequal measure. The coming of the light washed out the final traces of fear from his mind and Konnyaku felt himself to be a conqueror, a prince without a crown. He was light on his feet and almost felt like dancing a few steps.

As he drew closer to the area where Shigoto's family house was located, the destruction around him became more marked. Many of the buildings, mainly modest homes of favoured retainers, had evidently been looted as there were domestic items strewn here and there. A length of now trampled silk, pottery smashed, a heat scorched painted screen still smouldering where fire had not eaten into it. There were several corpses too lying unattended in the dirt. A hand with a stub of the forearm attached lay in the path in front of him had been detached from its rightful owner, and apparently tossed to one side, as a grim, obsolete object. One of the corpses, that of a fresh faced youth lay leaning against a timber palisade fence that threatened to topple over, as if it was only the resolute effort of the youth that preventing it from pitching over into the dust. Konnyaku went over and crouched down in front of the body. He wiped the sweaty palms of his hands on his clothing, and noticed for the first time that he had blood on them. The blood of others, faces he would never remember except perhaps in his dreams, without names and without opportunity to grow any older. As he looked into the now peaceful face of the youth, he was reminded of Shigoto, and shuddered at the thought of coming upon his corpse, pitched face down and stiffening in the dirt. He leaned in closer to the youth, and with a deft action picked up out a still sheathed, narrow bladed knife from the folds of the belt. The finely wrought scabbard caught in the cloth of the belt as he tugged at it, and as it pulled free, a small leather pouch with three silver coins revealed itself. Konnyaku looked up and down the street, but there was no one among the living to see him. He slipped the knife and the purse into the folds of his own belt. As he did, he could feel the welcome knot of his own purse still secure there, with the satisfying weight of the heavy silver pieces nestling in alongside it. He smiled again as he stood up adjusting his secret load, the coins would be sufficient to keep his family in food for several months. Yes, he had gambled and he had won, won handsomely indeed.

As he approached the house, or at least the place where he thought Shigoto's home to be he stopped. Fire had broken out, either by accident of war or deliberately, and a building had been virtually consumed whole. All that was left were charred still smoking timbers and the blackened rubble what had been someone's home. Now concern raced through his mind, if Shigoto's home had been burnt down, how would he know if anyone had been caught in the conflagration? The ashes were still smouldering, sending a stinking plume of grey smoke up into the sky, and he certainly did not want to be the one assigned the task of raking through the mess looking for a body. Somehow Konnyaku could not believe that Shigoto had perished in the fire: it was not something that he was prepared to countenance.

He stepped back and looked about him, weighing possibilities against likelihood, the gambler coolly assessing the fall of the cards exposed on the table. Then he saw another body lying at the front of a building a little further along the lane. The road was quiet, the air now stilled. He decided to investigate further, drawn on by the comforting weight at his waist and the chance that he may perhaps add to his hoard. As he drew nearer he could see that there was a body lying just inside in a smashed down doorway. All he could see was a pair of feet projecting back towards the entrance. The owner had apparently lived long enough to drag himself part way into the building. There was a pool of drying blood on the floor. He was about to reach down to turn over the first corpse with his foot, when he gasped in astonishment and shock.

"Shigoto! Shigoto, what the...!"

Konnyaku knelt at the side of his companion. Shigoto's head and shoulders were covered in blood. There was a deep wound to the back of his head and one arm trailed uselessly behind. He seemed to have been discarded like a broken toy, a child's abandoned doll. Lying still, unmoving and damaged seemingly beyond repair.

"Shigoto, no... not you, not you." For the first time Konnyaku felt something tearing at his heart, loosening the strictures he had put in place that had allowed him at least the grace of survival. Tears were welling up in his eyes, hot, hard barbs that made his eyes sting, and caused him to blink. For several moments he knelt there at the side of his fellow gardener, living through the agony of having someone close to him torn away. Guilt leaped up at him, as if the fire had reignited: it was he who had not stopped Shigoto running off. He should have gone after him, brought him back to be with the others, or at least gone with him and stood by his side to protect him.

"Shigoto, I'm sorry, so sorry," tears were falling now, rushing in thin rivulets down his cheeks, streaking the grime smeared over his face, catching at his jaw before dropping into his clothing. They fell among the dark splashes of dried blood, like rain dripping through the canopy trees onto dry ground below. Konnyaku reached out his hand to try and brush away the hair that had fallen across Shigoto's face. It was covered in thick dark fluid and the eyelids were so encrusted by dried blood that they had stuck together. He angrily and impotently waved away the flies already gathering in anticipation of a feast. The body was not cold yet, there was a trace of warmth to the skin, or had he imagined that? Suddenly hope sprang up in him, a desperate hope that something good, some slim chance existed of winning again. He pulled at the body, it shifted a little closer towards the entrance where there was more light. At first it seemed to move easily, then it seemed as if it were snagged on something. Shigoto's right arm was projecting further into the dark interior, and now Konnyaku could see that his hand had closed fast about something. As he peered closer he saw that the fingers had shut about a length of some cloth, and following the line of the unravelled cloth back into the room he saw that most of the rest of the material was lying trapped under another fallen body. Konnyaku stood and moved into the room and he realised that this body belonged to an elderly woman, mouth agape, frozen in time. Shigoto's fingers would not open to release the cloth, so he slipped his newly acquired knife from its scabbard and slashed roughly at the cloth, leaving a scrap lodged in Shigoto's grasp. Then looking one final time at the inert body of the old woman, he bent down and gingerly lifted the limp body of his companion into his arms. If there were even the slightest odds of saving him, he knew with absolute clarity what he had to do, and where he had to take him.

CHAPTER THIRTY

February 1595

'I am not dead', the realization began to form at the nacreous speed of a pearl binding itself atom by atom to a piece of grit. He was walking through a landscape and the sun was shining blindingly bright, all the leaves and branches seemed to being pulled out in one direction, as if by a strong horizontal wind. Everything except him was affected it seemed.

"Look, Mother," and as he effortlessly ran, his hand was trailing behind him among the long grasses, light sparked and played among the stems and waving leaves, sending flashes up into the air. "I can do it again, look, Mother, I can do it again." The wind did catch the sound of his voice, it stretched it out so thin that it could reach back to his childhood. These were the very first words he was saying, articulating who he was for the world, for his mother. Revealing himself as he was, this is what I feel. "I am what I feel, Mother." Running, always running, under the deepest blue sky, with the wind never touching him, perhaps he ran faster than even the wind itself.

He scrambled up the side of the hill, and as he climbed the grassy fields were receding away below him becoming more silvery than green with the increasing distance. The further he went the steeper the going got, and he was now obliged to use both his hands as well as his feet. The angle of the slope was severe enough that he knew if he attempted to stand up on his feet he would fall backwards, roll back the way he had just fought to come. When he looked over his shoulder he could see the fields below him wavering in the heat haze, his mother now the barest speck, sometimes visible sometimes not, it was hard to know for sure. He wanted to wave at her but he was holding on to roots that ran helter-skelter over the surface of the earth, and he did not want to relinquish his grip. There was a sound coming to him, a beating pulse, it appeared to be coming from somewhere above him, though it was difficult to locate the origin. He felt a flush of irritation rising in his chest as he realised if the sound was to increase in volume, as it threatened to do, then he would not be able to hear where he was going.

'I have to use all my senses. Not just rely on my eyes. My eyes don't see in the dark, they're too new for that, they have to get used to the light first. That's why I'm here. It's just something that has to be done, there's nothing much to do.' Shigoto paused as he clung to the roots; it was then he realised that more than one form of himself existed. 'I can speak to myself,' he thought with a degree of surprised amusement. Gathering himself again he pushed on upwards, as there was really only one direction to go. There were no tracks to follow; it was a matter of scrabbling upward against the wishes of gravity, that wanted nothing better than to tip him head over heels, again and again. Spin him away off into space before he even knew what was happening. Hug the earth, stay low, that was the way to move, where the whining wind did not hamper you and sound cannot get at you. Stay low, keep among the plants, it was the secret of success; all he had to do was stay within the realms of his own consciousness. If he raised his head enough and looked up, he could see a crest ahead, but he knew it was not the final summit that would come later. One step at a time was enough for now.

At the top he expected to be able to look out across the landscape spread out like a map about his feet. Instead he found the crown of the hill densely covered by trees; not that he cared too much at that point. He was tired from the effort of getting to the top. His body felt leaden, as if all the air had been drawn out; not just from his lungs, but from every part of his body, from the spaces between the muscles and the bones they were attached to, even from between his internal organs, everything was crushed and drowning under its own weight. His eyes, the only part of him that moved without hindrance looked about trying to take in where it was he had reached. This is what all the effort was about, to get here, to be here. It was a crushing disappointment at first: there was nothing to see, no view, no clear space, no sense of soaring like a hawk. Only trees, trees everywhere, growing so thick together he may as well have stayed in the grass fields where he was. They were trees though, because he could see the trunks, with their thick sinewy flaking bark, bifurcating branches emerging from the hard ground to become something, all reaching upwards, locking into each other to hold up the sky.

"What a disappointment, I thought I would be free here," he spoke to no one and no thing in particular. "It's strange, I expected it to be so different really. Not the way it is now. I suppose it's always been like this. It must have been this way, and it's just that it's taken so long to get here. I just need to rest. I'll be all right then. I'll wave back down to mother then, after I have rested, she won't be expecting me yet. Keep the sun from my face, I'll rest awhile."

Lying there he realised that he was not actually very comfortable, his legs were trapped under his body, and that was why he could not move. It took a great effort, but by contracting and expanding his muscles in turn from his toes up through his torso to his head, he was able to pull himself into a straight line again. It took all his concentration and strength, as he needed every set of muscles to move in the correct sequence before movement was detectable, even his eyelids had a part to play. Finally he found himself leaning with his back against the deep-fissured bark of a pine tree, the crown of which dissolved hazily into space above his head. He felt cheered to be where he was, and with his joy came the sweet aroma of optimism. 'I suppose its all a matter of patience really, that's all. Just having the patience to wait for the right moment,' he told himself. Now that his bare flesh was touching the trunk, he was able to feel the tree was actually alive. It was not just the static element of an architectural form as he had first assumed, rigid and immobile, but that there were internal currents skittering along those limbs. Deep within the branches were running streams of energy, busily hastening about their business, impatient of the slightest delay. In fact, it was unstoppable, since whenever the stream flow came up against some kind of an obstacle, it pooled as if to consider for a moment and would then rush off in an alternative direction, repeating this trick over and over until a way round the encumbrance was found. 'All that water. I could do with some water; my throat is dry after the climb up the hill. I suppose one day it will fall as rain, and then I could lie here with my mouth open and drink in all that I need. There will be enough for that.' Shigoto opened and closed his mouth, worked his lips, touched them with the tip of his tongue. 'All those streams,' he thought, 'all those streams running, it'll have to fall as rain again one day. Everything that goes up, comes down sometime soon."

"Shigoto, what are you doing here?" The voice was so familiar. "I've been waiting for you, you took so long. Did you get lost on the way somehow?"

"Mother?"

"No, don't be silly, I'm not your mother. Whatever made you think that?" The voice was so familiar, it reverberated as an echo in his mind, and with each pulse it became even more knowable. For a while the voice followed the pulsing rhythm that he could still hear, which had never entirely cleared his perception, though it had faded deeper into the background as he emerged among the trees at the top of the hill. The sound of the voice, soft, beguiling, tender and tempting even, now joined with the beating pulse and ran along the top of it. Hopping and skipping without care, it had been released by the pulsing bass beat, and raced along in its own time, stepping now and then lightly from one beat to the next. At times it shifted away from the constraints of time and hence rhythm and then it soared up and away lost in its own dreams, playing 'look-at-me' games with existence.

"Shigoto, I have been waiting patiently for you. Come, everything is laid out over here ready," there was almost a note of impatience, even annoyance, in the voice, but it was so sweetly syruped over that there was no way Shigoto could have taken it as a reprimand. He barely noticed the tone of admonition. "You are such a dreamer, but I knew that from the first. I read it in your eyes. It's what I wanted to find there, I needed to know that there were dreams inside you and that you weren't just empty and hollow. Come on, you've lain there long enough, it's time to come and join me, after all we came here to be together didn't we?"

Now the voice was sinuous and seductive; he was reminded of roots running across the surface of the ground covered with unfathomable pockets of velvety mosses. He looked up to try to locate the origin of the voice better, but a blinding stream of lights flickered in his eyes and it was too much effort to focus.

"My eyes are new, you see, they haven't hardened properly, there isn't a crust formed yet," he explained. Yet even as these words unfolded, images born in a newly formed light began to flood into his consciousness, now filling his sight as if a long night of sightlessness tipped over into the dawn of rebirth, and a new beginning.

"Everything is over here, all set out, ready," the voice trailed away, and he strained to track the direction with his burgeoning awareness, and so fix it against something he could find again, to locate it in a clearer knowledge when the right the time would come. "Nureba?" The question exploded in his mouth, and shockwaves ran through his body, expanding him, reinflating him once more, putting air where there should be air, opening up spaces where space was needed for shape and order to be maintained. For flow to occur once more. "Nureba, is that you?"

A low table was set on the broad flank of an outcrop of rock. It had been covered with a bright red felt cloth, with the corners neatly folded in and smoothed down by hand. Either side of the table was a cushion, deep green, as green as pines of late summer; a round cushion on the bare smooth rock. Across the table were scattered a profusion of black lacquered bowls, their interiors burnished golden, with delicate patterns of spring flowers etched also in gold against a limitless depth of black. Every bowl had a different kind of food in it. It was easy to see from where he stood at the table that the dishes contained his favourite foods. Nureba came and knelt gracefully on the cushion at the far side of the table, her head inclined downwards and a neutral expression across her face. She had such beauty, it radiated out from beneath her skin. The beauty was more than her body could contain, it leached out everywhere, and she carried it over her shoulders as a shawl.

"Come and sit," Nureba lifted a pale hand towards him, it hovered over the table and gold was reflected onto her skin from the bowls.

"Nureba, this is so beautiful," Shigoto folded himself on to the cushion at the opposite side of the table to her. "I was expecting to get a good view from here, I was going to wave to my mother in the grass field below, but then I lost sight of her. It was much steeper than I thought, and there were all these trees in the way. They are holding up the sky and I could not get my bearings, so I kept to the roots to make sure I did not fall again."

"There's no need to explain, it's not that important after all how we get here. It soon becomes a fact, then nothing can be changed ever again, it's fixed that way forever. I never realised that before, well, not until the table was fully laid out anyway. That's when I first noticed it I suppose. You are here now, that's the most important thing. Are you hungry?"

"This is all so very beautiful," his eyes were sweeping restlessly from one point on the table to another. "You've thought of everything, this is just the beginning too, the stars haven't come out yet, we've got all the time we need. Nureba, we can even create time when we need more. I should kiss you first, as a blessing for this abundance, even though there is such a throbbing pain in my head." Shigoto looked across the table, Nureba was as radiant as ever, her face now angled upward, she tilted her chin forward in defiance.

"No," she said firmly," that's not possible. You've got no blood in you right now. No, you stay there; you are not strong enough yet. When you do enter me, you'll need to be stronger than you are now. You'll have to give me everything; it will only work with everything in place. Listen…" Nureba raised her hand to stop him saying anything just then, one finger was delicately held up away from the others pointing into the azure sky. She was smiling broadly.

"I can't hear anything, "said Shigoto.

"Listen. There it is again. You are thinking too much to hear it."

This time when he listened he could hear the bellowing of an ox, it was some distance off, hidden from view by the landscape. Time and time again it called with a deep roaring sound that began somewhere in its ample gut and by twisting and turning upon itself came issuing out of its outstretched mouth as a low booming cry.

"It's Maguro Sensei," said Shigoto, "He'll know how everything fits together. He understands things I cannot even imagine right now. He sees beyond the horizon of my eyes. "

Then Sensei was standing a few paces away from the table looking towards him, and Nureba had closed her eyes in deep contemplation.

"Shigoto, I am sorry to disturb you, but there is something to show you, you will need this knowledge. It won't take long, then you can rest again when we are done. It's not far to move, and everything will be here when you get back. Even Nureba, I dare say. Come, come with me, now. We should be moving, if you stay too long then you might not be able to move again. All will be there to show you where you once were. There's more to it than that but I'll show you what I can, come."

Shigoto looked back across the table to take his leave of Nureba, but she had already gone, vanished, leaving but the slightest trace. Only the cushion with its barely noticeable indentation revealed where she had once been. He rose stiffly to his feet and realised they were unshod, scratched and bloodied where the skin had been torn into thin welts. Sensei had already moved off with his long easy strides, and Shigoto had to hurry to catch up enough to walk a few paces behind his teacher. He had meant to ask where they were going, but Sensei was leading him, so what was the point? He was being taken to find out, that was the purpose of the whole exercise. There would be no sense in chasing after a truth that was in you in the first place, after all where *would* you go to find it? Everywhere you travelled would only take you further away from where you wanted to be. 'Best not say anything, and keep silent. Accept and follow, after all you are the gardener's apprentice.'

They walked on through scrubby vegetation that rose as far as their waists at times, and Shigoto occasionally stumbled for a few paces to try and keep up with the relentless pace Sensei set. The track they were arrowing along had probably be scarred into the earth by animals, though none were evident now. He broke out into a sweat and had to wipe the back of his hand across his brow. Still, it did not prevent the sweat getting into his eyes and burning them, blurring his vision to the point everything started to swim. It was only the dark swinging form of Sensei's robes that kept him on track, and he stumbled on after his teacher.

"Don't touch your eyes," Sensei tossed a warning over his shoulder without turning around. "They need to form over again, they are too new to heal themselves yet. We are nearly there. There is little enough to see just here anyway."

They were moving downhill now, Shigoto could feel a lightness coming into his steps as they descended into a narrow valley. In a cleared space on the valley floor was a small square roof covered in charcoal grey tiles, the roof held aloft by a series of timber posts, there were no walls at all. Beneath the roof was a small circle of stone. When he got closer Shigoto saw that the stone had been cut, it was made up of five sections, each thicker than a grown man's thigh, each piece had been meticulously dovetailed together into a perfect empty circle. He stopped by the circle with his head sheltered by the crude roof. Sensei was standing next to him. Sensei had not so much as broken into the lightest sheen of sweat, in fact he barely seemed to be breathing at all. He turned to look at Shigoto, fixed him with a gaze that only Maguro Sensei could offer.

"It's a well," said Shigoto in a matter of fact tone, any trace of surprise now filtered out of his voice.

"Yes. Your father is in there, he's safe at last now, though he is in several pieces that can no longer be put together again. He cannot trouble anyone anymore and he will rest now. I have to tell you this, though you already know it; he is not your real father. He was only living behind the mask of being your father. He had no right to be where he was, and that's why nothing ever fitted for him. He must have been very uncomfortable as he was and maybe he tried too hard to break out. It's not only people that carry secrets with them, Shigoto, it's important that you know this, that you see this. The landscape holds secrets too; they are there in the ground you will walk on, in the rocks you will read and arrange, in the trees, in the water, always in the totality of these elements are there things being said and done, opened and closed, revealed and hidden to us. They surround us all, as a landscape they will bind us with cords so fine that we cannot not even begin to know or feel what is really before us. It's a shame that some things have to remain hidden, for if we could but see what we truly were, then we could begin to find the love necessary to begin to heal ourselves."

All at once Shigoto was looking from high up in the sky back down onto the earth; everything appeared miniscule, as if he were looking through a reversed telescope, except Sensei who remained entirely unchanged. There, far below, was the tiny roof over the well with its hard unyielding mouth, perpetually gaping and swallowing anything that may fall into its orbit, even light itself would be dragged down whole into its depths; this point of no return, a doorway between worlds, between points of knowing and not knowing.

"Don't take an unhealthy interest in dark water, if you know what I mean," Sensei was still talking to him, but it seemed as if he had not really heard everything, he felt as if he were a guest arriving late at a banquet, only arriving after the main decisions had been guiltily consumed. Yet there was something attractive about standing there next to that ring of stone, standing as close as possible and peering over the clean cut rim to look down into the blackness which indicated depth. But not only that, if you were tempted to stare down long enough, you would begin to become perfectly comfortable with the notion that 'down' could also mean 'up', or indeed any one of innumerable degrees between the two, and all of them would be true in the same time.

"So, who did you say is in the well, then?" he asked.

"Pieces, pieces that can no longer be put together."

"You mean my father?"

"It's all over now, the rain will come and wash all traces clean. In due course the water will appear sweet again, and salt and gravel will be spread to purify the earth."

"Does my mother know this?"

"She has taken into her hands all that she can carry. She has enough of everything in equal measure."

"Will the well ever be full again? Is there a bucket to lower to collect the water?"

"Everything has been thought of. Suffering though cannot be avoided, only relinquishing attachment to desire can still that particular flame."

Shigoto felt the need to turn away at that point, as the pulsing sound that had been dogging him for a while was growing more and more insistent; filling his ears so completely little room remained for anything else. The volume had been creeping stealthily upward while Sensei was there; if he turned his attention to the beats they shied slyly away, diminishing in volume to the point where the rhythm was the barest pinprick in a blank screen, but never quite letting go all together. Now the volume was again increasing steadily as if unafraid of any consequences, the fat, rounded tones jostling each other for space in an increasingly overcrowded and congested arena.

'I can't stay here,' Shigoto, reminded himself. 'There are things I need to do, things that I came for, of course.' But he could not focus on exactly what those tasks were. 'Errands, deliveries, messages, orders to be carried from here to there, something of that and all of those.' The strong drumming sound was throwing him off balance, the rhythm never coming down on the expected beat, which gave it a lop-sided, asymmetrical feel, all of its own. It made him feel nauseous as if his internal organs were beginning to awaken from a deep slumber, and were now cranking themselves up for action again, flexing the tube of muscle that had buried part of itself in the earth. 'No. I can't stay here. Move, move move!' he screamed at himself.

It wasn't actually so painful at first, but gradually waves of pain began to wash over him, crashing and bumping each other, pushing, cajoling, sometimes rolling him right over. He felt as if he were under water, and he would come blustering up to the surface to gulp down air in hungry mouthfuls, where the light was flat and hard. 'Move, move move!' he used the words as a whip-crack, snapping firecracker-bright in the air about him. 'I need to drink, I can't drown without a drink of water, my throat is so parched, my jaw aches, and if I could only reach the leaves I would lick the dew from them. So dry, so dry, after all. Burning in water... burning for water.'

Sensation was beginning to reawaken in Shigoto's body, pain flooding into him, pinning him as if a delicately mounted insect. But the discomfort also brought a modicum of consciousness with it. 'I am still alive. Not dead, not dead at all.' He could recognise himself at this different level of existence and he wished he could go back, rewind time to some earlier moment when everything required less effort from him. For the first time he became aware that his energy had a limit and that he was so close to the end of it. Death seemed to be smilingly holding out a hand to him, inviting him to make a step in that direction, or if not a step, then just to let go, relax his grip, open his hand, let everything go slack. That was all he had to do, it was so tempting, so very tempting to let go. Let everything slide, and he would slide along with it, Nothing would hurt any more. Nothing such as that would matter, and all attachments would be finally cut. 'So easy, just open your hand. Let go.'

He was part way there, when he realised that his mother was standing before him. The surprise of seeing her again checked the momentum of his slide. She was smiling, her hands held out in front of her body, the palms very slightly cupped and the fingers ever so gently tilted upward.

"Do you remember, Oku-*chan*, you were so proud when you explained to me the ideal shape of a branch when it is pruned? Do you remember that?" Her voice was light, sweetly coated and conversational in tone.

The question sent him reeling round and round. Out of control perhaps, but no longer sliding. "Why do you mention this to me now? I am dying, aren't I?"

"Is that what you chose in the end? You surprise me." Her voice chastised him in silky modulations. "There is an old pine out by a spring; it grows there alone, with only the spring water for company. It has been growing there a very long time. It too wandered across the face of the earth, constantly shifting and changing, before it found its place. The tree had been waiting far longer than you. Waiting for a gardener's touch. You made a promise to become a gardener, well, you have barely started. Your eyes have not opened yet. Ask Nureba, she knows."

"Is she here?" His voice was coming from a far distant place, one that was getting further away all the time, it was hard to make it out, it was so faint.

"She's waiting by the tree, for when you return to the world."

Then all images ceased, all trace of voices, words and meaning, with infinite patience coalesced into a single source of light;

until all that was left was a small ball of revolving light. A wind picked up, a gentle lilting zephyr to begin with that gradually gathered strength. It was blowing out from the light source, whence according to the imprint of its own creation light gave birth to sound. Sound so low in register and to all intents and purpose indistinguishable from light itself. At first it attracted no attention, it existed only in itself, but as the wind began to find some purchase, the sound cracked open up, jagged rents appeared in its sides, its skin tearing as the forces of division and expansion built inexorably inside. Now its translucent skin was being stretched, stretched to breaking point, and as the renting fissures began to give way, as they finally had to, burst open, so gaining in strength and beginning to form its own identity, the sound of a bellowing ox was released into the awakening sky. It was neither triumph nor disaster, but the cry of the self, finding the self.

CHAPTER THIRTY-ONE

March 1595

The chimerical light of dawn spread a softer haze across the room, silently bringing substance and form to the ill-defined interior as it gathered strength. A still and silent body covered by a thin cloth lay in the centre of the room. It was just possible to make out a gentle rise and fall in the region of the chest. A clenched hand slowly emerged from under the covering. It rose hesitantly at first, until the fingers opened and touched the drawn, ash-pallored face that was still half hidden by a ragged hem. The fingers collapsed in on themselves until the hand became a soft fist that rubbed at the pale cheeks and proceeded to gently knead sunken eye sockets. Preceded by a rapid intake of breath, then once again but this time with an increasing sense of urgency, the chest heaved and the wet sound of a cough broke the web of silence of the nascent day. Shigoto pushed himself half up on his elbows and looked about him.

"Are you awake?" The voice belonged to an older man.

Shigoto twisted round trying to catch the source of the voice, pin down its location, and as he did the pain suddenly returned, a sharp, jagging stabbing pain in his ribs that jerked his voice away, pushed it out of reach for a moment.

"Stay there. I'll make some tea. Stay where you are." The voice again, this time it was not forming a question, it was a command, and as if to enforce its authority it was lined by a polished steely edge that Shigoto knew well. He knew better than to disobey that voice, and he let his body softly collapse back on the floor. As the last traces of the darkness were being chased from the room, a smile formed involuntarily about his dry lips.

"Yes, Sensei," he said, but the words were formed so quietly they never had a chance to disturb the air even inches in front of his mouth. Instead they circled as an incomplete sentence about the space of his mind that was otherwise occupied with putting together an image of the room where he lay, and an awareness of himself lying in that room. He wanted to add something to the tail end of that sentence, but the words stubbornly refused to come, even in the bustling silence of his own mind. "Never mind', was all he could manage to think, 'never mind'.

Maguro Sensei came back into the room some minutes later, with a small wooden tray on which were two cups filled with fresh green tea. He knelt down and set the tray down on the floor near to Shigoto's head, then gently and with precise movements picked up one cup and slid it across toward the young man. From where he lay he could now smell the tea, with its promise of fresh fecund earth, overlain by a sweet, grassy bouquet.

"Drink your tea. It'll do you good," the voice had now lost its tone of stern command, and was mollified by a caring sensibility and concern. "Can you sit up on your own? Try to sit up yourself."

Shigoto dug his elbows once more into the *tatami* mats beneath him and heaved himself painfully up into a sitting position.

His head spun for a moment, and the pain in his chest rushed at him, as if it were a series of waves breaking in angry frustration against dark rocks of a shoreline. Sensei did not move to help him, but simply allowed Shigoto sufficient time to breathe easily again. When he judged the moment right he reached out with his long thin fingers and picked up the cup, and held it out to him.

"It's better, eh, this morning." It was a simple statement of fact.

Shigoto grunted, "Umm, thanks," then took the proffered cup in both hands. He cradled it for a moment, allowing the palliative warmth to seep into his skin, then he drank.

Maguro Sensei, teacher, mentor, and now his protector, watched his young charge drink the tea. His eyes were sharply focussed on the young man's face, weighing, assessing and interpreting the signs. In the aftermath of the attempted coup, he had taken in the battered, bleeding and broken body of the young man, and had watched over him as his body set about its task of repairing itself. When Konnyaku had arrived at his door with the bloodied and unconscious body of Shigoto, he had immediately directed that he be brought in. "Will she be here today, Sensei?"

Maguro Sensei's face clouded imperceptivity, his watching eyes narrowed.

"Just drink your tea for now. There will be some herbs to drink as well. Right now you must concern yourself with allowing your body to heal, Shigoto. Everything else will take care of itself."

"And my mother, will she come today? Will she be here today?" The tone of his voice rose as an underlying anxiety threatened to break through to the surface.

"Just drink your tea for now, eh," was all Sensei replied before he got to his feet. "I will go and prepare some herbs, then we can talk." He stood now looking down at the young man, his face impassive and unreadable.

Shigoto remained half sitting up, his body was screaming at him and chest aching. It felt tight as if bands of steel were threatening to crush the air out him, and his head swam with semi-exposed emotions and thoughts. He was dimly aware momentous things had happened, but he could not connect the pieces together, nothing quite fitted in place. He had stepped, or was it fallen, into a storm, and had been swept off by forces way beyond his control or imagination, yet somehow he had survived. Maguro Sensei was here, that was a certainty, a fixed point of reference, everything else was chaotic and beyond even recall as a faintest memory of tragedy and destruction.

He had the impression of time having passed, but he could not say for sure how much of it had flowed irretrievably past. That was part of the hindrance to him, his memories were so fractured and disassociated, that they were useless to gauge anything so precise and delicate as time. The light in the room was still thin, as if it too could barely muster the strength, but that was because the outer shutters were still drawn. When Sensei returned a few minutes later, he set down a tray holding a small bowl, in the bottom of which was a thick, dark and pungent liquid.

"I've been awake before, haven't I?" he said, his mind still as unfocussed as his eyes.

"Yes, many times in fact. Now drink this."

"How long have I been here? Where is Mother? Is she coming soon?" His voice was plaintive, searching for answers.

"Drink." It was a command this time, yet Sensei stayed where he was. This time he made no attempt to lift the bowl any nearer. Shigoto had to reach for it, and when he did the pains came again shooting along his outstretched limbs. He pulled the bowl towards him, and then with a grunt lifted it up to his lips. The liquid was as unsavoury as it looked, leaving his tongue feeling thick and clotted. It took three draughts but he downed the liquid without saying anything more, then lowered the bowl to the floor before finally letting slip of it with his fingers. He felt weakened, exhausted by the effort. He stayed where he was, letting the waves of pain subside and clearing his mind as they did. He looked up at Maguro Sensei.

Sensei moved away, and broke Shigoto's gaze. He walked over to where the night shutters had been pulled shut, and with a rapid twist of his wrist he slid them back. Shigoto blinked in the light.

When his eyes had adjusted to the new levels of luminescence in the room, Shigoto, with great care, pushed himself onto his hands and knees. He halted when he had manoeuvred around, panting with effort.

"I'm stronger, see…" he said when his breathing had returned to a steady rate.

Maguro Sensei had found two cushions and he tossed them down by the open space, which overlooked the small garden beyond.

"It's good that you are moving. You have been lying down a long while. Keep moving, it will get the energy flowing again. It'll hurt, there will be pain, but never mind, keep moving, and it'll help you heal. Make your way over here. See, the garden is looking good in this light. Come, come and look for yourself." Maguro Sensei sat on one of the cushions. He crossed his legs under him, and with one hand he tugged at the cloth of his *kimono*, straightening a seam here and a tuck there. All the while his eyes were focussed on the scene in front of him; he never turned his head towards where Shigoto was slowly moving like a broken insect toward the other cushion. Nor did he offer any assistance.

He allowed Shigoto to make himself as comfortable as he could on the cushion, and he waited until he observed that his attention was also directed outward toward the garden.

"You have been ill," he began, "Very ill, some thought you might not recover from the injuries you received. But, I am pleased to see that you have defied the doubters." He spoke in a formal manner, he was clearly choosing his words with great care. His voice was soft, slightly flat in tone, sometimes he allowed the tail of one sentence to almost slide into the next, but never quite enough for a true collision to occur.

"I don't know how much you remember, but as far as I am aware this is what happened:

"Konnyaku *san* found you at your mother's house. You were lying on the floor covered in blood, unconscious. He brought you here, and you have lain here since. Your wounds are healing well; you have had much attention in that respect. Kirifuda *san* has provided the necessary medicines to heal the flesh, and bones have been reset. It seems you got into a fight to protect your home from…" here he paused as if he were unsure of the term to use. Thieves, intruders, mercenaries or aggressors, any language is full of such terms, which mean one thing, and one thing only.

The pause lingered on the air, hung there between them like a thin band of incense caught in a momentary vortex.

"Your grandmother was also found in the house. She was already dead. Your mother has not been found since the attack on the palace. It is thought that she may have been taken hostage by the…" again Sensei tripped up over the word. "Some of those who carried out the attack escaped by the boats they had come to the island in. In the course of…."

The words suddenly appeared looming, cumulus-like, mushrooming hugely to Shigoto. He had been following the opening remarks carefully, and the words had had some sense of meaning, however detached it may have appeared, as if Sensei was talking about someone else, someone from another time and space all together. As the realisation that he was the subject of the remarks began to filter down through his consciousness, he felt the pain in his body disappear. He became aware of his body now expanding rapidly: he seemed to be filling with air that was stretching his frame to its limits. In what felt like milliseconds his body was filling the room in which they were, and started to escape the confines of space by leaching out into the garden. He saw Sensei sitting there by the window, his posture like a a rock. Was Sensei a rock in the garden? Had the interior of the room imploded and fused somehow with the garden outside? Was what had once been the exterior now the interior, or was it the other way around?

A hammering sound began filling his ears, rising from the floor below him, seeping into him as the pain returned pain-filled body, the not quite fully reformed flesh and bone. It was disturbing his concentration and he lost track of any logic in Sensei's remarks, which became audibly blurred, smeared, mashed into one another, broken down into pure pieces of slippery sound without meaning, and then they were lost all together. It was a wailing, a keening that was filling him now, all the way from a plaintive lowing, through to a high pitch open mouthed scream that sounded like someone trying to say, "No-ooo."

"She's, dead, too?" he gasped out eventually.

"Missing, presumed taken hostage. Oba-*chan*, your grandmother is dead, yes. And you are alive. Shigoto you are alive, take hold of that fact. You are alive, that has not been taken away from you. Your work continues. You are alive, you hear me?"

Shigoto looked out across the open space. The ground was flat, except towards the rear, where a dark-leaved hedge the height of his shoulder cut across the view. Towards the back of the garden small mounds of soil had been contoured to create some relief, the surface of the ground was covered by thick, lush moss in a continuous carpet. Here and there rocks pierced the verdant carpet; it may have been long distance views of bare rock summits or escarpments breaking out from a sea of vegetation.

There was barely any planting, except small groups of azaleas tightly huddled about a couple of the stone settings, but they appeared randomly, as if the creator had brought insufficient stock when building the garden initially. His gaze fixed on one of the rocks, and he clung on to it in desperation as emotion burst from within him, flooding out, twisting him inside out, before rolling through the garden wildly in full spate.

"Sit with your back straight." Sensei reached across and with a barely perceptibly movement of his hands touched Shigoto between the shoulders. It was sufficient for him to straighten his posture from where he had slumped with rounded, heavily burdened shoulders. "It's better for your chest, sit up, there, like that. Keep your head up, then the energy will flow in and out as easily as breathing, eh? Good. Good. Now breathe as you do when you meditate, or when you are pouring the tea." This time he left one hand resting at the top of Shigoto's back, between the shoulder blades, careful to avoid an area where a vivid jagged weal ran purple-black across the skin. The gentle pressure the hand formed warmed the skin and steadied him. Slowly, slowly the chest ceased its heaving sobs.

"And my father, did he... is he...?"

Sensei sighed, and the hand dropped away, and found its way to rejoin the other hand lying in his lap. They came together in such a way as to suggest they were enclosing an invisible ball of light.

"Your father, it is said, was one of the plotters of the uprising, that he had sided with Kezure Saeko against *his* father. He died during the chaos, struck down. That is what I have heard. He died fighting against his own Lord, a traitor, you might say. Kezure was captured, and he died by the sword the following day. A place of execution was set up in the field beyond the gardens, you know where the grassy field stretches out down to the sea. Kezure was not allowed the option of taking his own life; it was Lord Saeko's personal order. He was executed as a common criminal, a murderer. At least your father escaped that fate."

"That's where I would go with my mother, when I was very young," Shigoto interjected quietly. "We walked there many times, she stood and looked out over the sea, and I would run through the grasses."

Maguro Sensei remained imobile his focus was now directed back toward the garden again, his chest barely rising and falling, and his face untraceably neutral. He waited for Shigoto to continue.

"So, they have all gone then." Shigoto paused, transfixed by the enormity of the thought. "I am glad my father is dead. I hated him, and he hated me for some reason. He always did. Only my mother loved me really, that was just the way it was." He held the silence a moment. "I knew my father was plotting something, I just didn't know what. I overheard him at the teahouse one night; he was talking to someone, someone important. Someone wearing leather shoes, I remember that. I was nearly caught by them, I disturbed them somehow, and I nearly got found out. I hid under the floor and I saw the leather shoes."

"Kezure Saeko wore leather shoes sometimes. It was an affectation of his. They say the shoes came from a foreign trader." Sensei filled in the missing detail to encourage the young man to remember.

"At least my father chose for me to be a gardener. He did one favour for me. And Nureba? Tell me she is well." A lopsided, twisted wreckage of a smile was etched across his face.

"Indeed she is. She has been concerned for you and your recovery." The reply came back, and then they lapsed into an alliance of silence.

"Will I ever be a gardener again, Sensei?" asked Shigoto.

"Can you ever be anything other? You are alive, Shigoto. Your pulse beats on. In time these wounds will fully heal, and you will continue your work. Fortunately the gardens did not suffer, there was some damage done, buildings destroyed and damaged by fire. But you, you survived. There is a message, a teaching in that, you are not finished yet. Perhaps you are just starting, that's all. Hold on to that, it's right here in front of you."

"There's nothing in front of me … they have all gone … gone." Shigoto's head bowed under the weight of the grief that thundered down on him. Then the anger came, white hot and corrosive it swept through him, scouring him, stripping every trace of individual identity, until he felt himself reduced to a revolving sphere of pure malice. He hated the garden that he was looking at, it seemed utterly pointless and devoid of any meaning or sympathy. He hated his teacher, who sat there beside him abstract, unmoving as a mountain, whilst all Shigoto desired was for him to return his hand to where it had momentarily rested. He hated the light of day that was strengthening with each moment passing. He hated himself for surviving, when all else had gone, been smashed, obliterated, and even now being washed away by the receding tide, until all that would be left were memories, and what use were they? Anything of substance gone…

Maguro Sensei said nothing; he just continued to sit beside the young man. Eventually after several minutes had dragged by he turned to Shigoto.

"Go and lie down now for a while. Rest that body of yours, it will have to carry you on, so let it heal properly. Let it rest for the moment. Besides you will have a visitor later. Maybe this time you will be awake when the visitor comes, that would be nice." His voice was hushed and calm. It found its way through the hard crust of rage that enveloped his apprentice, and brought him back to where they were. The shape of his words shimmered and dissolved into the sounds of a breeze running in the tall bamboo growing beyond the hedge. The wind was beginning to stir into wakefulness, stretching itself lazily at the beginning of a new day. Shigoto wanted to ask Sensei who was coming, but a black tiredness crept through his body, and he wanted to lie down, to seek oblivion in sleep. He could not muster the energy to form the words, so he abandoned them. He began to push himself back round onto all fours, Sensei rose from his cushion, and standing above the crabbed body of his charge, he reached down and with surprising strength he lifted him to his feet and steadied him a moment. Together they shuffled the few paces back into the room to the place he drank his tea before rising. Then carefully and tenderly Sensei laid Shigoto down, and then he drew the thin cloth over the foetal form once more.

"Rest for now," he said. "There has been so much to take in, your bowl is overflowing, and yet still the river runs on without ceasing."

Even as he straightened, he could see that Shigoto had fallen asleep, his chest lifting and falling in a deep steady rhythm, the eyes shut tight to the light of the day.

"Good, rest, sleep, it will heal you. You will need strength for the work you have to do. It was not for you to die, it was not your time to begin again. There are many things for you to learn in this world yet, and much to be done. The truth is you have barely begun, barely begun at all."

Maguro Sensei left the sleeping form of Shigoto, and picking up the bowl drained of its restorative herbs, he crossed the small room and went to prepare an infusion for the patient's next dose. In a personal interview with the patriarch Lord Saeko, he had asked special permission to concentrate his time on the immediate restoration of the body and soul of his young apprentice.

"You seem particularly fond of the young man, Maguro Sensei," the elderly Lord Saeko had said, when he had proposed keeping Shigoto under his immediate care. "There are others who could be charged with his welfare. I would not wish that the gardens to suffer because of the madness that has visited us. At Hirame here, the Saeko family have been renowned for their gardens over many generations. There is no reason that this generation or indeed the next will fail in their duty in that respect." His voice was firm, if tired and frail.

They were seated in one of the reception rooms with its sparse decoration, the doors were slid back to fully open the room to a view across the main gardens. The walls were entirely composed of sliding paper screens, each panel decorated with a series of paintings reflecting the four seasons. From where he sat as Maguro Sensei looked towards Lord Saeko, he could not fail to see a massive pine tree that had been painted on the screens behind his Lordship. The thick twisted trunk appeared and disappeared behind a pattern of clouds of foliage, and here and there on the foliage the white paper had been left, to resemble a light fall of snow caught among the pine needles.

"Even in winter, the pine remains steadfast and noble," said Maguro Sensei, and he bowed low, so low his forehead brushed the bare polished boards of the floor. The old man looked across to Maguro Sensei.

"Do not try and flatter me with sweet words, priest. They do not fit the times we are living through. As you know I have renounced my position as head of the clan. That title has been passed on to Ito, now my only son. It is now for him to catch the flying arrows. I am an old man whose days are truly numbered, just like the snows of winter. If there is pleading and sweet words, then perhaps you had better reserve them for him."

"With respect, I was appointed originally by you Sire. Also it was through your intervention that the young boy Shigoto Okugi was made a garden apprentice."

"I do not wish to have the name Shigoto raised in my company. Do you hear," as he angrily slammed his fist on the gleaming floor before him. "That man caused this island loss and grief, not to mention this family and the son we have lost. I care about those things, Sensei. Unlike some I care what happens to every branch, every leaf of this family. I need not remind you of these things, you are a gardener after all under those priestly robes, are you not? That's why you were brought here in the first place. The gardens, Maguro Sensei, the gardens are your first consideration. I do not need to remind you of that fact."

"Yes, Sire, that is entirely clear."

"Well then …" then came a softening in his voice, as if the tendrils of compassion refused to allow his anger to remain. "Take care of the boy as you see fit. He is under your charge after all. Just make sure the gardens are not neglected because of this, that's all."

"You have my word, Sire," and again Maguro Sensei bowed so low, a dull reflection of his balding head appeared momentarily on the floor.

"How old is the boy now?"

"That I am not sure, Sire, I would say he would be eighteen or twenty years of age."

"Is he any use at all?"

"Shigo… the boy, shows great promise in spirit as a garden creator, Sire. That is part of the reason I sought out this audience with you. To make a special pleading for his welfare."

"I issued instructions that the boy is not to be tainted by the actions of his father. Is that not enough for you, priest? That whole chapter is closed now, whatever was said and agreed in the past is done with; gone, finished, ended. You Zen priests are keen on the expression that you do not walk in the same river twice, is that not correct?'

"It's true Sire, we never step in the same water when crossing a river, you are very wise."

"Wisdom is no substitute for knowing the future though, is it?"

"None of us can know that, Sire. It is given to us to deal with what is immediately in front of that. In Zen we speak about the eternal present, and we learn that the past and future are mere illusions, set to distract us from the path."

The elderly man waved his hand impatiently, "Enough philosophy, now is not the time for chatter and debate. I will speak with Ito, the decisions are his to make. I will suggest that your allowance is increased for the time you are tending the boy back to health."

"I seek no further allowance, thank you Sire, I have sufficient resourses to hand. Kirifuda san, your friend and companion at the Tea ceremony, has provided healing herbs. The boy will make a full recovery from his injuries; as for those injuries to his mind, time alone will reveal how well how that goes."

"Umm, he was never trained as a samurai, so I suppose not much can be expected. He is of better stock than one would imagine though. Just make sure the gardens do not suffer as a consequence of your attention being diverted elsewhere, that's all." Lord Saeko repeated. "When the boy is well enough, further decisions can be taken by others wiser than myself. You have heard what I have had to say, you may leave me in peace now, Sensei. You have a lot to do."

"Thank you Sire," and once more the pale reflection of Maguro Sensei's pate was briefly reflected on the dark highly polished boards.

Maguro Sensei left the room with a final deep bow before he stepped backwards through the opening onto the wide veranda. It ran across the front of the building enclosing one side of the Southern Courtyard, with its wide-open gravel space. Many times he had dispatched his young apprentice to sweep its surface. Beyond the courtyard he could see the Great Dragon Pond, the heart of the garden. Its surface, barely ruffled by the breeze caught the sombre grey tones of the clouded sky. It matched his mood, and he reminded himself as he walked how often it was that a garden reflected the mind of the viewer.

Sleep came as a balm of forgetfulness to Shigoto. At first he tried to keep it at bay, preferring the barbed stings of grief, but solace cannot be denied entirely, as nothing can ever be only one thing. Sleep came rolling in inexorably, as waves wiping smooth the beach. As he fell deeper and deeper into the seductive wiles of sleep long strands of memory, as insubstantial as wisps of smoke snaked past his eyes. He saw himself again running across an open field of late summer grasses, running in ever widening circles about his mother, her gaze fixed across the flat spread of the silver scaled sea. He saw Sensei, as insubstantial as the wind itself, yet as unyielding as a boulder lying on the streambed. In time all passes, this way or that. He wanted to ask, "Is that all there is?" The words would not form in his mouth but simply leached away into the blood-enriched soil he walked over, and then they were gone too.

"Is anything left apart from memories? Who will remember the memories, or is that when we truly die, when there is no one who remembers us anymore? Is that the end of the scent?" As he passed beyond words and questions he saw a headless man struggling to rise from his knees as the sound of birdsong rose, lamenting loss and the betrayal of hope. As he passed beyond recognising the images for what they were, he heard the baying of an ox, screaming out its last moments. It was the sound of the attenuated world beginning again, being born again of a sound, in the first light of day.

The ox was maddened with rage and dark unnamed bitterness raking at its heart, its nervous system, its gut, sinews and bones. It tossed its head up into the sky to thrash with unfocussed eyes at the stars that threatened it with their ancient light. It stamped its feet with the power of the earth cracking open, crepitating the bamboo forest, and making shrill birds flee for higher ground. In the undergrowth small mammals raced against one another, species against species, in search of shelter from the ensuing storm. The air came alive with billions of flying creatures, from the flea to the crane, taking to the wing, the backwash of their haste flattened the breeze to nothing. The ox hooked with his horn the moon, driving its point into the underbelly, its eyes bright red, shot with pulsing veins and tears for the past.

The ox stood rooted to the spot refusing to budge, even a moment to allow time its natural course. It locked its massive haunches against change, and scarred the earth for generations with its determination to refuse what was. It bent its head and pushed back with a force so great it felt its ribs break with the effort. But nothing would prevail, nor prevent the point of change from doing that which it can only do. Not even its voice, a rolling web of thunder and lightning leaving scorched plains and empty wells behind, could halt the moment when it came to do what it had to do. The one and only thing it could do.

The ox bellowed at the injustice of it all, and the dire sadness of it all. It tore at the grass with its hooves, ripped trees out by the roots leaving a trail of misery and destruction in its wake. All because of what? Because it could not have its own way, because it was denied the version of reality it craved so bad. The only truths that it knew were shredded by doubts of their veracity. No amount of tender words of endearment could be enough to heal the fabric that had been torn to shreds.

Except that sleep did come, the amnesiac slumber that soothed maddened eyes, eased the iron hard muscles and unclenched tooth from tooth. After the cry lit into the sky and sound came to break the waters, the wheel shifted in the mud, and the cycle shuddered into movement. The river flowed as it has always done, cutting here and there into softer banks, unperceptively grinding at the bedrock. When it was dammed it sought another way round, searching out the weakest point. Even when there was not an apparent weak point, it created one. First by osmotic seepage and underground transitions, so by gradually thickening to a trickle, it would find a way to continue. Once it had gained direction then the river itself followed, pouring through the gap in the defences, with a certainty that eventually would carry away entire mountains, grain by grain of sand.

The agency of change came as a sighting of the dragon moving across the sky. The scales of its tail glittering and flashing, whiplashing to and fro in a slivered streak of red, white and blue lights, like a river itself. In the blink of an eye it travelled thousands of days through landscapes lit up by lightning strikes, chasing its tail with the outstretched three-clawed feet, rasping tight whirlwinds followed in its wake. Forests were flattened, and lakes emptied, mountains shivered. When the earth joined with the dragon it rained and rained, so fiercely that the world was cleansed of its identity, the seas rose and lashed impotently against the shore, there was water everywhere, in the air, the wind, and the only sound was the running of water.

The dragon with its nest a bed of bleached bones was known by a name in every region on the earth. Ouroboros the 'Conqueror of Time', Philaletha the 'Dissolver of All Things', Derkein the 'Far Seeing One', Ierud the 'Slayer', or even, Kaishan the 'Mountain of Regret'. It knew nothing of its own identity, only the force of function that drove it on, bringing chaos and change to accepted order. The dragon was the renewer, the force through which the seed cracks open and the rapidly dividing cells both rise towards the light of space and sink into the dark tissue of earth. The dragon saw Shigoto lying helpless in the fabric of his dream, and it wished release for him. Tears of compassion welled in its huge, bulbous eyes, and where those tears reached the ground the trees rose to outlast empires, their canopies shrouded by clouds, the home of thousands of birds. One tear engulfed Shigoto, bearing him back to a beginning, to a point before time and sound. Grief would always remain with him, for that is the price for living on, to be thrust wanting into a future propelled by what has left behind forever. But for now one such tear washed him clean of what he had once been.

CHAPTER THIRTY-TWO

March 1595

"Well, look at who is here. It's Shigoto, he's back again." One of the two gardeners looked up from what he was doing, straightened his back, and turned in the direction of the outstretched finger of his companion. His face was like a paper sheet untouched by ink, untainted by any thoughts that may have been running through his mind. He was tall, much taller than the man standing next to him, broad across the shoulders, and he carried himself with the confidence of the certainty his own strength of limb. Konnyaku looked across to Shigoto as he approached.

"You better now?" The question was awkward and forced, as if neither words nor sentiment came particularly easily to him, as he spoke his eyes looked down toward the ground as if he was searching for something he had lost some time long before.

"Yes, thanks. Still sore sometimes, but all right. Sensei says I will start work again soon. I'll feel better when I am back at work."

The Gardener's Apprentice

Shigoto looked toward the tall figure of Konnyaku, it was the first time he had spoken with his fellow gardener since the coup attempt had taken place at Hirame Palace, since Konnyaku had scooped up the bloodied inert body and taken him to Maguro Sensei. Shigoto realised that there now existed a bond between them; an indebtedness that they both would have to come to terms with, and he had had ample time to think about that whilst he recovered. Now it was a question of beginning to negotiate his way through the reality.

"Hey, Shigoto, it's good to see you again, good to see you up and on your feet again." Kamaboku wore a smile that creased his tanned face. He radiated goodwill, shuffling from one foot to the other as if he could not contain his pleasure. Of all his fellow gardeners at Hirame Palace, Kamaboku was the one who was closest to Shigoto. It had always been so, ever since the first days of his time as an apprentice. Kamaboku had been the first one to hold out the hand of friendship and companionship to him. Whereas the other gardeners had always retained a certain degree of reservation in their dealings with him, Kamaboku had accepted him seemingly without any inhibition. It had been he that Sensei had assigned to show Shigoto the ropes as a gardener, to keep an eye on the new apprentice, and the two had forged a friendship over time. "I came one time to see you, but you were not well, you were not of this world. I am happy to see you again. It's good to see you up and about again, eh."

"It's the first time I have been able to get out, to see the gardens again. It's funny, I missed seeing the gardens as much as seeing you. Sensei did not want me to start going out until I was stronger." Shigoto wanted to explain, to begin to ensure that they understood what had happened, what had really happened.

"I heard you were pretty badly banged about," said Kamaboku, he looked towards the silent figure of Konnyaku standing nearby, as if to invite him to participate, but Konnyaku remained wordless caught somewhere between action and words. His eyes avoided looking directly at Shigoto, and his hands fidgeted restlessly with the smooth polished shaft of the digging tool in his hands.

Shigoto shrugged his shoulders. "Yes, some…" and the words trailed away in the air.

With that Konnyaku dropped the tool he was holding and with a few words that were scarcely audible he turned and walked briskly away, leaving Kamaboku and Shigoto looking anxiously in the direction of his silent retreating back.

"Oh, don't pay any attention to him," Kamaboku gestured in the direction Konnyaku had gone. "He's having one of his off days," he added with a wink. "So you are coming back to work soon then?"

"Yes, Sensei says I should be strong enough to start in a few days. To be honest I am getting tired of sitting about. You know how it is?"

"Sure, sure. Well it'll be good to have you back, eh. There's plenty of work to be done as ever. Sensei has not let up on that, troubles or no troubles, eh." Kamaboku stood before Shigoto, the smile lit up his face, and when he grinned broadly Shigoto could see a black gap in the row of teeth that were revealed by his parted lips.

Shigoto looked back again, but Konnyaku was already out of sight.

"You sure he's all right, Konnyaku I mean." He kept his voice low as if he were expecting Konnyaku to come suddenly charging towards him any moment.

"Sure, sure, right as rain. As I say, he's having an off day that's all, too much to drink last night. I heard he also lost some money gambling, that always makes him mad as anything, you know how he is with money an' all."

"I suppose so," Shigoto replied in a voice that revealed he was far from convinced by the explanation. "Has he said anything about me?" he asked.

"You mean about what happened back then?" Kamaboku spoke as if he were trying to dredge up from his memory the details of some event that had occurred so far back in time that it now required forensic skills to recover. He shrugged his shoulders in a helpless gesture.

"He saved my life, didn't he?" Shigoto felt a sense of exasperation building inside with the forcefully cheery attitude of Kamaboku. His leg was hurting him and his ribcage throbbed with a dull persistent ache. His own memory of that time was still a blur, where the details had been smeared and so distorted that he could not bring them clearly to his mind, and then the events of the time had become overlain with a fog of grief, that did not allow him easy access to clarity.

Kamaboku said nothing as the grin slowly faded, he raised his hands with palms upwards as if in a helpless salutation and then let them fall to his side again. They were silent for a moment, each held within the sphere of their own thoughts, as if weighing the effects and consequences of continuing the conversation. Finally Kamaboku broke through the silence like a diver breaking through the skin of the sea.

"Hey, Shigoto," his voice was hushed," you have to understand that there is this bond between you now, between Konnyaku and you. *On*, you know what I am talking about don't you?" Shigoto looked across at the face of his companion, the gaiety of a moment ago had gone, and there was seriousness in his expression now.

"*On*? You mean, honour, do you?" he said puzzled.

Kamaboku's brow creased as if he were trying to find the words to explain. "Not exactly, honour," he said, "it's more like a kind of debt, you know. Konnyaku saved your life, that's something that you will carry, and something that he will have to carry too. It's a bond between you now. It's something that the pair of you will have to deal with somehow. Konnyaku feels a responsibility for you, and that's a certain kind of burden. People react differently to things like that, you need to understand it that way." Kamaboku waved his hands in front of him in a gesture that seemed to suggest it was an inevitability that no one could do anything now to change.

"I would have done the same for him." Shigoto said, though even as the words emerged, the thought occurred to him that there was a question regarding the truth of what he had just uttered. A shiver ran down his spine, and he felt the throbbing in his chest intensify.

"You feel all right?" asked Kamaboku, "You look pale."

"No, I'm getting better, thanks. Fine. It's just my ribs, I've been walking more than I have done for a while, they're sore that's all. No, I'm fine, really." His voice emerged as if it had travelled a long way and was beaten down with exhaustion. "Anyway, I guess I had better let you get on with your work. I wouldn't like Sensei to think I am holding you back from your work."

The smile was back on Kamaboku's face now and his eyes had regained their usual sparkle and life. "That's all right, you know, no problem with that, eh. Work? There will never be an end to work, eh. Never an end, even when we are long forgotten old souls living with the spirits somewhere in the heavens, there will be someone here looking after this place, eh." Then he laughed out loud, and the sound of his laughter broke the mood, as if a stone had been thrown into a pond.

After their early morning meditation a few days later, Maguro Sensei was the first to arise, leaving Shigoto sat where he was. He went to the kitchen area reappearing a few moments later with a handful of foliage in his hand. He went over to the *tokonoma* alcove in the room and kneeling down before beginning to arrange a few green sprigs in a tiny vase. His slender fingers delicately teasing the foliage until he was satisfied at last. He sat back on his heels and without turning around he addressed Shigoto.

"You have not moved," he said simply. There was a long, deep sigh from Shigoto.

"I was just thinking that's all. I found it hard to meditate today. It's as if there is a conversation of ghosts in my mind, they do not give me any peace these days. Sometimes when I close my eyes I can see my father's face in front of me. My mother's too..."

Maguro Sensei turned and looked at Shigoto, this time his gaze did not burrow into him, but he observed him dispassionately, as if from a far place.

"If you are looking for the truth in all that has taken place, with your eyes and ears, then you will see and hear much, but understand little. The truth does not lie there. Do you think you can gauge the depth of the pond by looking at its surface? If you want to approach the truth, then you have to look inside yourself. Do not just concern yourself with the cause and effects and wonder about the apparent cruelty of fate. Look instead into the heart, the energy of things, go back to the source of all things. It can be a dark place, frightening even to point your eyes in that direction. But you have to start from there and begin to make your journey by placing one foot in front of the other. The only idea you need carry with you for that journey is that the destination itself is of no consequence. You, Shigoto, will never find yourself until you finally let go of everything, including all that which you imagine you are.

"After all what is it really concerns you in all this? Is it a fear of letting go of your self? You think now that now you are all alone, without parents, without roots; a sapling torn by the wind from the earth, without love, tenderness and affection to support you. Is that what you fear? Then you are mistaken. All that you seek is already inside you, the truth you are seeking is part of the very fabric of who you are, it's there in your bones, your tissues and your blood. You do not have to lift a finger, to reach outside of yourself to find the things that you seek. Let go of desire and all that you crave, all that sickens you will come pouring out of you as if it were a river in flood. You look at me with eyes that see me as your teacher, your *sensei*. Shigoto, I am saying to you that you are the creator of the world that you know. You have been offered a chance to go out into this world and create beauty, that's not something that is given to many, though it may be something that many search for. Realise that you are the master of yourself. See your breath as being the centre itself." The urgency in the voice lapped over Shigoto as if he were smooth, flat-washed sand.

For a long time Shigoto did not reply. He was struggling to take in the words of his teacher, to put them into some sort of order, to extract something of who he was from them, something he could recognise and cling onto. Sense, logic or certainty, nothing seemed to fit him any longer. Anything that would make sense would do, just something to build on, but he did not know what that might be. He realised that his teacher was trying to throw him a rope to drag himself from the pit of despair that he had tumbled into, yet he found that his fingers could not grasp the means to extricate himself. What seemed to him worst of all was that he had no idea how to reach out for the support.

After a long pause, all the while Sensei's eyes never left Shigoto's face, the tension gradually evaporating from his lips as he spoke. "I think that you are ready to return to work, Shigoto. It will be good for you to return to the gardens."

"Sensei, I am not sure the others will accept me now. I feel that in some way, because of the actions of my father I am being blamed for what has happened. That is something that I am not sure that I can carry. Konnyaku does not wish to speak to me. He cannot even bear to look me in the face. I wanted to thank him for bringing me here… when he found me hurt, he… but he just walked away. Kamaboku tells me it's because of the debt of *on*, that exists between us, and I do not know that I can ever repay him."

The Gardener's Apprentice

"Set all that aside for now. The cherry blossoms are nearly with us, and there is work to be done. You are a gardener after all. Now, do as your teacher tells you."

Bearing Sensei's instructions for the day, Shigoto set off leaden-footed for the palace buildings, in his heart the coming of spring held no great store of delight. He felt gloomy and defeated by the pressures that bore down on his shoulders; pinning him to the earth, even threatening to press him through its crust into what he could only imagine was an eternal morass from which there was no escape. He looked up into the sky and saw the clouds drifting above him and offered a silent prayer for help. He thought about Nureba who had come to help tend him as he recuperated from his injuries. 'If only I could find some way to speak to her. I would offer to marry her and we could maybe leave this place and start anew somewhere else.' Though where they might go and how they might support themselves was something he had no idea about. He had tucked away in a pocket of his tunic secreted away in a carefully folded small square of cloth, a wooden carving about the length of his little finger, that he had whittled during idle hours with a knife given to him by Tanuki. He had been pleased with his attempt at carving the Jizo figure, and had initially decided to give it to Sensei, and then the idea had come to him that he would offer it to Nureba instead. Now he carried it with him at all times, a hidden talisman, waiting for just the moment when he could make his offering.

Shigoto had been yearning for the company of Nureba. Yet the more that he felt a sense of love for her, the further away she seemed to be. What if he lost her altogether now? Maybe fate had not yet finished with him, but had merely taken a sideswipe at him, teased him with a passing blow. Ever since the time of the Wisteria dance when he had realised she was the dancer who had held him in such rapt attention, he recognised a feeling of love and passion for her. There had never had been opportunity to reveal to her what he felt. That was as much to do with the few opportunities they had to meet, as to the iron-fisted strictures his father had imposed. Nevertheless the "gift" of the handkerchief, with its now long evaporated scent, she had left for him to find, remained anchored in his mind as a symbol of an enduring bond between them. Nothing could change that knowledge, not now, above all not now. 'It's all that there is left,' he thought and brought his fingers up to rub an ache in his side. He kicked out at a small stone that lay in his path and heard it rattle dryly before it finally nestled into a channel that ran along the side of the path.

In the courtyard where Maguro Sensei had instructed him to work there was a cherry tree growing beyond the plastered wall, its branches thrusting into the still cool breeze, the thick clustered buds heavy with anticipation. Shigoto looked up at it, and then set down his basket and tools by his feet. The tears welled up in his eyes, and he felt his chest swelling to bursting point.

"Shigoto *san*."

The voice floated up into the air about him so softly that for a moment he did not realise that it was his own name. He turned around. Nureba was kneeling on the floor of the broad veranda that ran along one side of the garden. He had no idea how long she had been there. Except for her floating pale round face, the dark angles of her body were dissolving into the shadows.

"Nureba?" Shigoto looked about him. "What are you doing here? I was just thinking about you, and..." He looked around again. They were alone apart from the traces of wind in the trees. .... "And, there you are."

Her face softened into a smile, "I was passing, and I saw you standing there. It's good to see you back at work again."

Shigoto dropped his shoulders, nodded his head, his hands flapped at his sides. "Sensei wanted me to tidy up here. I have not done much yet. I just got here."

"I can see that," she said smiling softly. He was at a sudden loss to know where to begin, or what to say. Then one hand came up and his fingers clutched at the hidden figure beneath his clothing.

"The cherry will soon flower, the buds are just waiting for a warmer wind." He looked into her eyes, as he fell into the warmth of tender sensations. Nureba said nothing. "You have been good to me. You and Sensei, you have put me back on my feet again." He smiled at her. Nureba's gaze remained impassive, at least on the surface, yet drawing him in deeper, challenging him, waiting for him to move.

"I have something I wanted to give you. I thought about it, and I... I have not seen you in a while, that is." He stared down at the ground between them. Then he pulled out the small cloth bag in which the Jizo carving was secreted. He cupped it in his hands before thrusting it in her direction. Nureba stayed where she was, her face a pale moon in early morning light. Shigoto unwrapped the wooden figure and set it down upright facing her on the edge of the veranda. Then it seemed to vanish from his sight, until he was looking at her gazing down at the tiny figure she now held in her lap. He could not recall her having moved at all.

"I carved it myself," he said. Nureba was turning it in her hands.

"It's beautiful. You should give it to the temple. A Jizo..." her voice lost it self in the shadows.

"No, I thought to give it to you. As a 'thank you' gift. You... you were kind. I ... there is something other that I have been thinking of. Of how it would be to leave here, go somewhere else... my father, he has poisoned the air for me. He has left me to bear his guilt in many people's eyes. Nureba, I have to leave this island. I have got to leave. I want you to come with me."

The gusting wind rattled the branches behind him. Her eyes had never left the figure.

"It's beautiful," she said once more. "I will take it to the temple myself then."

"No," blurted Shigoto, "it's for you to have yourself. I wanted you to… to keep it yourself. I do not have much to offer you, our house burned down. I thought that we…"

"I will take it to the temple, then it will always be there. It will be there when you come back."

A sudden particularly vigorous gust caught in the cherry roughly shaking the branches, sending out a clattering sound. Shigoto looked back up into the sky behind him, where the weak spring sun was struggling to extract itself from the clouds. When he turned back again, there was only the empty cloth bag on the veranda. He was on his own again.

CHAPTER THIRTY-THREE

April 1595

As soon as the boat started to pitch and roll, a feeling of nausea started to spread like a contagion through his body. He fought it back as long as he could, then stumbled to the side and emptied himself violently into the white lacy froth the craft was cutting through. As he lay there he could see the black waves rising and falling before him. When there was no more to give, he dragged himself away and fell back on to the restless deck exhausted. This was his nightmare, terrors stalked his mind, and fear coursed in his veins; he was wet, cold and sick to the pit of his stomach. He screwed his eyes shut tight and fought with his terror, begging his body to relax. 'Be calm. Breathe. Just concentrate on breathing.' The image of Maguro Sensei loomed up behind his eyes. 'Oh Sensei, what have I done?'

How long he lay there he had no idea. Nothing changed, the rough wooden boards beneath his back continued to dance to a rhythm that was beyond his control, with sound of the wind among the taut ropes in his ears. He exercised the only option he had left: give in to it all, and abandon himself to his fate. Once he did the nausea retreated like a wave drawing back into itself, and he began to be able to predict the next moment when the bow of the boat would seem to hang suspended before throwing itself over the edge of a precipice, to eventually slam down onto something hard and unyielding. He kept his eyes screwed tight shut still, though now he could hear snatches of laughter. Cupping a hand over his eyes, he slowly separated his fingers and allowed himself to peer in between them. A blanket of blackness surrounded him, and there was nothing at first to see. A pinprick of white light pierced the gloom momentarily, then a vague recognition of the frilled edges of clouds appeared and disappeared like a phantom. 'Above me the sky and beneath the sea.' It was the sea that terrified him the most, its black infinity, home of unimaginable beasts waiting for him to slip beneath the waves into their world, not his. 'Air. I need to breathe. I need to breathe to live.'

The laughter came again, and this time he tilted his head forward enough. To see a crewman's face twisted in amusement looking at him.

"Not much of a sailor, are you?" He seemed utterly unconcerned, and spat a wedge of phlegm overboard. Shigoto shuddered. "My name is Daikusei. I told them it would not be smooth tonight. Don't worry, it gets worse than this sometimes, this is nothing to shit yourself over." There was no sympathy for his plight in the voice, and it provoked Shigoto to push himself up on his elbows.

"I'll be alright. It's not what I expected, that's all. I am starting to feel better. How long will it take from here?" Shigoto had to shout to make himself heard, and to make himself believe in his own words.

The helmsman laughed. "With this wind, we may get there before daybreak, or maybe not."

The Gardener's Apprentice

Shigoto pulled himself up into a sitting position, though he clung grimly on to a rope running beside him. He could see nothing in the night. The sky was as black as the sea. "How can you know which direction to go? It all looks the same to me. I can't even see the stars now."

"You're not a sailor, are you," and he spat again, and looked away.

"No, a gardener. I was an apprentice of Maguro Sensei."

"Trouble, is what I heard. Not that I give a damn about anybody else's business. I get paid to do mine, and that includes keeping my mouth shut. I don't care who you are or what you have done. I just said, 'you're not a sailor'. That's enough to know. We'll get there, when we get there. Just keep out of the way, that's all you have to do."

Shigoto pulled the shawl he had among a few meagre possessions tighter around his neck, and then looked around for someplace to crawl so that he could at least be in the lee of the wind and the spray. He craned his neck to peer into the blackness and not far behind him he thought he could just about make out what appeared to be another huddled human form. He cautiously pulled himself in that direction. When he had finally inched his way across the slippery deck to the shelter of a small bamboo screen mounted on the mid deck, he collapsed once again onto his back, and gave himself up to the crazed whirling and dipping, dancing darkness. Adrift and utterly helpless, all there was left to cling to was memory.

He closed his eyes again as a last defence against the forces unleashed around him, and one hand clutched at his stomach, whilst with the other he gripped tight to anything solid that he could reach. Then on the inside of his eyelids a dim point of light appeared, slowly, slowly getting brighter, until he grimly recognised the image of a familiar face looming before him.

❖ ❖ ❖

Maguro Sensei and Shigoto had been meditating as they so often did. When the allotted time span had passed they slowly rose, and then bowed to one another from the waist.

"Shigoto, perhaps you would like to make the tea this morning."

"Yes, Sensei. "Shigoto went to the room that served as a kitchen and found the necessary familiar items. He blew on the glowing coals beneath a heavy black iron kettle, but when he lifted the lid he could see the water was already hot enough for tea. He came back into the room where Sensei sat waiting and set the small warm teapot down on the tray with two cups.

"Pour the tea." He did, and Sensei keenly watched his every movement but Shigoto excelled now in the smoothness of his gestures. When he had poured some tea into both cups he sat back on the round cushion. Sensei lifted his cup with both hands and drank.

"Shigoto, I have been giving a great deal of thought to your situation here." Sensei fixed him with his most piercing gaze. "I know how things are for you. I have heard people speaking. There are those who wish you to carry the blame heaped upon Kanyu." It had startled Shigoto to hear his father's familiar name being spoken by Sensei. "I have learned things about your father since I have been on the island, possibly things that you do not know yourself, or have not been told."

"What do you mean Sensei?" Shigoto was puzzled. "My father was on the side of the rebels, he fought alongside Kezure, against his father. My father was a traitor, and I do not mourn his passing. He never cared for me. It was my mother who did that. My father, I do not think he even loved my mother." Shigoto's hand trembled slightly as he set his cup back down on to the tray.

"There is good reason that you should not carry the guilt of his actions," resumed Sensei; "He was not your real father. Your father was another man, not Kanyu. Most families have their secrets, those things that they would rather remain buried. The Saeko family is no different, and Kanyu's family agreed to him acting as your father for political gain. The Saeko needed to save what they saw as their honour. Reasons are not hard to find if you look carefully enough."

"I do not understand, Sensei. These things you say about my father. My mother, she never…"

"No, she wanted to shield you from all this." Maguro Sensei frowned. "There are many things still that I do not know. I am only telling you what I know of. But it's true the man who died as a traitor was not your real father. It was all a façade, a play of shadows on the wall. Of that I am sure. Though you carry his name there is no reason for you to also carry his guilt."

"So, why do people not leave me alone? Why does no one explain this, then they would understand?"

Sensei shook his head. "I do not know. As I say, all families have their secrets. Lord Saeko cannot come out and explain, he would be seen to lose face over the matter. These things are important when you hold people's lives in your palm. For better or worse, it's the way of the world we live in."

"So, who was my father?" Shigoto was staring back into the depths of his teacher's face. The expression, which was utterly neutral, never altered.

"I do not know for sure. It is something that is held tightly by those who know. Your mother, she never said anything to you?"

Shigoto shook his head. "No." He looked away, down towards the floor.

"I do not believe that your mother is dead, so you should not mourn for her. The likelihood is that she was taken as a hostage. As such she would be kept alive, as she would be worth more to them alive than dead. Maybe Kanyu wanted her out of the way for some reason, he could have planned on her being taken to the mainland, it is possible. I do not know these things for sure. It may be that she is working in the service of another family now."

"Bought and sold on as a slave, you mean," said Shigoto with considerable venom.

"I did not say that. I meant she is possibly alive somewhere and unable to get back to the island, that's all." Sensei's eyes narrowed slightly. "You should never lose the hope that she is alive. Say your prayers for her."

"I think of her everyday, though sometimes I lose her face. I cannot always bring it back as I used to. I do not know if I will ever see her again," said Shigoto.

"You are her son. The son she loved and sought to protect as a mother. That is one strand that we cannot untie, it is a part of who we are. That cannot be taken from you, even by fate." Silence filled the space between then, and the tea went cold in the pot. "I can arrange for a boat to take you to the mainland. From there you can travel to Kyoto. I will give you a letter of introduction to the abbot of Engen-in temple. It is the temple where I was brought up. Many fine gardeners have studied Zen there. There is only one direction for you to travel and that is onward. You have begun your journey as a gardener, and as an artist. I have seen that you have that light inside you, a light that glows in those destined to create. There is nothing other that you are beholden to any longer. You have been released from the ties that bind you now."

"It was a dream of mine," Shigoto smiled slowly at the thought of it. "I used to tell my mother I wanted to become a famous gardener in Kyoto. Like you, Sensei."

"Pah! I want nothing of fame. Please do not offend your teacher, not even in jest. No, Shigoto, strive to become a gardener, a real gardener that is, one who is an artist with rocks and water. That is someone who touches the soul of others, because he has critically looked into and understood his own being. Technique is all that I can teach you now, and you are well enough versed in the everyday duties of a gardener now. I have given what I can to you. From now on you will have to steal from those others who will be your teachers, until there is nothing left to steal from them. But keep searching, never stop searching for all that you do not know."

"But Sensei, there are so many things that you know," protested Shigoto. "Don't send me away, please."

"Shigoto, I am going to release you as a falconer does his charge. This is my last instruction to you as your teacher, your *sensei*. Tonight after it goes dark, make your way to the spring by the Lady Ketsudan Pine, you know where that is don't you? There someone will come to find you. He will be your guide, and he will bring everything you will take with you. Bring nothing with you, you understand. Leave all your possessions behind. Take nothing from the House of Gardeners, even leave your scissors behind, and take nothing with you at all. You will receive all you need. Speak to no one about this, not even Kamaboku."

"Kamaboku is about the only one who speaks to me anyway."

"And you are not to see Nureba. You must just leave. I will find the time to speak with her. She will understand." Sensei's eyes held Shigoto's attention as he spoke. "It would be very dangerous for her as well as you, but she will be staying on the island. Don't put her in any danger, not now."

❖ ❖ ❖

'Don't put her in any danger.' Those words revolved in his mind, as he lay huddled on the pitching boat. He *had* put her in danger, he had gone against his teacher's instructions, and had even used Kamaboku to get a message to Nureba to persuade her to meet him in the gardens that afternoon. "Sensei, I have failed you already." He spoke the words to the wind, which caught them from his lips and hurled them far out over the empty, angry sea. No one could have heard. But he knew the truth himself and he felt wracked by the guilt of knowing it. But she had come.

"We should not be meeting like this, someone may see us. It's not safe anymore, not for the moment anyway, you must understand." Nureba was anxiously casting her eyes about, concern and unease was written across her face. Shigoto had not seen her so anxious before, and it threw him off balance. He blustered out what he had to say.

"Nureba, I am to leave this island. I have spoken with Sensei about this. I have to leave, and get away from here. Everyone treats me as if I am some traitor, or that I have a disease they don't want to catch. I know people blame me because of what my father did. I just can't stay any longer. Listen, come with me. Let's get away from here. We can find somewhere we can live. Just say you will come with me."

Nureba shook her head, "It's not safe," she muttered. "I left quickly the last time because I thought I heard footsteps coming. Things will calm down in a while, people will forget, and time will heal."

"It'll never be the same," Shigoto said bitterly, "not now, not again. There are some things that cannot be undone. It's not like making a garden. Sensei will arrange get me to the mainland." Nureba gasped and lifted her hand to cover her mouth. "I thought that when you took the Jizo, it might mean you would come," he added, but she shook her head, as if she were trying to clear her thoughts.

"You know I cannot leave. There are things here, things that keep me here. Oh, Shigoto, if you go, will you ever come back?"

"You can come with me. We could make our way to Kyoto," he insisted, as frustration began to rise and thicken in his heart.

"I will take the Jizo to the temple. We will wait for you. Then you will always know that there is something here for you to return for one day. Now, I should go back."

He knew now that she would not, could not change her mind, he could hear it in her voice. It seemed as if a door was slamming shut, and he was on the outside. He put out one hand and gently laid it on her shoulder. To his surprise she felt feathery and slight, and Shigoto recognised an unexpected frailty, it made her all the more attractive to him. It was also the first loving gesture that he had made to her, and Nureba did not move nor shrug his hand away. She just shook her head. "It's not safe to be here, someone may see us."

"Come, I know places in the garden where no one but gardeners go." He wanted now to pull her impatiently along. She followed him as if in a daze, and had lost the orientation of her own will. Shigoto hurried along taking narrow paths and pressing deeper into parts of the garden she did not recognise. In a little time they came to an ancient pine, the tree grew beside a spring, with its lower branches sweeping down to the ground as if they were reaching out.

"No one comes here," said Shigoto as he crouched beside the spring. He cupped a handful of water into his mouth, before wiping the back of his hand across his face. "It's good water, here have some yourself." Nureba shook her head, but she was staring into the tiny pool.

"I can see your reflection in the water," she said quietly, her breathing had calmed after the headlong rush. The she looked up at him. "I cannot stay here, they will miss me, and questions will be asked."

Shigoto stood up and came over to where Nureba was stood.

"You could still come," he started to say, but she put her fingers to his lips and shook her head.

"No."

A pent up urgency broke within Shigoto, he reached out and put his arms around her and drew her into his embrace. He was looking into her eyes right until their lips touched, then he closed his eyes. They remained like that for a long moment.

"Nureba...?"

"No, don't say anything." She pulled her head back and once again brushed his lips with her fingers as if in disbelief, as to how far she dared travel. Shigoto dipped his head and sought her lips again with a hunger he had not felt before. This time he pulled her body into the folds of his.

It was only after they had after sunk down into the grasses, and he was pressing himself into her that he really knew what he was about to do, also that it was too late to resist. Nureba's hands were on his back, urging him, pulling him ever closer through the final traces. She gave a sharp cry as his hips jerked forwards then there was no space at all between them.

❖ ❖ ❖

'Is this my punishment now, did I sow seeds of guilt as well?' The wind was howling above his head, and the boat pitched and rolled its course through the steep black waves. The shrouded form next to him stirred, something was grunted, but the words were whipped away by the incessantly howling wind before he could hear them. The only other passenger on the boat pulled a hood tighter about his head and kept his back to Shigoto.

Shigoto had followed the rest of Maguro Sensei's instructions. After dark he went once again to the ancient pine by the spring. He imagined that he could still see the place where he and Nureba had lain hours before and made love among the flattened grasses. Then the guide had emerged silently from out of the nearby woods. Not a word was exchanged, the man (he assumed it was a man), had a dark hood folded over his head and his face was lost in its shadows. He moved sure-footedly without making any sound. He beckoned Shigoto on, and Shigoto wordlessly followed until they eventually reached the seashore. The man crouched down and gave a low whistle, a few moments later

The Gardener's Apprentice

a boat came nosing onto the shore. Shigoto's guide threw a cloth bag into the boat, then having helped Shigoto in, clambered over the side into the boat himself. The man had said nothing throughout the voyage only wrapped himself deeper into his cloth shroud for protection from the elements.

❖ ❖ ❖

The sea had calmed a little as the helmsman edged in closer to land. He reached forward and roughly shook Shigoto's leg as if he were ascertaining whether his cargo were still of this world or had passed into another. "Get yourself ready, we are nearly there. Stay where you are until I tell you to move. I'll take the boat as close in as I can, you'll have to make your own way from there." His words directed at Shigoto, but his eyes were searching the gloom. "No more talking now, every sound carries, even on a night like this." Now Shigoto was able to distinguish the unmistakable sound of waves crashing against a shoreline. It was pitch-black and he could make out nothing, except to register changes of rhythm in the boat and the sound of waves breaking. His heart was beating wildly in his chest as he looked up into the sky. There was just one star flickering with a startling brilliance in a moonless sky that had swallowed all other light.

A few moments later as Shigoto looked toward the helmsman he jerked with his thumb. Shigoto scrambled to his feet, and made his way unsteadily to the side of the boat. Waves were lapping up to its rail.

The stranger who had been the only other passenger leaned over to mutter to Shigoto, the cloth hood pulled down over his head to protect himself from spray and wind. "Jump overboard, the water will be up to your chest. I'll pass you your bag; keep it out of the water, and make for land as fast as possible. Then keep going, get away from the shore whilst there is still darkness."

The sailor who was looking away into the dark, lines drawn tight across his face, spat downwind. Shigoto pushed himself over the rail into the water.

"You know what fireflies are, don't you?" The man leaned forward over the rail and whispered hoarsely as he held out a bag to Shigoto.

"Yes, I used to catch them in my hands when I was a child." The boat was beginning to turn its bow away from Shigoto. The swell grasping greedily at his chest, the cold snatched at his breath. He was frightened and the fear slid icily down his spine. His arms were thrust up to the inky sky holding his bag above his head. His feet searching for something solid.

"Maguro Sensei gave me this message for you. 'Now you are a man, you are to make your own way in the world. Use the light of fireflies to find your path from here on. Good luck.'"

There was something familiar about the voice, but Shigoto, desperate to remain upright in the water could not grasp it immediately. It was only after the skiff had nosed away once more and was consumed by darkness that a name finally sprung into his mind. "Kamaboku," he muttered to himself. "Kamaboku." By then he was clutching the bag in his arms as the sea foamed and frothed in vain about his ankles, and he stumbled over a beach of smooth flat pebbles. A stranger on a strange shore.

Made in the USA
Columbia, SC
13 November 2017